# CITY of FORTUNE

## BERKLEY PRIME CRIME TITLES BY VICTORIA THOMPSON

### GASLIGHT MYSTERIES

MURDER ON ASTOR PLACE
MURDER ON ST. MARK'S PLACE
MURDER ON GRAMERCY PARK
MURDER ON WASHINGTON SQUARE
MURDER ON MULBERRY BEND
MURDER ON MARBLE ROW
MURDER ON LENOX HILL
MURDER IN LITTLE ITALY
MURDER IN CHINATOWN
MURDER ON BANK STREET
MURDER ON WAVERLY PLACE
MURDER ON LEXINGTON AVENUE
MURDER ON SISTERS' ROW
MURDER ON FIFTH AVENUE
MURDER IN CHELSEA
MURDER IN MURRAY HILL
MURDER ON AMSTERDAM AVENUE
MURDER ON ST. NICHOLAS AVENUE
MURDER IN MORNINGSIDE HEIGHTS
MURDER IN THE BOWERY
MURDER ON UNION SQUARE
MURDER ON TRINITY PLACE
MURDER ON PLEASANT AVENUE
MURDER ON WALL STREET
MURDER ON MADISON SQUARE

### COUNTERFEIT LADY NOVELS

CITY OF LIES
CITY OF SECRETS
CITY OF SCOUNDRELS
CITY OF SCHEMES
CITY OF SHADOWS
CITY OF FORTUNE

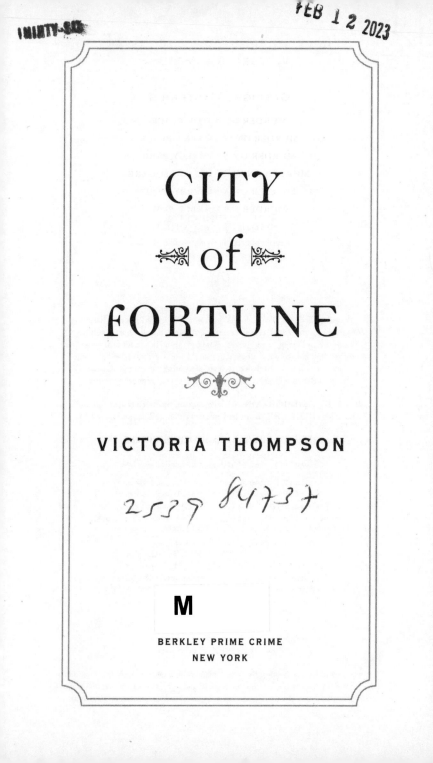

# CITY
### of
# FORTUNE

## VICTORIA THOMPSON

**M**

BERKLEY PRIME CRIME
NEW YORK

BERKLEY PRIME CRIME
Published by Berkley
An imprint of Penguin Random House LLC
penguinrandomhouse.com

Copyright © 2022 by Victoria Thompson
Penguin Random House supports copyright. Copyright fuels creativity,
encourages diverse voices, promotes free speech, and creates a vibrant culture.
Thank you for buying an authorized edition of this book and for complying
with copyright laws by not reproducing, scanning, or distributing any part of it
in any form without permission. You are supporting writers and allowing
Penguin Random House to continue to publish books for every reader.

BERKLEY and the BERKLEY & B colophon are registered trademarks and
BERKLEY PRIME CRIME is a trademark of Penguin Random House LLC.

The Edgar® name is a registered service mark of the Mystery Writers of America, Inc.

Library of Congress Cataloging-in-Publication Data

Names: Thompson, Victoria (Victoria E.), author.
Title: City of fortune / Victoria Thompson.
Description: New York: Berkley Prime Crime, [2022] | Series: A counterfeit lady novel
Identifiers: LCCN 2022025326 (print) | LCCN 2022025327 (ebook) |
ISBN 9780593440575 (hardcover) | ISBN 9780593440599 (ebook) |
Subjects: LCGFT: Novels.
Classification: LCC PS3570.H6442 C576 2022 (print) |
LCC PS3570.H6442 (ebook) | DDC 813/.54—dc23
LC record available at https://lccn.loc.gov/2022025326
LC ebook record available at https://lccn.loc.gov/2022025327

Printed in the United States of America
1st Printing

Book design by Kristin del Rosario

*To my fabulous editor, Michelle Vega,
who suggested I write a book featuring horse racing,
and to my wonderful agent, Nancy Yost, who told me I
could watch horse racing on TV any day of the week.
This one is all your fault!*

# CITY of FORTUNE

# CHAPTER ONE

BEING MARRIED HAD ADVANTAGES THAT ATTORNEY GIDEON Bates had never even considered during his bachelor days. For example, he no longer had to think of polite excuses when a client offered to introduce him to a marriageable daughter, as he was starting to suspect Mr. Sebastian Nolan was working his way up to doing.

"I'd like to arrange for a sum of money to be settled on my daughter, Irene," Nolan was saying. He was a large man, tall and substantial without being fat, and his weathered face indicated he had worked very hard for his fortune, although Gideon happened to know Nolan just spent a lot of time on the training track with his Thoroughbred horses. "Not so much money that she would draw the attention of fortune hunters but enough to ensure her a comfortable income and to sweeten the pot."

"Sweeten the pot?" Gideon echoed in confusion.

"I guess that's a poor choice of words, but I'd like to provide any potential suitors with a little incentive. You see, Irene is . . . Well, don't get me wrong. No man could want a finer daughter.

She's smart as a whip and has the disposition of an angel, but a girl needs something more. We're both men of the world, Mr. Bates, so I know you understand."

"I'm not sure I do, Mr. Nolan," Gideon hedged, afraid he understood only too well.

Nolan sighed. "A man wants a woman who's at least a bit . . . *attractive*. It shouldn't matter, of course, but we both know it does, at least to most men, and Irene . . . Poor Irene took after me when it comes to looks, instead of her sainted mother, God rest her soul. She's a wonderful girl but not one a man would look at twice, if you know what I mean."

Oh dear, poor Irene indeed if that's what her own father thought of her. Gideon didn't even have to imagine what his mother would say on the subject of females being judged on their appearance, and his wife, Elizabeth, would agree with her whole-heartedly. For his part, Gideon wanted to argue with Mr. Nolan, but he couldn't exactly take the high ground on this subject since his own wife was quite lovely. He also had to admit that it had been her beauty that originally attracted him before he fell in love with her spirit. Still, he didn't want to confirm such a shallow quality in his gender as a whole.

"I'm sure your daughter will have many suitors who find her quite appealing."

"I admire your optimism, young man, but she's twenty-three and hasn't had a suitor yet, which is why I want to give her a dowry of sorts. It's an old-fashioned idea, but it used to do the trick, and I don't see why it couldn't do so again."

"Perhaps we shouldn't call it a dowry," Gideon suggested. "I like the word you used, 'settle.' Perhaps we could call it a settlement."

"So, you can fix that up for me?"

"I have a few ideas on the subject, but I'd like to discuss them with my partners who have a lot more experience with things like this." Was that really true? He hoped so. "They may have some even better suggestions. If you give me a week, I can prepare a proposal for you."

Nolan actually clapped his hands together with satisfaction. "That's the ticket! I knew you'd figure something out."

"Please wait until I've actually done it to compliment me, Mr. Nolan," Gideon begged him good-naturedly.

"Of course, of course. I appreciate your attitude, Mr. Bates. You're married, aren't you?"

Gideon blinked at the abruptness of the question. "Why, yes, I am." So, his fears that Nolan wanted to fix him up with Irene had been unfounded.

Nolan fingered his luxurious beard thoughtfully. "I'm wondering if you and your missus might enjoy a day at the races. The Belmont Stakes are next Wednesday, and it should be a good show. Sir Barton is running. They say he's the best horse of this year, maybe of this century."

"Yes, I've read a lot about him."

"I'd love to have you and your missus join me. I've got a box reserved since I have two horses running that day."

"In the Belmont?" Gideon asked in surprise.

"Oh no, in other races. I don't have a horse that good yet, but I'm still building my stable."

"I knew you raised horses, but I didn't know you raced them."

Nolan shrugged modestly. "I took up raising them as a hobby when I first made some money, but I finally started racing seriously the past few years. How about it? Do you think your wife would enjoy a day at Belmont Park or is she one of those folks who don't believe in gambling?"

Gideon was pretty sure Elizabeth had nothing against gambling, and she might very well enjoy a day at the track. "I'm sure she'd be happy to accompany me," Gideon said with confidence, "but I'll need to check with her in case she has other plans."

"I understand. And how about your mother? Would she join us, too, do you think?"

"She very well might. That's nice of you to include her, Mr. Nolan."

"Nonsense. I've got to fill up my box, and I've been thinking Irene should meet some society ladies. You see, her mother died when she was born, so she spent way too much time running wild at the stables growing up, and I'm afraid she knows more about horses than she does about etiquette."

Gideon bit back a smile. He should probably admit that his wife wasn't exactly a "society lady," but she was quickly becoming one, and, in any case, her background was certainly none of Nolan's business. For her part, Elizabeth would probably love the idea of being a role model for Irene Nolan, and his mother would like nothing better than helping Irene polish her social skills. "I'm sure my wife and mother will be delighted to meet your daughter at Belmont Park next Wednesday."

Elizabeth LOVED GREETING GIDEON AT THE FRONT DOOR when he returned home from work at the end of each day. He was always as happy to see her as she was to see him, and they shared a few moments alone in the front hallway to demonstrate that happiness before removing to the parlor, where Gideon's mother waited.

"Have you seen the newspapers?" his mother asked the moment he entered the parlor.

His smile matched hers. "Of course I did. Newsboys were hawking extras on every street corner. Congratulations!"

"I hardly deserve congratulations," Mother Bates demurred. "I'm not solely responsible for the passage of the Woman Suffrage Amendment."

"You certainly did your part, though," Elizabeth said, and turned to Gideon. "We've been remembering our days in the workhouse and how many women made such important sacrifices to get this passed." Elizabeth had never thought being sentenced to six months of hard labor for demonstrating outside the White House would result in meeting the love of her life—or more accurately, his mother—but she would always be grateful.

"I suppose you'll be planning some kind of celebration," Gideon said.

His mother shook her head. "Probably not until it's been ratified. We've been disappointed too many times over the past eighty years, and ratification is far from certain."

"But surely, we can't fail now, and it won't take long," Elizabeth said. "We only need thirty-six states to approve it."

"I hope you're right," Mother Bates said. "But it will certainly take some work."

"If work is all it takes, I have every confidence it will be approved," Gideon said. "I've never seen people work harder for anything in my life."

Elizabeth drew Gideon down beside her on the sofa. "Now, what is *your* big news?"

"What makes you think I have big news?" he asked, obviously surprised and probably a little peeved that she'd noticed.

She sighed like a good wife who has been underestimated yet again. "You always get that little gleam in your eye when you have something exciting to tell us."

He narrowed that eye and pretended to glare at her. "Maybe that little gleam means something else entirely."

Elizabeth fluttered her lashes in mock innocence. "Oh no, when you mean something else, it is a completely different gleam."

Mother Bates cleared her throat to remind them they weren't alone. "Why don't you just tell us, dear?"

Gideon shook his head in mock despair. "How would you both like to go to Belmont Park with me next Wednesday to watch the Belmont Stakes?"

"Are you serious?" Elizabeth cried in delight. "Mother Bates, Sir Barton is running in the Belmont. He's the most fabulous horse."

"How do you know that?" Gideon asked, a bit surprised.

"I read the newspapers, and they've been full of reports of his victories this past month."

"Indeed," Gideon confirmed. "He's already won the Kentucky Derby, the Preakness and the Withers. They're calling him the horse of the century."

"My goodness, Gideon, I had no idea you knew anything about horse racing," his mother said with a smile.

Gideon gave her a pitying look. "No young gentleman's education is complete until he has lost his entire monthly allowance at the track, Mother."

She was absolutely delighted to learn this fascinating fact about her son. "I had no idea."

"Which was the whole point," Gideon said.

"And did you lose your *entire* monthly allowance?" Elizabeth asked, equally delighted.

"Sadly, more than once, which is why I no longer frequent the racetrack."

"Then what has kindled your suddenly renewed interest?" Mother Bates asked. "Is it this horse, Sir What's His Name?"

"A client has inspired it, Mother. He owns racehorses, and he has two of them entered in some of the other races on Wednesday, so he has invited all of us to join him in his owner's box."

"What fun!" Elizabeth said. "You must go with us, Mother Bates."

"But I don't know the first thing about horse racing. It isn't, as you might guess, a required part of a *lady's* complete education."

"You don't have to know a thing about it to enjoy it. The races are so exciting, and the horses are all just magnificent to watch. You'll also get to see a lot of rich women dressed up so we can gossip about their outfits."

"You do make it sound intriguing," Mother Bates admitted with a smile. "But did you say it's on Wednesday? Don't you have to work, Gideon?"

"I can take the day off because a client invited me, so it's really business."

Elizabeth shared a knowing glance with her mother-in-law. "Men have such a broad idea of what business is."

"And there's one more thing you need to know," Gideon said to change the subject.

"Oh my, that sounds ominous," Elizabeth teased him.

"Not ominous, but I think it's important. Mr. Nolan— Sebastian Nolan, he's the client who invited us—has a daughter named Irene."

"How lovely," Mother Bates said. "I assume she will be there, too."

"Yes, she will. Mr. Nolan would very much like for her to meet some society ladies who will set her a good example."

"Does she need a good example?" Mother Bates asked with a worried frown.

"Mr. Nolan seems to think so. You see, her mother died when

Irene was very young, and the girl spent more time in the stables than in the drawing room, if you know what I mean. Her father seems to think she's a little rough around the edges."

"I'm sure that isn't true," Elizabeth said, having no idea if it was or not but feeling compelled to defend the young woman. Elizabeth had a few rough edges of her own.

"Does he think we can improve her by our mere presence at the racetrack for one day?" Mother Bates asked skeptically.

"I think he'd like for Irene and Elizabeth to become friends, which would give Irene time to observe and learn from her."

"I hardly feel qualified to teach someone about society," Elizabeth said in dismay. "I'm still learning myself."

"Nonsense, my dear," Mother Bates said. "You know more about how to be a lady than most of the women I know. Irene Nolan would do well to learn from you."

Elizabeth gave her mother-in-law a grateful smile. Really, she was so very lucky to have such a wonderful woman in her life. But then, she'd learned to love Mother Bates long before she even knew Gideon existed, having first met her when they were in prison together for demonstrating for Woman Suffrage. "I don't know how much I could teach Irene, but I know she could learn a lot from you, as I have."

"If she even needs it," Mother Bates said. "Perhaps her father is just being too persnickety."

"He may be, but he's concerned because she's twenty-three and hasn't attracted a serious suitor for her hand yet," Gideon said.

"Maybe she doesn't want to get married," Elizabeth said. "Maybe she is actively discouraging their attentions."

"I didn't think of that," Gideon said. They all knew a young lady in that very situation, so it was a definite possibility. "But her father thinks it's because she's . . . Well, he doesn't think she's very pretty."

Elizabeth and Mother Bates both exclaimed their outrage.

"I know," Gideon said, waving his hands to calm them. "I agree. I'm just telling you what he said."

"He actually said that?" Elizabeth cried.

"I'm afraid so. Or at least he said no man would look at her twice."

"As if that were a woman's sole purpose in life," Mother Bates huffed.

"I didn't want to tell you," Gideon said, "but I thought it was important for you to know."

"And thank you for telling us, darling," Elizabeth said, taking his hand in hers. "This girl needs far more than lessons in deportment, and we are just the two females who can help her."

Gideon smiled and squeezed her hand. "I knew you'd accept the challenge."

THE TRIP OUT TO BELMONT PARK WAS QUITE PLEASANT, since the Long Island Rail Road had run an extension from the Queens Village station to the park itself, which made it easy for city dwellers to reach the track. A lot of city dwellers were taking advantage of it today, too. The crowd moving toward Belmont was already large, proving Sir Barton's appearance in the Belmont Stakes was quite a draw. The weather just happened to be perfect as well, sunny but cool for June with a high temperature forecast to be around seventy degrees.

"Mr. Nolan was so thoughtful to invite us to join him for lunch at the clubhouse before the races start," Elizabeth said as they strolled toward the entrance gate.

"Have you spent a lot of time at racetracks?" Mother Bates asked quite innocently. Few society mothers would need to ask such a question of their daughters-in-law.

"I wouldn't say I spent a lot of time there, but enough to know my way around." Elizabeth gave Mother Bates an apologetic smile. "My family has made a lot of money at the racetrack, but not from betting on the horses."

Far from being shocked, Mother Bates was intrigued. "Really? What do they do there?"

"Mother," Gideon said with mock sternness, "that is not something we should be discussing here." He glanced meaningfully at the crowd around them.

Elizabeth nodded her agreement. "And if you happen to see my father or my brother today, don't let on that you know them. They'll probably be working." If "working" was the correct way to describe what con men did for a living. Jake and the Old Man would certainly be at the track today with such a huge crowd. With any luck, their paths would not cross, however.

"Oh my, yes, I'll be very discreet," Mother Bates promised.

Elizabeth gave her a grateful smile. She really was fortunate. How many women would find it merely interesting to discover their daughter-in-law came from a family of con artists?

The clubhouse was already crowded with early arrivals. People had come to claim a good spot for watching the races, and all of them were hungry. Fortunately, Mr. Nolan had a reserved table and was waiting for them. He waved to catch their eye and they made their way over to the table. Elizabeth was disappointed to discover he was alone.

"I thought your daughter would be joining us," Elizabeth said after Gideon had made the introductions and they were seated comfortably around the table.

"She will be. She's gone down to the stables to check on our horse, Trench. He's running in the last race of the day, and she's worried about him."

"Does she have a reason to worry?" Gideon asked.

"Not really. Our trainer says he's in peak condition, but Irene is a bit anxious. Trench is her baby, and this is his first race."

"Trench seems like a strange name for a horse," Mother Bates said.

"I agree, Mrs. Bates," Nolan said with a smile. "He was born right around the time we entered the war, though, and folks were all naming their horses something to do with guns or battles or war in general. I wanted to name him Bullet, since it would make him sound fast, but Irene chose Trench. She didn't like names that sounded violent."

"I see. How interesting," Mother Bates said. "Naming your horses must be a lot of fun."

Mr. Nolan began telling her stories of how they had chosen names for their various Thoroughbreds through the years, pausing only when the waiter brought them a pitcher of lemonade and asked the gentlemen if they would like something stronger. When Mr. Nolan had engaged Mother Bates again, Elizabeth leaned over to whisper to Gideon.

"Do you think Mr. Nolan is looking for a bride for himself?"

Gideon choked on his lemonade, and by the time he had recovered, a young woman had made her way over to their table.

"I'm so sorry I'm late," she said with a smile.

Irene Nolan was a pleasant surprise. She was tall, like her father, and thin rather than slender, but she was certainly no plain Jane. Elizabeth couldn't imagine why her father thought no man would look at her twice. She might not be conventionally pretty, but her smile was glorious and her brown eyes twinkled with mischief. Her blond hair was the color of honey and refused to be tamed. Even this early in the day, errant curls were escaping their pins. She wore a tailored walking suit that was obviously expensive but designed more for comfort and ease of movement than for style, and a hat that shaded her face but was unencumbered with the usual trimming that would make it difficult to manage. Irene was obviously a very sensible girl.

The two men rose to their feet while Mr. Nolan introduced everyone. Irene took the empty chair between Elizabeth and her father. "I'm so glad you were able to join us. Have you ever been to the races before?"

"Gideon and I have, but Mother Bates is here for the first time," Elizabeth said.

"Oh good! I love explaining everything to newcomers," Irene said. "You'll have a wonderful time, Mrs. Bates, and this beautiful day will end perfectly when my horse wins the last race."

"Then Trench is all right?" Mr. Nolan asked.

To Elizabeth's surprise, Irene's glorious smile disappeared. "Mr. Quaid checked him again, and he even asked the vet to look at him. They both said he's sound as a dollar."

"I told you," Mr. Nolan said. "You worry too much."

"I can't help it." She turned to Elizabeth and Gideon. "I was there when he was born, and I knew the minute I saw him that he was special. You wouldn't believe how fast he is in training."

"I thought you said you didn't have a horse good enough to enter in the Belmont Stakes," Gideon teased Mr. Nolan.

"Trench is only a two-year-old. Next year he'll make everyone forget all about Sir Barton. You'll be telling your grandchildren that you were here today and saw him win his first race."

They all laughed at that pleasant prospect, and the conversation drifted to other topics. The waiter had just served them their lunch when someone said, "Mrs. Bates? Hazel, is that you?"

They all looked up to see the dapper middle-aged man who had approached their table.

"August, how nice to see you," Mother Bates said. "What a lovely place you have here."

"Is this your first visit?" he asked.

"Yes, it is. Mr. Nolan was kind enough to invite us as his guests today."

"I didn't think I'd seen you here before."

"You remember Gideon, of course," Mother Bates said.

Gideon had already risen, and the two men shook hands. "So nice to see you, Mr. Belmont. We're looking forward to watching Sir Barton."

"As are we all," Belmont said.

Gideon introduced Elizabeth. Belmont accepted her compliments about Belmont Park and then he said, "Good to see you, Nolan. You've got a horse running today, don't you?"

"Two, in fact," Mr. Nolan said. "Have you met my daughter, Irene?"

"Of course, the angel of our stables. I think you must spend more time there than most of the trainers, Miss Nolan," Belmont teased.

"You may be right, Mr. Belmont," Irene retorted. "I know a lot more than most of them, too."

"I don't doubt it. Is Cal Regan riding Trench today?"

"Of course, although I think a bug boy could ride him to a win," Irene replied with her dazzling smile.

"I don't know about that, but Regan should bring him in, for sure. That boy is a wonder."

"I'll tell him you said so," Irene said, obviously delighted by the praise for her jockey. "Have you given any more thought to the idea of an American Triple Crown now that Sir Barton has proven a horse can win three important races in a matter of a few weeks?"

August Belmont shook his head in mock dismay. "I've said it before, it's not my decision alone, but if it were, I'd designate the Withers, the Lawrence Realization and the Belmont as our Triple Crown."

"But they're all New York races," Nolan protested. "Sir Barton proved a horse can travel long distances and still win. Why, he won the Derby and then traveled to Maryland and won the Preakness in only four days."

"Not many owners would risk their horses like that," Belmont said, "and I can't blame them. Until they figure out how to make travel a little easier on the animals, I don't think America will have a Triple Crown."

Nolan and Belmont exchanged a bit more small talk, and then Belmont took his leave after exhorting Mother Bates to enjoy herself.

"You're friends with August Belmont, Mrs. Bates?" Mr. Nolan said in wonder.

"Acquaintances," Mother Bates demurred. "Nothing more."

Elizabeth wasn't fooled. They had called each other by their first names. Mr. Nolan probably wasn't fooled, either. He looked more than a little smug at having hosted a friend of August Belmont, who had built this racetrack and named it after his father, August senior.

"Is this Mr. Belmont related to our Mrs. Belmont?" Elizabeth asked.

"To Alva, you mean?" Mother Bates said. After her husband died, Alva Vanderbilt Belmont had used her great wealth to finance the Woman Suffrage movement in America. "Yes, August was her late husband's brother."

"But Oliver Belmont wasn't involved with the racetrack, was he?" Irene said.

"No, although Oliver was just as horse-mad as all the other Belmonts. When he built his house in Newport, the entire first floor was the stables for his beloved horses."

Everyone except Gideon expressed their amazement at such a thing.

"He kept his horses in the house?" Irene exclaimed in surprise.

"Not only that, but the stables were just as well appointed as the rest of the house, with gilding and tiled walls and stained glass windows and even a marble watering trough. And the house only had one bedroom, so Oliver never had to invite guests to stay the night."

"Unless they wanted to sleep in a horse stall," Elizabeth said. "I can't imagine Mrs. Belmont tolerating that."

"They had other houses in Newport, so she didn't have to, but she did convert the stables into a ballroom when she and Oliver married. Oh, I just remembered a funny story about the house."

"Do tell," Irene encouraged her.

"I'd forgotten all about it until this very moment. Alva was entertaining some friends at the Newport house one afternoon when a wagonload of tourists pulled up out front. She told her guests to be quiet and listen because the guide would often say something humorous. This time the guide said, 'Alva Belmont used to dwell in marble halls with Mr. Vanderbilt. Now she lives over the stables with Mr. Belmont.'"

Everyone laughed uproariously at that, and Irene had to wipe tears from her eyes.

"Mother Bates, I'm so glad you remembered that."

"So am I," Mother Bates admitted, recovering her composure with some difficulty.

"Mrs. Bates?" Another well-dressed gentleman had approached the table, but his smile wasn't quite as friendly as Mr. Belmont's had been.

Mother Bates didn't seem to notice that, however, as she obviously recognized another old friend. "Daniel, how are you?"

"I'm well. You look as beautiful as ever, Hazel."

Mother Bates smiled at the compliment. "And you are as big a liar as ever. Are you here to watch Sir Barton race?"

"I'm afraid it won't be much of a contest, but yes, I am."

"You know Gideon." The two shook hands and Mother Bates introduced Elizabeth to her old friend, Daniel Livingston.

"Do you know Mr. Nolan and his daughter?" Mother Bates asked. Elizabeth thought it a fair question, since Mr. Belmont had known them well.

Only then did Mr. Livingston so much as glance at Mr. Nolan and Irene, and his gaze lingered no more than a second before returning to Mother Bates. "We've met." Neither man made any effort to shake hands or even acknowledge each other. The tension was palpable, although Mother Bates gave no indication that she felt it.

"Do you have a horse in one of the races today, Daniel?" she asked him.

"Yes, but it's just a plater. Nothing like Sir Barton or Nolan's Trench. He has high hopes for that one, I hear."

Elizabeth noticed he was speaking of Mr. Nolan as if he weren't present, a deliberate discourtesy. Mother Bates knew it, too, if the tightness of her lips was any indication. Still, she tried to smooth things over. "Yes, Miss Nolan assures me a bug boy could win the race with Trench."

Mr. Livingston's eyebrows rose at that, perhaps because he wouldn't have expected Mother Bates to use a term like "bug boy" or perhaps because he didn't expect Trench to win the race. "We'll see, won't we?" Mr. Livingston said. He nodded to Elizabeth. "So nice to meet you, Mrs. Bates, and to see you again, Gideon. Hazel, always a pleasure." He nodded politely and strolled away.

"I'm sorry. I have no idea why he was so rude," Mother Bates said to Mr. Nolan and Irene.

"Quite all right," Mr. Nolan assured her, although neither of the Nolans looked like it was all right.

"I just . . . I've known Daniel for years, and he's always been somewhat of a curmudgeon," Mother Bates said, still trying to smooth things over. "It all started years ago. He was engaged to a young lady whom he apparently adored, but she threw him over and eloped with someone else, I believe. He's been angry at the world ever since."

The Nolans exchanged a glance, and Mr. Nolan dropped his gaze, obviously not wanting to respond. Irene said, "I believe that young lady was my mother."

"Oh my goodness," Mother Bates exclaimed.

Elizabeth was just as surprised, but it certainly did explain Mr. Livingston's behavior. "He doesn't seem to have forgiven you," she remarked to Mr. Nolan.

He had no answer for her, but Irene said, "It's ridiculous, re-ally. It's been almost twenty-five years. How could you bear a grudge for all that time?"

"It does seem excessive," Elizabeth agreed. "Surely, the woman he did eventually marry wouldn't have tolerated it."

"He never married," Mother Bates said.

"And my mother died when I was born," Irene added. "I've always thought he must blame us for that as well."

It really was a sad story, but they couldn't allow this incident to ruin their lovely day. "I'm sorry for him, but that's no excuse to spoil our lunch," Elizabeth said.

"You are absolutely right, Elizabeth," Mother Bates said. "So, let's change the subject. I now know two new racing terms, but I have no idea what they mean. Perhaps you could enlighten me, Miss Nolan."

"Let me guess," Irene said, obviously grateful for the new topic of conversation. "One of them would be 'bug boy.'"

"You are correct," Mother Bates said with satisfaction.

Mr. Nolan's smile was a bit stiff, but he joined in the fun. "The other one is probably 'plater.'"

"Exactly. Now, who is going to explain them to me?"

Gideon said, "I believe Miss Nolan said she loves explaining things to newcomers."

"And I do," Irene agreed. "A bug boy is an apprentice jockey. They're all very young, so they really are boys, and many of the jockeys are not much more than boys, either. You see, there are weight limits on how much a horse can carry, so the jockeys must be very small and light."

"I see," Mother Bates said. "I guess a lot of the boys eventually grow too large to ride."

"That's right, and even the ones who remain small enough to continue riding are still called boys, no matter how old they are."

"But you haven't explained the bug part," Mother Bates said.

"When the names of the jockeys are listed, the apprentice jockeys will have an asterisk beside their names. Someone apparently thought it looked like a bug, so they have become known as bug boys."

"How funny," Mother Bates exclaimed. "And what about plater?"

"That one isn't as clever, I'm afraid. Some of the races are selling plates, which means the winning horse is auctioned off, and horses who run in these races are called platers."

"Why would someone want to sell their racehorse?" Mother Bates asked.

"Probably because it didn't win many races," Elizabeth said.

"Or because the owner needs the money," Mr. Nolan said somewhat apologetically. "Training racehorses is an uncertain business at best."

"Mr. Livingston said he has a plater running today," Gideon said.

"And so do I," Mr. Nolan said. "Dodger is running in the first race."

"You're not going to sell Trench, though, are you?" Mother Bates asked.

"Of course not," Mr. Nolan assured her. "Trench is going to make our stable famous."

"Father thinks that when Trench wins the Belmont Stakes next year, we'll be invited to Mr. Belmont's house for tea," Irene said with a twinkle.

Her father was not amused. "You can joke if you like, but I've seen it before. When you have a winning horse, people in society treat you with respect."

Elizabeth didn't think a winning horse would make Daniel Livingston treat Mr. Nolan with respect, but she knew better than to say so.

Before she could say anything at all, Mother Bates said, "Your father is probably just thinking of your future, Miss Nolan. I'm sure he'd like to see you recognized by the best people."

Irene gave her father a loving glance that softened his disgruntled frown. "You're right, Mrs. Bates, but I think I'm already recognized by the best people. They're the ones working down at the stables and taking care of my horses. I don't care much for anyone else's opinion."

Elizabeth reached over and covered Irene's hand with her own where it lay on the table. "I knew we were going to be great friends. Now tell me which horses you think are going to win today so we'll know how to place our bets."

# CHAPTER TWO

❧

THE GROUP REACHED SEBASTIAN NOLAN'S BOX WELL IN TIME for the first race at two thirty. Except for the brief unpleasantness with Daniel Livingston, Gideon was enjoying watching his mother's excitement as she learned all about horse racing. He was also enjoying watching Elizabeth charm the Nolans. She might not have been born into society, but she was masterful at managing the many traditions that set that class apart and preserved their exclusivity, no matter how silly and hidebound those traditions might be. She was a wonder to observe.

His mother and Irene took the two front seats in the box, and Gideon sat down beside Nolan in the back row. Elizabeth sat alone in the middle row so she could more easily participate in his mother's racing education.

"My trainer may join us to watch the races," Nolan said, indicating the empty seat beside Elizabeth. "But he'll be busy the rest of the time, keeping an eye on Trench."

The "box" wasn't anything like a box at the theater or the opera. Only a three-foot-high wooden barrier separated the boxes from each other, and they could see and easily converse with people in the adjacent boxes. Gideon greeted several people he knew.

His mother was asking about the hedges in the inner track. She couldn't understand how the horses could run with hedges blocking their way. Irene and Elizabeth explained that track was for the steeplechase races. The second race of the day was a steeplechase and his mother seemed quite pleased she would get to watch one.

"I'll never get used to seeing the horses running the opposite way on this track," Nolan said.

"I know. I think August Belmont just enjoys being different." Belmont had decreed that the races at Belmont Park would be run clockwise, the way most racetracks were designed in England, even though all the other American tracks ran counterclockwise. "Do you think the horses get confused?"

"A few do, and they simply can't race here."

Gideon glanced at his program. "Are you going to bet on Dodger?"

Nolan smiled. "I never bet. That's a fool's game. The odds on Dodger are too low anyway. He's the favorite in his race."

"I see." The program listed projected odds for each of the horses and Dodger's listing indicated Nolan was correct. Still, the odds always changed as the bets were placed and the race drew closer.

"Should we bet on your horse, Miss Nolan?" his mother asked.

"I'm sure he's going to win, but I wouldn't advise you to bet on anything unless you're willing to lose your money."

"That's good advice, Mother," Gideon said.

"I can afford to lose a few dollars," his mother assured them. "How would I go about placing a bet?"

"The wagering area is no place for a lady nowadays," Mr. Nolan said quickly. "If you really want to place a bet, Gideon or I will do it for you."

"Why can't I go myself?" his mother asked, obviously disappointed to miss this part of the racing experience.

"Perhaps you remember a few years ago when the anti-gambling forces managed to close down the racetracks completely, because if people can't bet on the races, they aren't nearly as much fun to watch," Irene said.

"Yes, now that you mention it, I do remember that," Mother Bates said. "But the tracks are open again now."

"Yes, but only here in New York State, and only because the courts here ruled that . . . Well, it's complicated, but wagering is now a free-for-all because we have to pretend that placing a bet with a bookie is just two individuals making a private bet."

"And as a consequence," her father continued, "the wagering area is no longer the orderly place it used to be, with bookies having their own booths with the odds posted publicly. Now the place is bedlam with every man for himself, and it's certainly not a place you should be, Mrs. Bates."

His mother decided she would forgo the pleasure of betting rather than inconvenience Gideon and Mr. Nolan, so they settled back to watch the preparations for the race. The weather was still fine, and the track was dry. At last, the horses began the parade to the starting barrier.

"They really are magnificent animals," his mother exclaimed. "Which one is Dodger?"

"The third one in line. Our lead jockey, Cal Regan, is wearing the yellow silks."

"He's going to ride Trench later, too, isn't he?" his mother asked.

"Yes, Cal is one of the best jockeys around," Irene said with more than a little pride.

"I see Mr. Livingston's horse is running in this race, too," Gideon said.

"That would be his plater," his mother said knowledgeably.

"Yes," Irene confirmed, "but he doesn't stand a chance. Cal will bring Dodger home."

"What is that thing blocking the track?" his mother asked. "It looks like a giant badminton net. Don't tell me the horses have to jump over that. It's much too high."

"That's the starting barrier," Irene explained. "The horses have to line up behind it, and when all of them are in place and standing still, the starter—see the man with the flag—he lowers the flag he's holding, and they quickly raise the barrier, and the race begins."

"Not all the horses seem to be cooperating," his mother observed.

"Which is why we get a lot of false starts," Mr. Nolan said. "It's an imperfect process."

"And not a very safe one," Gideon said. "I've seen the barrier catch a jockey's chin when it goes up and throw him clear off his horse."

"I've seen worse things than that," Mr. Nolan said. "But it's the system we have, and we must work with it."

They watched intently as the horses took their places and shifted restlessly. Gideon observed that the starter must be very careful so as not to give one horse an advantage over another. One horse backed away from the barrier and the rider had to bring him forward again. If the barrier went up while the horse was moving, he would have a decided advantage over the others who would have to start from a dead stop. But at last, all the horses were in place and the starter dropped his flag. The barrier flew up without mishap and the horses darted forward.

The entire crowd of twenty-five thousand shouted, "They're off!" in unison.

"Racing is all strategy, Mrs. Bates," Irene explained, raising her voice to be heard over the shouts from the crowd. "Usually, you want to ride as close to the inner rail as possible, because that's the shortest distance around the track."

"And Mr. Regan has brought Dodger right to the rail already," his mother shouted in delight. "But why isn't he in front?"

"That's another part of the strategy. The front-runners are going flat out, and it's difficult for most horses to keep up that pace for over a mile."

"I see, so they get tired and drop back."

"Exactly," Irene said, her dazzling smile showing her approval of her student's cleverness.

"Which one is Mr. Livingston's horse?" his mother asked.

"The one in dark blue silks," Gideon said.

"Oh, look, he's coming right up beside Dodger," his mother said.

The horses had reached the far turn and Livingston's horse was running neck and neck with Dodger. The two horses ran practically in lockstep around the turn and when they reached the final stretch, the two horses who had been in front gradually dropped back and Dodger and the Livingston horse took the lead.

Gideon fully expected one or the other to pull ahead now, since the jockeys would urge the animals to their best efforts in the final push for the finish, but to his surprise, they remained side by side as if attached somehow.

"What the devil?" Nolan cried. "Why isn't Cal making his move?"

Irene was yelling something, too, some instruction that the jockey couldn't possibly hear over the din from the crowd, which was screaming almost in unison for one or the other horse to prevail. And still neither jockey responded, although Gideon thought he saw Cal Regan raise his whip and strike the other jockey. That couldn't be true, though. Why would he strike another jockey?

Gideon was so focused on the two horses running in tandem that he almost missed a third horse that came galloping up on their outside. On the home stretch, there was no longer an advantage to running along the rail, and this jockey easily passed the two others and left them more than a length behind as he crossed the finish line.

Nolan was shouting invectives down on his jockey for not taking advantage of his perfect position to easily win the race, and to Gideon's horror, he kicked the wooden barrier separating their box from the one next to it, making the whole wall shake. Irene turned to her father, her face chalk white, her mouth open in shock, and Elizabeth and his mother were also gaping at him. For a moment, Gideon was afraid he might have to restrain him, but fortunately, Nolan quickly realized he had frightened his guests and visibly got control of his temper.

"If you ladies will excuse me, I need to speak to my jockey," Nolan said, remembering his manners with obvious effort. "Irene, stay here with our guests."

Irene voiced a protest, but Nolan was already gone. Gideon gave a moment's thought to his responsibilities and realized he had none, so he obeyed his instinct. He followed Nolan, eager to learn what had happened and to make sure the man didn't lose control again. The crowd was thick, but Nolan used his bulk to force his way through, and Gideon had only to follow in his wake until they reached the area where the horses were being cooled down. One of Nolan's stable boys had taken Dodger's head to lead him around while the jockey, who had dismounted, was having a heated discussion with a man in a suit who must be the trainer.

"Cal!" Nolan shouted, obviously furious, but when the jockey turned, he was even more furious.

"I'm sorry, Mr. Nolan, but Hawkins hooked his leg over mine. I couldn't do a thing."

"He hooked your leg?" Nolan echoed in amazement. "Who would dare try a dirty trick like that here at Belmont Park?"

"Hawkins would, or Livingston," the man Gideon had identified as the trainer said bitterly. "Hawkins wouldn't do it on his own, that's sure."

Nolan cursed. Only then did he realize Gideon had followed him. "Bates, what are you doing here?"

"I wanted to know what happened, too," Gideon said. He turned to the jockey, who was a remarkably handsome young man who stood nearly a head shorter than Gideon even though he was obviously well out of his teens. He had been one of the lucky bug boys who didn't grow out of his job. "I thought I saw you hitting the other jockey."

"I did," Regan said, still so angry his words sounded breathless. "I was shouting at him to let me go, and when he wouldn't, I used my crop on him. But he must've had his orders not to let me win."

"It doesn't make any sense," the trainer said. Gideon remembered his name was Quaid. "Why would Livingston give an order like that? It meant his horse didn't win, either."

"But nobody else would do it without Livingston's approval," Nolan said.

Did Livingston hate Nolan that much? And what a petty revenge for a broken love affair that happened a quarter century ago.

"Livingston didn't care about winning," Nolan said. "He just wanted to keep Dodger back."

Gideon couldn't imagine why that would matter to a man like Livingston, but he couldn't very well ask a question like that in such a public place. They had already been overheard by everyone who was in the cool-down area—jockeys and trainers and stable boys and owners alike. The story would be all over the track in a few more minutes, Gideon was sure. He glanced around to see if Livingston himself was there, but he had apparently chosen to enjoy his triumph elsewhere.

Livingston's jockey was there, though, and he came striding over. "Are you accusing me of something, Regan?"

"We'll be filing a complaint against you, Hawkins," Quaid said. "You might pull a stunt like that at some bush-league track, but jockeys act civilized here in New York."

"And I'll be filing a complaint because Regan hit me with his whip, and I've got the welts to prove it."

"Yeah?" Regan taunted. "Let's see them."

Since Regan had struck Hawkins on his backside, Hawkins could only glare. "You'll be hearing from the commissioners." He strode away.

"You want me to file that complaint, Mr. Nolan?" Quaid asked.

Nolan sighed. "Let me think about it. I want to see if Livingston is stupid enough to file first. If either of us do, they'll probably suspend both jockeys and that won't help anybody."

"I doubt Livingston will want people to know what Hawkins did," Gideon said. "Everyone would be sure Livingston had ordered it."

"Maybe Livingston doesn't care what people think of him," Nolan said. Now he sounded bitter, too.

"People like Livingston always care what people think," Gideon said. He turned to Regan. "I'm sorry things went so badly for you, but it was a good race up until then."

Regan sighed. "Thanks."

Nolan remembered his manners and introduced Gideon to

Regan and Quaid. They commiserated a few more minutes and then Gideon and Nolan headed back to their box.

"I know you were certain you'd win that race," Gideon said, remembering this had been a selling plate. "But at least you don't have to auction Dodger now."

Nolan shook his head. "I needed to sell him. Things have been . . . tight lately."

Gideon remembered Nolan wanted to make a settlement on Irene and wondered how the race money would have figured into that. He had a few questions for Mr. Nolan, but they would have to wait for a more private place.

E LIZABETH AND MOTHER BATES HAD BEEN DOING THEIR BEST to calm Irene, but nothing they could say helped at all. She was furious at how the race had gone and couldn't understand the jockey's behavior, but even more interesting was her determination not to blame him for whatever had gone wrong.

"You seem very fond of Mr. Regan," Mother Bates observed gently as Irene dabbed at the tears she couldn't seem to control.

Irene's head jerked up at that. "What do you mean?"

Mother Bates was a little surprised at Irene's reaction, but she said, "You mentioned how much you think of the people who work for your father, so naturally, I thought you also meant Mr. Regan."

That seemed to placate Irene a bit. "Yes, well, Cal is . . . I've known him for such a long time. He was only thirteen when he came to us. He ran away from home because he wanted to ride horses, and Father gave him a job mucking out the stables. I was eleven, and I still thought mucking out the stables was great fun, so we became friends."

"Then you grew up together," Elizabeth said.

"Yes, I guess we did. He slept in the house and ate his meals with us."

"He was like a brother to you then," Mother Bates said.

"Yes, like a brother," Irene agreed too quickly, and neither of them missed the way the color rose in her cheeks when she said it. Cal Regan was evidently more than a brother to Irene and wasn't that interesting? No wonder she said she cared more about what the people in the stable thought of her than what society people did.

A few of those inhabiting the surrounding boxes had expressed their regrets to Irene over Dodger's loss, and she had replied stiffly to each one. Owners, she explained to her guests, were supposed to pretend that they didn't care if their horse won or lost and greet either outcome with calm acceptance. Elizabeth could easily see that Irene's concern was only for Cal Regan, though, and not whether her horse had won or lost.

After what seemed an age, but which couldn't have been more than a few minutes because the horses were just lining up for the next race, Gideon and Mr. Nolan returned. Irene was on her feet immediately. "What happened?"

Mr. Nolan sighed wearily. "Hawkins hooked Cal's knee and wouldn't let him go."

"*What?*" Irene cried in horror. "Why on earth would he do a thing like that?"

"I suppose because he didn't want Dodger to win," Mr. Nolan said, sinking down into his chair.

Mother Bates looked hopelessly confused, so Elizabeth explained. "This Hawkins, who I assume was the other jockey, brought his horse up beside Dodger and hooked his leg over Mr. Regan's. That made it impossible for Mr. Regan to pull ahead because if he did, he'd be swept off Dodger's back and into the path of the other horses."

"Good heavens, he could have been killed," Mother Bates said.

Had that been the intention or was this Hawkins simply trying to prevent Cal Regan from winning the race?

"I can't believe Cal didn't do something," Irene said. She had sunk back down in her own chair, obviously flummoxed by this news.

"He did," Gideon said. "He hit Hawkins with his whip. I saw it myself, and he admitted it, too, but Hawkins still wouldn't let him go."

"That son of a . . . Oh, I'm sorry, ladies," Mr. Nolan mumbled.

"Why would this Hawkins fellow do something like that?" Mother Bates asked.

"We'd have to ask him, but it's pretty easy to figure out," Mr. Nolan said. "Livingston must have thought that I needed the money from auctioning off Dodger, so he told Hawkins to do whatever he could to make sure Dodger didn't win the race."

"Even though it meant his horse didn't win, either," Irene said. "What a horrible man."

"Irene, didn't you tell me that owners aren't supposed to care whether their horses win or lose?" Mother Bates said in that voice she used when she was trying to teach Elizabeth a valuable lesson in deportment. Elizabeth leaned in to be sure to hear what she said, and Irene responded instinctively.

"We can care," Irene clarified. "We just aren't supposed to show it."

"Then let's not give Daniel Livingston the satisfaction of seeing us downcast, shall we? I for one am very interested to see how horses can race while jumping over hedges."

Indeed, the horses entered in the steeplechase were lining up on the inside track. Irene somehow managed to smile. "I think you'll be impressed."

Mother Bates turned and said over her shoulder to Mr. Nolan, "By the way, in spite of everything, Dodger finished in the money."

Elizabeth didn't bother to cover her laugh at Gideon's shocked expression, and even Mr. Nolan looked surprised, but not to find out that Dodger had come in third, a nose behind Livingston's horse, which was joined to him. Rather, they were surprised to hear Mother Bates rattling off racing terms like an old hand.

Meanwhile, she had turned back to the race preparations. "Where is the barrier for this race?"

"They don't use a barrier for steeplechase," Irene patiently explained. "The horses just line up."

"Sort of like an honor system," Mother Bates mused.

Elizabeth did hide her smile at that. She didn't want her mother-in-law to think she was laughing at her, even though she was.

The steeplechase was just as exciting as Mother Bates had expected, and afterward they chatted with some friends who stopped by the box before the next race. The Harlem Selling Stakes was third on the schedule, and Mother Bates insisted on betting two dollars on Matinee Idol because he had such a charming name. Sadly, he came in last, so everyone told her she wasn't allowed to bet on Trench when the time came. Then, at last, it was time for the Belmont Stakes.

"Only three horses in this race?" Mother Bates lamented as they paraded to the starting line.

"There were two more entered, but they scratched," Gideon explained. "That means—"

"I know what it means," his mother informed him loftily. "Irene already explained it to me. But why would you scratch a horse from such an important race?"

"They might have been injured in training, but more likely it was because no one can beat Sir Barton, Mrs. Bates," Mr. Nolan said kindly. "Mr. Coe originally entered three of his horses, just to make it a real race, but he's had to scratch one of them, and Pastoral Swain was scratched as well."

"That doesn't seem very sporting," Mother Bates complained. "You'd think they'd at least want to challenge Sir Barton."

"It's possible no other horse *can* challenge him, Mrs. Bates," Irene said. "Even the program says Sir Barton is the champion of his age."

They watched as the horses paraded to the barrier.

"He's a beautiful animal, isn't he?" Irene said of the chestnut stallion.

"He's smaller than I expected," Gideon said. "You wouldn't think he could be so fast."

"Less weight to carry," Mr. Nolan said.

"With only three horses in the race, at least all of them will finish in the money," Mother Bates remarked.

"Now you're just showing off, Mother," Gideon said, making her laugh.

The course for the Belmont Stakes was a strange, fishhook shape, and it started on the practice track at the far end of the park so it could end in front of the grandstand. Everyone stood and craned their necks to see the start so very far away. The horses stood in a perfect line for just a moment, and the starter caught them there, dropping the flag so the barrier could fly up. "They're off!" the crowd yelled.

Sir Barton was running before the other two horses even knew what was happening, giving the impression he had broken right through the barrier, but his jockey wasn't about to let him take the lead so early. Johnny Loftus held him back and to the crowd's amazement, he let Natural Bridge take the lead by two lengths, with Sweep On following two lengths behind. Just as if they had choreographed the race, they held this perfect symmetry all the way around the training track.

"Why isn't Sir Barton winning?" Mother Bates shouted above the din of cheers from the crowd.

"Johnny Loftus is just giving us a show," Irene replied, laughing with pleasure.

Then the horses reached the spot where the training track joined the main track for a straight run of nearly a half mile to the special finish line, and Johnny Loftus gave Sir Barton some signal invisible to everyone else. Sir Barton roared away with such speed the crowd seemed to gasp in unison. He opened so large a gap that Johnny actually slowed Sir Barton down as they approached the finish line. Sir Barton still won by six lengths.

Even though the race had never been a real contest and the opponents nothing more than shills, everyone present knew they had seen greatness. In spite of having been held back for half the race and being slowed down at the end, Sir Barton had set a new American record. A second round of cheers erupted when the numbers were posted on the infield sign.

"Ladies," Mr. Nolan said with some satisfaction, "you have witnessed history."

Some of the people in the boxes began to leave after Sir Barton had received his accolades in the winner's circle. There were still two races to be run, but for most, the excitement was over with the running of the Belmont Stakes. All that was left was a claiming race for three-year-olds and upward and the final, which was a maiden race for horses at least two years old that hadn't yet won a race. This was to be Trench's big moment, so naturally Mr. Nolan's guests weren't going anywhere.

While they waited for the fifth race to begin, Mr. Nolan ordered some beverages for them to enjoy. From their box, they had a good view of the apron below, the area between the track and the grandstands, where the general public mingled and watched the races. Elizabeth had purposely not spent much time watching the people come and go in that area, because she was afraid she might see someone to whom she was related. She was chatting with Irene when Mr. Nolan startled them. The sound he made was somewhere between a gasp and a groan, and Elizabeth turned in alarm, terrified she would see him clutching his chest and falling to the ground.

Instead, he was half out of his chair and leaning forward in an attempt to see something down on the apron. His face was white and his expression shocked.

"Father?" Irene cried. "What is it?"

"Nolan?" Gideon asked, laying a hand carefully on Mr. Nolan's shoulder. "Are you all right?"

Nolan shook his head as if to clear it and sat back down in his chair, although his gaze never left whatever he'd been staring at. "I'm fine. It's only . . . That woman. She looks just like my late wife."

"Which woman?" Irene asked, turning eagerly back toward the apron. Of course she'd be interested, since she had never known her mother.

"The one in the pink dress," Nolan said. "She . . . I know it can't be her, but . . . She does resemble Mary. It was a bit of a shock, I'm afraid."

Elizabeth was looking, too, because how could she resist? She saw a woman in a mauve walking suit, something a man might call a "pink dress."

"Is that the one?" Irene asked eagerly. "The lady standing with that tall man in the top hat?"

"Yes," Nolan said, recovering himself now. "I can't believe how much she looks like your mother. It's uncanny."

But what was really uncanny, to Elizabeth, at any rate, was that she knew the tall man in the top hat. She knew him very well. He was, in fact, her father.

G IDEON SAW HIM, TOO. HE WONDERED IF MR. MILES KNEW his daughter was sitting in one of the owner's boxes. He also wondered what Mr. Miles was doing today. Since his father-in-law made his living by conning people out of their money, that was probably why he was here, although he would have done better to mingle with the people in the grandstands instead of those down on the apron. But the lady he was with, the one who apparently resembled the late Mrs. Nolan, did seem prosperous. Maybe she was his mark. Cheating a female seemed low even for a con artist, but Gideon supposed if you had no scruples, such a thing could hardly matter.

Like everyone else in their box, Gideon watched the woman, although surely she would eventually feel them all staring at her and look up and catch them at it. Irene was actually leaning forward in her seat, making no secret of her interest. Eventually, Mr. Miles and the woman strolled away. Perhaps they had decided to leave like so many others or perhaps Mr. Miles had spotted a new mark. At any rate, they soon disappeared into the crowd.

Gideon sighed with relief and so did Mr. Nolan. Irene, on the other hand, was disappointed. "Was Mother really as beautiful as that woman?" she asked, turning in her chair to face her father.

"Even more so," Mr. Nolan said loyally. "And you look just like her."

Irene shook her head in despair. "He's such a liar," she informed

Gideon's mother. "I wish we could have spoken to her. Maybe she's some long-lost relation."

As usual, Gideon's mother was sensitive to the undercurrents of emotion and realized Mr. Nolan didn't really want to discuss the subject. She picked up her program and said, "This next one is a claiming race. What does that mean?"

Although Irene clearly would have liked to continue discussing the mysterious woman who looked like her dead mother, she knew she mustn't ignore her guests. She proceeded to explain that any of the horses in a claiming race could be purchased by "claiming" it prior to the start of the race. The owner would receive the set sale price and any money earned if the horse finished in the money.

Several of the entrants had scratched, so only five horses ran. Daddy's Choice took an early lead and was never challenged.

As soon as the race ended, Irene rose from her seat, obviously intending to leave. Gideon assumed she'd want to go check on Trench and his jockey before their race.

"Let's walk down to the paddock and watch the horses being saddled," Mr. Nolan said before she could speak.

"Can we?" Gideon's mother asked, delighted.

"I'd love to meet Trench in person," Elizabeth said.

Irene smiled at that, although Gideon noticed her smile was a bit strained. Plainly, she was still a little worried about her horse or maybe it was her jockey. "I would be happy to introduce you. Shall we?" She motioned for the other ladies to precede her, and they filed out of the box and made their way to the grassy area where the horses gathered before each race to be saddled and mounted.

"I can't get over how beautiful they all are," his mother marveled as they made their way past the other horses to find Trench. "What makes their coats so shiny?"

"They oil them, Mother," Gideon said. "Although I've never understood why they go to all that trouble just to make them look nice."

"All part of the show," Nolan said with a knowing smile. "There he is. That's Trench."

The ladies recognized the yellow silks Cal Regan wore and they made all the appropriate remarks about how beautiful Trench was. He was indeed. A dark gray with white stockings and a white blaze on his face, he stood out from all the other horses and not just because of his unusual coloring. He seemed taller and larger and gave the impression of being carved from living stone. Gideon had no trouble at all understanding why Nolan had placed all his hopes on this animal.

Irene had hurried on ahead and she was already beside Trench, in earnest conversation with Mr. Quaid and Cal Regan.

"I can't find a thing wrong with him, Miss Nolan, and neither could the vet," Quaid was saying.

"He worked out fine this morning," Regan confirmed, obviously anxious to put her mind at ease.

Irene reached up and gently stroked the enormous stallion's face as if he were a lapdog. "I just have this feeling . . ."

"Females and their feelings," Mr. Nolan said in an attempt to lighten the mood, but Irene scowled. "Quaid knows what he's doing, Irene, and so does Cal. If they say he's good to go, then we have to trust them."

"It'll be all right," Regan said softly. "I'm going to win this one for you."

Irene gave him what she might have thought was a grateful look in return, but even Gideon could see she felt more than gratitude for the jockey. She might tower over him, but she obviously cared for him, and he undoubtedly returned her feelings.

Could the two of them be in love?

Gideon glanced at Nolan to see if he had noticed, but he was too busy looking over his horse. What would Nolan say if he thought his daughter was in love with a jockey? Probably what any wealthy father would say if his daughter was in love with the chauffer. Jockeys as good a Regan earned a generous salary, but their careers were too often cut short by injury or simply by the bad luck of losing too many races. Nolan would want much more security than that for his only child. Irene would know that, of course, and she couldn't possibly be seriously involved with Regan.

The call came. "Riders up!"

"We need to get back to our box so we can see the race," Nolan said. "Come on, Irene. Cal will take it from here."

Irene cast the jockey one last longing look and then followed the rest of them as they made their way back. Gideon was glad to see his mother link arms with Irene as they strolled. She would do her best to calm the girl. Gideon gave Elizabeth his arm.

"Do you think there's something wrong with the horse?" she asked him quietly so Irene wouldn't hear.

"I have no idea, but surely the trainer wouldn't let him race if there was."

"Racehorses are such delicate creatures, for all their strength. So many things can go wrong with them."

"Let's hope it's just prerace jitters on Irene's part."

The horses were parading by the time Nolan and his group found their places again. They watched as each horse reached the barrier. It seemed to take an age for them all to line up, although it was probably no more than a minute or two. The remaining crowd yelled, "They're off!" as the barrier flew up and the horses darted forward. It was a slow start, and Regan kept Trench from taking the lead, allowing the speedsters to charge ahead and wear themselves out. They had just rounded the first turn when he gave

Trench his head. The stallion started to pull away from the pack when something happened.

They were all on their feet immediately, trying to see, but the horses were on the far side of the track and the rail was in the way. One thing was for certain: Six horses had come out of the first turn, but only five were entering the final turn. None of those five jockeys wore the Nolan yellow silks.

"What happened?" Irene cried. "Where are they?"

Then they saw Trench. He had risen and staggered away from the rail, and to their horror they saw he was dragging Cal Regan, whose foot was caught in a stirrup.

Irene screamed, and she was running away from the box and down to the track before anyone could stop her. Nolan ran after her without a word.

# CHAPTER THREE

"Y<small>OU'D BETTER STAY HERE</small>," <small>GIDEON TOLD ELIZABETH AND</small> his mother. "I'll see if I can help."

Elizabeth would have been a good support for Irene, but they couldn't leave his mother all alone, and Gideon couldn't imagine his mother running out across the track and the infield to where Trench and Cal had fallen. He silently asked Elizabeth if she understood, and she nodded.

"Yes, go," she said. "We'll be fine."

Since Belmont Park was specifically designed to keep spectators from accidentally or purposefully getting out onto the track, Gideon had to run a good way to find a break in the fencing. By then the race was over, and he wasn't the only one running across the track, ducking under the rail and then crossing the infield to deal with the rail again before reaching the far side of the track.

Fortunately, many people had been watching the race from the infield and some had immediately hurried to rescue Cal Regan, corralling Trench and freeing Cal's foot from the stirrup. No one could do much more for him, however, except keep Trench a safe distance away. Oddly, this wasn't much of a challenge since the horse seemed to have broken down in some way and was standing docile.

Irene had pushed her way through the crowd gathered around the injured jockey, and she was pleading with them to do something as Regan groaned in agony. His right leg was twisted at an odd angle and blood seeped out of the top of his boot to soak his silk pants and puddle in the dirt.

Her father was there, too, standing over Regan and wringing his hands helplessly. Gideon saw Quaid had taken charge of Trench, who was able to walk, although he hung his head in an uncharacteristic way.

"Are they bringing an ambulance?" Gideon asked Nolan, whose stricken gaze kept darting between the injured jockey and the cowed horse.

Nolan turned to Gideon as if he'd never seen him before. "What?"

"An ambulance. They need to bring up an ambulance to get Regan to a hospital. That leg is badly broken."

"They don't have ambulances here," someone said, as if Gideon were an idiot to even suggest such a thing.

No ambulance at a place where jockeys were routinely thrown or otherwise injured, sometimes grievously? "There must be something," Gideon argued. "This man needs medical attention immediately."

"Maybe the vet should just shoot him," some wag suggested darkly.

Gideon turned to see who had made such a horrible suggestion, but the onlookers retreated a few steps at his fury, refusing to meet his eye. He gave up and turned back to Nolan. "You can't just leave him lying there."

"I . . . I sent someone to see if they could find a truck or even a wagon," Nolan said, his attention finally focused fully on Regan. "What on earth happened?"

"What happened?" Gideon repeated, raising his voice so the crowd could hear him. "Did anyone see what happened?"

"He just collapsed," one man said.

"Yeah," another confirmed. "The horse, he kind of lurched sideways and hit the rail, then fell down. Regan lost his seat, but his foot was caught. He got dragged a bit before we could catch them."

"He needs a doctor," Irene cried. She was sobbing now, cradling one of Regan's hands in both of hers. "You have to do something."

"We'll take care of him," Nolan promised rashly, although no one had lifted a finger to do anything of the kind.

Gideon's heart ached for the jockey, but he made no move to help, afraid that in his complete ignorance he would do exactly the wrong thing and cause even more damage.

Some of the other jockeys from the race had made the complete circuit to come back to see what happened. Everyone wanted to know what they'd seen. The two jockeys whose horses had been in front hadn't even known anything was wrong until the race was over. The rest confirmed what the other witnesses had seen. No one had even been close enough to have caused the accident. It seemed that Trench had simply fallen for no apparent reason.

Gideon was starting to think he should go himself to find some means of transporting Regan when they heard the roar of a motor, and a battered truck rattled down the track toward them. It was obviously a vehicle used to transport hay and whatever other equipment was needed around the track. It was filthy and decrepit and Gideon wondered how far the sputtering engine would take them, but no one else seemed alarmed.

Half a dozen men stepped forward to lift Regan into the truck bed. His screams were testimony to a lack of gentleness, but finally he was securely placed. Irene started to climb up after him.

"You can't go," Nolan said.

"I'm not leaving him," Irene said fiercely.

"I'll go."

"Then we'll both go," she said. She hoisted herself up into the truck bed with no regard for the delicacy of her outfit or maidenly modesty.

Nolan gave Gideon an apologetic look. "I'm sorry, but—"

"No need to apologize. Take care of Regan. We'll be fine," Gideon assured him.

"Father, hurry!" Irene shouted. Her face was white and her eyes wild. Plainly she was terrified for Regan, and she had every right to be.

Nolan climbed up behind her and shouted for them to head for the nearest hospital. The driver took off, stirring up a cloud of dust that sent the spectators scattering. Gideon strode over to where Quaid and some stable boys were tending to Trench.

"Is he hurt?" Gideon asked.

"Not that I can tell right now. His legs seem fine, and he doesn't act like he's in pain, but he's not breathing right. I'm afraid he's broke down somehow."

"I don't suppose they have an ambulance for horses here, either," Gideon said, not bothering to hide his anger.

Quaid smiled sadly. "If the horse can walk, you take it back to the stables. If it can't walk, you shoot it and haul it away."

"I guess Trench is lucky he can walk then."

Gideon watched for a long moment as Quaid and the others

led Trench back down the track toward the stables. The crowd had dispersed now that the drama was over, and all that remained was a dark stain in the dirt where Regan had bled. That meant a really bad break where the bone had come through the skin, which had to be terrible news for a man who made his living with his body.

Shaking his head, Gideon began to retrace his steps to where Elizabeth and his mother awaited his return.

H OW HORRIBLE," MOTHER BATES SAID WHEN GIDEON EX-plained what he understood about what had happened.

"I can't believe they didn't have an ambulance to take him to the hospital," Gideon said. "Apparently they make no provision at all for injured jockeys or horses."

Elizabeth shook her head. She knew many more shocking things about the lax way racetracks were operated and how little concern there was for the well-being of horses or jockeys, but she didn't see the need to mention them now. "Do we even know which hospital they took him to?"

"Nolan just ordered the driver to the closest one. We can probably figure it out."

"Or contact Mr. Nolan tomorrow," Mother Bates said sensibly. "There's no use following them now. There's nothing we can do for the poor man."

"You're right," Elizabeth said. "We should just go home. No one will know anything about Mr. Regan until morning, and we'd just be in the way at the hospital."

The last of the crowds were filing out of the park as they made their way to the train station. The ride home was crowded, and they had no chance to talk, although those around them were full of conjecture about why Trench might have fallen. Elizabeth had some ideas of her own.

When they finally got home, Elizabeth made them sandwiches since the servants had been given the afternoon off.

"This certainly isn't the evening I had envisioned," Mother Bates said as they sat round the table with their impromptu supper.

"I know," Elizabeth agreed. "We should have been celebrating Trench's victory with the Nolans." She noticed Gideon seemed lost in thought. "What is it, darling? You're being awfully quiet."

"I was just thinking about something Nolan said. He was really counting on Dodger winning the selling race this afternoon. I got the impression he needed the money."

"That seems strange," Mother Bates said. "Aren't people who own racehorses extremely wealthy?"

"That's what I thought," Gideon said, "and Nolan always gave me the impression that he was. In fact, he wants me to set up some kind of settlement for Irene as a sort of dowry to entice potential suitors."

"Good heavens, what a thought," Elizabeth said. She was gratified to see Mother Bates's frown of disapproval as well.

"I know, it's a bit high-handed, but it indicated to me that he had the money to fund such a thing, but now . . ."

"It's easy to lose money racing horses," Elizabeth said. "People start out rich and invest a lot of money in horses that *should* be winners but turn out not to be. You see, no one knows how a horse will perform until it does, and most of them never develop into champions."

"Mr. Nolan seemed so sure that Trench would be a champion, though," Mother Bates said.

"Maybe that was wishful thinking," Gideon said.

"We may never know, depending on what happened to him out there today. In any case, maintaining a stable is quite costly," Elizabeth said. "You have to feed the animals and pay a lot of people to care for them and exercise them and train them."

"I imagine things were especially tight when the reformers closed down all the tracks and nobody was making any money at all racing," Gideon said.

"That's true," Elizabeth agreed, "and the purses have been much smaller in the years since then, too, so even if you win, you aren't seeing the same profits."

"The purses?" Mother Bates echoed. "You mean the money the horses win?"

"Yes, that's right."

"Why would they be smaller now than before?" Mother Bates asked.

"Because of the way the reformers have restricted the betting," Elizabeth explained. "The bookies used to pay the track rent for their betting boxes, but now they're only allowed to stand around the wagering area and chat with people in some pretense of making a friendly wager with an acquaintance."

"So, the tracks have lost a lot of income," Gideon said, "and they no longer have money for the larger purses for the winners."

"I see. So that means the owners don't make as much money even when their horses win."

"And it still costs just as much to operate a stable," Elizabeth said. "That could explain why Mr. Nolan is feeling the pinch."

"He also sold his business years ago," Gideon said. "He may have been quite wealthy then, but without any new income and the expense of keeping his horses . . ."

"I can see why he might be anxious," Mother Bates said. "Seeing Trench go down like that must have been a shock in many ways."

"Yes," Elizabeth said. "He'd naturally be concerned over a horse and rider he cares about, but their accident also means a substantial financial loss to him. I just hope he intends to support Mr. Regan while he recovers."

"You mean he might not?" Mother Bates asked in amazement.

"A lot of owners wouldn't," Gideon said. "The jockeys are contracted to ride and if they can't ride and make money for the owners, they're on their own."

"But surely Mr. Nolan will support Mr. Regan," Mother Bates said. "Irene said he's like a member of the family."

But Gideon was shaking his head. "You didn't see his injury. I didn't, either, not really, because of his boot, but I could tell it was very bad. I'd bet he'll be in the hospital for weeks, maybe even months, and then there's the question of whether he'll ever be able to ride again."

"How awful," Mother Bates said.

"No worse than any other job, though," Elizabeth said. "If a worker is injured and can't work anymore, his employer fires him and hires someone to take his place."

They all knew this was true, and for a long moment, no one spoke as they considered the injustice of such a system.

Elizabeth said, "I was glad to see Irene went with Mr. Regan to the hospital."

"That did surprise me," Mother Bates said, "but I also saw how they looked at each other down in the paddock. I have a feeling those two are very much in love."

"I noticed they seemed fond of each other," Gideon said, "but surely Irene Nolan wouldn't seriously consider marrying a jockey."

Elizabeth gave him a pitying look. "They've known each other since they were children."

"Then maybe she thinks of him as a brother," Gideon argued.

Mother Bates covered a smile, and Elizabeth shook her head

sadly. "I promise you I never looked at Jake the way Irene looks at Cal Regan."

"Ah, but you don't like your brother," Gideon argued.

"I detest him, but I also love him dearly. Believe me, it's an entirely different emotion than what Irene feels for Mr. Regan."

Gideon frowned. "I wonder if Mr. Nolan knows or at least suspects."

"He gave no indication of it, dear," Mother Bates said.

"But he was particularly interested in protecting Irene from fortune hunters. Could he have meant Cal Regan?"

"It's possible, I guess," Elizabeth said, "but I think Mother Bates is right. I don't think Mr. Nolan has realized Irene's feelings for Mr. Regan are deeper than ordinary affection."

"I can't imagine he'll be pleased," Gideon said darkly.

"Probably not," Elizabeth said, "especially after all that talk about wanting a winning horse so society people would accept them. I think Mr. Nolan imagines Irene marrying the scion of some old New York family, like I did."

"I'm hardly a *scion*," Gideon protested.

"You are definitely a scion," Elizabeth teased.

"In any case," Mother Bates said, smiling at their banter, "Mr. Nolan wouldn't approve of such a match, and Mr. Regan's injury won't help matters."

"I just hope he doesn't suspect anything until Mr. Regan has recovered," Elizabeth said. "I'd hate for him to abandon Mr. Regan because he wants to separate him from Irene."

"What an awful day for the poor Nolans," Mother Bates said. "I'd almost forgotten the earlier race where that jockey prevented Dodger from winning."

"Oh my, I had, too," Elizabeth admitted.

"Do you think Trench's accident might not have really been an accident?" Gideon asked.

"Didn't you say no other horse was near them when Trench fell, though?" Mother Bates said.

"That's true."

"There are a lot of other ways to sabotage a horse," Elizabeth said.

"Such as?" Mother Bates asked with interest.

"Drugs. Somehow altering the saddle or bridle. Even loosening a shoe can cause a horse to lose a race."

"Bribing the jockey is another one," Gideon said, "although I think we can rule that out in this case."

"It's hardly likely Mr. Regan would have put himself in so much danger, that's true," Elizabeth said.

"Although that Hawkins fellow could have been bribed," Mother Bates said.

"More likely, he was simply ordered to keep Regan from winning," Gideon said.

"But if someone gave Trench a drug or interfered with him in some way, that would probably involve bribing someone who works in Mr. Nolan's stable," Elizabeth said.

"And we don't have to wonder who might have done such a thing," Gideon said. "Daniel Livingston is too obviously the choice."

"Oh, I dearly hope he isn't responsible for Trench's accident," Mother Bates said. "That would just be too much."

Elizabeth reached over and covered Gideon's hand with hers. "I think you and I need to find Mr. Regan tomorrow and go visit him. I can't rest easy until I know what really happened."

Gideon gave her an adoring look. "I know what you're thinking, but there's no way you can make this right by running some kind of con."

"Who said anything about running a con?" she asked with feigned outrage.

"No one yet," Gideon admitted, "but I know it's just a matter of time."

THE TWENTY-MILE TRIP OUT TO QUEENS WAS LESS FESTIVE the next day. Except for a few special events, the running of the Belmont Stakes marked the last day of racing at Belmont until September, so the train wasn't crowded with revelers. Gideon hadn't been happy about taking another day off work, but Elizabeth assured him his partners would understand his wanting to support a client during a very difficult time. Locating the hospital wasn't too difficult, and they found Irene sitting beside Regan's bed in a ward with several other men in various stages of recovery. Someone had put a screen around Regan's bed to afford him a little privacy, but Elizabeth and Gideon had no trouble spotting him. His right leg was encased in an impressively large cast. Mercifully, he seemed to be asleep.

"How kind of you both to come," Irene told them in a whisper, rising from the straight-backed chair she'd been sitting in. She still wore the same clothes she'd had on yesterday, her hair was a mess, and her eyes were bloodshot from lack of sleep. Plainly, she'd spent the night by Regan's side. She motioned them away from the bed so they wouldn't disturb him. "How on earth did you find us?"

"I telephoned the racetrack. Someone there was sure this was the right place," Gideon said. "How is he doing?"

Irene's weary face fell. "It was a very bad break. Both bones in his calf. He was in surgery for hours, but the doctors think he'll be able to walk again when it heals."

"Just walk?" Elizabeth echoed in dismay.

Irene's forced smile was painful to behold. "That is all we can hope for, apparently. The doctor says Cal won't ever ride again, at least not in a race."

"Doctors don't know everything," Elizabeth said. "Mr. Regan seems like a very determined young man. He might well make a full recovery."

"I pray you're right, but . . ." Her voice broke, and Elizabeth instinctively wrapped her arms around the young woman and allowed her to weep on her shoulder for a few minutes.

But Irene Nolan was too well-bred to make a spectacle of herself for very long. She quickly pulled away and mopped her tears with a bedraggled handkerchief she drew from a pocket. "I'm terribly sorry. I don't know what came over me."

"Have you been here all night?" Elizabeth asked.

"Yes, but . . . I couldn't leave him alone, could I? Father stayed, too."

"Where is he now?" Gideon asked.

"He went to check on Trench. We'd planned to move all of our horses to Jamaica today, but now . . ." The racing schedule moved around the various tracks every few weeks. Jamaica was next and then Aqueduct.

"Where were you staying?" Elizabeth asked.

"We've been renting a house near Belmont, and we planned to stay there for another month, until the racing shifts out to Empire City because Jamaica and Aqueduct aren't that far away."

"At least you don't have to pack up there, too," Elizabeth said. "I think you need to go home and at least get a change of clothes. I can go with you."

"I can't leave Cal," she protested.

"Gideon will stay with him, won't you, darling? At least until your father returns."

"Of course," Gideon said. "You should get some rest as well. You won't be any help to Regan if you collapse yourself."

Irene cast an anxious look at the patient. "But if he wakes up and finds me gone—"

"I'll tell him my wife kidnapped you," Gideon assured her with a smile.

She smiled wanly back. "You must be sure the nurses give him his medicine, so he isn't in pain."

"I promise."

"Come along, Irene," Elizabeth said.

They had turned to leave when Mr. Nolan entered the ward. He looked a bit better than Irene. He had obviously stopped by the house to shave and change clothes, but his face was just as haggard.

"Father, how is Trench?" Irene asked, hurrying to him.

"It's . . . I don't honestly know," Nolan said. Only then did he seem to notice Elizabeth and Gideon. "This is a surprise. You didn't have to come all this way."

Gideon and Elizabeth assured him it was no hardship at all and that they hoped to be of some help.

"Did you find out what happened to Trench?" Gideon asked.

To their surprise, Nolan's expression hardened to fury. He glanced around as if making sure no one was listening and lowered his voice. "I can hardly believe it, but . . . he was sponged."

Elizabeth and Irene gasped, but Gideon plainly had no idea what that meant.

Elizabeth said, "Someone put a sponge up Trench's nose. Horses can only breathe through their noses, so a blocked nose means they can't get enough air and they . . . well, they collapse, the way Trench did."

"How do you know that's what it was?" Irene asked.

"Quaid found the sponge. He said he remembered that you had been worried about Trench all day, and he admitted he also thought something wasn't quite right, even though they couldn't find anything to be concerned about. He said he tried to think what someone could have done to make him break down and . . ."

"We should have scratched him," Irene said in dismay.

"You couldn't have known," Elizabeth said.

"How is he now?" Irene asked. "Do you think he'll be all right?"

"We won't know for a few days, at least."

Elizabeth turned to Gideon. "Sponging can ruin a horse."

"If he only had it in for a day or two, he might recover," Nolan said, but they could tell he was trying to convince himself as much as them.

"How could something like that happen?" Gideon asked, angry on behalf of his friends.

"Easily," Elizabeth said. "Racetracks don't have much security. Pretty much anyone can wander around the stable area day or night."

"Unless you post a guard on your horses, they're at the mercy of anyone who happens by," Nolan said.

"And even if you post a guard, he could be bribed," Irene said. "We don't pay anyone at the stables enough to keep them honest."

"Can you punish whoever did this?" Gideon asked.

"I'm not sure how you'd do that," Nolan said, "but it probably doesn't matter because I don't think we have a chance of finding the guilty party."

"It would have taken two people," Irene said. "One to put in the sponge and one to hold Trench. No horse would stand still for something like that."

"Then maybe you'd have a chance that one of them would talk," Elizabeth said.

But Nolan just gave her a pitying look. "Not if it would get him in an equal amount of trouble, and that would mean being banned from racing for life. All they have to do is keep their mouths shut. Chances are, there were no witnesses or none who would come forward at any rate."

"But we know who's behind it," Irene said, her cheeks now blooming with color from her fury. "Daniel Livingston is the only person in the world who might want to see us ruined."

Nolan glanced around again. "Don't say things like that, Irene. You may be right, but we can't prove it, and Livingston won't take too kindly to being accused."

"I don't need to prove it. I know he's the one, and I'll never forgive him for what he did to Cal." Her eyes filled with tears again and her father's dismay turned instantly to panic.

"Don't cry, sweetheart. Cal is going to be fine. You'll see," he assured her with enough desperation to cause his listeners to doubt his conviction.

"I was just going to take Irene home for a little rest," Elizabeth said.

"I'm only going to change my clothes," Irene insisted. "Then I'm coming right back."

"There's no rush," Gideon assured her. "I'll be here. Mr. Nolan, perhaps you should go with Irene as well. You both look like you need some sleep."

Mr. Nolan refused Gideon's suggestion and said he'd stay with him at the hospital while the ladies went back to the house the Nolans were renting.

Elizabeth found a cab to take them. The rental was a ramshackle affair, one of many that were temporarily let out by their owners during the racing season to make extra money. Elizabeth insisted Irene take a bath while Elizabeth investigated the larder for possible meal ingredients.

Elizabeth found eggs and bread and some wilting vegetables she could chop up for an omelet. When she had everything ready to go into the pan, she went to check on Irene, who had fallen asleep in the tub.

Elizabeth chastened her as she knew Mother Bates would have. A person could drown in the tub if they weren't careful! Elizabeth snatched up a towel and helped Irene from the tub, and in the process, she noticed something Irene probably had not intended her to see.

She helped Irene into a dressing gown and brought her into the kitchen while Elizabeth prepared the omelet. By the time Irene had finished eating, she was practically asleep sitting up, so Elizabeth had little trouble encouraging her to go to her bed for a short nap. Since Elizabeth had no intention of keeping her promise to wake Irene in an hour, she settled in to wait.

As she had expected, Gideon had apparently finally convinced Mr. Nolan to go home as well. He came in quietly and started when he found Elizabeth sitting in the parlor.

"Irene is asleep. I thought it best not to wake her, although she was anxious to get back to Cal."

"The nurses are taking very good care of him, so there's no reason we need to be there with him every minute," Mr. Nolan said, sinking down onto the sagging sofa with a weary sigh. "The doctor thinks it will be months before Cal is healed up."

"Irene said there is some question about him being able to ride again."

Nolan nodded grimly. "A jockey needs strong legs. I've seen boys who broke their legs come back and do just fine, but never after a break like this."

"Perhaps Mr. Regan will surprise us all."

"Yes, well, we'll see, I suppose. In the meantime, Mrs. Bates, I told your husband I would send you back to the hospital so the two of you can head on home to the city before it gets too late."

"I hate to leave Irene without saying good-bye."

"She might sleep through the night, and I know you don't want to be stuck here until morning. I'll give her your regards."

"I know you both think a lot of Mr. Regan," Elizabeth said. "Irene told us you practically raised him."

Mr. Nolan smiled at that. "Yes, he was just a boy when we found him hanging around the stables. That was at our farm up near Saratoga. Nobody worked harder than Cal did. He wanted to prove that even though he was small, he could do the work of a grown man."

"I'm sure his size made him a good workout rider, too."

Nolan nodded enthusiastically. "Most of the boys grow too big to keep riding, but not Cal. He told me his father was short and he hoped he would be, too. It's a sin how light the jockeys have to be, but I don't make the rules, and it certainly helps if they're small like Cal."

"Irene said she grew up with Cal," Elizabeth said just to see what he would say.

"I let her spend too much time at the stables. Turned her into a tomboy, I'm afraid."

"Turned her into an expert horsewoman," Elizabeth argued. "You said yourself she knows more than you do about it."

"She probably does. Many's the night she's sat up with a sick horse, her and Cal alone in the stable, working together. I couldn't have had a son any more devoted to my animals."

Did he mean Irene or Cal or maybe both of them? "Irene and Mr. Regan seem very fond of each other."

"I expect they are. Like brother and sister."

Elizabeth managed not to flinch. "Then you'll continue to support Mr. Regan while he recovers?"

Nolan was obviously shocked by such a direct question, especially because it came from a female whom he hardly knew. "I know my responsibilities, Mrs. Bates," he said stiffly.

"I'm sorry, Mr. Nolan. It's none of my business, but I'm sure it would be a comfort to Irene to know that."

"Irene knows I wouldn't turn my back on Cal, not after all that boy has done for us."

"You're very generous."

He didn't look like he appreciated the compliment very much. "I should get you back to the hospital, Mrs. Bates." Plainly, he wasn't happy with her anymore.

"If you could summon a cab for me, I'll be on my way. Please tell Irene she may call on me for anything. I'm happy to help."

Mr. Nolan got a cab there as quickly as he could, and Elizabeth was soon back at the hospital. Gideon reported that Cal Regan had woken up in pain and the nurse had dutifully administered another dose of something very powerful that put him back to sleep again. He hadn't even noticed that Irene didn't come when he called out for her.

"How interesting that he did that," Elizabeth said.

"Yes, he seemed very sure she would be right by his side."

"I had a little chat with Mr. Nolan," Elizabeth reported while they waited for another cab to take them to the train station. "He has no idea Irene and Cal are in love."

"I can believe that. A man sees what he wants to see. I'm sure Nolan isn't interested in seeing that his daughter has fallen in love with an employee."

"Yes, not even an employee who is like a member of the family."

"People do use that expression," Gideon mused, "but they rarely mean it."

"What do you mean?"

"When they are making their wills, for example. They'll say some servant or other is like a member of the family, but you can be sure the servant won't be receiving an equal share of the estate with the real family members."

"Yes, I can see that, but Mr. Nolan may have to change his mind about Cal Regan."

"Then you think Irene can convince him to accept Regan as a son-in-law?"

"I'm thinking he won't have much choice. Unless I'm very much mistaken, Irene Nolan is with child."

# CHAPTER FOUR

HOW CAN YOU BE SO SURE, DEAR?" GIDEON'S MOTHER ASKED Elizabeth that evening when they had finished reporting on their visit with the Nolans. "I didn't notice a thing."

"I helped her out of the bathtub," Elizabeth said. "She's very thin everywhere else, but there was no mistaking that tummy."

Gideon knew little of female conditions and understood even less. "Maybe it's something else. Even if she's in love with Regan, wouldn't she be too sensible to risk conceiving a child out of wedlock?"

Both women gave him a pitying look.

"People in love seldom behave sensibly," his mother said. Gideon couldn't help his wince. He'd behaved less than sensibly any number of times because he was in love with Elizabeth.

"She may even have done it on purpose," Elizabeth said, "since she knows her father is unlikely to give his blessing if they simply ask for it."

"I guess I can see that," Gideon admitted. "Nolan would hardly refuse to allow Irene to marry if she's expecting a child."

"Mr. Regan's injury will certainly have ruined their plans, though," Elizabeth said. "Mr. Regan was undoubtedly earning a generous salary from Mr. Nolan, and he'd earn extra money riding horses for other owners when none of Mr. Nolan's horses were running, so he probably thought he could easily afford to keep a wife."

"A wife and child," his mother corrected her.

"But now, Regan can't ride for months and perhaps he never will again. How can he hope to support a family?" Gideon asked.

"I'm sure he hasn't had time to think about all of this yet," Elizabeth said. "He just had surgery and he's hardly even been awake more than a few minutes at once, but I'm also sure Irene has been thinking about nothing else."

"Poor thing, she must be frantic," his mother said. "I wonder when they intended to inform her father. She won't be able to hide her condition forever."

"Yes, it's a difficult situation," Gideon said, "but it's really none of our business."

The two most important women in his life gave him another pitying look.

"But we hardly know them," Gideon added, already sure that his protests were futile.

"One thing I've learned from the Suffragist movement is that women are always at a disadvantage in this world, and we need to help each other whenever we can," Elizabeth said, earning an adoring smile from her mother-in-law.

"How can you hope to help in this case, though?" Gideon asked, trying to sound reasonable. "You can't offer a crippled jockey a job. You can't shield Irene Nolan's condition from being found out."

His wife and his mother exchanged a knowing glance, and Elizabeth smiled sweetly. "You're absolutely right, darling. We can't do either of those things, but we can befriend her, which might be the kindest thing of all."

Befriending didn't sound too bad. Gideon had to agree it was a good compromise.

Before he could say so, his mother said, "How shall we approach this then?"

"I was thinking we could take some treats to the hospital for Mr. Regan," Elizabeth said. "Perhaps some fruit or cookies, things they probably don't serve him there."

"Yes, and then we can engage Irene in a serious conversation to find out how we can really help her," his mother said.

Gideon frowned. "I thought you had decided you can't really help her."

Elizabeth reached across the table and patted his hand. "We decided we couldn't hire Mr. Regan or keep Irene's secret, but who knows what other assistance we could offer?"

"That is what friends do for other friends," his mother said, as if she were instructing a small child.

"Don't forget, Mr. Nolan is a client. I have to be very careful," Gideon said.

"We're hardly likely to divulge any confidential information about him, since we don't know any," his mother said.

"Well, except that he wanted to provide some kind of dowry for Irene without attracting fortune hunters," Elizabeth added.

Gideon pinched the bridge of his nose, certain a headache would be forming there soon. "I never should have said that."

"And we certainly won't mention it," his mother assured him.

"Especially since Mr. Nolan confessed to you that he's broke," Elizabeth added.

"He didn't say he was broke, just that things were tight," Gideon said.

"Perhaps we can get some clarification on that," Elizabeth

said, "but not by asking Irene for details about her father's financial situation. That would be terribly rude, wouldn't it, Mother Bates?"

"Indeed it would," she agreed. "One can inspire the sharing of a lot of confidences simply by being sympathetic, however. If Irene is feeling as desperate as we assume she must be, she will be glad to learn someone cares."

"I still can't understand why you're so determined to help her," Gideon said.

His mother glanced at Elizabeth and said, "Because we can, dear."

I N THE END, THEY WAITED UNTIL SATURDAY SO GIDEON COULD go with them to the hospital. They had managed to find some berries at the Gansevoort Market. Mid-June wasn't the best time for fresh fruits since most of them wouldn't ripen for at least a month, but Mother Bates made some cookies to round out their offering.

They discovered that Cal Regan had been moved to a private room, and Elizabeth decided he must be doing better if he had the energy to argue with Irene.

"I told you, I don't need a private room. Do you know what they charge for this?" he was saying as they reached the doorway.

"I have no idea how much it costs, but I won't have you in a ward where you might catch something from the other patients."

"I'm not going to catch something, and if we spend all my money on the hospital, we won't be able to—" he said but stopped when he noticed his visitors in the doorway. "Are you looking for somebody?"

Irene turned at the question and saw them. "How nice to see

you." She hurried to greet them. "Although I'll never forgive you for not waking me up the other day, Elizabeth."

"I'm perfectly happy to remain unforgiven if the rest did you some good."

"I'm sure you know it did. Cal, you remember Gideon and Elizabeth Bates and Gideon's mother. They were at the track with us on Wednesday."

Cal smiled in acknowledgment. "I remember. Reenie said you came to visit me the next day, too." He glanced at Irene with what could only be called adoration. "I'm sorry I slept through it."

"I'm sure you were much happier being asleep," Gideon said, moving to Regan's bedside. "How are you doing?"

"It hurts like the devil, even when they give me something, but it could be worse, I guess."

"Yes, it could," Irene said. "You might've been trampled to death."

Regan gave Gideon a conspiratorial look. "That's her way of cheering me up."

"I'm glad to see your spirit is intact, at least," Elizabeth said. "And what a good idea, moving him to a private room, Irene. I'm sure he'll get a lot more rest here than in a ward."

"They're ganging up on me, Bates," Regan said.

"Let's send them away, then, shall we?" Gideon said good-naturedly. "I know Elizabeth thinks Irene should get a little fresh air."

"I should, too," Regan said with a mischievous grin, "but I'll be happy to just have a little peace and quiet."

Irene gave him a mock glare but turned back to her guests with a smile. "I would love to go for a short walk if Mr. Bates will sit with Cal."

"I'd be delighted," Gideon assured her.

Irene put on her hat and gloves and the three ladies made their way out of the hospital and into the sunshine.

"How is he really doing?" Mother Bates asked when they were clear of the building.

"They won't know until they see how the bones knit," Irene reported in dismay. "The surgeon is sure he'll be as good as new, but the other doctors think he might never walk right again."

"How annoying," Elizabeth said. "But at least there's some hope for a full recovery."

If Irene shared that hope, she gave no indication.

"This terrible accident must have spoiled all your plans," Mother Bates said.

"Yes, we had great hopes for Trench, and a few of our other horses are coming along, too. With Cal riding, we were sure we'd win some races this summer."

"Is that what's most important to you, just winning races?" Elizabeth asked.

Irene smiled wanly. "It's what's important to Father."

"But what about *your* plans?" Mother Bates asked, her expression completely innocent. Elizabeth would have to practice that. "Your plans with Mr. Regan, I mean."

"I don't know what you're talking about," Irene said warily.

"I think you do," Mother Bates said. "It's clear the two of you are in love."

"And it's only natural for two people in love to want to marry," Elizabeth said.

Poor Irene looked poleaxed, so Elizabeth had mercy on her. "Shall we sit for a while? There's a bench up ahead."

With a sigh of relief Irene sank down onto the bench while Elizabeth and Mother Bates sat on either side of her. Now Irene looked almost frightened. Her gaze kept darting back and forth between the two other women as if she expected something untoward.

Elizabeth didn't think what they had to say was untoward, but it would probably shock Irene.

"As Elizabeth said, we assume that you and Mr. Regan wish to marry," Mother Bates said gently.

Irene's gaze dropped and she appeared to be studying her shoes with an inordinate amount of interest. "I don't suppose it would do any good to point out that is none of your business."

"Oh, dear me, no, it wouldn't. Gideon already tried," Mother Bates said. "But please believe that Elizabeth and I understand completely, and we are willing to assist you in any way we can."

"I can't imagine you could be any help at all," Irene said so sadly that Elizabeth wanted to put her arm around her new friend.

"You underestimate us," Elizabeth said. "Did I happen to mention how I met Mother Bates in the first place?"

"Of course you didn't, my dear," Mother Bates said cheerfully before Irene could reply. "She would probably not have welcomed us so cordially if she knew we were a couple of jailbirds."

"What?" Irene asked in amazement.

"Yes," Elizabeth confirmed solemnly. "We met in prison."

Mother Bates gave Irene a few moments to absorb this startling news and then said, "We were sentenced to six months of hard labor at a workhouse for demonstrating for Woman Suffrage outside the White House."

Irene blinked a few times as she made sense of this. "How . . . how awful for you."

"It certainly wasn't pleasant," Elizabeth agreed, "but it did lead to my meeting Gideon, so all's well that ends well."

"And we want your story to end well, too," Mother Bates said.

"Are you ready to admit that you and Mr. Regan are more than just friends?"

Irene chewed her lip for a long moment. Finally, she said, "I've been in love with him since I was eleven years old."

"May we assume he feels the same way?" Elizabeth asked.

"He . . . He believes he shouldn't love me."

"Has that stopped him?" Mother Bates asked.

"I . . . No, it hasn't, although he keeps insisting it will never work. My father will never give his consent."

"But you're of age, aren't you?" Elizabeth said. "You don't need his consent."

"He would cut me off without a cent, and he would fire Cal."

"If Mr. Regan is as good a jockey as we have reason to believe, he'll be able to find work elsewhere," Elizabeth said.

"I keep telling him that, but he also feels he owes my father for taking him in and giving him a chance in the first place. He doesn't want to steal me away and rob Father of his best jockey into the bargain."

"He wouldn't have to feel guilty if your father fired him," Elizabeth reminded her.

"It makes so much sense when you say it, but when I say it to Cal, he talks about loyalty and honor and a bunch of things that don't really matter at all, and he won't be moved. He also says even if he can earn a good salary as a jockey, he can never hope to provide for me the way my father has, and now, well, we can't even be sure he'll ever ride again."

"We must believe he will make a full recovery," Elizabeth said with more confidence than she felt.

"Yes, we must," Mother Bates said. "And when he does, is that what you would expect him to do, support you in the same style your father does?"

"Of course not, but there's no reasoning with him. He grew

up with nothing except his pride, and he refuses to marry me until he can give me the kind of life my father has."

"Does he have some idea of how he could do that?" Elizabeth asked.

"He knows he can't ride forever, so he's been saving up to start his own stable. He could train horses for other owners and raise a few of his own, too."

"A very worthy plan," Elizabeth said, "although it could take years and then never really succeed."

Irene gave a long-suffering sigh. "I've mentioned that to him."

"I gather," Mother Bates said thoughtfully, "that Mr. Regan is not feeling any sense of urgency. Could this be because he doesn't know about the baby?"

This time Irene looked terrified, and she might have actually bolted, but Elizabeth took her hand and held it rather firmly. "I . . . I don't know what you mean," Irene tried.

"I never would have guessed if I hadn't helped you get out of the bathtub," Elizabeth said. "If Mr. Regan doesn't know, I'm sure no one else has guessed yet, either."

"But it won't be long until guessing won't be necessary," Mother Bates said.

This was finally too much for Irene, and she began to weep. Both Elizabeth and Mother Bates offered her handkerchiefs in turn, and both were soaked by the time she had exhausted herself.

"I'm sorry. I seem to cry at everything lately," Irene said, mopping the last of her tears.

"You're expecting a child," Mother Bates said wisely. "That makes a woman more emotional than she would ordinarily be."

"And you have been through a lot the past few days," Elizabeth added. "The question is, How are you going to solve this dilemma?"

"I . . . I should have told Cal weeks ago," Irene admitted, "but

I kept thinking he would realize that waiting years to marry was a terrible idea. I guess I wanted him to marry me because he chose to, not because he had to, and now . . ."

"And now telling him would only add to his troubles, which must be nearly overwhelming at the moment," Mother Bates said.

"Yes, I couldn't give him one more thing to worry about."

"He's very lucky to have you," Elizabeth said.

"Do you think so?" Irene asked in all sincerity.

"Don't be silly. Of course I think so."

Mother Bates had been giving the matter some thought. "Do you think your father would be understanding if you told him about the baby?"

Irene's horrified expression told them the answer before she could even speak. "He would probably disown me. He's been lecturing me since I was a little girl about guarding my virtue from unscrupulous men, and he's voiced his opinion of *fallen women* enough times to convince me he wouldn't tolerate one in his house."

"You're far from being fallen," Mother Bates said, "and you might be judging your father too harshly. It's easy to condemn something in others that you would excuse if it were your own child."

"I'd like to think you're right, Mrs. Bates, but if I tell him and find out you're not . . ."

"Yes, you'd be even worse off."

Elizabeth said, "However, it occurs to me that all your problems could be solved by a large sum of money."

"That's probably true of most problems," Irene said wanly.

"You may be right, but in this case, we're sure it's true."

"Do you have an idea, dear?" Mother Bates asked her.

Elizabeth smiled. "Not yet, but I'm sure I'll think of one eventually."

D O YOU KNOW WHAT HAPPENED OUT THERE ON THE TRACK?"
Gideon asked Cal Regan after they had exchanged the usual
pleasantries and Cal had answered his questions about the injury
itself. "It was impossible to see from where we were since you
were on the far side and the rail was blocking our view."

Regan rubbed a hand over his face. "It happened so fast, but
then, those things always do. I was holding Trench back, saving
him for the final stretch, but I decided to let him go a little on the
back stretch and when he started to pull ahead, he . . . I'm not
sure I can even explain it. He just stopped or as close to it as a
horse can when he's running almost full out. He fell against the
rail and knocked me out of the saddle, but I couldn't get my right
foot out of the stirrup."

"I guess that's how you broke your leg."

"I've been trying to remember. Could be it broke when I hit
the rail and that's why I couldn't kick it free, but I don't guess it
matters much."

"No. Thank God none of the other horses trampled you."

"Or tripped over us. I would've hated for somebody else to get
hurt because of my mistake."

Gideon frowned. "It wasn't your mistake. Didn't anybody tell
you about the sponging?"

Regan sighed. "They did and that surely was the reason Trench
broke down. My *mistake* was not believing Reenie when she said
something was wrong with Trench when she watched him work
out that morning."

"It's my understanding that it's virtually impossible to detect
when a horse has been sponged," Gideon said. He knew this because Elizabeth had explained to him and his mother everything
she knew about this horrible crime.

"Yeah, the vet didn't find it, even after Reenie said there was something wrong with Trench. Mr. Quaid and I didn't, either."

"Will it cause Trench any lasting damage, do you think?"

Regan shook his head. "Nobody knows. I've heard it can ruin a horse, especially when they don't find it right away. Imagine if you could only breathe half the air you usually breathe and then somebody made you run."

"No wonder Trench stopped. He must be a smart fellow."

"Smartest horse I ever rode. If he's ruined . . ."

Gideon gave Regan a moment to compose himself before asking, "Do you have any idea who might have done it?"

To Gideon's surprise, Regan turned his head away and pressed his lips tightly together, as if he was trying to hold back his reply.

"I suppose it's impossible to know since anyone could have gone into Trench's stall," Gideon tried.

"It's not impossible to know," Regan said, turning back to Gideon. His face had reddened, and Gideon realized he was furious.

"Then you found out?" Gideon guessed.

"Mr. Nolan doesn't have a lot of enemies. He hasn't had that much success in racing yet. But he brought one with him from the old days, and that one really bears a grudge."

"Then you think Livingston was behind it," Gideon said.

"Do you think it's a coincidence that Livingston's jockey hooked me to keep me from winning the first race and then Trench loses because he was sponged?"

"No, to me it actually seems to indicate Livingston is responsible."

"We'll never prove it unless somebody confesses, but Mr. Nolan told me Toby, one of our bug boys, quit us yesterday. He said Daniel Livingston offered him more money."

"And this Toby would have had access to Trench."

"Yeah. He probably needed help, but I'd bet a year's pay he was in on it. Why else would he leave so sudden?"

"Going to Livingston is suspicious, too. But if he can be bribed, maybe you could bribe him to turn on Livingston."

"Not likely. They'd probably blackball Toby from racing altogether if he confessed to sponging, and Livingston would get a two-week suspension from racing and only if we were very lucky. More likely, he'd get no punishment at all. The owners don't like to punish each other."

"That hardly seems fair."

"Racing isn't usually fair, Mr. Bates."

"How about Mr. Nolan?"

"What about him?" Regan challenged.

"Doesn't he want to go after Livingston?"

Cal sighed. "Owners hate accusing other owners of things like this. It can backfire, and I don't think Mr. Nolan wants any more trouble right now."

That did not seem like the right attitude to Gideon, but he decided not to say so. "Irene tells us you've been with them since you were a kid."

Regan blinked in surprise at the sudden shift of subject, but he said, "That's right. I ran away from home when I was thirteen. I wanted to ride horses, so I went to a racetrack and started offering my services."

"I don't expect you got a lot of takers," Gideon said with a smile.

"You'd be surprised. They pay you fifty cents to do a morning workout and they let you sleep in the stables with the horses. Not many grown men are willing to work for wages like that, but a boy can live on fifty cents a day if he's got a free place to sleep."

"I thought you lived with Mr. Nolan growing up."

"Reenie did tell you about me, didn't she?" He seemed pleased by that, "His trainer used me a lot. Saw I had a way with the horses and told Mr. Nolan. He decided I could be a jockey and set out to see I got the chance."

"That was kind of him."

Regan gave a little snort. "He's not kind. I worked hard for my keep."

"You ride for other owners, too, don't you?"

"When Mr. Nolan doesn't need me."

"I know you have a good reputation with the other owners. You ever think of leaving Nolan?"

Regan frowned and Gideon decided he'd gone a bit too far, but there was no help for it now. "I think about it, but Mr. Nolan gave me my chance. He gave me a place to live and treated me good. Like I said, he isn't a kind man, but he's fair. That's about all a boy can hope to find in this world."

"And you got to meet Miss Nolan, who is probably your biggest fan," Gideon said with what he hoped was nonchalance.

Regan didn't reply for a long moment, and Gideon realized he was attempting to figure out if there was some hidden meaning in that statement. Since there was, Gideon tried not to look guilty, but he wasn't as good at this as Elizabeth, so he wasn't sure how successful he was.

"Miss Nolan is the finest woman I know," Regan finally said, obviously not willing to admit his true feelings for Irene to a stranger. "If she was a man, she'd be a top trainer, even at her young age."

"Yes, her father shares your opinion. He told us she knows more about horses than he does."

"I don't doubt it."

"Maybe the two of you should go into partnership," Gideon said. "You could have your own stable."

Regan laughed mirthlessly at the suggestion. "Yeah, Reenie

could train the horses and I could ride them." He gestured toward his enormous cast. "And we'd use the millions that I saved being a jockey to buy some breeding stock."

"Wouldn't Mr. Nolan help?" Gideon asked.

"You mean help his daughter start a rival stable?" Regan scoffed. "Not likely."

"Maybe Miss Nolan will have some sort of dowry when she marries," Gideon said.

Regan's eyes narrowed. "Who is she going to marry?"

Gideon didn't have to feign surprise. "My wife seems to think she's going to marry you."

Regan opened his mouth to reply, but nothing came out.

Gideon gave him time to find his tongue and when he didn't, Gideon said, "I'm sorry if I spoke out of turn, but Elizabeth was so very sure."

"I . . . Miss Nolan isn't going to marry a crippled jockey," Regan said quietly.

"I'm sure her father wants the best for her, which is why I thought you wanted to start your own stable."

Regan was scowling now. "You're a lawyer, ain't you? That's what Reenie said. Is this some kind of legal trickery? Are you trying to cheat me somehow?"

Now it was Gideon's turn to be confused. "Certainly not. Why would I?"

"I don't know, but lawyers are always tricking people into doing things. It's Mr. Nolan, isn't it? He doesn't want to pay for my hospital, does he?"

"If he doesn't, he hasn't said anything about it to me," Gideon assured him, but Cal was not to be placated.

"He's not going to pay me, either, I'm sure of that. I have a contract for twelve thousand a year, but only if I can ride. And I know he was counting on Trench winning that maiden race and auctioning off Dodger. He don't talk about money, but you can tell when an owner is feeling the pinch. He starts letting people go and selling horses and—"

"Has Mr. Nolan started letting people go?"

Regan frowned. "Well, no, not yet anyway, but I've seen racing ruin more than one millionaire. It's a very expensive hobby and it's a bankrupting profession." Regan sighed. "I'm never going to marry anyone if I can't get out of this bed and back on a horse."

"I don't think you'd make weight with that cast," Gideon said in an attempt at levity.

Regan looked up in surprise and laughed. "That's funny." Racetrack officials set strict limits on how much weight a horse could carry. Horse and rider could be disqualified if they didn't meet the standard, which is why jockeys had to be small and light. "I guess you're right. But I don't know how I'll lay in this bed for weeks without going crazy."

"I'm sure Irene will do her best to keep you entertained."

Regan looked away. "I can't let her waste her time on me anymore."

"You may not be able to stop her. She cares for you, Regan. It's obvious. She's not going to leave you here to rot."

"What makes you such an expert on women?" Regan scoffed.

"A little experience, although I'll bet if you asked Irene, she'd tell you the same."

Plainly, Regan would rather break his other leg than do such a thing.

"I'm wondering," Gideon said, although he had not been wondering at all, "if you and Irene had the money, would you really set up your own place?"

"Why do you care?"

"I'm just curious," Gideon lied. It wasn't exactly a lie, because he was a little bit curious, but still, Elizabeth would be so proud.

"There's no use thinking about it because we don't have the money and we aren't likely to get it. If I have to pay my hospital bills, I'll be broke. Her father isn't going to give us any money, and even if he would, I wouldn't take it."

"Why not?" Gideon asked with interest.

"I never took a handout in my life, and I'm not going to start now. I earned every dollar I ever had. Either I make it on my own, or I don't make it."

Gideon frowned. Helping Cal Regan might be more difficult than they'd thought.

S HALL I INVITE YOUR FATHER FOR DINNER?" MOTHER BATES asked Elizabeth after they had traveled back to the city and shared what information they had gathered from Cal and Irene.

Elizabeth noticed that Gideon frowned. He liked her father well enough, in spite of his occupation, but he was also worried about his mother falling under the Old Man's charm. Elizabeth knew Mother Bates was much too smart for that, but she didn't bother to explain it to Gideon. If he was worrying about his mother, he'd have less time to worry about his wife. "I think I'll just pay him a visit at his office."

Mother Bates was surprised. "Does he have an office?"

"Oh yes. It's in the back of a saloon. Didn't I ever mention that?"

"You visit your father in a saloon?" Gideon asked, outraged. She'd obviously made a mistake mentioning this, although she hadn't realized he didn't know.

"I don't go into the saloon," Elizabeth explained patiently. "There is a separate door in the back, so you can't be seen going in."

"But a *saloon*," Gideon repeated, apparently a little stunned.

"That's what she said, dear," his mother reminded him sweetly.

"It's Dan the Dude's place. All the grifters gather there. He rents out the back room to them. If somebody comes in from out of town, they go there to see if anybody can use them for something."

"Sort of like a lonely hearts matchmaking service," Mother Bates observed.

"I'm sure it's nothing like a matchmaking service," Gideon said.

"Oh, but it is," Elizabeth said. "I never thought of it that way, but often you'll need a specific type of person for your con, and you can go to Dan the Dude's to find him. If you don't find the right person, someone will know someone, and you can send for them."

"How interesting," Mother Bates said. Gideon thought his mother was far too impressed with how con men worked, but Elizabeth saw no harm in it. Mother Bates was hardly likely to start selling yokels the Brooklyn Bridge or something.

"At any rate, I think I need to talk to the Old Man alone, but you're perfectly welcome to invite him for dinner anyway. You know how he loves seeing me living in this house with the scion of an old Knickerbocker family."

Gideon gave her a disgruntled frown, which made her laugh.

"Do you have an idea, dear?" Mother Bates asked.

"I'm still thinking," Elizabeth said. "Was Mr. Regan really sure that Daniel Livingston was behind the sponging?"

"He was, but he has no proof. Maybe if we talked to this bug boy, Toby, we could find out for sure."

"Toby is hardly likely to talk to us, especially since he'd face such a harsh penalty if he did sponge poor Trench," Elizabeth said.

"I can't believe Daniel would do such a horrible thing or at least order it done," Mother Bates said.

"How well do you really know him, though?" Elizabeth asked.

"Not well at all for the past twenty years or more. He keeps to himself, and everyone snickers about him behind his back because he's still in love with a dead woman who threw him over for another man."

"Then you can't be sure his disposition hasn't completely soured to the point that he would endanger Mr. Regan and Trench and whoever else was involved in that race just to get a little revenge."

"And don't forget Livingston's jockey hooked Cal Regan in the first race," Gideon said.

"He wouldn't have dared do that without permission from his employer."

"It doesn't look very good for poor Daniel, does it?" Mother Bates said with a sigh.

"No, it doesn't," Elizabeth said. "I think he's going to have to pay for his sins."

# CHAPTER FIVE

⁑

S UNDAY WAS THE USUAL WHIRL OF CHURCH AND SUNDAY DIN-
ner and then visits from friends, so Elizabeth couldn't go see
the Old Man until Monday. She knew better than to call on him
too early, but she set out after lunch. She wondered what the gossip columns would say if someone reported she was seen slipping
into an alley beside a saloon. Fortunately, the gossip columnists
spent little time in this neighborhood, so none of them were likely
to see her.

Reaching the side door, she knocked the coded knock. The
viewing panel in the door slid open a few minutes later and then
the door opened immediately. "Nice to see you, Contessa," Spuds
said with a grin that only deepened the wrinkles that gave him
his nickname.

"It's nice to see you, too. Is the Old Man in?"

"He is, but he has an appointment soon." Which meant he
would be participating in a con somewhere in the city.

"Then I'll be quick." Elizabeth went down the short hallway

into the main room. A few men were playing pool at one end, and they greeted her cheerfully. The Old Man came out of the adjoining room that served as his office. As always, he wore a bespoke suit, and his silver hair was neatly styled.

"Lizzie, what a nice surprise."

"Spuds says you have an appointment later. I can come back if you need to go."

"I can spare you half an hour, I think."

He escorted her into his cluttered office and cleared the chair beside his desk for her. "Now what can I do for you?" he asked as he sat down in his own chair.

"First of all, you can tell me who that woman was."

"What woman?" he asked with creditable innocence.

"The one I saw you with at Belmont." As if he didn't know.

He smiled his most charming smile. "I must admit, I was a bit surprised to see you and Gideon there as well. Is Gideon interested in horse racing?"

"Not at all, but one of his clients had some horses running that day and invited us to join him in his box so we could see Sir Barton in the Belmont Stakes."

"Yes, Sebastian Nolan." At her raised eyebrows, he added, "I inquired when I saw you with him. You're not thinking of conning him, are you?"

How interesting that he assumed she was running a new con. "Any reason I shouldn't?"

He shrugged. "He had a horse in a selling race. That might be a bad sign."

"Did you see the last race that day?"

"No, we left early, but I read about the accident."

"That was Nolan's horse as well, and it was no accident. He was sponged."

He shook his head. "A nasty practice."

"Yes, it is. And his horse in the selling race lost because another jockey hooked Cal Regan."

He seemed surprised at that, although you could never be sure. "That sounds like a conspiracy."

"Yes, it does. So, now that you know why I was at the races, are you going to tell me who that woman was?" She was well aware he had tried to distract her from her original question.

He smiled sheepishly. "I suppose I should have introduced you."

"It's not too late. Is she going to be my new stepmother?"

He nearly choked at that, which allayed any fears Elizabeth had on the subject. "Heavens no. She's a . . . colleague."

"She's a grifter?" Elizabeth asked happily.

"I'm sure she would object to such a common term, but yes."

"Where is she from?"

"Most recently San Francisco."

"So, no one here knows her."

"Hopefully not."

"Does she have a specialty?"

"Several, but why are you so interested in her?"

"This is quite a coincidence, but she strongly resembles Mr. Nolan's late wife. That was how I happened to see you in the crowd. Nolan saw her and pointed her out to his daughter."

"Paulina will be interested to know this, I'm sure."

"But we're not going to con Mr. Nolan."

*"We?"*

Elizabeth smiled benignly back at him. *"I* am not going to con Mr. Nolan, but I do have a new project."

The Old Man frowned and studied her for a long moment. "Paulina isn't kindhearted or generous, Lizzie. She won't want to waste her time on one of your do-gooder projects."

"I wouldn't expect her to. She can take her regular cut. I'm planning on a big enough score for everyone to be happy. The question is, Can Paulina handle something that size?"

"Paulina can handle anything. What did you have in mind?"

"Nothing yet. It never occurred to me that Paulina was a grifter. Seeing her with you, I naturally assumed she was a mark, so I have to reconsider everything. Is she involved in something here?"

"Not yet. She's just getting the lay of the land, I think."

"What did she do in San Francisco?"

"She was running a variation on the Drake inheritance."

"Do people still fall for that old chestnut?" she scoffed.

"Like dominoes, I am happy to report. There's a couple out in the Midwest signing up farmers by the wagonload to finance the legal battle to free Sir Francis Drake's mythical fortune for his rightful heir."

Elizabeth shook her head. "How long ago did Sir Francis die anyway?"

"Centuries ago, I'm sure."

"But you said this Paulina woman was running a *variation* of the Drake con."

"Yes, she claims to be the heir to a great fortune herself, but she can't touch it until some future date for some reason. In the meantime, she accepts loans to support herself, promising to repay them at a high interest rate."

Elizabeth shook her head. "Greed is such an unpleasant character trait."

"And so many people have it," he said with a smile.

"Does she plan to run it here?"

"She hasn't shared her plans with me. As I said, she's getting the lay of the land."

"And you just happened to take her to the races?"

He smiled at that. "She asked me to escort her. She enjoys them, she says."

Elizabeth considered how best to proceed. "Mother Bates suggested I invite you for dinner some night."

"I am always delighted to visit your happy home, Lizzie."

"And perhaps you could bring Paulina with you."

"Are you thinking you can persuade her to offer her services?" he asked with amusement.

"I told you, she can take her usual cut. Why should she care if I give mine away?"

"Perhaps I should warn her that you will try to convince her to give hers away, too."

"Perhaps you should. I'm sure she'd participate just to prove I could never succeed."

"Oh, Lizzie, I'm afraid you've gotten a little too sure of yourself."

"But isn't that a common trait among grifters?" Elizabeth asked with an innocent grin.

"Not the ones who are successful."

"We'll see."

G IDEON KNEW HE HAD CROSSED SOME INVISIBLE LINE HE never even knew existed when he realized he had agreed to invite a female con artist to dine with his mother. How had this happened? And the worst part was, his mother was thrilled.

"I'm not exactly sure how to act," his mother was telling Elizabeth as they waited for their guests to arrive that evening.

"Just treat her as you would any other dinner guest, but don't give her any money," Elizabeth replied with a mischievous grin.

Even Gideon had to laugh at that. "Are you going to enlist her tonight or will that happen later?" he asked.

"I'm sure the Old Man has warned her of my plans, although he doesn't know any details yet."

"Did you tell him about Irene and Cal?" his mother asked.

"Heavens no. He wouldn't care, and their situation doesn't matter in the slightest."

"But won't she want to know why we're doing this?" his mother asked with concern.

"Probably not, and she's doing it for the money," Elizabeth said patiently. "That is the very best reason of all, as far as she is concerned."

"Oh, I suppose you're right. I forget not all con artists are like you, dear."

"Yes, Elizabeth is one of a kind," Gideon said with some pride, earning a grateful smile from his bride.

The sound of the doorbell alerted them to the arrival of their guests. They were all on their feet, waiting expectantly when the maid announced them. "Mr. Miles and Mrs. uh, Mrs. de la Shav . . ." The poor girl stopped, turning helplessly to Mr. Miles for assistance.

"Senora Paulita Padilla y de la Fuente viuda de Chavez," he rattled off with such ease that Gideon wondered if he had made it up on the spot. She certainly looked the part. She was a tall woman with a lush figure. She wore a gown of some sort of deep red gauzy material that fell in intricate folds over a black under-dress, and her ebony hair was adorned with a fancy comb and a small lace veil. She looked like every American's fantasy of what a Spanish aristocrat would look like, making Gideon wonder about the switch from Paulina to Paulita.

Elizabeth betrayed no surprise at the moniker, but his mother couldn't hide her astonishment. Still, she quickly rose to the occasion.

"We are so glad you could come, Senora," she said, going to meet the two.

"Allow me to introduce everyone, Senora," the Old Man said. He swiftly did so.

Gideon's mother invited them to sit, and Gideon offered them drinks. The Senora asked for sherry, as was proper, and he poured out some Scotch for the Old Man. Elizabeth and his mother also chose sherry, and Gideon fortified himself with a generous dollop of bourbon.

"Elizabeth didn't tell me you were from Spain," his mother was saying to the Senora.

"I was born there, although I have lived all over the world. My father was a diplomat, you see, and my late husband simply loved to travel."

"You don't sound very Spanish," Elizabeth observed archly, making Gideon realize that the Senora should probably be affecting a Spanish accent to convince people of her country of origin.

But the Senora didn't seem bothered by the implied criticism. "I learned at a boarding school in Switzerland. They did not allow us to speak with an accent."

How very convenient. Gideon took a sip of his bourbon so he wouldn't be tempted to speak in any accent at all.

"I'm sorry," his mother said. "I'm afraid I didn't catch your name, or rather I'm afraid I don't know which of your many names to use."

"Ah yes, Spanish names can be somewhat difficult. It is because we try to tell you so very much with just our name. Paulita is my given name. It means small," she said with a self-mocking smile, since she was anything but small. "Padilla was my father's name. Fuente was my mother's maiden name, and Chavez was my late husband's. Viuda comes before his name, and it means *the widow of.*"

"How interesting," Elizabeth said. "I'll have to figure out what my name would be in Spanish."

Plainly, the Senora didn't know what to make of that, so Gideon quickly said, "What brings you to New York, Senora?" Might as well give her a chance to practice her story on the rubes.

"I am looking for a place I can settle down," she said without blinking an eye. "I have never known a real home. My husband's family has an estate outside of Madrid, but I never felt at home there, and his brother is now the master, so I am free to go wherever I like."

"What a lovely opportunity for you," his mother said as if she believed this fairy tale. "I think you'll find our city very welcoming."

"Yes," Gideon agreed. "New Yorkers adore wealthy, fashionable widows."

That earned him a glare from Elizabeth and a raised eyebrow from her father, but the Senora was only amused. "So I have been told. Mr. Miles has made me very welcome."

The Old Man smiled in acknowledgment.

They chatted for a while as Gideon's mother asked the Senora questions about her life that the Senora answered with a pack of amazing lies that no one except perhaps his mother believed but which were impressive just the same. Finally, the maid announced that dinner was served. Gideon escorted their guest into the dining room and the Old Man offered his mother an arm. Elizabeth brought up the rear.

Dinner was a cozy affair. The Senora made polite conversation, returning his mother's interest by asking about their family and what Gideon did for a living and how long he and Elizabeth had been married. Elizabeth happily described the wedding trip they had taken to the Caribbean. The Senora had, of course, visited there as well and they compared notes on what they had seen.

Gideon hadn't been sure what to expect, but it seemed like a normal dinner party as long as everyone pretended to believe whatever everyone else said. It was a bit disconcerting but also entertaining.

His mother had set up a card table in the parlor, but no one was really interested in playing, so after supper, they took their seats before the fireplace again. Elizabeth was the first to break the spell of their imagined personas.

"Is this how you play it? That you're a wealthy Spanish widow?"

Paulina smiled. "How direct you are, Mrs. Gideon."

"Oh please, call me Elizabeth."

"And you must call me Paulina, although only when we are alone," she said graciously.

"That goes without saying. Has my father told you any details?"

"I don't *know* any details," he protested. "She was remarkably secretive," he added to Paulina.

"Just because *I* didn't know any details, either," Elizabeth said. "But I think I have it all worked out now."

Gideon managed not to wince, and he noticed his mother was beaming with pride at her daughter-in-law's cleverness.

"Do you have a mark in mind?" Paulina asked.

"Yes, and I've determined that he's well worth the effort."

Paulina allowed that she would be delighted to hear all about him, and Elizabeth told her so much about Daniel Livingston that Gideon marveled. Even his mother seemed surprised at how much she knew, although surely his mother had been the main source of information.

The Senora was also particularly interested in learning about Irene and Cal's situation and how it fit into the plan, which surprised Gideon since Elizabeth had been convinced she wouldn't care about them. The Senora might have been intrigued by the romance of it, although she didn't really seem like the type to

Gideon. But then he was the first to admit he didn't really understand women all that well.

"I've never run a matrimonial con before," Paulina mused when Elizabeth had told her everything she knew about the family history.

"You don't have to—" Elizabeth began, but Paulina stopped her with a wave of her hand.

"I know, that part isn't really necessary, but I think I shall enjoy it. Men who are in love have no sense at all."

"That has been my experience," Gideon said, earning a fond look from Elizabeth and amused ones from everyone else.

"They also tend to be more generous," the Old Man remarked.

Paulina smiled wickedly. "And that has been *my* experience."

D OES THE SENORA *WANT* ME TO WRITE ABOUT HER?" CARRIE Decker asked with a confused frown. Carrie had come for tea on Friday afternoon at Elizabeth's invitation.

Elizabeth gave the reporter what she hoped was a reassuring smile. "I know it's difficult to imagine someone wanting their name to appear in the gossip . . . uh, I mean *society* columns, but Senora Chavez is anxious to meet the right people in the city, and I convinced her that a mention in your column was the quickest way to introduce her." Elizabeth had met Carrie a few months ago when she had caused Elizabeth all sorts of problems by announcing her and Gideon's upcoming wedding in her column. Carrie hadn't meant to cause the problems, though, and Elizabeth had cultivated the friendship in case she ever needed Carrie's assistance. Now she did.

"She'll get invitations from the climbers, too," Carrie warned. Newly rich people eager to rise in society would consider entertaining someone like the Senora a real social coup.

"I can sort out the invitations," Elizabeth assured her. Or rather Mother Bates could do it. Senora Chavez would associate only with the wealthiest and most dastardly members of society.

"Do you think I could meet her?" Carrie asked. "I could interview her." Poor Carrie, she aspired to be a serious news reporter, but as a female, she had very little chance of attaining that goal.

"She isn't comfortable talking to reporters," Elizabeth said quite truthfully. "But I'm sure I can answer all your questions about her."

Carrie smirked. "And if you can't, you'll make something up." Carrie had seen Elizabeth do that very thing.

"And you will have a delicious scoop. No other newspaper will even know Senora Chavez is in town until they read it in your column."

Carrie sighed, knowing when she was defeated. "I have a lot of questions."

"I assumed you would," Elizabeth said, and she settled back to answer every one of them.

SINCE HER NAME HAD NOT BEEN MENTIONED IN CARRIE Decker's column, Elizabeth had not expected to be questioned about it, so when her best friend, Anna Vanderslice, came straight over to her after church on Sunday, she was a little surprised.

"Did you see what Carrie Decker wrote about that Spanish lady in her column?" Anna demanded. Anna looked especially lovely in an apple green frock that emphasized her slender figure.

Elizabeth couldn't quite read her expression, though. It was somewhere between amused and confused. "What Spanish lady?"

But Mother Bates, who had gathered her things in time to

join the conversation, ruined any efforts Elizabeth might have made at ignorance by saying, "Do you mean Senora Chavez?"

Anna gave Elizabeth a triumphant smile. "Is that what her friends call her? I couldn't imagine they used that amazingly long name Carrie put in her column."

"Spanish names have to give a lot of information," Mother Bates explained with more than a little pride because she knew this interesting fact.

"What makes you think I had anything to do with the story about the Spanish lady?" Elizabeth asked, trying once again to claim ignorance.

Anna smiled. "Actually, I didn't. I just wondered if you'd seen it because it was so very interesting, but now it is clear to me you know all about it."

Elizabeth sighed and Mother Bates had to cover a smile. Gideon, blast it, was grinning like a loon. "I am obviously losing my touch."

"Anna, why don't you and your mother join us for Sunday dinner," Mother Bates said. "Then Elizabeth can tell you all about Senora Chavez."

"What a wonderful idea," Anna said, and scurried off to inform her mother of the invitation.

Mrs. Vanderslice was happy to join her old friend for dinner. They were pleased to see she had apparently gotten over her obsession with contacting her late son, David, through a medium and seemed to be more like her old self once again. After the meal, she and Mother Bates retired to the library to catch up, leaving Gideon, Elizabeth and Anna some privacy to discuss Senora Chavez's story.

"It all started when one of Gideon's clients invited us to watch the Belmont Stakes with him in his private box."

Anna frowned in confusion. "Is that an opera?"

"Hardly," Gideon said with amusement. "It's a horse race."

Anna did not look one bit less confused. "Oh. When you said 'private box,' I thought . . ."

"Yes," Elizabeth said. "I can see how you would. It's an important horse race, so Gideon and I and Mother Bates spent the day at Belmont Park with Mr. Nolan and his daughter, Irene. The owners have private boxes, although they are nothing like the ones at the opera house."

"I would love to see a horse race," Anna said. "Are they absolutely thrilling?"

"Absolutely," Elizabeth assured her.

"But what does a horse race have to do with the Spanish lady?"

"A lot," Gideon said, "but we'll never get to it if you keep asking questions."

Anna gave him a mock glare and said, "I promise not to ask a single question until you're finished."

Elizabeth told her about the races and how Daniel Livingston's jockey had hampered Cal Regan from winning the first race and how Trench had fallen because he was sponged—Anna had to break her promise not to ask questions a few times—and how Irene and Cal were in love and Irene was expecting a baby. Elizabeth finished up with, "And the only way to help Irene and Cal is to get them enough money to start their own horse farm."

Anna frowned. "I can see that, and you're probably trying to figure out how to con her father or someone out of the money, but who is the Spanish lady and what does she have to do with all of this?"

"What Elizabeth failed to mention," Gideon said, "is that while we were at the races, we happened to see Mr. Miles with a lady that Mr. Nolan said strongly resembled his late wife."

"And is *she* the Spanish lady?" Anna asked hopefully.

"Yes, she is."

"Ah," Anna said, nodding, although she still looked confused.

"And we think that Daniel Livingston is behind the dirty tricks being played on Mr. Nolan's horses," Elizabeth added.

"I gathered as much, but what does that have to do with the Spanish lady?"

"Daniel Livingston was engaged to the woman Mr. Nolan married," Elizabeth said.

"She threw Livingston over to marry Nolan," Gideon clarified. "Livingston has never forgiven Nolan."

"Or Irene," Elizabeth said, "because Mrs. Nolan died after giving birth to her."

"My goodness, how like a melodrama. And you said the Spanish lady resembles Mrs. Nolan?"

Elizabeth nodded. "Yes, she does. And it seems Mr. Livingston still cares for Mrs. Nolan, if his need for revenge is any indication."

Anna was still confused. "But how will you convince this Spanish lady to get involved in your plan, whatever it is?"

"Oh, I forgot to mention that she is a, uh, *colleague* of my father's," Elizabeth said.

"Oh, she's a con artist, too," Anna said with more enthusiasm for the topic than Elizabeth liked to see in her friend.

"As it happens, yes."

"And she is going to help you con someone? Who is it? Mr. Nolan or Mr. Livingston?"

"Anna, you know you shouldn't be interested in Elizabeth's cons," Gideon tried.

She dismissed his concern with a scowl. "Elizabeth's cons are paying my college tuition."

"*Jake* is paying her college tuition," Elizabeth hastily explained at Gideon's frown.

"Jake says I earned a share of the score," Anna explained, "but for some reason he and Elizabeth don't want to corrupt me with the ill-gotten gains."

"The score?" Gideon echoed, not sure he'd heard her correctly. How many society girls knew con artist slang?

"Isn't that the right word for it?" Anna asked Elizabeth.

"It is exactly the right word for it, but I see we are failing in our efforts to not corrupt you," Elizabeth said.

Anna waved away her concern. "The question is, How can I help with this Spanish lady business? And Freddie will want to help, too." Frederica Quincy was Anna's dear friend who might actually be more than a friend, but Elizabeth had chosen not to pry into Anna's personal life.

"I'm sure you and Freddie can't help at all," Gideon said with more hope than confidence.

"At the moment, I don't see a role for you and Frederica," Elizabeth tactfully confirmed. "Although I do appreciate your willingness to help."

"But you'll call on us if you need us," Anna said with a confidence that made Gideon cringe. "Now tell me what you're planning."

"We're planning to introduce Senora Chavez to society," Elizabeth said. "I don't suppose your mother is on friendly terms with Daniel Livingston."

"Is he the one you want to con?" Anna guessed. "Mother doesn't socialize much since David died, you know."

The mention of Anna's dearly departed brother silenced all of them for a moment. David had been Gideon's best friend, and they all felt his loss.

"I understand that Mr. Livingston doesn't socialize much himself," Elizabeth said to guide their thoughts away from David. "Our plan is to introduce the Senora to society and establish her and then arrange for her to encounter Mr. Livingston somehow."

"I'll ask Mother if she knows him," Anna said.

"Mother Bates knows him, so maybe your mother does, too, although Mother Bates said she hadn't seen him in a long time. He recognized her, though, and he spoke to us at the racetrack"

"Then wouldn't it be natural for her to invite him to a party or something?" Anna said. "To renew the acquaintance perhaps?"

"I don't know. Would it?" Elizabeth asked Gideon.

Gideon sighed in a way Elizabeth recognized as resignation. "It would if she wanted to get involved in a con."

"Well," Elizabeth said briskly to let Gideon know that had not been her intention at all, "if it comes to that, but we'll probably find another way for him to encounter the Senora."

"Is she really Spanish?" Anna asked.

"I doubt it," Gideon said.

"I know she doesn't sound very Spanish," Elizabeth said apologetically, although she shouldn't have to apologize for the Senora's failure to fake an accent. "But that's because she went to a Swiss boarding school."

"What does that have to do with having an accent?" Anna asked.

"Nothing at all unless a con artist says it," Gideon said. "Then it makes perfect sense."

Elizabeth chose to ignore that. "Anna, I really don't want to involve you in any more cons. It isn't something a young woman like you should be doing."

"But without any college classes to keep me busy this summer,

I need something to do. Besides, it isn't something a young woman like *you* should be doing, either," Anna pointed out.

"Thank you, Anna," Gideon said with heartfelt sincerity.

Elizabeth ignored that, too. "Now tell me, who are the most despicable members of society, because the Senora needs to meet them."

I MUST APOLOGIZE IN ADVANCE, SENORA," MOTHER BATES SAID to Paulina on Tuesday afternoon. Paulina had joined her and Elizabeth for tea so they could advise her on which invitations to accept. As Elizabeth had expected, she had received more than a few already as a result of Carrie Decker's column. "Elizabeth says I am to advise you on which of these are the least deserving of your company."

The Senora smiled beneficently. "She knows my preferences well. These are the cards I have received as of today." She handed a small stack of envelopes tied with a red satin ribbon to Mother Bates.

"What are your plans?" Elizabeth asked pleasantly as Mother Bates examined the invitations.

"I want to make some friends in the city."

"Wealthy friends, I assume."

"Yes, and male. Females, I have learned, seldom have control of any money worth mentioning, and even when they do, they aren't going to give it to another woman."

"But you said you've never run a matrimonial con before," Elizabeth reminded her.

Paulina smiled. "Love is not the only reason a man might give a woman money."

"Ah yes, the Old Man said you run a variation of the Drake inheritance, and that you are the heir."

"But I cannot access my inheritance for several years because of circumstances beyond my control."

"And men who aren't in love with you agree to support you until then?" Elizabeth didn't bother to hide her skepticism.

"Of course not, but as I said, they do agree to lend me money against my future inheritance."

"At exorbitant interest rates," Elizabeth said. "That makes perfect sense."

"Yes, because greed is so much more powerful than love can ever be."

"It is, at least, more long-lasting."

"And far less fickle," Paulina agreed. "I am not as young as I was, and these things take time, so I cannot rely on my charms. I was in San Francisco for almost five years."

"Good heavens, that's amazing." What con men called a "long con" might take a few weeks or even months, but Elizabeth had never seen one go on for years. She desperately wanted to know how much Paulina had taken during those five years, but it was rude to ask.

Paulina shrugged off Elizabeth's admiration. "It is a game only a female can play. These rich men think they can take advantage of a woman alone and she will not realize she is being cheated."

"And they never suspect that a woman could outsmart them."

Paulina smiled. "Never."

"Yes," Mother Bates said, reminding them she was there, "men are always underestimating women. They never expected we'd win the vote, for example, and now it's just a matter of time before the amendment is ratified."

"The amendment?" Paulina echoed in confusion.

"The constitutional amendment that will give women the right to vote. Congress just passed it," Elizabeth said. Was it possible Paulina was unaware of the long struggle for Woman Suffrage?

"Oh yes, I have read about that, but I do not understand why women want to be involved in politics. Such a sordid business."

Elizabeth had to smile at a con artist criticizing another "sordid business." "We believe that women will have an uplifting influence once we win the right to vote."

Paulina shrugged this off as well. "I think you will find that uplifting politicians is very heavy work."

"I'm afraid you are correct, Senora," Mother Bates said tactfully. "I have chosen the invitations I think you will find the most helpful."

Paulina seemed glad for the change in topic. Mother Bates had chosen three of the eleven cards and described the people who had issued them. They were millionaires, all married couples and nominally respectable but not particularly honest. Elizabeth realized Mother Bates had chosen people whose characters were questionable enough to make them deserving of being cheated. Elizabeth had never been prouder of her.

"Are none of them bankers?" Paulina asked when Mother Bates had finished her descriptions.

Mother Bates frowned. "I didn't see any."

"I'm sure you'll meet some soon enough," Elizabeth said. "These three are all excellent choices."

"There was one more that I . . . Well, I wanted to ask you first, Elizabeth." Mother Bates handed the card to her.

Elizabeth smiled when she saw the name: Westerly. The Westerlys had already provided her family with a nice little score in their efforts to associate with European aristocracy.

"Didn't Rosemary marry a baron?" Elizabeth asked.

"That's what the announcement said," Mother Bates confirmed.

"You have, uh, done business with these people before?" Paulina asked with interest.

"Yes, and . . . Well, it seems the Westerlys are still interested in entertaining distinguished European visitors. I think you should accept this invitation, too."

# CHAPTER SIX

"WE NEED AN AUTOMOBILE," ELIZABETH TOLD GIDEON AS the cab carried them to the Westerlys' home on Friday evening.

"Are you trying to put me out of business, ma'am?" the cab-driver asked over his shoulder.

"Not at all," Gideon replied for her, "because we are not getting an automobile." They had had this conversation before.

"It would be much more convenient than always trying to find a cab to take us places," Elizabeth pointed out.

"Motors are expensive and where would we keep it?" Gideon said.

"In the old stable. Heaven knows we don't use it for horses."

She was right, of course, and motors weren't so expensive that they couldn't afford one. In fact, he knew Elizabeth could easily buy one with her own money that she had brought with her into their marriage. Gideon didn't like to think how she had earned that money, which was another reason he didn't want to spend it on buying a motorcar. He didn't say any of that to her, though. He never wanted her to think he judged her for her past because he didn't.

"I suppose you'd want to drive it yourself, too," Gideon said.

Her face lit up, making him want to kiss her, but he refrained. They'd already outraged the cabdriver enough for one evening. "I would always defer to you, darling. You know that."

"I don't know anything of the kind, but I would like to experience that just once in our marriage, so perhaps I will buy you a motorcar just so I can."

She laughed at that. "Are you saying I'm not an obedient wife, darling?"

Gideon cleared his throat meaningfully. "We are attending a party at the Westerlys' house in spite of my objections."

"You didn't really object, did you? I mean, you asked me whether I really thought it was a good idea and I did think it was a good idea, so that should have allayed your concerns."

"She's got you there, mister," the cabdriver said.

"She's always got me," Gideon said with a sigh.

"You'll enjoy yourself," she assured him. "You'll see."

They had made a point to arrive right on time so they would be there to see everyone else come in.

"What are you going to say if the Westerlys ask you if you've heard from Percy?" Gideon whispered to her as they made their way to the parlor where Mr. and Mrs. Westerly were greeting their guests. Lord Percy had supposedly been an old friend of Elizabeth's and had jilted the Westerlys' daughter and cheated Mr. Westerly out of a small fortune.

"They won't ask," Elizabeth said with a confidence he didn't think she had a right to feel. "They'll want to pretend he never existed now that Rosemary is a baroness."

Gideon frowned, certain she was wrong, but when they reached the Westerlys', Mrs. Westerly greeted them with a smile that looked almost genuine. "Elizabeth and Gideon, I'm so glad you could come tonight." As usual, she was wearing a gown that was decidedly too youthful for her, and while it fit to perfection, it did little to flatter a figure that had thickened with age.

"Thank you so much for inviting us," Elizabeth said. "I was happy to see the announcement of Rosemary's marriage. To a baron, I believe." She made it sound like a question and Gideon somehow managed not to roll his eyes.

"Yes, a baron," Mrs. Westerly said. Her smile had faded just a bit, but she was determined to put a good face on it. "There is no estate, just a small manor house, but Rosemary has great plans for it."

"I'm sure she does," Elizabeth said ingenuously. "It must be difficult for you, though, having her so far away in England."

"We're coping," Mr. Westerly chimed in, and from his expression, Gideon would have bet real money that he didn't miss Rosemary all that much.

"I'm looking forward to introducing you to our guest of honor," Mrs. Westerly said, obviously eager to change the subject. "Senora Padilla y de la Fuente viuda de Chavez is anxious to make new friends in the city."

They had decided not to tell the Westerlys that they were already acquainted with the Senora, so Gideon said, "We're looking forward to that as well. We don't often see visitors from Spain in the city." There, he'd managed that without telling a single lie.

"I'm sure we will see more foreign visitors now that the war is over," Mr. Westerly said. He was a portly man who obviously thought his opinions were important and always correct. "In fact, we'll probably be overrun with people trying to escape Europe."

Since Gideon knew perfectly well that the Senora hadn't come from Europe at all, he simply smiled and nodded and moved on.

"You see," Elizabeth reminded him when they were out of earshot, "they didn't even ask about Percy."

"Is a baron better than an earl?" Gideon asked. Rosemary had believed Percy to be an earl.

"Heavens no. A baron is the lowest one on the list of aristocratic titles. And you heard Mrs. Westerly, he doesn't even have an estate. But at least Rosemary got a title, which was what she really wanted." Elizabeth stopped and turned to Gideon in surprise. "Is that Logan and Noelle?"

"It certainly is." They headed for the couple who were standing by themselves in the hallway.

After greetings had been exchanged, Elizabeth said, "I must say, I'm surprised to see you here."

"You mean you're surprised the Westerlys invited us," Logan said. Logan and Rosemary had been engaged, and she had thrown him over for Percy.

"I think," Noelle said in her delightful French accent, "they wish us to see their triumph to entertain this Spanish lady." She had met Logan in France during the war and come over as a French war bride afterward.

"And probably to show they don't care a fig that Logan married someone else now that Rosemary has her baron," Elizabeth said.

"Yes," Noelle agreed with a twinkle. "Not a fig."

"It just occurred to me, do you know something about this Spanish lady?" Logan asked Gideon with a suspicious frown.

"I know very little about her," Gideon said quite truthfully.

"But after this evening, I'm sure we'll all know her very well,"

Elizabeth said with her usual tact. "Did you hear that she's an heiress?"

"She is wealthy, you mean," Noelle said.

"So it would seem," Elizabeth said with a straight face.

"Although it's rude to discuss such things," Gideon reminded Elizabeth.

"In some circles it is," Elizabeth replied unrepentantly.

"Is the Spanish lady going to disappear like Percy did?" Logan asked with interest.

"My goodness," Elizabeth chided him. "Lord Percy didn't *disappear*. He's not a ghost. He simply went to Europe to escape his creditors."

"As one does," Gideon added with a smirk.

Logan turned to Noelle. "I think we are going to be well entertained by this Spanish lady."

"Noelle," Gideon said quickly to distract them, "your English is improving every time I see you."

Noelle smiled and blushed at the compliment, and they began to discuss subjects that did not involve the Spanish lady, to Gideon's relief. Some other friends arrived and joined them, and they were deep in conversation when a hush seemed to fall over the assembly. They turned to see the maid had opened the door to the Senora, who had obviously taken great pains to look her part.

She was clad, head to toe, in black, and her gown was amazing. The fitted bodice was a series of sequined fish scales that tapered to below her waist. Her long sleeves were lace, and her skirt was a mass of sequins and lace that ended just above the toes of her satin slippers with their jeweled buckles. On her head she wore a magnificent mantilla—made of the same lace as her dress—that was mounted on a comb that stood a good six inches or more from the crown of her head. Around her neck was a thick lace choker and a large gold cross hung from it, drawing attention to the barest hint of cleavage that showed above her modest neckline.

A young woman had accompanied her, and she had obviously been dressed with deliberate care so as not to upstage her companion. Although she was younger and nearly as beautiful as the Senora, her gown was a pale yellow and of a simple design, meant to fade quickly from memory. The maid directed them into the parlor, where the Westerlys waited to welcome their special guest.

"Who is that girl with the Senora?" Gideon asked no one in particular.

"I'm sure we'll find out soon enough," Elizabeth said. From her expression, he knew she wasn't nearly as surprised as he was. "Just try to enjoy yourself, darling."

Mrs. Westerly had taken charge of the Senora and was leading her around to meet everyone. She began with those she considered the most important among her guests, which meant that Gideon and Elizabeth were among the last to be approached, along with Logan and Noelle. Mrs. Westerly obviously thought she was doing them a great favor by making the Senora known to them, if her smug smile was any indication.

"Oh, and may I present the Senora's sister, Senorita Olinda Padilla," Mrs. Westerly added as if it were an afterthought. Plainly, she found the girl to be unnecessary to her purposes.

Olinda smiled sweetly and murmured something unintelligible without making eye contact with any of them. Up close, Gideon realized she looked very familiar and was apparently painfully shy, although that might have been an excuse not to look people in the eye so they wouldn't get a good look at her. He couldn't imagine what purpose she would serve in the Senora's plans, but he supposed he would find out soon enough.

"Mrs. Carstens is a French war bride," Elizabeth informed the Senora.

"Then you are newly married," the Senora said with a smile. "My best wishes to you both."

"Were you fortunate to escape Spain before the war?" Noelle asked.

"Yes, I was. I love to travel, you see, and luckily, I was visiting America when it started. I, uh . . ." She looked around as if to see if anyone were eavesdropping, which, of course, many people were. "Well, I must avoid Spain for a while, until things are settled with my brother-in-law."

"Family disputes can be difficult," Mrs. Westerly said.

The Senora smiled apologetically. "Disputes involving an inheritance are always difficult, but enough talk about that. No one is interested in my troubles. This is a party, and I do so want Olinda to enjoy herself."

Olinda's pained smile indicated that might be impossible, but Elizabeth said, "We'll be happy to take her in hand and make sure she does."

Olinda had completely stopped smiling and even looked a bit panicked by the time Elizabeth took custody of her and spirited her away along with Noelle. Mrs. Westerly directed the Senora to the last group of guests remaining to be introduced, leaving Gideon and Logan to their own devices. They set off to find themselves a drink and some more friends to speak with. Sadly, Mr. Westerly found them before they were able to surround themselves with the protection of other guests.

"What do you think of the Senora?" he asked them.

"She's a rather impressive woman," Logan said. "What do you know about her?"

"She's filthy rich," Westerly said with confidence. He didn't even bother to lower his voice.

Logan and Gideon had no reply to such rudeness so they both chose to take a sip of their respective drinks instead.

"There's some problem with the inheritance, though," Westerly said in response to their silence.

"What kind of problem?" Gideon heard himself asking, although he would have sworn he didn't really want to know. Etiquette made terrible demands on a man.

"The kind that makes estate attorneys rich," Westerly said smugly, "or at least that's what I understand."

Since Gideon was an estate attorney, he knew Westerly would expect him to inquire further, and Logan would certainly think it odd if he didn't. "That's . . . interesting."

"She inherited her husband's entire estate when he died. It was in his will, but his brother is contesting it. They're an old family and don't want the property going to an outsider. They've been fighting it in the courts for a couple years now, but I understand he has finally agreed to a settlement." Westerly was awfully well-informed, considering he couldn't have known the Senora for more than a few days.

"That's good then," Gideon said, knowing full well it couldn't possibly be good.

"Yes. He's going to be satisfied when his son marries the Senora's sister, that little girl she brought along with her tonight. They've just been waiting until she turns eighteen."

"I see," Gideon said, although he didn't see at all.

"Yes, the Senora hasn't been able to touch any of the money since her husband died. Because of the court case, you know. The judge sealed everything. But it won't be long now. Just a few more months until the girl is old enough. Then the Senora gets all the money, and the brother gets the estate in Spain. The boy and girl will be their heirs, so they'll get it all in the end and it will remain in the family."

"Seems a bit medieval, doesn't it?" Logan asked.

"That's the way they do things in Spain," Westerly said with a confidence he shouldn't have felt. "Things are very old-fashioned there."

Gideon could think of a half a dozen things that could go wrong with an arrangement like that, but he didn't bother to point them out since he knew none of this story was true. "I'm sure the Senora will be happy to have everything settled."

Westerly chuckled. "The rest of us will be, too."

"The rest of who?" Gideon asked in confusion.

Westerly glanced around to make sure no one was near enough to hear him and then he leaned in so only Logan and Gideon could. "Those of us who loaned her money. She's a bit strapped from all the legal wrangling and she doesn't have any sense at all about interest rates."

Gideon managed not to wince. "Are you saying you lent her some money?"

Westerly shrugged. "At twenty percent, I'd be a fool not to. Everyone is doing it."

Gideon didn't bother to hide his astonishment, and Logan actually gasped. "Aren't you taking advantage of her?" Logan asked.

"She's a foreigner, and besides, she can afford it. You might offer to lend her something yourself. You don't want to miss out on an opportunity like this."

Westerly obviously thought his work was done because he took his leave, moving on to bestow his presence on some of his other guests.

"I can't believe he'd take advantage of a woman like that," Logan said. "Or anyone at all, for that matter."

"It is despicable," Gideon had to agree, although he didn't bother to explain exactly what it was he found despicable.

"Does that sound right to you?" Logan asked. "Legally, I

mean? If her husband left everything to her, shouldn't that be the end of it?"

"I'm not familiar with Spanish law." Which was completely true, although it didn't begin to answer Logan's real questions. Poor Logan didn't even know what the real questions were.

"Yes, I guess other countries do things differently," Logan said with a sigh. "Still, to cheat a poor widow like that . . ."

"Senora Chavez isn't exactly poor," Gideon said.

"She will be if she has to pay twenty percent interest on her loans."

"Westerly may have been exaggerating."

"Let's hope. And that young girl. I wonder how she feels about being married off like that."

Gideon couldn't help smiling. "Probably the way you felt about marrying Rosemary Westerly."

Logan groaned and Gideon slapped him on the back. "Let's find someone to talk to who doesn't know anything about the Senora and her problems."

D ID YOU LEARN ANYTHING NEW THIS EVENING, DARLING?" Elizabeth asked. They were snuggled up in the backseat of the cab as it carried them home from the Westerly house.

She couldn't see his expression in the dark, but she could imagine it. "Westerly has loaned the Senora some money."

"*Already?*" This was impressive, even for someone as accomplished as Paulina.

"At twenty percent interest."

"He must be thrilled."

"He seemed to be. He's apparently not the only one, either."

"Oh my, the Old Man did speak highly of Paulina's skills."

"What is the story about, uh, the girl she had with her?"

"Just that she's the Senora's sister."

"But not *Paulina's* sister."

"Of course not. She doesn't have the same . . . I don't know what to call it. Presence?"

"Yes, 'presence' does describe Paulina," Gideon said.

"Although the girl is playing her part rather well."

"So far, at least. Westerly told us all about her. She's going to marry the dead husband's nephew and the two of them will inherit the estate and the money."

"I can tell from your tone that you don't think this is a good plan."

"It wouldn't be, if it were real. I keep wanting to advise the Senora to protect her interests."

"Because you're such an honorable man, my darling. You would do better to advise her not to accept loans at twenty percent interest."

"I would if I thought she had any intention of repaying them."

Elizabeth smiled in the dark and snuggled a little closer to Gideon.

"How is this supposed to help Irene and Cal, though?" he asked after a few moments.

"We need to arrange for Daniel Livingston to meet the Senora."

"Then he'll lend her money, too?" Plainly, Gideon didn't like this idea one bit.

"Doesn't he owe Cal for injuring him so severely?"

"Yes, but . . . I guess I can't really defend Livingston. He deserves whatever he gets."

"And so do Cal and Irene. How do you feel about visiting the racetrack again?"

"Is that the only place the Senora can encounter Livingston?"

"Your mother hasn't found anyone she knows who is on intimate terms with him, so he isn't likely to accept a social invitation."

"Then I guess we'll have to go to the track, although I can't keep leaving the office in the middle of the week."

"I'll see what I can do," she promised.

T HE FOLLOWING MONDAY, ELIZABETH AND MOTHER BATES made the trip out to the hospital in Queens to visit Cal Regan. They were not surprised to find Irene at his bedside, although she looked as if she were merely visiting now instead of sleeping in the chair beside him every night.

"How nice of you to come," Irene said, jumping up to greet them.

As before, they had brought some fruit and sweets—a cake this time—that Cal could enjoy and share with his nurses.

"I never know whether to bring a man flowers when he's in the hospital," Mother Bates told Cal.

"You can't eat flowers, Mrs. Bates," he replied with a grin.

"So true," Elizabeth agreed. "How are you doing?"

Cal simply groaned his frustration. Irene said, "The doctor predicts he'll be in a cast for the rest of the summer, at least."

"How tiresome," Elizabeth said. "We brought you some newspapers, too. Sunday's edition of the *Times* has a nice story about the Dempsey-Willard fight coming up on Friday."

"I don't know how you can have a *nice* story about a prizefight," Mother Bates said, earning a chuckle from Cal. "I can think of a lot better ways to celebrate the Fourth of July."

"So can I," Cal agreed, "but since I can't ride, I won't be doing any of them."

"Elizabeth, why don't you take Irene for a little walk. I'm sure she could use some fresh air, and I'll keep Mr. Regan company. I'll be happy to listen to all your complaints about the hospital and commiserate with you."

"I shouldn't leave him," Irene protested. "I have to be at the track this afternoon. Father is running Rainmaker in the fourth."

"Mother Bates will entertain him," Elizabeth assured her.

"Go on, Reenie," Cal said, "and don't worry, Mrs. Bates isn't going to steal my heart while you're gone."

"Don't be so sure, young man," Mother Bates chided him as she shooed Irene out of the way so she could claim the bedside chair.

Elizabeth took Irene by the arm and, ignoring her feeble protests, guided her out of the room. When they were outside, Elizabeth said, "Do you go to the track every afternoon?"

"Most days, and I always go if we have a horse running. Father likes for me to check on the horses, too. Not that he doesn't trust Mr. Quaid, but after the sponging incident, he wants my opinion in case they try it again. Mr. Quaid did miss it with Trench."

"How is Trench doing?"

"He seems to be recovered, but we won't know until he races again. Father is going to give him some more time, just to be sure."

"I certainly hope he doesn't have any lasting damage."

They walked for a few moments in silence before Elizabeth said, "Do you often see Daniel Livingston?"

Irene frowned. "What do you mean?"

"I mean how much time does he spend at the track? Do you see him there very much?"

"He usually comes if he has a horse running, of course, and also if there's a big race. I'm afraid I haven't been paying much attention to whether he's at the track or not since Cal got hurt."

"But you said he usually comes when there's a big race, like the Belmont with Sir Barton," Elizabeth guessed.

"Yes." Irene winced. "Or I guess if he's interested in sabotaging one of our horses."

"I'm sure you're being very careful."

"Yes, Mr. Quaid has been sleeping at the stable since we moved them from Belmont. We've hired some guards, too, but if someone is really determined, they can still find a way."

"Let's see if we can distract Mr. Livingston from wanting to harm your family at all."

"How on earth can you do that?" Irene asked.

"I'm not sure yet," Elizabeth lied, "but I think if we can make sure Mr. Livingston is at the racetrack on a particular day, we can find a way. There must be some big stakes races coming up for the Fourth of July holiday."

As Elizabeth had expected, Irene knew exactly which races were scheduled. "There's the Clover Stakes on the Fourth, but the really big one is on Saturday, the Tremont Stakes. It has a six-thousand-dollar purse and that new colt who's winning everything is running in it."

"Which colt is that?"

"Man o' War. He's only a two-year-old but people are already comparing him to Sir Barton."

"And it's on Saturday, too. Gideon particularly asked me to schedule our racetrack outings on the weekend from now on."

"Did he?" Irene asked with amusement.

"He did, indeed. Just between us, I think he enjoyed himself, even if he didn't bet. I don't suppose there's any way you can make sure Livingston is at the track on Saturday."

Irene gave the matter some thought. "I suppose I could ask around. Someone might know his plans."

"Perhaps you could start a rumor that Mr. Livingston is afraid to face your father after what happened to Cal and Trench."

"My goodness, that would be certain to bring him out," Irene said with a smile.

"Be sure everyone knows you'll be in a box on Saturday for the Tremont. If you'll invite us to join you again, I think we can ensure Mr. Livingston encounters a major distraction."

"What kind of distraction?" Irene asked with a worried frown.

"The less you know, the better, but it will definitely take his mind off you and your father."

W HEN WILL I BE ALLOWED TO ENTERTAIN THE SENORA?"
Mother Bates asked Elizabeth as the cab carried them to the Senora's hotel, a small and very exclusive establishment just off Fifth Avenue.

"You need to officially meet her first," Elizabeth said. "But even then, I'm not sure you should be closely involved with her."

"Why not? It seems like everyone on the social register wants to be her dearest friend."

"Not everyone on the social register has a con artist for a daughter-in-law," Elizabeth reminded her.

"That is hardly common knowledge, my dear."

"And it won't become common knowledge if we aren't closely associated with cons."

"But won't many people be taken in by her? We will just be yet another family of victims."

Elizabeth gave her mother-in-law a horrified look. "You don't plan to lend the Senora any money, do you?"

"Certainly not, but we could claim to have done so. No one is likely to question that."

Elizabeth almost laughed out loud. "I wonder what Gideon would think of such a plan."

"Oh, I know he doesn't approve of lying, but I wouldn't actually lie. I could just indicate I am very disappointed when the Senora disappears and let people form their own conclusions."

Elizabeth sighed. "Please don't tell Gideon your idea."

Mother Bates smiled serenely. "I wouldn't dream of it."

The doorman at the hotel greeted them warmly and showed them inside when they told him they were visiting the Senora. She had invited them for tea, and they were not her only guests that day.

The Senora's suite was quite large, as it was the penthouse. The furnishings looked like something Marie Antoinette would have chosen for her palace, all curlicues and gold leaf, and an elaborate display of crustless sandwiches and tea cakes had been set up on the sideboard. The Senora must have realized that her Spanish attire would clash with the suite's French decor, so today she wore an afternoon gown of pale green silk chiffon with a ruched waist. Her figure was too full for the prevailing fashions, but this particular gown was a lovely compromise.

Elizabeth introduced Mother Bates to the Senora for the benefit of the other guests, even though they had already met, and then they greeted the four other women who had arrived before them. Elizabeth was not surprised to see Mrs. Westerly was among them. Mrs. Westerly, however, seemed very surprised and not at all pleased to see them. Perhaps she didn't consider them worthy of the Senora's attentions.

Elizabeth also greeted Olinda, who was once again wearing a gown designed specifically to be unflattering. Although it was embroidered and embellished, it was a nondescript shade of brown that didn't suit her at all, and her golden hair was scraped into an unbecoming chignon. Olinda managed a feeble smile for Elizabeth but otherwise gave the impression she would rather be anywhere else but here among the fashionable and older ladies of the Senora's acquaintance.

The ladies chatted about the usual topics: the weather, the foibles of their friends, and what social events they were planning to attend, which included a lively discussion about the upcoming Fourth of July celebrations being held around the city. They drank copious amounts of tea and finished off nearly all of the edibles.

"Olinda, where will you live when you marry?" Mrs. Westerly asked just as Mother Bates got up to use the washroom, which was located adjacent to the Senora's bedroom. Up until now, the bedroom door had remained closed.

Olinda's lovely blue eyes widened with terror at being directly addressed, and her gaze darted to the Senora in a silent plea for help.

"Olinda and Hernando will officially live in Spain at the Chavez family estate," the Senora answered for her, "although I expect they will visit many of the countries Olinda and I have toured these past few years."

"Is the estate very large?" Mrs. Westerly asked. Even Elizabeth winced at the question. Honestly, is that all the Westerlys thought about?

"Large enough," the Senora replied tactfully. "And how does your daughter like living in England, Mrs. Westerly?" she countered.

"She finds it . . . quaint," Mrs. Westerly decided. "There are so many rules one must follow as a member of the aristocracy." She said the word as if it were delicious on her tongue.

"Ah yes," the Senora said, ignoring Mrs. Westerly's reference to the aristocracy into which her daughter had married. "Europe does love its rules. That is why I so enjoy being in America. A woman has much more freedom here."

"And even more now that we will soon have the vote," Elizabeth added.

"Women have been able to vote in New York for a while now," one of the other women pointed out.

"But when the amendment is ratified, *all* the women in the country will be able to vote."

"Only if the amendment is ratified," the woman said. "It has a long way to go."

"Perhaps not so very long," Elizabeth said. "Look how many states have ratified it already."

"But many others won't ratify it at all."

Elizabeth had opened her mouth to continue the argument when Mother Bates emerged from the bedroom looking amazed. She had left the door wide open, too. "My goodness, Senora Chavez, that is an impressive safe."

The Senora looked a little abashed. "Yes, it is, I'm afraid."

"Do you have a safe in your room?" Mrs. Westerly asked in surprise. "How odd. Most hotels will keep your valuables in their safe if you have the need."

"I do not keep my jewels in that safe, Mrs. Westerly," the Senora explained patiently.

"And if she did, she'd hardly need a safe that large," Mother Bates said. "It's taller than I am, and it must weigh a thousand pounds."

"More than a thousand, unfortunately," the Senora admitted.

"Excuse me, I need to use the . . ." one of the other women said, with a vague wave of her hand. She jumped up and headed toward the bedroom, ostensibly to use the washroom but obviously to get a better look at the safe in question, which was just visible through the open door.

"I'm sure it's none of our business why you have such a large safe in your hotel room," Elizabeth said, certain there must be etiquette rules about discussing such things, even in America, and she wanted to be seen to be the first to obey them.

Fortunately, none of the other ladies cared about such things in the face of such a juicy bit of potential gossip. Mother Bates, who seemed to be enjoying the attention her discovery had brought her, said, "And what are all those seals for? It looks like it would be impossible to open the safe without breaking them."

The Senora sighed. "That is the intention, you see. I . . . Well, it is embarrassing to discuss, but I know you ladies will respect my privacy." She hesitated, as if waiting for someone to confirm this naïve belief, and Elizabeth was gratified to note that every woman still in the room falsely assured her they would. "My late husband left me his entire estate, but his brother has contested the will. He and his family have moved into the castle, and he is claiming it for his own. All I could do was retain the funds my husband had left. I removed them from the bank so my brother-in-law could not get possession of them through some nefarious means and put them in this safe. I thought the money would then be mine by law, but the judge decreed that I could not touch it until the case was settled, so he put those seals on the safe and it cannot be opened until he makes his decision."

"And you brought that enormous safe with you from Spain?" Mother Bates asked in astonishment.

"I had no choice. If I left it behind, my brother-in-law could have hired someone to break into it and rob me. He would deny involvement and I would have nothing. So, I keep the safe with me, where I know it will remain untouched. But I must ask you not to share my secret. I would not want word to get back to my husband's family about where the safe is kept."

Elizabeth joined the other women in pledging their secrecy, but she was positive she was the only one who intended to keep that promise.

# CHAPTER SEVEN

THE BATES FAMILY CELEBRATED THE FOURTH OF JULY AT THE campus of Columbia University, where the New York Military Band gave a concert that evening. Gideon had been reluctant to attend one of the many orations being held during the day, since they promised to be lectures condemning those deemed less than patriotic for opposing the recent war and who now were demanding fair treatment for workers. The ban on fireworks or explosives of any kind in the city made for a quiet evening, and the city itself seemed practically deserted, since the heat and the fireworks ban had sent thousands out to Coney Island and the other beaches. The newspapers reported that many, like the Bates family, had avoided the lectures and instead attended the various concerts or the entertainments held at the stadium of the College of the City of New York.

Gideon's choice of the concert had pleased his wife and mother, so everyone was in a good mood the next morning when they boarded the train for Aqueduct Racetrack, thus named because it had been built on property that belonged to the Brooklyn Water Works, home to the conduit that carried water to the city of New York. It was the only racetrack actually located in the city and was only eight miles from Belmont Park. Like Belmont, it also had its own train station for the convenience of racing fans.

The ladies, even the Senora, wore white dresses and broad-brimmed hats in deference to the heat. Gideon envied them, since he would be sweltering in his suit all afternoon. The forecast was for a high of eighty-nine degrees today, even hotter than yesterday when most of the city's population had fled to the shore.

"Do you think we'll see your father today?" he asked Elizabeth as the train carried them out to Queens.

"We might see him, but I'm sure he'll be busy. I told you, he's not involved in this at all."

"I'm surprised Olinda didn't accompany us," his mother said to the Senora. Gideon had flipped one of the seat backs so the four of them could face one another as they rode.

"She is not needed here, at least not yet," the Senora said. "Besides, she sunburns easily and didn't want to ruin her complexion."

"I'm very anxious to see how she *is* needed," his mother said with enough enthusiasm to make the Senora raise her finely arched eyebrows.

To her credit, she did not comment on it, however. "I am wondering just how much I really look like this dead woman. Did you know her, Mrs. Bates?" she asked.

"I did, but it's been almost twenty-five years. I'm not sure I would have even noticed the resemblance if Mr. Nolan hadn't pointed you out."

"She would have been much younger than I when she died, too," the Senora mused.

"Only by about ten years, I would think," his mother said

tactfully. The Senora was clearly at least forty while Mary Nolan would have died before she was twenty. "At any rate, Mr. Nolan found the resemblance astonishing. Mr. Livingston probably will, as well."

The Senora frowned. "And you are sure the only way to reach this Livingston is through the Nolans?"

Elizabeth sighed. "We tried everything we could think of, but no one we know really socializes with Mr. Livingston anymore. Since Mr. Nolan stole the original Mary away from Mr. Livingston, we think Mr. Livingston will be eager to return the favor once he sees you with Mr. Nolan."

"I will, of course, encourage Mr. Livingston to do just that, but Mr. Nolan may not give up easily."

"I'm sure you can discourage him," Elizabeth said. "Besides, from what we know, Mr. Nolan isn't anywhere near as rich a mark as Mr. Livingston. He's hardly even worth considering."

"If you say so," the Senora said, although Gideon didn't think she looked completely convinced. "Do you remember anything about this woman Mr. Nolan married? What she was like?"

His mother gave the matter some thought. "She was a lovely girl, but she wasn't like the rest of us."

"In what way?"

"In the way that we were all bred to be subservient and compliant and to defer to the men in our lives."

"As all women are," the Senora said with a smirk.

"It was even worse when I was a girl, but Mary always had a rebellious streak."

"Did she?" the Senora asked with interest.

"I don't mean she did anything outrageous or got in trouble at school or anything like that. She was just a bit . . . She chafed at all the rules. We all did, of course, but she admitted it and questioned them. I think . . ."

"What do you think, Mother Bates?" Elizabeth said, leaning forward in her seat.

"I think she may have just been looking for an opportunity to rebel without totally scandalizing society. She wouldn't want to ruin herself forever. She wasn't that much of a rebel, but I think she wanted to be noticed in some way."

"So, she jilted her fiancé," Elizabeth said.

Gideon's mother frowned. "I don't believe she did it on a whim. I think she was genuinely fond of Mr. Nolan, but even still, you can't imagine how shocking it was. Marriages were very thoughtfully arranged in my day. Young men would never make an offer to an unsuitable girl, and once betrothed, the families would make sure the marriage took place."

"Unless there was some sort of scandal," Gideon said, remembering a few tales he had heard through the years.

His mother nodded solemnly. "And even that wasn't enough in some cases. New York is a surprisingly small town if you just consider the society families. Everyone knows everyone else, and if you insult a family, it can start a feud that lasts for generations."

"And all the members of both families will feel honor bound to keep the feud going," Gideon added with some amusement.

"How awful," Elizabeth said. "But I can see why one would hesitate to humiliate a member of an influential family."

"And yet, this Mary did that very thing," the Senora mused. "Mrs. Bates, you said she really was fond of Mr. Nolan, the man she eventually married."

"It seemed so, although they were married for only a few years before she died, so it's difficult to know for sure. And, of course, they had moved out to the country, to his horse ranch, and we didn't see them very often after that. Sebastian was certainly besotted with her, though, and if the truth were told, he was more than a little proud of having gotten one up on Daniel Livingston, too."

"I'm sure that didn't help Mr. Livingston forgive them," Elizabeth said.

"Not at all," his mother agreed. "And Daniel made sure everyone knew he wasn't forgiving them. He expected all his friends to turn their backs on the Nolans, and many of them did, at least until Daniel all but withdrew from society after Mary died."

"I wonder why he did that," Elizabeth said.

"I've wondered, too," his mother said. "I think he may have realized his outrage no longer had a purpose if Mary was dead. He would just look foolish, so he chose to escape notice altogether."

"How very sad for all of them," the Senora said. "This Mary seems like a woman who would have had an interesting life if she had the chance."

"Her daughter is a truly modern woman," Elizabeth said. "I think Mary would have been proud of how she turned out."

"Even though she's hoping to marry a jockey?" Gideon challenged with an amused smirk.

"Would that really be so awful?" the Senora asked.

"It wouldn't be the most brilliant marriage, but he's a very successful jockey," Elizabeth felt compelled to say.

The Senora's usually complacent expression briefly expressed sorrow, but only briefly. "Yes, Cal Regan. He was very good, but they say he will never ride again."

"Which is why Elizabeth wants to con Livingston. Didn't she tell you?" Gideon said.

"Yes, she did tell me," the Senora said. "I must admit, however, it is not clear to me how this will benefit the Nolan girl and her jockey."

No one spoke for a long moment. Gideon's mother knew better than to speak for Elizabeth, and Gideon had already put his foot in it. After a long, painful moment, Elizabeth said, "I am donating my cut to them."

The Senora opened her mouth and then closed it again before finally saying, "All of it?"

"Yes, all of it. They want to start their own breeding farm."

The Senora needed a few minutes to come to terms with this amazing admission. "The Old Man did warn me you were rather unorthodox."

"And you wouldn't have believed him if he told you I don't keep my share of the cons I run."

"You don't keep any of them?" the Senora asked in amazement.

Elizabeth glanced at Gideon, silently acknowledging his influence on her. "Not anymore."

The Senora studied Elizabeth for a few moments. "I don't suppose the Old Man donates his share."

"Sometimes he makes a contribution," Gideon said, unable to resist.

The Senora now seemed genuinely shocked. "I hope you don't expect me to do that, too."

"Certainly not," Elizabeth said.

Gideon managed not to laugh out loud at the blatant lie. Elizabeth fully expected the Senora would make a donation when all was said and done. She would even do so gladly, if Gideon knew anything at all about his wife's powers of persuasion. But there was no point in saying so now.

The Senora continued to quiz his mother for every detail she remembered about Mary Nolan until they reached the Aqueduct station. The noontime sun was merciless, but the ladies had brought parasols. Gideon envied them their summer finery, although he knew the corsets they wore were almost as uncomfortable as his three-piece suit.

In spite of the heat, the crowd was respectable. Not as large as for the Belmont Stakes, but at least fifteen thousand were in attendance at a track that comfortably seated eight. They made their way to the shaded clubhouse, where Mr. Nolan and Irene were waiting to join them for lunch. All Elizabeth had told Irene was that they were bringing a fourth person with them, so Gideon wasn't at all surprised at Nolan's stunned expression when he saw the Senora stop at his table.

"I HOPE YOU DON'T MIND, MR. NOLAN, BUT I INVITED MY FRIEND Senora Chavez to join us," Elizabeth was saying. She pretended not to notice how Mr. Nolan's jaw had dropped and how he seemed too stunned for normal human speech, at least for the moment. "Senora, may I present Sebastian Nolan and his daughter, Irene?"

Irene looked almost as stunned, but she was obviously made of sterner stuff than her father. "What a pleasure to have you join us. Please, sit here beside me," she added, indicating the chair between her father and herself.

The Senora obeyed and Mr. Nolan was able to pull himself together enough to remember to hold the chair for her. "I do love the races," she informed them. "Back in Madrid, my late husband kept a racing stable, and it was so much fun watching the horses run even when they didn't win."

Mr. Nolan couldn't seem to take his eyes off the Senora, a situation she acknowledged only with the kindest of smiles before turning her attention to Irene, who also seemed a bit awestruck.

"Do you have any horses running today, Miss Nolan?" the Senora asked Irene.

"Yes, two," she said and launched into a description of them and their merits. The Senora asked questions that revealed her understanding of horseflesh, delighting Irene and apparently striking Nolan even more mute than before.

The waiter came to offer them beverages and when he left, Nolan said into the momentary silence, "You're Spanish."

The Senora turned to him with her placid smile. "Yes. I am on a prolonged visit to your country, however."

"I saw you before. At Belmont Park." Elizabeth would have found the intensity of his gaze disturbing, but the Senora was undaunted.

"Yes," Gideon said in an effort to keep the conversation going. "We went to watch Sir Barton run."

"And you remembered me?" the Senora said. "How flattering. That was weeks ago."

"That race was thrilling, wasn't it?" Elizabeth said. "Even without suitable competition, Sir Barton managed to set a course record. Now I'm afraid no other comparable horses will challenge him."

"Are there any comparable horses?" Mother Bates asked.

"I thought we came to see one that might be," Elizabeth said. "Irene told me Man o' War might be even better than Sir Barton."

"Are you a widow?" Nolan asked the Senora, apropos of nothing.

She looked at him in surprise. "Why yes, sadly, I am." If she was disconcerted by his continued interest, she gave no sign of it. She merely turned back to Irene, who was speaking again.

"Do you know the story of Man o' War? He was bred by August Belmont himself. Mr. Belmont had already enlisted in the army, even though he was long past the age to be drafted."

"Everyone thought he was quite noble to volunteer to serve," Mother Bates said.

Irene waved away Belmont's nobility. "Which is why Mrs. Belmont named the foal Man o' War, in honor of Mr. Belmont. At any rate, he usually trains his horses himself, but since he was overseas and didn't know how long he would be away, they sold all their stock, and Samuel Riddle bought Man o' War."

"I'm sure poor August is sorry he sold the colt," Mother Bates said.

"And I'm sure a lot of other horsemen are sorry they didn't buy him," Irene said.

"Do you know," Mr. Nolan said, still staring at the Senora with an intensity that should have set her hair on fire, "you look just like my late wife."

"Father," Irene chided him in dismay.

"Well, it's true. Why shouldn't I say so?" he asked, still not taking his gaze off the Senora.

"No reason at all," the Senora said with a gentle smile. "I've been wondering why you seemed so interested in me, although I'm sure my ordinary charms could explain it."

The others chuckled politely, but Nolan didn't even seem to hear. "You couldn't be her, though."

"Of course not," Irene said a little desperately. "How could you even think that? Mother has been dead for over twenty years."

"And the Senora is from Spain," Mother Bates said kindly.

"Mary would be forty-two," Nolan said, ignoring her.

"And the Senora is plainly much younger," Mother Bates said, although no one really believed it.

But none of this deterred Nolan from continuing to stare at the Senora until the waiter brought their lunch and he had to at least pretend to eat. The Senora tolerated his attention and distracted herself by speaking with the rest of the people at the table. Elizabeth was starting to question her decision to introduce the Senora to Livingston through the Nolans, though. Was the Senora going to be able to discourage Mr. Nolan enough so he would lose interest in her?

Gideon expressed a desire to discuss the races being run that day and asked Mr. Nolan's advice. He gave it grudgingly between bouts of staring at the Senora.

For her part, the Senora engaged Irene in conversation about their stables and about Cal Regan's condition. She had, she explained, been at the track when he was injured and was concerned, even though Elizabeth knew perfectly well Paulina and the Old Man had left before the last race.

"Trench could have given Man o' War a run," Irene lamented. "We would have entered him in the Tremont if he'd won that day at Belmont."

"Did you ever find out what caused the accident?" the Senora asked.

"The horse was sponged," Nolan said, his bitterness evident.

"Dear heaven," the Senora cried. "How awful. Did you discover who did it?"

"Daniel Livingston," he said without hesitation.

Everyone at the table stared at him, amazed that he would make such a claim in a public place. Elizabeth glanced around to see if anyone had overheard. Fortunately, no one seemed to be paying them any mind.

"Father," Irene said in a fierce whisper, "you can't say things like that."

"Why not, if it's true?"

"We don't know for sure it's true."

"I know it is."

No one had an answer for that, but Mother Bates rescued them by noting it was nearly race time and they should be getting to their seats.

Mr. Nolan offered the Senora his arm, ignoring everyone else.

Gideon escorted his mother and Irene, and Elizabeth followed behind.

"I feel like I should apologize to the Senora," Irene said softly. "I've never seen Father behave like this."

"I imagine it was a shock to see a woman who so closely resembles your late mother."

Irene glared at her father's back for a long moment. "He's not acting shocked. He's acting like an idiot."

"I'm sure he'll get over it," Elizabeth said, making it as much a prayer as a statement. She hadn't really planned on what she would do if Mr. Nolan's interest in the Senora continued beyond their initial meeting. Elizabeth supposed the Senora could con him along with all her other victims, but she didn't really want the Nolans to be victimized, since the whole idea was for Irene and Cal to be better off when this was over. Of course, Irene and Cal weren't likely to be among the Senora's victims, so maybe it didn't matter if Mr. Nolan made a fool of himself, so long as it didn't interfere with Livingston's involvement.

Mr. Nolan made sure the Senora sat beside him in the back row of the box. Irene and Mother Bates took the two front seats, and Elizabeth and Gideon sat in the middle row. Mr. Nolan was running Dodger in a later race in another attempt to sell him, so they were able to enjoy the first few races without worrying about who won.

The Senora insisted on placing a bet in the first race when she saw one of the horses was named Irene. She must honor her hostess, she claimed, and sent Mr. Nolan off with her two dollars.

"I'm so sorry," Irene told her when he was gone. "I'm sure you must be uncomfortable with all the attention my father is giving you."

"Nonsense. I haven't been admired this much since I was a

young girl," the Senora said with a smile. "I am finding it quite gratifying."

Elizabeth wondered if that could possibly be true, but she couldn't exactly challenge the statement. In any case, the Senora gave every indication that she was thoroughly enjoying herself. Like every other lady in the park, she was lazily fanning herself as she delighted in the bustle of the crowd around her. Several friends had stopped by to greet Mother Bates or Irene, and they both made certain to introduce the Senora to each and every visitor.

Elizabeth was beginning to despair that their plan would work when a gruff voice greeted Mother Bates.

"Daniel, how nice to see you," Mother Bates said with some surprise.

Irene had gone completely rigid at the sight of him, and Elizabeth wished she could snatch the poor girl out of the box and take her as far from Daniel Livingston as possible.

"How dare you show your face here?" Irene asked.

He glanced at her in surprise. "It's a public racetrack, Miss Nolan. I've as much right to be here as you do."

"Until you're banned from racing entirely," she snapped, rising to her feet. She squeezed past Elizabeth and Gideon to escape the box, leaving Livingston frowning after her.

"I've never been very popular with the Nolans," he said by way of apology to Mother Bates.

She, being conscious of her role in this little drama, said, "Senora Chavez, may I introduce an old friend of mine, Daniel Livingston?"

Livingston lifted his gaze to see the lady in question, and to Elizabeth's surprise, he looked as poleaxed as Mr. Nolan had been.

The Senora simply continued to wave her fan in easy arcs and lazily lowered her gaze to the gentleman in question. She gave him a small nod of acknowledgment, but he didn't return it. He looked too stunned to even think of such a thing. After several tense seconds, he said, "Mary?"

The Senora tilted her head in a silent question.

Mother Bates rose to the occasion. "Oh my goodness, I see you've noticed the resemblance as well. Doesn't she look like Mary Nolan? Sebastian saw it immediately, although I have to say, I didn't notice until he pointed it out."

"You're not . . ." Livingston said, his face creased into a baffled frown.

"She is Paulita Padilla y de la Fuente viuda de Chavez," Mother Bates said. "She is visiting America. Aren't we lucky to have such a distinguished guest?"

Livingston needed another moment to collect himself, but when he did, he glanced around as if verifying his location. "This is Nolan's box, isn't it?"

"Yes, it is," Mother Bates said.

"And you are friends of his?" he asked, his gaze drifting back to the Senora, who seemed to be paying him no attention. Obviously, he remembered seeing them in Nolan's box before.

"Yes, he invited us to watch the Tremont Stakes with him today," Gideon said.

"Oh, hello, Bates," Mr. Livingston said absently. Plainly, he was still trying to figure out what was going on. He looked up at the Senora again, but she was busy watching the crowd and ignoring him. He glanced back at Mother Bates. "And this lady is a friend of his?"

"The Senora is a friend of *ours*," she said, "and Mr. Nolan was kind enough to allow us to include her today."

Livingston nodded as if answering some unspoken questions. "What did you say her name was?"

"Paulita Padilla y de la Fuente viuda de Chavez, but you may call her Senora Chavez."

"Chavez," he muttered, moving around to the entrance to the box so he could squeeze by Gideon and Elizabeth and enter. "Senora," he said when he had reached her. "It is a privilege."

She looked up at him as if she hadn't noticed him before and languidly offered him her hand. "Mr. Livingston, is it?" she asked.

"Yes. Yes, it is. I . . . What an honor to have you visiting us. You're Spanish, are you?"

She smiled tolerantly. "I am from Spain, yes. Madrid."

"You . . . What brings you to America?"

"I was visiting when the war started, and I could not go home," she said. "Perhaps now . . ."

"Oh no, you mustn't leave now. You must let us show you around our fair city."

"Us?"

He smiled what he must have thought was an appealing smile. "Me. You must allow me to show you around. I . . . I should like to get to know you."

"I would enjoy that very much," she said without the slightest trace of enthusiasm.

"Would you?" he asked. Apparently, he'd noticed her disinterest.

"Oh yes. I should love to make some friends here in America."

"Friends?" he echoed as if he'd never heard the word before. "Of course. I'd be happy to introduce you to my friends."

"That would be very nice. Do you enjoy the races, Mr. Livingston?"

"I . . . I have my own stable."

"Is that so? My late husband raised racehorses in Madrid."

"I would love to show you my stables. I have some of the best breeding stock in the country."

The Senora smiled tolerantly. "I understand everyone who raises horses says this."

"In my case, it is true. I would be happy to prove it to you—"

"*Livingston*," Mr. Nolan fairly shouted as he approached the box with Irene in his wake. Plainly, she had gone to fetch him. "What in God's name are you doing here?"

Livingston straightened and returned Nolan's glare. "I'm speaking with Senora Chavez."

"Well, you can stop speaking to her. She doesn't want to be bothered, and I'll thank you to leave my box."

"The Senora seemed perfectly happy to speak with me, and wouldn't she be a better judge of that than you?"

"She is in my box, so she is under my protection, and I intend to protect her from you, now get out before I have you thrown out."

"Mr. Nolan," the Senora said with a small smile. "Mr. Livingston was not bothering me at all. I found him very pleasant, but this argument is very unpleasant. Perhaps you two gentlemen could simply agree to postpone it for a later time so we can all enjoy the races."

The two gentlemen in question drew up to their full height and glared at each other, but neither dared say another word in anger. Livingston nodded to the Senora. "I am glad to have made your acquaintance, Senora Chavez. I am sure we will meet again soon."

"I will look forward to it," she said.

Livingston took his leave of the Bateses and exited the box, pausing to look back longingly at the Senora when he was safely away. For her part, she simply smiled at Nolan as if nothing untoward had happened. "Did you place my bet on Irene?"

"I did indeed," he said, entering the box and resuming his seat next to her, "and you got good odds, too, but don't be too disappointed if Irene doesn't finish in the money."

The Senora's languid gaze drifted to where Irene Nolan was taking her seat beside Mother Bates. "I'm not concerned about winning. I only wished to pay tribute to your charming daughter. She would make any father proud, would she not?"

To Elizabeth's consternation, Nolan needed to think about this for a minute. "Oh sure. Irene is a good girl, all right."

Faint praise indeed and Elizabeth almost cringed. At least Irene didn't seem to have heard it. Gideon had, though, and his raised eyebrows revealed his opinion of Nolan.

Mother Bates turned around in her seat to address everyone in the box. "I must apologize for Daniel Livingston. I never dreamed he would make such a scene or I would have snubbed him."

"It isn't your fault, Mrs. Bates," Irene assured her. "I should have been prepared since I was pretty sure he'd be at the track today."

She exchanged a look with Elizabeth, reminding her it had been Elizabeth's idea to make certain he was present. By now Irene would have realized that the Senora was the distraction Elizabeth had planned for Livingston. At least that part had gone off, although not without some drama.

"Is that the man you suspect of sponging your horse?" the Senora was asking Nolan.

"Yes, he is."

"Why do you not report him to the authorities? I assume America has a way to deal with such things."

"We do, but . . . It's difficult for them to determine who is right in cases like this. Livingston would only have to claim he knew nothing about it, even if we could prove one of his employees did it, and so far we haven't been able to do that."

"I see, yes, it is difficult."

Irene pointed out that the horses were parading up for the first race, a selling race for fillies and mares three years old and up, and all talk turned to speculation on which one might win. They all decided to root for Irene since the Senora had bet on her. The horses spent five minutes getting lined up at the barrier, a wait that seemed interminable, but finally the race was on. Irene showed some speed, but not enough, and she finished fifth, with Adele taking first place.

"I'm sorry," Irene told the Senora in jest, and the Senora took the apology in the spirit in which Irene offered it.

"I am sure *you* always finish first, Miss Nolan," she said, her words obviously sincere enough to bring a blush to Irene's cheeks.

Elizabeth frowned. Why was the Senora cultivating Irene? She understood perfectly well that Irene had nothing worth taking and that continuing a relationship with the Nolans was a waste of time. But then maybe the Senora was simply gracious to everyone, just the way Mother Bates was. Elizabeth should probably emulate them instead of worrying about why they were so nice to other people.

The next race was the Glendale Steeplechase Handicap, and Mother Bates declared the steeplechase her favorite of all the races. Only three horses ran for the two-thousand-dollar purse, but everyone enjoyed Mother Bates's enjoyment.

The third race was the Tremont Stakes, and all conversation turned to Man o' War. He was making his fifth start in under a month, and he had won his first four races easily. Could he possibly make a good showing after being raced so often, though? And he was carrying 130 pounds, far more than the other two horses in the race, and this would be his first race at six furlongs. Would he falter under the greater weight and distance? He was hardly facing a challenge, though. Rocking Horse had scratched, and Ace of Aces wouldn't offer a contest. He had been entered at the last minute just to earn the three hundred dollars he would get for finishing third. The crowd also had little confidence in the other horse entered, Ralco.

The three horses stood at the barrier for barely a minute and then they were off. Man o' War took the early lead and his jockey, Johnny Loftus, never even asked him for speed. He finished one lazy length in front of Ralco and twenty-one lengths ahead of Ace of Aces.

"What do you think, Irene?" Elizabeth asked. "Is Man o' War better than Sir Barton?"

"There's only one way to find out," Mr. Nolan said before Irene could express her opinion. "But I'm guessing neither owner will consent to a match race this early in Man o' War's career."

"He's certainly a fine-looking horse," Irene said to Elizabeth. "So much bigger than Sir Barton, but you can't always tell from that."

"His jockey would not let him run," the Senora said. "Why is that, do you think?" Plainly, she had addressed this question to Irene.

Irene would have answered, but Nolan beat her to it. "He doesn't want people to know just how fast Man o' War can go. If we knew, nobody would ever race against him."

The Senora ignored him. "Do you agree, Irene?"

Irene turned to face the Senora. "I think Loftus is just treating his horse right, asking him to give enough to win and no more. There isn't an additional prize for winning by a bigger margin. Simply winning is the ultimate prize, so why risk your horse for more?"

The Senora smiled a mysterious smile for just a second, almost as if she was proud of Irene's logic, and then she turned to Nolan and asked him a question about the race that she undoubtedly knew the answer to, but he was much too full of himself to realize it and began pontificating. Even Irene rolled her eyes.

The fourth race was the Brookdale Handicap, and Mr. Nolan had a horse entered. They all walked down to the paddock to see Hopscotch saddled and to admire him.

Elizabeth kept watching the crowd, wondering if Daniel Livingston would attempt to speak to the Senora again. She did catch a glimpse of him in the paddock, but he made no move to approach them. She gave a sigh of relief, wondering what Nolan might do if Livingston tried to engage with the Senora again.

"Should I place a bet on your horse, Mr. Nolan?" the Senora asked.

"I never advise people to bet on horse races, Senora," he said.

"But surely, you think your horse is going to win," she argued.

"I always think so, but I am not always right."

"Ah yes, that is so. But I feel I must place a bet on Hopscotch. Mr. Bates, could you do it for me?"

Gideon was only too glad to try, although the time was getting short.

Gideon made it back to the box just as the horses were lining up at the barrier, and he had to apologize to the Senora. The lines were too long, and he wasn't able to place her bet. Then the barrier shot up and the crowd yelled, "They're off!"

They all shouted for Hopscotch and although he seemed to get off to a slow start, he methodically worked his way to the rail and pulled away in the final stretch to win by a length.

"Now I'm really sorry I didn't place your bet, Senora," Gideon said, shaking his head.

"I will always be grateful for your efforts," she swore, laying a hand over her heart and making everyone laugh.

Irene and Mr. Nolan hurried down to the winner's circle, leaving their guests to watch from the box. Elizabeth was so intent on seeing Hopscotch and his owners receive their honors that she didn't notice Daniel Livingston had approached their box again until he spoke.

"Excuse me, Senora, but I overheard you say you wanted to

place a bet on the last race, so I took the liberty of placing one for you. Here are your winnings."

"Mr. Livingston, I do not know what to say," she replied, obviously nonplussed, but Elizabeth noticed she accepted the packet Livingston handed to her.

"You don't need to say anything at all."

"But you bet on Mr. Nolan's horse," she marveled.

"I bet on the best horse, and the best horse won. Congratulations, Senora. I hope I will see you very soon."

With that, he sketched her a small bow and disappeared into the crowd.

The Senora looked down at the packet Livingston had handed her. The bills were neatly wrapped in a handkerchief. When she looked up, she was smiling that mysterious smile again.

"Mr. Livingston knows how to make himself remembered."

# CHAPTER EIGHT

⟞⟐⟞

ELIZABETH KNEW THAT MEN WOULD SOMETIMES PLACE BETS on behalf of their lady friends, but the class of those women was usually quite a bit lower socially than the one the Senora had claimed for herself. Of course, Elizabeth's experience with socially prominent folks was limited to recent years and had never included attendance at the racetrack, but she was reasonably certain society ladies were not expected to give their *favors* in exchange for such favors.

She gave Gideon a questioning look and found him staring back at her with an equally baffled expression.

"Mother Bates, how should the Senora respond to Mr. Livingston's, uh, generosity?" she asked.

To Elizabeth's dismay, Mother Bates seemed equally bemused. "I really have no idea. On the one hand, it seems extremely thoughtful of him to place a bet for her. That's exactly what she asked Gideon to do, remember."

"Except I was using her money to place it at her request,"

Gideon said. "Livingston used his own money and did it without her permission."

"Yes," Mother Bates said with a sigh, "which makes me question the propriety of it."

"Perhaps it was very rude of him to do so," the Senora said, not breaking her Senora character even though no one who didn't know her true identity was listening, "but I am a foreigner, and I am unfamiliar with American customs. I can pretend to be flattered by his attentions. This is what we were hoping for, is it not? For Mr. Livingston to take an interest in me?"

"He certainly seems to have done so," Mother Bates said with a wan smile.

"And he did promise to see you again," Gideon said. "So, the Senora is probably right. She can take offense if she likes or not take offense if it suits her purposes better."

"Perhaps I will question it just to make him more determined to prove himself," the Senora mused.

Elizabeth wasn't sure she liked that idea, but this wasn't really her con or even an area where she had experience, so she had to trust the Senora knew what she was doing. Gideon pointed out that the Nolans were returning, so they had to drop their discussion.

Both Irene and her father looked happy. Mr. Nolan had obviously been pleased with the win, even though the purse was only $2,500. People kept stopping him to shake his hand as he and Irene made their way back to the box. His guests took their turns congratulating both of them as well.

"Your jockey gave Hopscotch a good ride," Elizabeth told Irene.

She smiled a little sadly. "Cal could have done even better, but I can't complain about a win, can I?"

"No, you can't," her father said a little too sternly.

"You should have bet on your own horse, Mr. Nolan," the Senora said. "I did very well."

To Elizabeth's surprise, she held up the packet Livingston had given her. Although it was still wrapped in the handkerchief, it was plainly a stack of bills.

Nolan's smile turned quizzical. "I thought Bates wasn't able to place your bet."

"He wasn't," she said quite innocently. "But Mr. Livingston placed one for me. I thought that was quite thoughtful of him."

"*Livingston*," Mr. Nolan said, nearly spitting the word. "That son of a—"

"Father!" Irene chided.

Nolan had half risen from his seat, but he sank back down at Irene's warning.

"I thought you would be flattered, Mr. Nolan," the Senora said. "Mr. Livingston bet on your horse. In fact, he informed me that he bet on the *best* horse, so that is a compliment to you, is it not?"

"Yes, it is," Irene said before her father could deny it. "Although I hope you weren't offended when Mr. Livingston dropped a bundle of money into your lap."

"He was much more gentlemanly than that, Miss Nolan," the Senora assured her. "But it is plain to me that you and Mr. Livingston are not friends, Mr. Nolan. Perhaps you would tell me why that is, in case it should change my opinion of him."

"You already know he sponged my horse," Mr. Nolan said stiffly. "I think that explains my feelings for him and tells you what your opinion of him should be."

"Ah, but you said you have no real proof, and you have not explained why you think he would have done something terrible to your horse. Plainly, you and Mr. Livingston have much bad blood between you."

Nolan frowned and crossed his arms, silently resisting her request, but Irene said, "Honestly, Father, she should probably know before one of you embarrasses her."

"She already knows she looks like your mother," he replied, refusing to even look at the Senora.

"But why should Mr. Livingston . . ." the Senora began, and trailed off as if suddenly recalling something. "Your mother," she said to Irene. "Her name was Mary?"

"Yes," Irene said.

"Mr. Livingston called me Mary and Mrs. Bates remarked on my resemblance to your mother. I did not think that strange since many people must have known her, and Mr. Livingston could certainly be one of them."

"He knew her rather well," Irene said, earning a black look from her father, which she ignored. "They were engaged to be married until she met my father."

Elizabeth could have believed the Senora had never heard this story before. She seemed surprised and a bit delighted.

"How romantic," she said to Mr. Nolan. "You stole her heart."

"Mr. Livingston didn't think it was romantic," Irene said. "And he's hated my father ever since."

The Senora shook her head. "But that was such a long time ago, and your poor mother, didn't you tell me she has passed?"

"Yes," Irene said. "She died when I was born, and Mr. Livingston blames *me* for that, so he has had excellent reasons to brood on his fury at both of us for all these years."

The Senora couldn't seem to take her eyes off Irene. "Your mother . . . she died in childbirth?"

"Sadly, yes."

"And you have no memories of her?" the Senora pressed. Elizabeth frowned. What was she getting at?

Irene, however, seemed undaunted by the intensity of the Senora's gaze. "Although I know it's impossible, I sometimes imagine that I do. I remember this beautiful woman—"

"Irene, no one cares about your memories," her father said. "I must apologize, Senora. I don't know how the conversation got so maudlin."

"Because the Senora wanted to know why Daniel Livingston hates you so much," Mother Bates reminded him mercilessly as Elizabeth reached out and took Irene's hand in silent comfort. Irene's cheeks were scarlet, but she had obviously learned not to respond to her father's slights.

"And now she does know why he hates me," Mr. Nolan said. "He was jealous and spiteful, and he never got over the fact that Mary preferred me. Now can we talk about something else?"

Elizabeth was only too happy to oblige. "Don't you have a horse in the last race, Mr. Nolan?"

They discussed that race and the other one still to be run, although no one really cared much. Nolan's horse was in a claiming race, which meant he hoped it would be sold. It wasn't, but it did win, earning about a thousand dollars.

Elizabeth kept glancing around after the race ended, hoping Mr. Livingston hadn't taken the opportunity to place another bet for the Senora. Thankfully, he did not make another appearance.

Mr. Nolan invited his guests to join him for supper to celebrate, but the ladies were too exhausted from the heat and begged off.

The Senora thanked Mr. Nolan for allowing her to share his box, and if she was a little more fervent in her gratitude than the deed deserved, Mr. Nolan didn't notice.

"I am honored that you graced us with your presence today,

Senora. I hope you will let us know whenever you wish to attend the races so we can be sure to reserve a box."

"You are too kind, Mr. Nolan."

"And may I also hope that we will encounter you at other times? I would very much like to call upon you when I am in the city."

"You flatter me, Mr. Nolan. If I am free when you are in town, I should be happy to see you."

Mr. Nolan seemed a bit nonplussed by such a lukewarm promise, but to his credit, he refused to be discouraged. "I will try to make it soon."

"And I would always welcome a visit from your charming daughter," she added, giving Irene a fond look.

Irene seemed a bit startled to be singled out, but she said, "I rarely go into the city, Senora."

"Then your father must take you when he goes." She turned back to Nolan. "If you bring Irene, I will promise to be free."

Nolan only managed a surprised blink before the Senora walked away, joining the Bateses as they made their way to the station for the train ride back to the city.

They had little opportunity for conversation on the train since it was so crowded. Once in town, they decided to share a cab, dropping the Senora at her hotel first, so they could speak more freely before separating.

"What will happen next?" Elizabeth asked the Senora when the cab had pulled into traffic.

She smiled sweetly. "I am not a fortune-teller, but I am sure both Mr. Nolan and Mr. Livingston will attempt to see me. Since neither of them know where to find me, they will be forced to consult one of you."

"But you won't be encouraging Mr. Nolan," Elizabeth said.

"Why not?" she asked with apparent surprise.

"Because . . . We don't think he has enough money to be worth the effort," Elizabeth said.

The Senora shrugged. "Perhaps not, but his pursuit will encourage Livingston. Livingston will not want to lose this time."

"I think she's probably right, dear," Mother Bates said. "You saw how jealous they both still are of each other over a woman who merely *resembles* Mary."

"Yes, but . . . Remember, we're doing this to help Irene, and impoverishing her father won't help her at all."

"I promise I will not harm Irene," the Senora said with some amusement.

This did not reassure Elizabeth, but she had no authority to order the Senora to spare Mr. Nolan from her con. Besides, the whole purpose of this exercise was to make Irene and Cal independent of her father, so his financial situation should not affect them at all.

"I think it's time for me to hold a dinner party in the Senora's honor," Mother Bates said.

Gideon didn't even bother to hide his horrified reaction to such a thought, but the Senora said, "I would be delighted if you would do so. Perhaps you could invite both of my suitors as well. I should like to see them together once more to judge which one is the most appealing."

"It may well be the only way to get Livingston back into society," Elizabeth admitted reluctantly.

"And do not worry, Mr. Bates," the Senora said. "Nothing untoward will happen at your home."

Gideon sighed. "I don't believe anyone has ever made me a promise like that before."

"Then you should feel reassured," Elizabeth said with an encouraging smile.

"Hardly," he said with resignation. "Because no one has ever *needed* to make me a promise like that before."

HOW MANY PEOPLE SHOULD WE INVITE TO YOUR DINNER party, Mother Bates?" Elizabeth asked the next day after they'd finished Sunday dinner and were relaxing, reading the newspapers in the family parlor.

Gideon groaned aloud. "I was hoping you'd forgotten about that."

"It will be fun, dear," his mother said with a smile. He remembered how much she had once loved entertaining her friends, back when his father was alive. He should be glad to see her taking an interest in the social activities she'd neglected in her widowhood. If only those social activities didn't involve a certain female con artist who wasn't his wife. "I was thinking we should have at least a dozen. My table will seat twenty, if necessary, but I don't want the Senora to feel overwhelmed."

"I doubt Paulina ever feels overwhelmed," Gideon muttered. "I'd just like to be sure we have enough able-bodied men to break up a fight if Nolan and Livingston come to blows."

His wife and mother didn't even blink.

"Shall we make a list?" Elizabeth jumped up and went to the desk his mother used for her correspondence. After rummaging around, she came up with a pencil and some paper. "The three of us, of course," she said, scribbling down their names.

"And Roger Devoss to partner Mother," Gideon said. He ignored his mother's glare and Elizabeth's giggle. Mr. Devoss was a senior partner in Gideon's law firm, and he was always fruitlessly trying to attract his mother's interest.

"Put a question mark beside Roger's name," his mother said.

Elizabeth did no such thing. "The Senora, of course, and the Nolans and Mr. Livingston."

"Logan and Noelle Carstens," Gideon said. "So Elizabeth and I have someone to talk to while everyone else is trying to fool each other."

"Should we invite the Westerlys?" his mother asked.

"I don't think you should pass up an opportunity to remind Mrs. Westerly that you are her match when it comes to entertaining the Senora," Elizabeth said.

"And since she didn't include me when she had her party, I don't owe her an invitation. That means she'll be in my debt if she attends."

"I doubt she would miss it for the world," Elizabeth assured her.

"How are the numbers?" his mother asked.

"So far we're even, six men and six women."

"Oh dear, what about Olinda?" his mother asked. "I suppose we must include her, too."

"What about Olinda?" Anna Vanderslice asked as she breezed into the room unannounced.

"Anna," Elizabeth cried in welcome, jumping up to greet her friend. "I thought you and your mother had plans this afternoon."

"Mother's plans were to visit some of her most boring friends, so I decided I had a headache and should stay home."

"I'm happy to see you are fully recovered," Elizabeth said.

"I'm not recovered. I felt I needed a walk in the fresh air to clear my head."

"The fresh air is about a hundred degrees today, isn't it?" Gideon asked with a grin.

"Which is why I had to take refuge at your house. So, tell me what you need to include Olinda in."

"Mother Bates wants to have a dinner party for the Senora," Elizabeth explained.

"And we must include her younger sister, Olinda," his mother added.

"I'm still wondering why the Senora needs a sister," Anna asked, taking a seat next to his mother on the sofa.

"Perhaps she simply *has* a sister and the girl travels with her," his mother said.

Elizabeth gave this some thought. Gideon could tell by the way she wrinkled her lovely nose that she really needed to figure something out. "Olinda does have a role in the con, though. Remember, the Senora won't receive her husband's fortune until Olinda marries her husband's nephew."

"Oh yes," his mother said. "I'd forgotten that part. It's so difficult to remember all of it."

"I have that problem, too," Anna confided. "But you must include poor Olinda in your dinner party. Since she's doomed to an arranged marriage, I'm sure she hardly ever gets to have any fun."

"She will, of course, not be marrying anyone, and this dinner party will definitely not be fun," Gideon said darkly.

"Don't be silly, darling," Elizabeth said. "People are always highly entertained by prizefights."

"Are you having a prizefight at your dinner party?" Anna asked in amazement.

"Not by design," his mother said. "Gideon is afraid the Senora's two spurned lovers will come to blows."

"Then you must show me the guest list so I can be certain my name is on it," Anna said.

"We are still compiling the list," Elizabeth said, whisking the paper into a drawer and slamming it shut.

"If you don't invite me, I'll simply show up. You can't possibly forbid me to attend."

Elizabeth sighed in mock defeat. "Then let me explain the situation to you. If you attend, we will need to invite another man, and we are already one man short if we include Olinda."

Anna understood the problem instantly, but she said, "Doesn't Gideon know two single men who would be interested in meeting a Spanish heiress?"

"I probably know a dozen such men," Gideon said tightly. "The question is, Do I want them involved in this?"

"They'd hardly be involved," his mother argued.

"They would be if the Senora took a loan from them."

That silenced all further objections.

After a few awkward moments, Anna said, "Perhaps we should keep this an intimate family affair."

"What do you mean?" Gideon asked, barely able to keep the tremor from his voice.

"I mean Elizabeth could invite her father and her brother. What could be more natural?"

THIS WAS A TERRIBLE IDEA," GIDEON SAID FOR WHAT ELIZabeth was sure was the one hundredth time. He was standing behind Elizabeth, who was sitting at her dressing table, putting the finishing touches on her hair. He was leaning over so he could see himself in her mirror and trying to tie his bow tie.

"We should entertain more often," she said. "You look so handsome in evening clothes."

"I will promise to wear them every night if you swear you will never make me go through something like this again."

"Really, darling, how terribly rude of you. You are supposed to mention how lovely I look in my finery as well."

"You look like a goddess, as you well know, and we will need divine intervention if the Westerlys recognize Jake as their daughter's erstwhile fiancé."

"They aren't going to recognize him," Elizabeth assured him for what she *knew* was at least the hundredth time.

"But he *was* engaged to their daughter," he reminded her.

"For only a few days," she reminded him right back. "And he was an English lord then. I've seen it before. People are so easily fooled by the most elementary disguise, and Jake's disguise was far from elementary."

"At least Logan and Noelle already know him as your brother because they were at our wedding."

"And they knew Jake as Lord Percy, too, and never realized he was the same person. I'm telling you, we have nothing to worry about."

Gideon gave his tie one final tug and dropped his hands to his sides. "I'll just be glad when this evening is over," he said with a sigh. "Now come give me a kiss before you put on your lip rouge."

THE OLD MAN HAD STOPPED BY ANNA'S HOUSE TO ESCORT her to the party. They walked over since it was only a few blocks and the evening was pleasant. This made them the first to arrive.

"Is there anything I should know before everyone gets here?" Anna whispered as she greeted Elizabeth.

"The less you know, the more surprised you will be," Elizabeth said with a conspiratorial smile. "And thank you for suggesting we invite Jake and the Old Man."

Anna's blue eyes widened in apprehension. "Oh dear."

"Just act surprised," Elizabeth said.

Anna had no further opportunity for questions because the

maid had escorted the Westerlys into the parlor. Mrs. Westerly was telling Mother Bates she had recently received a letter from her daughter, the *baroness*. Mother Bates tried to look suitably impressed, and Elizabeth had to admit she did a good job of it. Society ladies had to lie just as well as con artists did at times.

Mr. Westerly found Gideon, who gratified him by immediately offering him a drink. Soon Logan and Noelle Carstens arrived, and then Mr. Nolan and Irene came in. Elizabeth greeted all of them, but she noticed Mr. Nolan's gaze kept darting to the doorway.

"The Senora has not arrived yet," she told him. "I think she likes to make an entrance, so don't expect her until the last minute."

Irene covered her smile, but Mr. Nolan did not find her amusing and he wandered off to the sideboard where Gideon was serving the drinks.

Elizabeth introduced Irene to Anna and the Carstenses. Irene was fascinated to learn that Noelle was a French war bride, and they were soon chatting away like old friends.

Mr. Devoss had come in while Elizabeth was with Irene, and finally, Daniel Livingston appeared in the doorway, hesitating as if uncertain of his welcome. Mother Bates went over to greet him, and Elizabeth knew the moment Irene saw him, because everyone in the room heard her gasp.

Like everyone else, Livingston looked to see who was in distress, and when he recognized Irene, his gaze quickly found Nolan. The two men glared at each other across the room for a long moment during which all conversation ceased as the tension between them seemed to actually vibrate in the air.

Mother Bates, rising to the occasion as usual, said, "Daniel, you know Sebastian Nolan, I'm sure. The Senora expressly requested that both of you be invited this evening."

Plainly, both men were shocked by this information but neither wanted to challenge Mother Bates or, even worse, the Senora, especially in front of all these people. Livingston simply nodded once as if to acknowledge the request and Nolan threw back the dregs of his drink with the air of a man preparing to do battle.

"Can I get you a refill?" Gideon asked smoothly, as if nothing untoward had happened in his home, because, of course, nothing had. Yet.

Elizabeth had been counting, and she knew they were now expecting only three additional guests. Then she heard the doorbell, and she exchanged an anticipatory glance with her mother-in-law. Many of those here tonight had witnessed the Senora's entrance at the Westerlys' party, and they were all poised to be impressed once again.

The Senora did not disappoint. Tonight, she wore a gown of deep purple satin with a black lace overlay. Unlike most women, who bound their breasts to conform to fashion, the Senora had cinched her waist with a sequined cummerbund that only accented the fullness of her figure. Once again, she wore a lace mantilla mounted on a large mother-of-pearl comb above her elaborate hairdo, which only added to her amazing appearance.

So impressive was she that hardly anyone noticed poor little Olinda, who hovered behind her. Olinda wore a stylish gown in a ghastly shade of green that made her look as if she might have been seasick. Elizabeth winced before moving to help her mother-in-law welcome their guest of honor.

"Hazel, my dear friend," the Senora said when she saw Mother Bates, and greeted her with a kiss on both cheeks. "You are so kind to invite us."

Plainly, Mrs. Westerly was a bit shocked to see the Senora greet Mother Bates by her first name and call her a dear friend, but no one else thought it strange.

"And thank you for adjusting your plans to welcome Senor Chavez, since he has just arrived in the city and knows no one." The Senora turned to indicate the young man who had entered behind Olinda.

He was slender with auburn hair, which he wore a little too long, probably so it would curl delightfully around his handsome face. He wore what Americans probably imagined was evening wear in Spain. His satin pants were a bit tighter than American men would ever wear them, accentuating his muscular legs and hugging his private parts with loving care. His jacket was only waist-length, and the lapels, cuffs and hem were heavily embroidered with gold and silver thread. Ruffles down the front of his shirt spilled out of the opening of his jacket, but somehow the effect wasn't at all feminine. His only flaw was a small scar that puckered the otherwise smooth skin of his left cheek.

"Merciful heavens," Anna whispered behind Elizabeth.

"Or someplace," Elizabeth replied, but she hurried to Mother Bates's side.

"Senor Chavez?" she asked, giving him her best welcoming smile.

"Hernando Chavez y Ramirez," he supplied in a charming accent, "but I understand you Americans prefer simpler names, so Senor Chavez is acceptable."

Elizabeth resisted the urge to thank him sarcastically, and fortunately, the Senora continued the introductions. "Hernando is my nephew, or more correctly, my husband's nephew. He is also betrothed to my sister, Olinda."

Hernando, as one would expect, cast the tiny Olinda a loving glance, which she returned with a murderous glare. While everyone was still blinking in surprise, Gideon swooped in and invited Hernando to have a drink, an offer he eagerly accepted.

The Senora was obviously pretending she hadn't noticed Olinda's reaction, so Elizabeth decided to pretend as well. "Olinda, we're glad you were able to come. Let me introduce you to some of my friends. I think you already know Logan and Noelle Carstens. . . ."

This move left Mother Bates alone with the Senora, which also meant Mother Bates was the Senora's only protection from her would-be suitors, who instantly swooped in with grim intent, but Elizabeth wasn't worried. Those two females could probably have taken charge of the Great War combatants and forged an acceptable peace treaty in far less than the six months it took them, if given the chance.

Elizabeth didn't even have to watch what was going on because Irene was watching, even though she was ostensibly having a conversation with the Carstenses and Anna, and her expressive face betrayed every emotion. The one it was betraying as Elizabeth introduced Olinda to her was terror.

"Is something wrong, Miss Nolan?" Logan Carstens asked in alarm.

Irene apparently didn't even hear him. "Elizabeth, did the Senora really insist that you invite both my father and Mr. Livingston?"

"Oh yes. She said . . . Now let me think. What exactly did she say?"

"Something about seeing them together so she could know them better, wasn't it?" Anna said innocently.

Elizabeth gave her a grateful smile, since Anna had made that up on the spot. "Yes, I believe that was the spirit of what she said."

"Do you know a reason they should not be together?" Noelle asked in her still-broken English.

"Yes," Irene said, her eyes filling with terror again. "Because they might murder each other."

"Nonsense," Elizabeth said. "People simply don't resort to violence at dinner parties." Even if Gideon thought they might.

"Because if they did," Anna said, "there would hardly be anyone left alive in New York City."

That made everyone except Irene laugh. She was still watching the two men with the Senora with an air of anguish.

"I'm so sorry. I know I was supposed to distract Mr. Livingston from bothering your family, but my plan seems to have done just the opposite. If it makes you feel better, I'll go over and see if I can break up the group," Elizabeth said.

"Oh, please do," Irene said.

Elizabeth excused herself and made her way back to where the Senora was still standing with her two admirers, who each looked as if he could cheerfully cut the other's throat.

"Senora, how lovely to see you."

The Senora greeted Elizabeth with the same exuberance she had greeted Mother Bates.

"If I could steal you away, Senora, I believe there are a few guests you haven't met yet, and the others would love to renew your acquaintance, I'm sure."

"Yes, I cannot allow you two gentlemen to keep me from meeting everyone else," the Senora said, dismissing them with a wave of her hand, and allowed Elizabeth to lead her over to meet Mr. Devoss, who had declared himself enamored of all things Spanish and eager to discuss some of them with her.

Satisfied that Mr. Devoss would monopolize the Senora for a few minutes, Elizabeth strolled away, glancing around to see what had become of Livingston and Nolan. She jumped when a voice said from right behind her, "What are you up to, missy?"

*Missy?* Elizabeth turned, ready to chasten whoever had shown her such disrespect, and came face-to-face with a furious Daniel Livingston.

"Perhaps you've forgotten my name, Mr. Livingston. I'm Mrs. Gideon Bates."

"I know your name, girl, but I don't know your game. You and Nolan are cooking something up between you, though. I'm sure of that."

"I have no idea what you're talking about."

"It's plain as the nose on your face. Why would you have invited me here except to make me look bad?"

Elizabeth had several options. She could have looked around and caught the eye of any gentleman in the room with a silent request to be rescued. She could, in fact, have simply turned her back on Livingston and walked away, fairly safe in the assumption he wouldn't go so far as to lay hands on her to keep her close enough to continue his tirade. But she chose to keep her feet planted right where they were and her gaze fixed firmly on Livingston until she found out exactly what he thought was going on. "Mr. Livingston, you are insulting your hostess in her own home," she said as quietly and gently as she could. "What could I possibly do to make you look any worse?"

He jerked as if she'd slapped him. "I . . . I didn't do no such thing."

"You certainly made me uncomfortable, and I suppose if you thought I was trying to undermine you in some way, you might be justified in doing so. However, I can assure you, I have absolutely no interest in making you look good, bad, or indifferent. Whatever made you think I did?"

"I . . . I . . . You're friends with Nolan. I saw you in his box at the track. Twice."

"Mr. Nolan is one of Gideon's clients. He invited us to watch the Belmont Stakes."

"And then you were at Aqueduct with Mary."

A chill ran up Elizabeth's spine. Did he really think the Senora was Mary Nolan?

"Do you mean Mary Nolan?" she asked, not even having to pretend to be confused. "Because Mary Nolan is dead."

He closed his eyes and shook his head, as if to clear it. "The Senora, I mean. What were you doing there with her?"

"Mr. Nolan had seen her at the track the day they ran the Belmont Stakes and remarked on her resemblance to his late wife. He wanted to meet her, so we took her with us to the track the next time we went." A slight bending of the truth, but Livingston was hardly likely to ever hear otherwise.

"Then if you're helping Nolan, why did you invite *me* here?" he demanded.

"I believe my mother-in-law already told you. The Senora specifically requested that you both be invited."

He was still glaring at her, but now he just looked confused.

"Tell me one thing," Elizabeth said. "Why did you assume I was the one making some kind of plot against you?"

"Because Hazel is much too good a person to do something like that and Gideon is much too honest."

He was right on both counts.

"And you think I'm neither good nor honest?" she asked, not having to feign her outrage because she always liked people to believe she was both, even when she was lying through her teeth.

"I don't know you well enough to judge, and you were the only one left."

Not the answer she had expected, but she supposed it was fair. "Mr. Livingston, if you truly want to impress the Senora, you should stop being angry for no reason at all and concentrate on being charming. She did, after all, have you invited here so she could better judge your character."

Before he could reply, their maid announced that dinner was served.

# CHAPTER NINE

*"*SENOR CHAVEZ, SHOULDN'T YOU BE PAYING SOME ATTENTION to your betrothed?" Gideon asked after he had refilled the young man's glass.

"The Senorita does not care for my attention, I am afraid," he said sadly.

Mr. Westerly had come over for a third refill of his own glass and overheard the Senor's complaint.

"I can't believe that," Westerly said, slapping Chavez on the back with more force than was necessary. Chavez was lucky not to lose his glass, although he did lose a bit of its contents. "Good-looking fellow like you, I bet all the girls are crazy for you."

"All but the one I am being forced to marry," Chavez said.

"Forced?" Westerly echoed rather loudly. Several heads turned to see what he was shouting about. Why did drunk people always speak so loudly?

"Is that not the right word?" Chavez said with a frown. "I am not willing to marry her, but I must."

"I believe it is what we would call an arranged marriage,"

Gideon said, hoping to placate Westerly before he caused a scene. Westerly glanced over to where Elizabeth was trying her best to interest Olinda in conversing with the other guests. "That's right, an arranged marriage. But she's not too bad-looking. Why are you so reluctant?"

Chavez took a sip of his whiskey. "I should like to choose my own wife, and if I did, I would choose one who is willing to marry me. That Olinda, she is like a snake whenever I get near her."

"A good-looking fellow like you, she should be grateful," Westerly said.

"But she is not," Chavez said sadly.

"You need to charm her, boy," Westerly advised.

"Yes, because if Senor Chavez does not marry the fair Olinda, the Senora will not receive her inheritance and she won't be able to repay your loan to her," Gideon pointed out. He was amazing himself with how easy it was to participate in all this without telling a single lie.

Westerly was still drunkenly considering this when dinner was announced.

"Excuse me," Gideon said. "I must escort the Senora into dinner."

THE GUESTS PAIRED UP AS MOTHER BATES HAD INSTRUCTED them after Gideon gave the Senora his arm and Mr. Devoss, as the second-most-honored guest, gave Mother Bates his. The Carstenses and Westerlys escorted each other's partners. Mr. Nolan escorted Olinda, and Senor Chavez took Irene. The Old Man took Anna, and that left Livingston to escort Elizabeth. If she had known what a boor he was, Elizabeth would have selected a different escort when they sent out the invitations, but at least he looked a bit chastened after her set down.

"You must excuse my behavior, Mrs. Bates," he said as they waited for the rest of the couples to form and make their way to the dining room. "I am not often in society, and I have obviously forgotten my manners."

"I understand you withdrew after Mary Nolan died."

He actually winced at that. "It still pains me to remember her. But do not fear for my reason, Mrs. Bates. I am well aware that Mary is dead."

"Which must be why seeing the Senora was such a surprise."

"It was more of a shock, especially seeing her with Nolan. For a moment, I thought . . . Well, it doesn't matter. As soon as I realized she couldn't possibly be Mary, I was interested in her for herself alone."

Elizabeth doubted that, but she said, "It's easy to see how the Senora could inspire that reaction. She is quite amazing."

"I hardly know her but that has been my impression as well. You see, that is why . . ."

"Why what?" she asked, managing not to sound too eager to learn the answer.

He frowned with determination. "Why I can't let Nolan win this time."

The last of the other couples were out the door, and Livingston offered her his arm.

"I wish you good luck, Mr. Livingston," she said.

"That is very generous of you, Mrs. Bates, considering Nolan is your friend."

"His daughter is my friend, not Mr. Nolan."

They had reached the dining room. The men were allowing the ladies to find their seats, as etiquette demanded. Elizabeth and Mother Bates had spent a lot of time carefully arranging the seating chart, and hand-lettered cards at each place indicated who was to sit where. Married couples must never be seated next to each other because the attraction of attending a dinner party was the opportunity to converse with someone who wasn't one's spouse. Once all the ladies had found their places, the men started to hunt for theirs.

Elizabeth knew where everyone had been placed, but she wasn't surprised to see Mr. Nolan and Mr. Livingston heading for the head of the table where the Senora had been seated at Gideon's right. They couldn't expect to sit at the head of the table, but the seat to her right would be reserved for a man and both of them hoped they had been assigned that chair.

Livingston had apparently understood the etiquette of it better than Nolan, because Elizabeth watched him barge through the men still lingering to give the ladies time to find their places. His gaze scanned the place cards as he went and he snatched up one as he passed and when he reached the seat beside the Senora, he set it down there. She couldn't see what he had done with the one that had been there, but she had a feeling no one would ever find it.

He nodded to the Senora and gave her what he probably thought was a charming smile. Elizabeth was gratified to see he had taken her advice, even though he looked more wolfish than appealing.

In the meantime, Mr. Nolan had located his seat and was obviously miffed to find himself seated on the opposite side of the table from the Senora and across from Anna Vanderslice, who was sitting on Livingston's other side, too far away for easy conversation with the Senora. After a few more minutes everyone had found their places except Mr. Westerly.

"There's no card at this seat," Anna said, indicating the empty chair beside her.

"Then that must be mine," Westerly said, moving to claim it.

"But it can't be," Mrs. Westerly said. "Hazel would never have seated us together." And she hadn't, because, of course, Mother Bates had put Mr. Livingston there—about the same distance from the Senora as Mr. Nolan was. How clever Livingston had been to move his card to the place he really wanted to sit.

Elizabeth glanced at Mother Bates to see if she would chasten Mr. Livingston and send him back to his proper seat, but she was simply observing the situation with a rather bemused smile.

"I would trade with you, but that would hardly solve the problem," the Old Man told Westerly with a smile of his own. He was sitting on the other side of Mrs. Westerly.

"Then I'll trade with you," Logan said generously.

Elizabeth sighed because he was on her left. With Mr. Nolan on her right and Westerly taking Logan's place, her evening seemed doomed to crushing boredom. She gave Mr. Livingston a sharp look, but he merely grinned, still wolfish and unrepentant.

As soon as Mr. Westerly and Logan changed seats, everyone sat down. Their maid and the extra girl they had hired to help tonight began to serve the dinner, which Mother Bates had planned with care.

The first course was anchovies on toast. They would have preferred oysters, but it just wasn't safe to serve them in a month without an *R*. The conversation began with Elizabeth speaking to Mr. Nolan on her right since Mother Bates and Gideon started by conversing with the honored guests on their right sides. That dictated with whom all the other guests could speak. This meant Elizabeth would spend the first half of the meal conversing with Mr. Nolan.

Unfortunately, Mr. Nolan was even more angry than Elizabeth could have expected. The way he was glaring at Mr. Livingston, who now sat next to the Senora, should have turned Livingston to stone.

"How is Trench doing, Mr. Nolan?" she asked in an attempt to draw his attention with a topic near to his heart.

With obvious effort, he turned to her. "He seems to be all right. We've run him a few times and he did well. We won't know for sure until we race him, though."

"Irene must be relieved. Mr. Regan, too."

Nolan frowned. His anger hadn't abated much, but now he seemed angry about something else. "If I had a good jockey, we could race him tomorrow, but now . . ." He jammed a triangle of the anchovies on toast into his mouth and chewed vigorously.

"I'm sure Mr. Regan would much prefer riding Trench to lying in a hospital bed."

"And he would be if he hadn't been so careless."

Elizabeth almost choked on the bite she had just taken. When she had safely swallowed it, she said, "You can't blame Mr. Regan for the accident."

"Not for the sponging, no. I know who to blame for that, but every jockey knows better than to fall off his horse."

Elizabeth forgot herself long enough to let her mouth drop open in shock before remembering her manners and closing it with a snap. Mr. Nolan didn't even notice. He was too busy glaring at Livingston who, Elizabeth noted with dismay, was completely ignoring Anna, with whom he should have been conversing, and trying to seize the Senora's attention from Gideon. Gideon, bless his heart, was doing his best to keep her attention on him, but she couldn't help being distracted by Livingston's relentless efforts.

The maids removed the appetizer plates and delivered the mock turtle soup. Mr. Nolan muttered something under his breath, but Elizabeth really didn't want to know what he'd said so she didn't ask.

"Have you hired someone to take Mr. Regan's place while he recovers?" she asked, hoping to engage him.

"That boy will never be right again," Nolan said, still angry. "The doctors all say so."

"How awful," she tried. "Irene still seems to be holding out hope, though."

"She's too sentimental. There's no place in racing for a broken-down jockey."

"But isn't Mr. Regan like a member of your family?" she asked with wide-eyed innocence.

"He works for me, like everybody else. If he can't work, he can't work for me. It's as simple as that."

Elizabeth somehow managed not to express her outrage. "That seems harsh. Couldn't he work in some other capacity?"

Nolan turned the force of his anger straight at her. "Why are you so concerned about Cal Regan? I can't see that he's any of your business."

Elizabeth couldn't help reflecting that Nolan was the second of the Senora's admirers who had been rude to her this evening. The Senora was certainly accomplishing her goal of attracting the most despicable members of society. Elizabeth didn't give Mr. Nolan the satisfaction of backing down, however. "I know Irene is very fond of Mr. Regan."

"She's fond of the horses, too, but she understands when we have to get rid of one."

Elizabeth couldn't help it. She widened her eyes at Mr. Nolan. "Are you planning to put Mr. Regan down?"

This time it was Mr. Nolan who almost choked, and he hadn't even taken a spoonful of soup.

He stared at her for a long moment and then he finally said, "You are an unusual woman, Mrs. Bates."

"Thank you, Mr. Nolan." She glanced over at where Livingston was still trying to claim the Senora's attention. Logan Carstens, bless him, had noticed Anna's plight and included her in his conversation with Mrs. Westerly. "Mr. Livingston was quite clever to move his place card, wasn't he?"

"Clever? More like devious, that dirty, rotten—" Elizabeth noticed his free hand had closed into a fist, as if he wanted to strike someone, probably Livingston.

"Mr. Livingston told me he doesn't intend to lose this time." Take that, Mr. Livingston.

Nolan's eyes narrowed as he studied her face. "He doesn't intend to lose what?"

"To lose out to you with the Senora, or at least that is what I understood him to say."

"Why would he say something like that to you?" She wasn't sure if his outrage was for Livingston or for her.

"One might well ask. I believe it was because he thought I was somehow putting him at a disadvantage by inviting both of you here this evening."

That seemed to please Nolan. "It was bound to," he said immodestly.

Elizabeth could have argued, but what was the point? "May I ask why you are both so intent on winning the Senora's affections?"

With terrible timing, the maids chose that moment to remove the soup course and deliver the fish course. The salmon with green peas looked almost too good to eat. Elizabeth was afraid Mr. Nolan had forgotten her question in the interim and was trying to figure out another way to ask it when he said, "I can't speak for Livingston, but I simply find the Senora fascinating."

"How interesting that the first female you take an interest in after more than twenty years happens to resemble your late wife, though."

"There's nothing interesting about it. I liked Mary's looks, so why shouldn't I like a woman who resembles her?"

Elizabeth could have pointed out that human beings were so much more than their outer appearance and just because the Senora looked like Mary didn't mean she was like her in any other way, but she decided logic would be wasted on Nolan. She chose to annoy him in a slightly different way. "And I suppose you think that because Mary chose you over Mr. Livingston, the Senora will choose you as well."

Elizabeth had expected another flash of annoyance, at least, but instead he frowned with what could only be dismay. "She will if she's smart," he said with far less confidence than Livingston had shown.

"I'm sure she is quite intelligent, but women often follow their hearts in matters of romance. Isn't that what your late wife did?"

For some reason this made his frown deepen, exactly the opposite reaction she had expected, since she thought she was paying him a compliment. "Yes," he said without a trace of conviction. Now what did that mean? If Livingston was still distraught over losing Mary all those years ago, shouldn't having won her be a source of pride for Nolan?

Sadly, Elizabeth had no opportunity to find out. Mr. Nolan turned his attention to his fish and pretended not to hear her attempts to continue the conversation. Then the maids were clearing the fish course and delivering the meat course, filet of beef with mushroom sauce, green beans and pickled peaches. This meant that Mother Bates would be turning the table by literally turning her attention from the guest on her right to the one on her left.

Elizabeth allowed herself a moment of pity for Mother Bates, whose task would be to get more than one sentence out of Olinda, and then allowed more than a few moments of pity for herself, who would have to converse with Mr. Westerly.

At least he wasn't likely to mention more than once that his daughter was a baroness.

Gideon actually sighed with relief when his mother turned the table. Vying with Daniel Livingston for the Senora's attention was an exercise in futility. First of all, Livingston was relentless, and second of all, the Senora's entire purpose was to encourage his attentions, so she wasn't resisting very much. The result had required virtually no effort on Gideon's part to make their honored guest feel welcome.

Now he turned to Hernando Chavez y Ramirez, who seemed to be enjoying his filet.

"I didn't know Spaniards had red hair, Senor Chavez," Gideon said.

Chavez looked up in surprise. "I am certain there are many things about the Spaniards that you do not know, Senor Bates. My ancestors are from Castile. Many Castilians have red hair."

"That is true," the Senora said, obviously having ignored Livingston long enough to overhear. "Catherine of Aragon had red hair."

The name sounded familiar, but Gideon couldn't place it. "Who?"

"She was a Spanish princess who was King Henry the Eighth's first wife."

"Oh," was all Gideon could manage. European royalty and their spouses had never been one of Gideon's favorite topics. Perhaps he should find something else to talk about. "What business is your family in, Senor Chavez?"

Chavez straightened in his chair as if affronted. "We do not engage in business, Senor Bates."

Gideon merely smiled. "But don't you have an estate? You must raise something there, at least."

After an awkward moment, Chavez said, "Olives. And grapes."

"Do you make your own wine?"

"For our personal use only," he said with a derisive sniff.

So much for that topic. "That is an interesting scar you have there."

Chavez bristled. "An affair of honor, sir. My opponent took unfair advantage."

"How awful for you," Gideon managed.

"Not as awful as it might have been. He was aiming for my throat."

So much for that topic, too. "What brings you to America?"

"I thought you must know. It seems everyone in New York already knows the most intimate details of my family and their affairs."

"If you mean the dispute over the Senora's husband's estate, I've heard something about it."

"Then you know that Olinda and I must marry."

"Yes, when she turns eighteen."

"Which she will do very soon, and that is why I am here. My father was afraid my aunt would refuse to return her to Spain when the time comes, so he sent me here to—what is that quaint American expression?—tie the knot."

"I would have thought your family would want your marriage to be a big event in Spain." Assuming the Chavez family really existed, owned a large estate and was socially prominent in Spain, but none of that was true.

"We will have a celebration when we return, but the important thing is for us to be married. It is only then that the estate can be settled to everyone's satisfaction."

"Everyone's?" Gideon challenged.

Chavez smiled. "To my father's satisfaction, at least."

"Does no one consider your feelings?"

"Firstborn sons are not permitted to have feelings, Senor Bates. We do what is best for the family."

"Oh, Hernando, you are such a baby," the Senora scolded him, choosing to ignore Livingston once more. "Few men would consider marriage to a beautiful girl like Olinda a hardship."

Livingston seemed far from pleased at losing the Senora's full attention, so he chose to insert himself into the conversation. "Why must Senor Chavez marry your sister, Senora?" Contrary to Hernando's theory, Livingston apparently didn't already know the story.

She smiled apologetically. "We should not be discussing our family business at a social occasion."

"But I would like to know. I would like to know everything about you, Senora," Livingston assured her with what he must have thought was an adoring smile. Gideon winced because it looked less adoring than possessive.

"I am sure you would not like to know *everything*," she said with a flirtatious smile in return. "A woman must have some mystery about her, no?"

"But surely you can't object to telling me your family history."

"Yes, Tía Paulita, tell him our family history," Chavez said with a slightly less than sober grin.

"Our family history goes back many years," the Senora said. "Mr. Livingston does not wish to hear all that."

"I think he just wants to know about my marriage to save the family," Chavez said. "If you will not tell him, I will. My uncle was the oldest son. He died and left everything to his wife, my tía Paulita." He nodded to the Senora. "But my father could not allow the Chavez estate to go out of the family, so he claimed it for himself."

"Stole it, you mean," the Senora said sweetly.

"One cannot steal what you already own," Chavez replied just as sweetly.

The Senora simply shook her head, whether in denial or bemusement, Gideon couldn't say.

"I see," Livingston said, obviously believing that he really did. "And if you marry the Senora's sister, the two families will be joined again."

"That is the plan," Chavez said, "and the family fortune will belong to all of us once more."

"Who does it belong to now?" Livingston asked, obviously forgetting it was rude to discuss money in polite society.

The Senora smiled with what might have been pity. She probably thought Livingston was an idiot. "As Hernando explained, I inherited everything."

"But," Chavez said, "my father now lives on the estate, as is his hereditary right, and the money is in a safe sealed by the Spanish courts where no one can touch it until Olinda and I marry, which is what we have all agreed."

Obviously, this intrigued Livingston. "Where is this safe now?"

"It is in my hotel room," the Senora said.

Livingston seemed greatly surprised by this, as well he might be, but he smiled as if he had just learned something momentous. "It's *here*? In the city? Then, I don't see the problem. If the safe is in America, the Spanish courts no longer have jurisdiction over it, and possession is nine tenths of the law."

"Actually, that's not strictly true," Gideon felt compelled to say, but no one paid him any mind.

"I am sure the Spanish government would object if Tía Paulita disregarded their judgment," Chavez said, plainly outraged. "As would my father and I."

But Tía Paulita seemed more than intrigued by the idea. "Are you saying the Spanish court's ruling has no power here?"

"What could they do to you if you claimed the money that your husband left you?" Livingston asked with the confidence of a man who has no understanding of the intricacies of the law.

"But Tía Paulita would not do such a thing," Chavez said with more hope than assurance. "If she did, she would never be able to return to Spain, where she would be regarded as a thief and probably thrown in prison."

"Maybe she doesn't want to return to Spain," Livingston said. "Maybe she'll decide to settle down right here in America. She could marry and have a happy life."

But Paulita didn't look quite so sure. "Never to return to Spain," she mused. "I cannot imagine."

"Of course not," Chavez said, still angry. "You would never be happy to remain here among the"—he glanced around the table with contempt—"among the Americans."

"Oh, I think she could be," Livingston said, and for once his smile looked genuine. "I could make sure you are, Senora."

"Mr. Livingston, you astonish me. We hardly know each other," she demurred.

"I feel I have known you all my life," he said with more enthusiasm than originality. "We have so much in common, too." Perhaps he really believed that, since she looked so much like his lost love.

"What could you possibly have in common with her?" Chavez scoffed.

"Racehorses. I have my own stable. She would feel right at home there."

"In your *stable*?" Chavez asked with a sneer.

"Hernando, you are being a boor," the Senora said before

Livingston could respond. He would have been less kind, judging from the ugly shade of red staining his cheeks.

"In any case," Gideon felt compelled to say, "I don't think the Senora would be wise to open a safe that has been sealed by the Spanish government." Which would have been true, if the Senora's safe had really been sealed by the Spanish government.

"Especially since Hernando and Olinda will be marrying very soon," the Senora said. "That will settle everything."

Gideon knew this was a bald-faced lie, but he merely smiled. He also caught the frown his mother was giving him from the other end of the table, which reminded him that a conversation among four people at the dinner table was unacceptable. Their raised voices were probably distracting the other guests as well. Nolan was definitely eavesdropping, judging from his thunderous expression, although he would have had to shout to reply.

Gideon was about to try ending his interaction with Livingston and the Senora when Livingston said, "How much money is in this safe anyway?"

The Senora looked suitably shocked, and Chavez nearly choked on the wine he had just sipped.

Livingston didn't seem chagrined. "I was just wondering if it's really enough to worry about."

The Senora gave him a pitying look. "It is enough to worry about, Mr. Livingston. Now may we change the subject?"

Fortunately, the maids were descending to remove the meat course and deliver the French salad and lemon pie, the first of the three dessert courses. Gideon sat back with a sigh. What was he going to talk to Chavez about for the rest of the meal?

He need not have concerned himself. Chavez was only too delighted to give Gideon his opinion of everything he had seen so far during his brief sojourn in New York. Nothing in the city pleased him, apparently. Everything was too new and too modern and much, much too tall. Why did anything except a church steeple need to rise above the roof of a church? Gideon had no answers and was obviously not expected to give any as Chavez rambled on and on through the ice cream and nut cake course, the fruit and candy course and the final coffee service that would enable them to stay awake after eating such an enormous meal.

Finally, his mother laid her napkin on the table and rose, signaling it was time for the ladies to leave the men to their cigars and port. The gentlemen stood while the women filed out, and when they were gone, Gideon offered around a box of cigars, which he didn't care to smoke himself, and the maids set out the glasses and bottles so the men could serve themselves an after-dinner drink.

Gideon was well aware that the presence of the ladies had probably been the only thing preventing Sebastian Nolan from climbing over the table to literally assault Daniel Livingston in retaliation for claiming the Senora's attentions during dinner. Now the responsibility for preventing that would fall to Gideon.

"Very clever, Livingston," Nolan said as the other men were puffing on their cigars.

"I don't know what you're talking about," Livingston said.

"Why, I believe he's referring to the way you managed to claim the seat next to the Senora," Westerly said. "Damned cheeky of you, I must say, but I suppose all is fair in love and war, eh?"

"Nobody is at war," Gideon tried.

"Are you interested in the Senora, Mr. Nolan?" Logan Carstens asked, obviously unaware of the hornet's nest he was poking.

"She is a good friend, and I don't like seeing her harassed by the likes of Livingston," Nolan said sourly.

"He did not appear to be harassing her," Hernando Chavez said. "In fact, I think she enjoyed his attentions."

Gideon wanted to punch him, but that would definitely set the wrong example to his guests.

"The Senora is certainly capable of avoiding unwanted attentions without any assistance," a voice from the other end of the table said, and Gideon realized his father-in-law had said it.

"You know the Senora well, Mr. Miles?" Logan asked in surprise.

Everyone turned to the Old Man expectantly. "We are acquainted, yes."

"Wait a minute," Nolan said with a ferocious frown. "I knew you looked familiar. You were with her at Belmont that day."

"Belmont Park?" Mr. Devoss asked with interest, probably remembering Gideon had taken the day off to attend the Belmont Stakes. "The racetrack?"

No one paid him any mind.

"When was that?" Livingston demanded.

"The first time I saw her," Nolan said, not even noticing his nemesis was the one who had asked, because his attention was now riveted on the Old Man. He probably thought he had another rival for her affections. "What were you doing there with her?"

The Old Man smiled benignly. "Watching the races, of course. The Senora had expressed a desire to see Sir Barton run in the Stakes, and I was happy to escort her."

"And how do you happen to know her?" Livingston asked, apparently prepared to share in Nolan's suspicions of him.

"I met her during the war. She's been in this country for several years, I believe."

"But not in New York," Mr. Westerly said. "She distinctly told me this is her first visit to the city."

"Yes, I believe we met in Baltimore, although it may have been Chicago," the Old Man said. "I travel quite a bit, and so does the Senora."

"And are you one of Tía Paulita's admirers, too?" Chavez taunted.

"What man could not admire her?" the Old Man said, making Gideon wince again, but the Old Man smoothed the ruffled feelings by adding, "but I am not interested in her romantically, if that is what you're asking. We are merely friends."

"So how much money does she have in this safe of hers?" Livingston asked, startling everyone.

"What safe is that?" Mr. Devoss asked. Obviously, he had not been eavesdropping on the Senora's earlier conversation.

Mr. Westerly took it upon himself to explain the situation. He got a few details wrong, but Chavez quickly corrected him.

"You're a lawyer, Devoss," Livingston said. "Couldn't the Senora just open the safe and take the money out now that she's got it here in America?"

Gideon caught Devoss's eye and realized his senior partner was amused that Livingston had overlooked the fact that Gideon was also an attorney. Gideon felt no obligation to explain that he had already tried to answer this question. "I would have to examine the laws to see what applies here. It sounds like a complicated case."

Which was probably what Gideon should have said.

"Anytime you're dealing with foreigners, it's a complicated case," Westerly lamented.

Chavez slammed his glass down on the table. "Are you insulting me, sir?"

Westerly looked over at him in astonishment. "Certainly not, young man. I'm, uh, thinking about my daughter. She's married herself a British lord."

Logan coughed, probably to cover a laugh, and Gideon didn't so much as dare to glance at him.

"I suppose that might be complicated," Mr. Devoss said, unaware of the undertones.

"And none of that answers my questions," Livingston said impatiently. "Does anybody really know how much money she's got stashed in that safe? And what's to stop her from just taking it out and claiming it?"

A long silence fell. Nolan glared at Livingston, but Gideon noticed he didn't chasten him this time. Nolan certainly wanted to know the answers to those questions himself. If the truth were known, every man at the table probably did, too. Curiosity was a besetting sin of the human race, and no one here was immune.

Finally, Chavez said, "We cannot be certain of its exact value, of course, because the war changed so many things, but my uncle left his widow over ten million pesetas."

"Ten *million*?" Westerly echoed in awe.

"And how much is that in real money?" Livingston asked.

"As I said, the war has changed much," Chavez said. "We would need to consult an expert."

"And what on earth is a peseta?" Logan asked. "It sounds like a fancy dessert."

"It is a Spanish dollar, I believe," the Old Man said, although he might not believe that at all. One could never trust a word he said.

"I thought the Spanish called their money pesos," Nolan said, obviously confused.

"That's Mexico," Westerly said wisely.

"Spain, Mexico, what's the difference?" Nolan asked no one in particular.

Gideon could only gape at him, horrified at his ignorance.

"There is a great deal of difference, sir," Chavez said tightly.

"But the important thing," Livingston said, "is that the lady has ten million of them if she can get them out of that safe."

# CHAPTER TEN

I'M SO SORRY YOU WERE IGNORED DURING DINNER," ELIZABETH said to Anna Vanderslice as they made their way from the dining room to the parlor where Mother Bates had arranged to have tables set up for cards or games when the men joined them later.

Noelle Carstens was walking with them, and she let out a lovely trill of laughter only a Frenchwoman could master. "I could not believe that man was so brazen. Such a thing would never happen in France."

"Such a thing should never have happened here," Elizabeth said, "but I suppose Mr. Livingston cares little for niceties like good manners."

"And I didn't mind because I'm sure I wouldn't have enjoyed my intended dinner partner any better," Anna said, glancing around to make sure Mrs. Westerly wasn't close enough to hear. "And your darling husband was kind enough to include me in his conversation with Mrs. Westerly, Noelle."

"He is a good man," Noelle said with a mock solemnity that sent them all laughing again.

Elizabeth noticed that Irene was trying to make conversation with Olinda with little success. "Someone should rescue Irene," Elizabeth whispered to Anna.

"I'll see what I can do with Olinda," Anna said with a sweet smile and moved toward the pair.

Mother Bates, the Senora and Mrs. Westerly had already reached the parlor and seemed to be waiting for the rest of them before claiming seats. Mrs. Westerly was probably angling to sit next to the Senora, but that lady had other plans.

"Miss Nolan," the Senora said. "Come and sit with me. I want to know how Mr. Regan is doing."

Irene seemed surprised at being singled out, but she obeyed, joining the Senora on one of the sofas. Mrs. Westerly was left to sit with Mother Bates on another.

"Do you speak any Spanish?" Elizabeth asked Noelle as they claimed some chairs a little apart from the rest of the group. This could be important to know.

"No, I am sorry. I can understand a little because we share some words, but not much. I did ask Olinda if she speaks French. She does, but badly."

"Then it's fortunate she speaks a little English, although I'm still not sure how much she understands. She hardly ever says a word."

"I know. She seems so unhappy."

Elizabeth nodded. "It must be difficult to live in a foreign country against your will and then be forced to marry somebody you don't even like."

"She does not seem to like Senor Chavez, does she?" Noelle said with a frown.

"Not at all, which is a shame since their marriage will solve so many problems for their family."

"Maybe she is just stubborn. She would not like anyone chosen for her. But she might come to care for Senor Chavez."

"If he makes an effort to woo her," Elizabeth said.

"Woo?" Noelle echoed with a frown. Plainly, her English vocabulary did not extend that far.

"Court. Try to please. Win her heart."

Noelle nodded. "Yes, but he does not seem to like her, either."

Elizabeth sighed. How did she get into this conversation? But Noelle had no idea this was all a fiction, so she had to keep up appearances. "I don't suppose it's any of our business, really," she tried in an effort to change the subject.

Noelle gave her a knowing look. "But you do like to see people happy."

Elizabeth had to smile at that. She had gone to great lengths to see Noelle and Logan happy. "Yes, I do, but I'm afraid the only way to make Hernando and Olinda happy is to separate them, and that would be a disaster for the Senora and the rest of her family."

"They have a choice between a big disaster or a small one, no?"

Elizabeth shrugged. "Maybe something will happen to save them. We can hope." She glanced over to where Anna and Olinda still stood near the doorway, deep in conversation. "Anna seems to be making friends with Olinda."

"I wonder what they are saying. Olinda never speaks more than two words at a time."

The sound of the Senora's laughter distracted them. She had obviously found whatever Irene had just said hilarious.

"You must share the joke, Senora," Mrs. Westerly said since all the other conversations had come to a complete stop.

"It is not a joke. It is just Miss Nolan's description of Mr. Livingston's behavior tonight. What did you call him, Miss Nolan?" she asked, her eyes dancing with laughter.

"A horse's patoot," Irene said without a hint of chagrin. "He is, too. I couldn't believe the way he stole Mr. Westerly's place card."

"He does seem determined to capture your attention, Senora," Mrs. Westerly said.

The Senora waved away Livingston's determination. "He thinks he must be in love with me because I look like my dear Miss Nolan's late mother."

"I know that's what people are saying, but I couldn't believe it's actually true," Mrs. Westerly said.

"Are people saying this?" the Senora said with a frown. "I should not like to be the subject of such gossip."

Which was a bunch of malarky since the Senora's whole purpose in being in the city was to engender gossip, but Elizabeth simply nodded sympathetically.

Mrs. Westerly obviously didn't want to displease the Senora so she quickly said, "I should have said I heard it from one or two people. I'm sure not many are even aware that you resemble Mary."

"Did you know Mrs. Nolan?" the Senora asked Mrs. Westerly.

"I did. Everyone knows everyone in New York, but it was a long time ago."

"Does the Senora really look so much like Miss Nolan's mother?" Noelle asked.

"I suppose so, but . . . Well, we're all older, aren't we? How do we even know what Mary would look like now?"

"Yes," the Senora said. "Perhaps I only look the way Mrs. Nolan looked then, not the way she would look now."

"What was she like, Mrs. Westerly?" Irene asked. "My mother, I mean. I never knew her at all."

Mrs. Westerly obviously didn't like the question. "It's so hard to remember. . . ."

"But you must remember something," the Senora said. "Am I like her in other ways?"

"She was . . . Well, you must understand, eloping with Sebastian Nolan when she was engaged to Daniel Livingston was quite a scandal. Young ladies are held to a high standard of behavior, and she behaved very shockingly."

"Then you did not approve of her," the Senora said.

"It really wasn't my place to approve or disapprove," Mrs. Westerly said quickly and turned to Mother Bates for help. "You must remember Mary Nolan better than I do."

"She was a brave girl," Mother Bates said. "She defied everyone and everything for love."

"Was she happy with her choice, do you think?" the Senora asked.

Plainly, no one had given this matter any thought at all.

"I think I always just assumed she had to be," Irene said. "I know my father has mourned her every day since."

"Has he?" the Senora asked with interest.

"Oh yes. He can hardly bear to speak of her. That's why I don't know much about her at all."

"And that must be why he has been so interested in getting to know you, Senora," Elizabeth said. "Perhaps he believes you can help him overcome his grief at losing her."

"What a terrible thought," Mother Bates said, surprising all of them.

"Why so?" Irene asked.

"Because no woman wants to be loved on those terms. A woman wants to be loved for herself alone."

"You are a wise woman, Hazel," the Senora said. "I should like to be loved for myself alone. I hope you young ladies feel the same."

The young ladies assured her that they did.

"I'm glad you aren't fooled by Mr. Livingston's interest in you, Senora," Irene said.

"Then she shouldn't be fooled by your father's interest in her, either," Mrs. Westerly said.

"I have been accused of many things, but never of being a fool," the Senora said with a smile. "Now tell me, Irene, how Mr. Regan's leg is mending."

Since those who cared about Cal Regan already knew and those who didn't care weren't interested, the ladies resumed their own conversations. Soon the men joined them, smelling of liquor and cigars. Elizabeth observed how the mood in the room changed drastically with the men's arrival, and all female-centered subjects were instantly dropped in deference to them.

Mother Bates explained what games were available to be played, and she also had several decks of cards for those so inclined. The Senora expressed an interest in playing bridge and both Mr. Nolan and Mr. Livingston eagerly agreed to partner her. Mother Bates tactfully accepted the Senora's invitation to be the fourth since no one else indicated they wished to enter such a fraught group. The Senora suggested that she and Mother Bates be partners and play the men, since the Senora didn't wish to show favoritism by choosing one over the other to be her partner.

The men were plainly displeased, but the Senora pretended not to notice and set about to shuffle the cards with a tiny bit of clumsiness that Elizabeth felt was very likely feigned.

The Old Man asked Westerly and Devoss if they'd like to play a little poker and Gideon felt obligated to join them, although he suspected Elizabeth's father would fleece them all.

The only men left were Hernando Chavez and Logan Carstens, but Noelle had already chosen a silly board game that she and Logan could play against Hernando and Olinda. Plainly, the two Spaniards weren't best pleased to be paired at the same table, but Noelle seemed determined to encourage the engaged couple to interact. Perhaps her French blood made her a romantic or perhaps she enjoyed tackling hopeless causes. Either way, Elizabeth was prepared to enjoy the show.

That left Elizabeth to host Anna, Irene and Mrs. Westerly at the fourth table. They all agreed they didn't want to play bridge, so Elizabeth suggested Panko, the card game developed in London to promote Woman Suffrage and named in honor of Emmeline Pankhurst, the leader of Woman Suffrage in England. Since it was similar to gin rummy, the others agreed cheerfully, although Mrs. Westerly might have only been pretending.

Elizabeth found herself losing hand after hand, since her attention was so divided. She kept trying to listen to the conversation at the Senora's table as well as the one where Olinda and Hernando were playing the Checkered Game of Life with Logan and Noelle.

Making Livingston and Nolan partners in the bridge game virtually guaranteed that Mother Bates and the Senora would win. Two men less likely to follow each other's lead or take cues from each other hardly existed. Their snide remarks and angry outbursts often caused the other guests to stop what they were doing and turn to look, as if expecting a fight to break out at any moment. The Senora would never allow that, of course, and Mother Bates probably knew just how to avoid it, so Elizabeth wasn't too worried about that table actually coming to blows. She wasn't so sure about Hernando and Olinda, though.

The two were plainly out of patience with each other and only maintaining a minimum of decorum for the sake of their hosts. No one knew what they were saying to each other because they spoke in rapid-fire Spanish and they kept their voices low, but the tone was unmistakable, as were the angry expressions on their faces.

"It's just a game," Logan cautioned more than once.

Hernando had apparently taken great delight in sending Olinda to "jail" on one of his early moves, and she had taken great offense. And no one else in the room could ignore the roar of triumph later when Hernando landed on the Matrimony square already occupied by Olinda.

"English, please," Noelle begged as Hernando spoke to Olinda in Spanish.

He smiled slyly. "I could send you back to jail, *mi prometida*, but I would much rather marry you."

Olinda hissed something obviously scathing, but Hernando's smile only deepened. "In fact, I do not think I will wait any longer. My new American friends have warned me that I cannot trust the laws in this country to protect my family fortune, so I'm afraid I dare not wait to make you my wife. We will be married as soon as it can be arranged."

Plainly, Olinda did not share Hernando's enthusiasm. She jumped to her feet, and in case anyone hadn't already noticed the altercation, knocked over her chair with a bang in the process. She fired off what must have been a scathing retort that brought Hernando to his feet as well. He replied in kind, and mousy little Olinda drew back her hand and slapped him resoundingly across the face.

The other men had also risen because years of good breeding demanded they stand when a lady does, but none of them made a move to intervene. Everyone seemed frozen in shock except the

Senora, who may have been accustomed to such displays of emotion.

Hernando held a hand to his flaming cheek, his expression murderous, and Olinda glared back at him with similar intent. Then the Senora grabbed Olinda by the hand and began pulling her toward the door.

"I am so sorry, my dear Hazel," she said as they made their way through the room. "I make no excuse for my sister, whose behavior is inexcusable, but I fear I must take her home before she disgraces me completely."

Olinda tried to argue with the Senora—or at least that's what it sounded like, but it was in Spanish, so no one could be sure—but the Senora stopped the girl with a word and never missed a step. Mother Bates hurried over and pulled the bell rope to summon a maid to assist them, since the girls would be otherwise occupied at this hour, not expecting any guests to leave so early.

"I'll see them out," Elizabeth said, hurrying to do just that.

She found them in the foyer. Olinda's defiance had faded under the Senora's fury, and from the way her lower lip was quivering, Olinda gave every indication she would burst into tears at any moment.

"Tell her not to start bawling," Elizabeth whispered to the Senora, glancing at the parlor door to see if anyone had followed them out.

The Senora smiled and shook her head. "She can understand what you say."

To prove the point, Olinda stuck her tongue out at Elizabeth, who almost laughed out loud. "I see neither of your suitors wanted to deal with a hysterical female."

"They are both cowards," the Senora said cheerfully.

The maid had finally appeared, and Elizabeth instructed her to fetch the Senora's and Olinda's wraps. The Senora thanked her again for a lovely evening and ushered Olinda out. Elizabeth waited until she was sure they had had time to get out of sight before returning to the party.

All the men rose to their feet again when she entered.

"Is everything all right, darling?" Gideon asked.

"The Senora is taking Olinda home. We thought it was for the best."

"But not soon enough," Hernando said, still rubbing his cheek.

"Perhaps if you treated her better, she wouldn't feel the need to slap your face," Elizabeth said sweetly.

Gideon made a strangled sound in his throat and even Mother Bates had to cough to keep her composure. No one else seemed to find her remark funny, however.

"Are you all right, Senor Chavez?" Mother Bates said when she could speak again. "Perhaps a cold compress . . ."

"I need no treatment for wounds of honor inflicted by a mere girl," he claimed. "I am sure you no longer find me pleasant company, however, so I will also take my leave."

He thanked his host and hostess profusely if a bit incoherently, and his exit seemed to spur Livingston and Nolan to action. With the Senora gone, neither had a reason to remain. Gideon saw them all out in case the two deserted lovers should at last come to blows. Happily, they satisfied themselves with a few glares before exiting the house.

Since all the tables were now shorthanded, all games were abandoned, and small groups began to form to discuss what had happened.

"Did anyone understand what they were saying to each other?" Mrs. Westerly asked. "It hardly seemed like a lovers' quarrel."

"I believe you would need two lovers to have a lovers' quarrel," Irene said with a hint of irony. "I don't think either of them would qualify."

"It's so tragic," Anna said with a little too much heartfelt dismay. Elizabeth would have to give her some instruction about that. "They are both young and attractive and in any other circumstances, they might have fallen madly in love."

"Do you really think Olinda is attractive?" Mrs. Westerly asked. "I mean, she always looks so unpleasant. . . ."

"She's just unhappy," Anna argued.

"As any girl would be if she was being forced to marry so someone else could get rich," Irene said.

"Exactly," Anna said.

Mr. Westerly, Mr. Devoss and the Old Man had remained at the poker table, and Elizabeth noticed they were still playing in spite of everything. She frowned at the large pile of chips in the center of the table, and she frowned even deeper when her father displayed his cards and gathered the pile of chips to himself.

He caught her glare and smiled benignly. "It's penny ante, my dear."

At least she didn't have to worry about her father conning her guests out of their fortunes at the poker table in her own parlor.

"Even I can stand losing with those odds," Logan said, and slapped Gideon on the back when he returned from seeing the three men out. "Let's join them, shall we?"

The women continued to analyze the events of the evening while the men played several more hands before deciding they had enjoyed themselves enough. The Westerlys, the Carstenses and Mr. Devoss left together. Elizabeth looked around and realized Irene was the only person not in on the con who remained, but that meant they still had to maintain the fiction.

"Did your father forget you and leave you behind?" Elizabeth asked, taking a seat beside Irene.

"He did ask if I wanted to go with him, but I didn't want to leave so early." She smiled a little wickedly. "I didn't want to miss anything else that might happen."

"You should have said something," Anna said. "We would have made sure to embarrass another person just for your entertainment."

They all laughed at such a preposterous notion.

"But surely you aren't going to return to Queens tonight all by yourself," Elizabeth said.

"No, we took a hotel suite for the night since we expected to be out late, so I don't have far to go."

"And who is looking after Mr. Regan while you're gallivanting around the city?" Mother Bates asked with a smile to show she was teasing.

Irene tried to smile in return, but to everyone's horror, her expression collapsed into tears, and she began to sob uncontrollably.

Elizabeth threw her arms around the poor girl and cast a desperate glance around the room to see who or what might help. Mother Bates had already headed over to the sideboard, where Gideon had poured drinks earlier in the evening, to fetch something calming. Anna had pulled a handkerchief from her pocket, and Gideon and the Old Man had gotten completely out of their way.

After Mother Bates had supplied a glass of brandy, and Anna's handkerchief, along with Elizabeth's and Mother Bates's, had mopped up the worst of Irene's tears, they were finally able to make sense of the words she had been trying to say between sobs.

"I'm so sorry," she stammered. "I didn't mean to make a spectacle of myself. . . ."

Elizabeth patted her hand. "Something terrible must have happened for you to be this upset, so you must tell us because you need our comfort."

"I don't know. . . ."

"Tell us," Mother Bates said quite firmly.

Irene sighed in defeat. "My father fired Cal. He said a jockey who can't ride is no use to him. He has also refused to pay the hospital bills, which means that Cal will have to use up all the money he's been saving to get his own stable."

"So the two of you can be married," Elizabeth added, in case anyone had forgotten.

"I have a little money of my own," Irene said, still dabbing at her eyes. "But Cal won't accept a penny even from me."

"If you were married, it would be his money, too," Gideon pointed out reasonably.

Irene gave him a pitying look. "He won't marry me for my money, either. He's the most stubborn man I ever knew."

"Now, now," Mother Bates said cheerfully, "you must not have known many men. They're all like that, full of misplaced pride and intractable as a mule."

"Not all of us, Hazel," the Old Man said from where he'd been playing solitaire at the poker table. "I'm perfectly willing to marry a woman for her money if I could only get one to offer."

Mother Bates, Irene and Anna laughed, but Gideon and Elizabeth glared. It was wasted on the Old Man, though, since he didn't even look up.

Elizabeth couldn't help wondering why Irene didn't just tell Cal Regan she was having a baby. Surely, that would motivate even the most prideful man to do the right thing. But Irene knew him better than Elizabeth did. Maybe the thought of a child would be too much worry on top of everything else he was concerned about at the moment. Lying helpless in a hospital bed must be incredibly difficult for a man as active as Regan had been. She didn't want to question Irene about this delicate subject in front of so many people, though.

"When you're feeling better, Miss Nolan, I would be happy to escort you back to your hotel after I see Miss Vanderslice home," the Old Man said.

"I really don't—" Irene tried, but a chorus of voices shouted her down.

"You can't go wandering around the city alone at this hour, no matter how close your hotel is," Anna said. "With Mr. Miles at your side, the only danger you will face is being charmed into proposing to him."

W E MUST PLAN THE WEDDING," THE SENORA SAID. SHE had called at the Bates house the next afternoon, and she was fortunate to find Mother Bates at home as well as Elizabeth.

"So soon?" Elizabeth said.

"I know. I did not intend for things to end so quickly here. I stayed in San Francisco for almost five years."

"My goodness," Mother Bates said. "That is a long time to pretend to be someone else."

The Senora smiled. "I am always pretending to be someone else, Hazel."

"That must be exhausting," Mother Bates marveled.

"One gets used to it. Now, the wedding."

"I suppose it will have to be at a church," Elizabeth said.

"Oh yes, a Catholic church. They will insist on a real priest, too."

"They?" Mother Bates echoed.

"The priests. But it does not matter since there will be no wedding."

Mother Bates shook her head in confusion. "But I thought that's why you came, so we could plan it."

"We must plan it, but it will not happen. Do not worry. It will all work out. Do you know a Catholic church?"

"Not personally, but we'll find one," Elizabeth said. "Shall it be a big wedding?"

"Only the bride and groom and their attendants, but we must invite many people. If I cannot stay here long, I must have many people witness the wedding."

"Why is that, dear?" Mother Bates asked.

"Never mind," Elizabeth said. The less her mother-in-law understood, the better. "Do you have a list?"

"Oh yes." She reached into her purse and pulled out a folded piece of paper.

Elizabeth looked it over, impressed by the number of names and by how few of the people on it she even liked. "They may not all be able to attend. We're not giving them much notice."

"They do not need to attend, but I think they will. I owe all of them money, and they will want to see Olinda and Hernando wed."

Elizabeth couldn't help it. Her jaw dropped open. "You owe *all* of them?"

The Senora sighed dramatically. "Americans are so generous."

Mother Bates had been looking at the list over Elizabeth's shoulder. "Why would all of these people lend you money?"

"Because I am penniless until I can open the safe. They know I am desperate, so they try to take advantage of me by charging me usurious interest rates."

"That's scandalous," Mother Bates exclaimed, clearly outraged on the Senora's behalf.

"Yes, it is," Elizabeth said with just the slightest smile, "so it's a good thing the Senora has no intention of paying back any of this money."

Mother Bates needed a moment, but in the end, she shook her head to clear it and said, "Of course. I just forgot."

The Senora graciously did not comment.

Mother Bates considered the list and the issue for another moment. "How much money do you supposedly have in your safe?"

"I usually do not specify because that would limit how much I could borrow, you see."

"I do see," Mother Bates said happily. "That makes perfect sense."

"But this time, my dear Hernando"—her tone clearly indicated he was not really dear to her at the moment—"told the gentlemen who were here last night that I have ten million pesetas."

"That sounds like a lot of money," Mother Bates assured her.

"Do you know how much a peseta is worth?"

For a second, Elizabeth thought her sweet mother-in-law was going to hazard a guess, but in the end, she said, "I have no idea."

"Neither do I," the Senora said. "But someone might, so we must end this quickly, before someone starts making entries in a ledger book and adding them up."

Elizabeth looked at the list again. "I'll add some of the society people you met whose names aren't on here, just so it doesn't look like you only invited people who gave you money."

"I already put Sebastian and Daniel on the list, as you can see, although neither of them has loaned me money yet."

"They haven't?" Mother Bates said. "I thought Daniel was your main target. No, that's not the right word. Mark, that's it. Daniel was your main mark."

The Senora smiled benevolently. "Hazel, you are a treasure. You remind me of . . . Well, never mind. But I do so enjoy your company. I shall miss you."

Mother Bates was obviously touched. "I shall miss you, too. Perhaps we can meet somewhere later for a real visit when all of this is over."

Elizabeth knew such a thing would never happen, so she quickly said, "When do you want to schedule the wedding?"

"Next Saturday, I think. A week from today. I need to give Sebastian and Daniel time to propose to me."

"Both of them?" Mother Bates exclaimed before Elizabeth could.

"I thought we weren't going to, uh, involve Mr. Nolan," Elizabeth said.

The Senora gave Elizabeth a pitying look. "You did mention that impoverishing Sebastian would not be in Irene's best interest, but I fail to see how that is true. When she marries Cal Regan, Sebastian will most likely cut her off completely, in which case she will get nothing from him anyway. At least if we manage to separate him from some of his money, Irene will get your share of it or so you led me to believe."

Elizabeth stared at her for a long moment. "You'd give me a cut of Nolan's score, too?"

"Of course. You roped him, and you told me you were giving your share of Livingston's take to her, so I assumed you'd do the same with her own father's money."

"What if he's as broke as we suspect?" Elizabeth asked.

"He still has those beautiful horses, doesn't he?"

Mother Bates frowned. "What would you do with horses, Senora?"

"Why, sell them, of course."

But this was a lie, as Elizabeth well knew. Con artists usually restricted themselves to cash. Even gold was awkward since it was heavy and so easily faked. Some of the oldest cons involved painting lead bars, and a con artist never wanted to be on the wrong end of a fake-gold-bar con. Taking something as difficult to convert into cash as a racehorse was simply asking for trouble. Nothing slowed you down more than a score that had to be fed and watered. "Are you serious?"

The Senora smiled to show she wasn't, not really. "Are you

worried about me, Elizabeth? Do you think I am losing my reason?"

"I did for a moment, yes."

"But," Mother Bates said with a sly grin Elizabeth had never seen her wear before, "I can't help thinking how pleased Irene would be if *she* owned her father's horses."

The Senora did an excellent job of acting surprised at this amazing observation, which made Elizabeth sure she had already thought of it herself. "Why, Hazel, we will make a grifter out of you yet."

Elizabeth winced at Mother Bates's delighted expression. She would have to make sure Gideon never found out about this conversation. "Cal Regan won't be best pleased to learn Irene owns her own racing stable."

"Then he will have to reconsider his priorities," the Senora said. "If all else fails, Irene can simply hire him to be an exercise boy."

"Which would teach him some humility," Mother Bates said.

"But which would hardly promote a happy marriage," Elizabeth said.

The Senora nodded. "I should speak to Irene about marriage. We are already seeing many children born out of wedlock as a result of the war, and we will see more before we are done. Too many young men did not return to marry their paramours, and society will learn to accept these children. If a woman has money of her own, she need not even fear society."

"But what if Irene really wants to marry Cal Regan?" Elizabeth argued.

"And what if he does not want to marry her? She said herself he is full of pride. Perhaps he is not man enough to humble himself for her."

Elizabeth had no answer for that. She should probably talk to

Irene herself, before Paulina did. Elizabeth could make a good case for marriage and at least balance the Senora's arguments. Of course, if Cal was stupid enough to reject a woman like Irene and his own child over some foolish pride, he probably didn't deserve either of them.

When had helping other people become so complicated? It never had been before.

"Elizabeth," Mother Bates said kindly, "you can only do what you can do. The rest is up to Irene and Mr. Regan."

"And Irene will do what is best for herself," the Senora said with a confidence Elizabeth didn't think she had any right to feel. "In the meantime, we must arrange for Sebastian and Daniel to be alone with me this coming week so they can propose."

# CHAPTER ELEVEN

I KEEP TELLING GIDEON WE NEED A MOTORCAR," ELIZABETH said as she and the Senora strolled from the train station to the Empire City Race Track. They opened their parasols against the brutal midday sun, but the umbrellas were inadequate to the heat. "We could have driven out and not had to swelter in the train."

"It is a long ride to Yonkers, but one must go where the racing is. I don't understand why they can't just always race in one place, but one must adapt. Besides, we would also have been sweltering in your imaginary motorcar and been windblown as well."

She was right, of course, but Elizabeth still wanted a motorcar. "How did you get Mr. Nolan to invite you out to the races so quickly?" Only two days had passed since the Senora had mentioned her plans for Nolan to propose.

"Irene had said that Sebastian was thinking of entering Trench in the Frivolity Stakes. There aren't a lot of races for two-year-olds that have a decent purse and aren't selling or claiming races, so I encouraged him to take advantage of it when we were playing bridge at your house."

"And then you mentioned you'd like to watch Trench win, I suppose."

The Senora shrugged. "I couldn't say such a thing in front of Daniel. I telephoned the hotel later that night to apologize to Sebastian for Olinda and Hernando's behavior. That was when I mentioned how much I would enjoy watching Trench run."

"I don't see why you needed to bring me along, although I do enjoy the races."

"Irene will be there. A man is hardly likely to offer marriage to a woman with his daughter looking on."

"So my job is to keep Irene busy."

"Keep her company, at least. Actually, I would far rather spend my time with Irene, but needs must."

"She is a delightful girl. I hope she and I can remain friends when this is over."

"I hope so, too, and I don't know why you couldn't. No one will suspect your part in all of this."

"I certainly hope not. Mother Bates is determined to let it be known she was one of your victims as well. That should clear us of any suspicions."

"I always knew Hazel wasn't the Goody-Two-shoes she pretended to be."

Elizabeth looked at the Senora in surprise. "What do you mean by that?"

But the Senora was waving at someone and apparently didn't hear her. "Isn't that your father?"

Elizabeth winced at the thought, but it wasn't the Old Man, after all, so they moved on to the luxurious confines of the clubhouse, where Mr. Nolan and Irene met them for lunch.

Irene seemed to have recovered from her emotional outburst on Saturday night, and no one would have suspected her inner turmoil from her outward expression. She greeted her two guests with genuine warmth, and if Mr. Nolan reserved his warmth for the Senora alone, Elizabeth had no complaints.

After they had exchanged pleasantries and inquiries about the train ride out and observations about the weather prediction for the day—eighty-five degrees and fair—and how that would affect the racing conditions, Elizabeth turned to Irene.

"How are you feeling about Trench today?"

Irene smiled the first genuine smile she had seen from her in a while. "He seems to be doing just fine. Mr. Quaid checked him for sponging just this morning, and we've kept a close watch on his feed. He's been training well, and he had a good run this morning."

Elizabeth turned to the Senora. "Perhaps we should place a wager on him."

Mr. Nolan smiled at that. "I will never advise you to wager foolishly, but I think Trench will finish in the money today at the very least. The odds might not be good, though, since he'll be the favorite."

"We do not care, do we, Elizabeth?" the Senora said recklessly. "We are betting for the excitement. One is much more interested in a race if one has wagered on it. Don't you find that to be true, Mr. Nolan?"

"How many times do I have to remind you to call me Sebastian? And yes, that is true, although as an owner, I don't have to wager to feel an investment in the race."

"Yes, you do stand to win a lot if Trench gets the victory," the Senora said, studying her program. "I see the purse is almost fifteen hundred dollars. I wonder how many pesetas that is?"

"Probably not many," Mr. Nolan said cheerfully. "But it doesn't matter. It's a respectable purse in these dark days when our government has seen fit to regulate racetrack betting practically out of existence."

"And you will place bets for me and Elizabeth, Sebastian?" the Senora said, making a little show of using his first name.

"I will be happy to do so. But first let's enjoy our lunch. Trench doesn't run until the fourth race, so we have plenty of time."

Several times during lunch Elizabeth felt the urge to ask after Cal Regan, but she decided to wait until she and Irene were alone or at least until Mr. Nolan wasn't around. She would need to remove Irene from her father's presence as often as possible to facilitate the Senora's plan, so she would have plenty of opportunities.

After lunch, they made their way over to the stands and found the box Mr. Nolan had reserved for them. Irene and Elizabeth sat in the front two seats while the Senora and Mr. Nolan took the two farthest back, leaving the two in the middle empty, which was as much privacy as anyone could get when sitting in the grandstands watching horse races.

"Senora, I'm afraid I can't keep the secret a moment longer," Elizabeth said with a sly glance back at her. "Is it all right if I tell them?"

"Since they are invited, I see no reason why not, and you will save me the trouble of finding an appropriate way to bring up the subject," the Senora replied with just a hint of resignation.

"Invited to what?" Irene asked.

"A wedding," Elizabeth announced a little too loudly, then clamped a hand over her mouth. "Oh dear, I didn't mean to invite everyone here!"

"Yes, please keep your voice down," the Senora teased. "I am not prepared to entertain half of New York at the reception."

Plainly, Mr. Nolan had gotten the wrong idea completely, as they had intended, and he looked suitably horrified. "Are you getting married, Senora?"

The Senora somehow managed to look equally horrified. "I? Whatever makes you think such a thing?"

Mr. Nolan obviously wasn't quite sure how he had reached this conclusion, judging by the way he stuttered and stammered. When he ran down, Irene said, "Then who is getting married?"

"Why, Olinda and Hernando. I thought you would know, since they have been betrothed for so long."

Both Irene and Mr. Nolan were speechless at this revelation. After a long, awkward moment of silence, Irene finally managed to say, "Even after that terrible argument they had on Saturday?"

The Senora shrugged away the terrible argument with one shoulder and a flick of her wrist. "I find that romance is much more interesting when it is mixed with passion, don't you?" She didn't wait for a response. "Olinda and Hernando know their duty. The sooner they marry, the sooner the family disputes can be settled. Then Olinda will produce an heir, and she and Hernando can begin to live separate lives, and everyone will be happy again."

"And what about you, dear lady?" Mr. Nolan seemed compelled to ask. "Won't their marriage leave you all alone in the world?"

She gave him a grateful smile. "You are kind to think of me, but I am not important. As soon as Olinda and Hernando sail for Spain as man and wife, I will have accomplished everything I was entrusted to do. Then perhaps I will consider my own future."

When Mr. Nolan would have argued with her, Elizabeth said to Irene, "Shall we walk down to the paddock and watch the horses being saddled?"

Irene blinked in surprise, but she readily agreed. She probably didn't enjoy watching her father mooning over the Senora, either.

Irene wore a broad-brimmed hat that shielded her from the sun as well as Elizabeth's parasol, but they still strolled slowly toward the paddock in deference to the weather.

"How is Mr. Regan doing?" Elizabeth asked when they were far enough from Mr. Nolan's box that he wouldn't hear.

Irene's pleasant expression evaporated in the heat of her anger. "That idiot! He was so determined to walk that he tried it without the crutches. The doctor had been letting him walk around his room with crutches for a few minutes each day to build up his strength, and he decided he didn't need them anymore, so, of course, he fell."

"Did he hurt himself?" Elizabeth asked in dismay. Cal Regan might well be an idiot. Maybe she shouldn't be encouraging Irene to marry him, after all.

"Luckily, no, except for his pride, which was severely damaged. The doctor even took him off walking with the crutches for a few days to teach him a lesson. He could have rebroken his leg," she added in disgust.

"Let's hope he won't do anything else foolish," Elizabeth said. "I suppose you gave him a lecture about it."

"I wanted to, but I was crying too hard. I think that upset him more than if I'd yelled at him, though. He's not used to seeing me cry because I never used to. But now . . ."

"Yes, Mother Bates did say you'd be more emotional *now*." Elizabeth knew better than to specifically mention Irene's pregnancy in public, where they might be overheard.

They'd reached the paddock, and they spent some time admiring the horses and watching the slight variations in the saddling ritual among the different trainers. Only four horses were running, so they had time to examine each of them closely. Then the jockeys mounted, and the horses headed out to parade to the starting barrier.

As Elizabeth and Irene headed back to the box, Elizabeth said, "Your father seems quite taken with the Senora."

Irene sighed. "I keep reminding him that just because she looks like my mother doesn't mean she's like her in any other way, and there's no guarantee she could even care for him in return, but nothing I say seems to make any difference. I thought he would burst with excitement when she telephoned us yesterday to apologize for Olinda and Hernando."

"You don't suppose he's in love with her, do you?" Elizabeth said to see what Irene might reply.

"I think he's in love with my mother's memory. I just hope he doesn't make a complete fool of himself over the Senora. I can't imagine why she would be interested in him."

"She isn't exactly discouraging him, though, is she?"

Irene frowned. "I think she just enjoys attending the races."

"She could attend the races with anyone," Elizabeth said. "My father, for example."

Irene smiled at that. "Yes, but she may prefer sitting in an owner's box."

Elizabeth smiled back. "I hadn't thought of that, but you may be right."

But when they approached Nolan's box, they saw he was holding her hand in both of his and their heads were so close, they were nearly touching. The Senora's expression was solemn, and Nolan's was intense, but only for a few moments until they became aware of Elizabeth and Irene approaching. They broke apart and Mr. Nolan managed a smile of greeting.

"Who looks good in the first race, Irene?"

"I'd pick Afternoon if I was betting. He's carrying the least weight and it's a fast track."

"Irene has a good eye for a winner," Mr. Nolan confided to the Senora.

"Irene is quite gifted in many ways," the Senora said, giving Irene an admiring glance. "You are truly blessed to have her."

Plainly, Irene wasn't used to such lavish praise, and she actually blushed. Her father, however, just looked nonplussed.

"Yes, of course, I mean, I always say she's as good as any son could be," he managed, earning a disapproving look from the Senora and a true glare from Elizabeth, which he didn't even notice. For her part, Irene didn't even seem surprised at her father's left-handed compliment.

"Look, they're lining up," Irene said, turning to the track, where the horses were taking their positions at the starting barrier. This effectively ended all discussion of Irene's virtues, which had probably been her intent. The horses lined up quickly and the starter sent them on their way after only a minute. The crowd yelled, "They're off!" and those sitting rose to their feet to cheer on their favorites. Afternoon's jockey held him back as the other horses wore themselves out sprinting for the early lead. Then he let Afternoon go at the stretch turn and he easily passed the early leaders to win.

"How did you know he'd win?" Elizabeth asked, knowing full well how unpredictable horse racing could be.

"Lucky guess," Irene said, but she was beaming with pride.

"Perhaps you should ignore your father's rule against betting," the Senora said. "You could do quite well."

"I'm not always right," Irene said modestly.

"And she doesn't have money to throw around," her father said sourly, as if he resented her little victory.

"She would if she won," the Senora said with a smile to soften her words.

Mr. Nolan seemed unable to resist that smile, even though he plainly disagreed with her. "And I did promise to place a bet on Trench for you, didn't I?"

"Yes, you did. And one for Elizabeth, too. Do you think that would be a sensible use of our money, Irene?" the Senora asked.

"If there is ever a sensible way to bet on the horses, then yes, it is," Irene said with a smile of her own. "Trench is going to win today. I just know it."

"Should we walk down to see how he's doing?" Elizabeth asked, seeing another opportunity to leave the Senora alone with Nolan.

"If you'd like. Senora, would you like to go, too?" Irene asked.

"It's much too warm to go walking around today," she said. "Please give your jockey my best wishes, however."

Elizabeth and Irene found Trench dozing in his stall, as if completely unaware he would be racing today. Mr. Quaid was sitting outside the stall, his wooden chair leaning back against the wall so he could doze, too, in the summer heat.

"Ain't nobody been near him since the last time you checked, Miss Irene," he reported, "and nobody's seen a trace of Livingston at the track today. He's not got a horse in any of the races, so I didn't expect he'd be around."

"It's just as well," Irene said, then to Elizabeth, she added, "with the Senora here."

"Yes, we don't want a scene, do we?" Elizabeth said. "Or anything to mar Trench's victory."

"He knows he's racing today. I can tell from the way he's holding his head. He always looks a little prouder when it's a race day."

Elizabeth thought that was probably nonsense, and from Quaid's expression, he did, too, but no one disagreed with her. "Who is riding him today?"

Irene named a jockey Elizabeth had never heard of. This wasn't surprising, since she didn't really follow horse racing that closely, but Irene couldn't say enough good things about the boy. All jockeys were called boys, no matter their age, but this one really was young, only seventeen. He'd already won a number of races, though, which was why he had been given Trench to ride.

"No one expects much from Trench today after what happened the last time, but I know he's going to do just fine," Irene said. "Maybe I should bet on him myself."

"A few dollars couldn't hurt," Elizabeth said.

But Irene just shook her head. "Father will be placing the bets. Do you really think he'll place one for me?"

Elizabeth understood. "I'll double my bet, then, and if I win, you'll get half."

"You don't have to do that," Irene said. "Besides, if you lose, I might not even be able to pay you back."

"You won't need to pay me back. Besides, Trench is going to win, isn't he, so there's no risk to me."

Irene just shook her head. "I don't suppose I can stop you, and I'm the one who guaranteed Trench will win, so I shouldn't even try."

"Exactly," Elizabeth said.

They made it back to the box just as the horses were lining up for the next race. The Senora seemed to be making a lot of progress with Mr. Nolan, who had been so deeply engaged in conversation with her that he hadn't even noticed when Elizabeth and Irene returned. The Senora had to clear her throat and withdraw her hand from his, and when she did, he seemed annoyed by the interruption.

He didn't look like a man who had successfully proposed to the woman he loved, though. He looked frustrated and anxious, but perhaps that was all part of the Senora's plan. The second race was a selling race featuring horses that Mr. Livingston would probably have called platers, but every race was exciting, with a winner and runners-up and losers, and the crowd cheered as if it were the Belmont Stakes all over again.

At the Senora's urging, Mr. Nolan went to place their bets between the second and third races. She didn't want him to wait and possibly not get the bets down in time. Before he left, he ordered some lemonade for the ladies to enjoy. It was a welcome refreshment in the heat, which was oppressive even in the shade of the grandstand.

"I hope my father isn't boring you, Senora," Irene said when conversation about the various races lagged.

"How could he be boring me?" she asked with an amused smirk. "His adoration is so flattering."

"Men probably make fools of themselves over you all the time," Irene said, "so I suppose you're used to it."

"If you pay attention, you will notice that men make fools of themselves over many things. Sometimes it is a woman, but not always."

This made Irene smile, as the Senora had obviously intended.

"I see you understand," the Senora said. "Is this because Mr. Regan has behaved foolishly as well?"

Irene told her about Cal's misadventures with the crutches.

"Are you sure he did not injure his head in the accident, too?" the Senora asked with mock concern.

"Sometimes I'm sure he must have," Irene said, letting her anger show a bit.

Elizabeth could see the Senora wanted to give her some advice, but since the Senora wasn't supposed to know about Irene's pregnancy and any advice would undoubtedly involve telling Irene to break the news to Cal Regan to get him moving in the right direction, Elizabeth couldn't allow her to mention it.

"How exciting that Olinda and Hernando are actually getting married," Elizabeth said to change the subject. "What will you do when you finally have access to your inheritance, Senora?"

The Senora raised her eyebrows to let Elizabeth know she understood what she was doing. "I have not allowed myself to think about that. What do *you* think I should do, Irene?"

Irene looked appropriately surprised at being consulted on

such a matter. "I have no idea. You should do what you want to, not what somebody else suggests."

"I wonder what you would do if you suddenly had a fortune at your disposal," the Senora replied.

"Me? That's easy enough. I would start my own stable and raise racehorses."

"But you are already doing that, are you not?" the Senora asked.

Irene shook her head. "I do a lot of the work at my father's stable, but he makes the decisions. Sometimes he takes my advice and sometimes he doesn't and when I'm right, he resents it and when I'm wrong, he gloats."

"And he doesn't even pay you," Elizabeth said.

"He does not pay you?" the Senora echoed in outrage.

Irene smiled wryly. "He gives me housekeeping money. He says everything will be mine someday, and that will be my payment."

"You do not sound so sure, I think," the Senora said.

"My father is in good health, so I'm not likely to inherit anything for a long time, and in the meantime . . ." Irene shrugged.

"And what in the meantime?" Elizabeth urged.

Her smile vanished. "Many racing stables go under and the owners end up penniless."

Neither Elizabeth nor the Senora had an answer to that.

Seeing their shock, Irene must have felt compelled to explain. "You see, there's a reason why most successful owners are millionaires. They have unlimited income, so they can afford to waste a good bit of it raising and training horses that might never earn a penny, and far too many of them don't."

"But I thought your father was quite wealthy," the Senora said. Elizabeth didn't remind her that she had warned her about this very thing.

"He was when we started, but he sold his company so he could devote himself to racing. That meant that his only source of income became the horses themselves. It doesn't take long to run through a fortune, especially if your horses aren't winning races."

"And that is why your father had such high hopes for Trench," Elizabeth said.

Irene just nodded.

"But you said you would start your own stable if you had your own fortune," the Senora said.

"I know, it must sound crazy, but it's what I love and what I know how to do and . . . Well, it sounds immodest, I suppose, but I think I could do a better job than most owners at managing things. I've seen the mistakes my father and others make, so I know how to avoid them."

"Then I hope you get your fortune," the Senora said. "You deserve your chance."

"And wouldn't it be pleasant to watch a woman succeed where so many men have failed?" Elizabeth said.

They were chuckling over this vision when Mr. Nolan returned.

"I hope you remember I advised you against betting if Trench doesn't finish in the money," he said as he took his seat next to the Senora.

"I will, of course, remember," the Senora said, "because you will most certainly remind me."

He smiled sheepishly at that. "I was thinking more of Mrs. Bates. Her husband might not be happy that she lost so much at the track."

Elizabeth had given him twenty dollars but had not mentioned to Mr. Nolan that half of that was being wagered on Irene's behalf. "I'm not worried about Gideon's reaction, Mr. Nolan, so there's no reason for you to be."

The Senora asked Mr. Nolan what odds he was able to get, and she kept him chatting until the third race began. They watched Marchesa II eke out a win although she was visibly tiring at the end. That led to a discussion, mostly between Irene and her father, over the logistics of the race, but it lasted only a few moments before the Senora reminded them they needed to go down to the paddock to see Trench being saddled for the next race.

All four of them made their way down. The crowd seemed to be affected by the name of the race. The owners and trainers and jockeys were all quite cheerful for the running of the Frivolity Stakes, and even Mr. Quaid was smiling.

"Look at him, Miss Irene," he said as they approached. "Trench can't wait to run."

"I told you he knew it was a race day," Irene said, reaching out to pat Trench's flank. He snorted at her, as if reprimanding her for holding him back.

A short fellow wearing the Nolan silks stood nearby, grinning ear to ear. Irene introduced Harvey Wallace to Elizabeth and the Senora.

"Are you going to win today, young man?" the Senora asked.

"Yes, ma'am, I am," Wallace promised, making them all laugh.

No wonder people loved horse racing so much, Elizabeth thought. Even she could feel the excitement and anticipation that seemed to vibrate in the very air. Hope and promise easily overcame wisdom and common sense, since only one horse would win this race, yet all the owners expressed the same confidence.

The call came, and the riders were hoisted into their saddles to begin the parade. Elizabeth and her group watched Trench start off, then hurried back to the box. Irene and Elizabeth led the way with the Senora and Mr. Nolan close behind.

Although she wasn't trying to listen, Elizabeth couldn't help overhearing Mr. Nolan say, "When we're married, you'll be able to do this every day."

Elizabeth glanced at Irene. Had she heard it, too? She gave no indication, thank heaven.

So, the Senora had already succeeded in her mission, although how she could expect Livingston to propose now when she was already engaged to Nolan, Elizabeth had no idea. She was sure the Old Man would advise her to sit back and watch a master at work, so that's what she would do.

The horses were just reaching the starting barrier when the group arrived at their box, and they didn't even bother to sit down as they waited for the starter to send the barrier flying up. It seemed to take forever for the horses to all stand still, but finally the flag dropped and the barrier flew and the horses ran. The crowd roared, "They're off!" and the four of them in the Nolan box shouted Trench's name.

The race started cleanly and Krewer set the pace. Wallace held Trench in check as the other horses strained to catch Krewer. Trench was being outrun when they reached the stretch turn, but that's when Wallace let him go. He took off then, driving past the other horses to take the lead. Krewer gave up. Romany tried to sneak up on Trench but didn't have enough to overtake him, and Luke's Pet swerved wide coming out of the turn and lost too much ground. Trench was running away when he crossed the finish to win handily.

Irene was screaming and Elizabeth threw her arms around her friend. "I thought you weren't supposed to show excitement when you win," she shouted into Irene's ear over the din of the crowd.

"Another thing I'd change about racing," she shouted back.

Then they turned to see how Mr. Nolan was taking his victory. He was beaming, of course, but otherwise managing to contain his excitement. Then to what was probably Irene's surprise, he took the Senora's hand and pressed a kiss to it.

"Come with me to the winner's circle," he said.

"That is Irene's place," she said, shaking her head. "And how can we keep our secret if I go with you?"

He frowned, obviously disappointed, but he called, "Irene!" and headed out without waiting for her. Elizabeth wanted to smack him, but she contented herself by thinking how heartbroken he would be when the Senora left him.

When Irene was gone, too, Elizabeth moved up next to the Senora. "Did he already propose?"

"Yes, while you and Irene were visiting Trench." Elizabeth would have expected her to look more gratified, but she didn't even look pleased.

"How are you going to get Livingston to propose if you're already engaged?"

"We are *secretly* engaged." The Senora smiled grimly. "No one must know until after Olinda and Hernando are married."

"I see. That makes sense, I guess. Are you going to meet Livingston at the track, too?"

"I do not think so. We cannot let Sebastian see us together, can we? Even a secret engagement would be strained by that."

"Yes, it would. And speaking of secret engagements, if only Irene had one, I'm starting to wonder if my share of the score will be enough for her and Cal to start their own stable."

"It is concerning, is it not? We will do the best we can for her, of course, but she is a sensible girl and will not overextend herself, I think."

"Or waste her money betting on the horses," Elizabeth said. "I only wish the odds had been better on Trench."

"Do not worry about Irene," the Senora said. "I think she can take care of herself."

M R. NOLAN WAS IN A DECIDEDLY GOOD MOOD WHEN HE returned from the winner's circle, and he had even given Irene his arm for the walk back to their box. They were stopped many times for congratulations, and Nolan seemed as much gratified by that as pleased by Trench's victory. Of course, one of his goals for winning races, in addition to the purses, was the social recognition.

When they reached the box, he allowed Irene to precede him. Then he took a seat in the empty row between where Elizabeth and Irene sat in the front row and where he had been sitting with the Senora in the back row. "Paulita, we need to share our news with Irene," he said.

The Senora glanced around to see if anyone was paying them any attention, but the horses were parading up for the next race and there were quite a few of them, so the crowd's attention had shifted to the track and the winners of the last race had been forgotten. "I suppose we must, Sebastian."

Irene had no experience hiding her emotions, and her concern was easy to read. She really had no idea what he was talking about, Elizabeth realized with dismay. This was the worst part of the con, Irene's distress at believing her father meant to marry a woman they hardly knew. At least Irene would eventually find out it had been a ruse, but for now . . .

"The Senora has agreed to become my wife." Nolan's obvious pride in this announcement only increased Irene's shock, although to her credit, she did try to put on a good face. She liked the Senora, after all, and wouldn't want to hurt her. "That's . . . What a surprise. I had no idea."

"And you must continue to have no idea," the Senora said. "We are not to speak of it until after Olinda and Hernando are married. Nothing must interfere with that."

"Since you insist," Nolan said with a slightly annoyed smile. "I still don't see how it could interfere, though."

"Hernando may think you will take control of the fortune and squander it," the Senora said. "If so, he could refuse to marry

Olinda and prevent me from taking possession. It is better to stay silent until the marriage takes place."

"That makes sense," Elizabeth said. "Everything about the Chavez family is a little unsteady right now, so there's no reason to give anyone a reason to change their minds about anything."

"I . . . I suppose I should wish you happiness," Irene said, obviously still trying to make sense of this. "I mean, I do wish you happiness."

"If you are concerned about having a new stepmother, you need not worry," the Senora said with one of her beneficent smiles. "I have no intention of trying to control your life."

"I'm glad to hear it, since my father already does enough of that," Irene replied with a small smile.

"What does that mean?" he asked in apparent surprise. "I just do what a father is supposed to do."

"Of course you do, my dear," the Senora said without much sincerity.

"Show her the ring," Nolan said in what was an obvious attempt to change the subject.

The Senora frowned. "I don't know . . ."

"Show her. Show them both," he said, warming to the subject.

"What ring?" Irene asked with another worried frown.

"The engagement ring," Nolan said. "You don't think I'd propose without an engagement ring, do you?" Such rings were newly fashionable and always exchanged by the very rich.

With obvious reluctance, the Senora pulled off her left glove to reveal a sparkling if old-fashioned diamond ring.

The ring was truly lovely and shouldn't have inspired the horrified gasp from Irene.

"That's my mother's ring!" she cried.

Her father silenced her with a glare. "It *was* her ring and now it's mine to do with as I please, and I please to give it to my fi-ancée."

Plainly, Irene did not want to give the Senora offense, but she was also clearly upset.

"I'm sorry, my darling," the Senora said quite sincerely. "I didn't realize . . . I know it must be a shock to see your mother's ring on another's hand."

"Yeah, it was a shock, all right," Nolan agreed with deter-mined bravado. "You should've seen Paulita's face when I put it on her finger. I guess she never expected something like that from a fellow like me."

"It was a . . . surprise," the Senora agreed with a tight smile.

Elizabeth would have thought the Senora would be pleased to receive expensive jewelry as a bonus to her con, but she seemed oddly not pleased. She had already pulled her glove back on to conceal it. But perhaps she was just worried about someone else seeing it and guessing at the secret engagement.

"Irene, I hope this news has not upset you," the Senora said. "I want us to be friends."

"We are friends," Irene assured her. "It was just a surprise, that's all. I . . . I should like very much having you as a member of our family." If she sounded less than enthusiastic, no one could blame her.

Nolan smiled a big, satisfied grin at that, but Elizabeth could manage only a small smirk since she knew the Senora would not be part of anyone's family if she could possibly help it.

# CHAPTER TWELVE

"I CAN'T BELIEVE I'M GOING TO A DINNER PARTY AT DANIEL LIV-ingston's house," Gideon's mother said. "No one has been in his house in twenty years."

"It's probably not much of a party," Elizabeth said. She and Gideon were accompanying her to the corner where they could more easily flag down a cab to take them to Livingston's. "I have visions of Livingston announcing he and the Senora are engaged and then ushering all of us out."

"Let's hope he does, because it will probably be pretty boring otherwise," Gideon said. "Whom can he invite, after all, if he and the Senora are supposed to keep their engagement a secret?"

"I'm sure the Senora has given him a list of trusted friends," his mother said. "She won't want to spend a boring evening, either."

"She would have *had* to supply the guest list," his mother said, "because I don't think Daniel has a friend left in New York."

"Don't be too shocked, but I believe the Old Man will be there," Elizabeth said.

Gideon almost tripped on the sidewalk. "Your father is going to Daniel Livingston's engagement party?"

"He's going to the Senora's party. They're old friends, remember? He may also be your mother's dinner partner."

"How delightful," his mother said, just to annoy Gideon, he was sure.

"Mr. Devoss told me he was coming," Gideon said, "so he'll probably be your partner."

"There's no reason to be cruel, Gideon," his mother chided him. "Is that a cab?"

Gideon flagged it down and gave the driver the address.

"Whoever is there, I'm sure it will be a small group with no known gossips included," Elizabeth said.

"Which means the Westerlys will not be there," Gideon said.

"Thank heaven for that," Elizabeth said.

"Will Olinda and Hernando attend, do you think?" his mother asked.

"Hernando can't know about the engagement, so I'm sure they won't be there."

"That's a pity," Gideon said. "I'm sure they could be depended upon to break up the party early with another argument."

"If it means that much to you," Elizabeth said with the flirty smile that made him want to kiss her, "you and I could have an argument. I could even slap you if you like."

"I don't think we'll have to go that far," Gideon said with a mock glare. "Claiming a headache should be enough."

"Now stop this, you two. I'm sure it will be a lovely evening," his mother said.

Gideon glanced at Elizabeth and quickly looked away since he could see she was about to burst out laughing. There was no reason to make his mother feel bad. Let her enjoy her fantasy as long as she could.

A rather decrepit family retainer dressed in a suit that had gone out of style ages ago opened the door when they arrived at Livingston's home. The place had a decidedly neglected air, even from the outside. Although it was in good repair, the small front yard sported none of the flowers or shrubs that graced the minuscule lawns of its neighbors and made them appear welcoming. Inside, the atmosphere was a bit musty, as if the doors and windows were seldom opened.

The butler took the ladies' wraps and escorted them into the parlor where Livingston and the Senora awaited them. The room was dark with heavy velvet drapes and bulky horsehair furniture harkening to a bygone era. If Livingston had not entertained in twenty years, he hadn't redecorated in far longer than that.

The other guests had already arrived, and to their surprise, Anna Vanderslice was among them. The Old Man had escorted her to this event as well, and the two of them had been conversing with Mr. Devoss when they walked in.

Greetings were exchanged, but no one offered congratulations or mentioned the engagement. In point of fact, the invitation had made no mention of it, either, and no one here should have known of it at all except for the happy couple.

Livingston was a bit rusty with his hosting skills, but his aging butler managed to serve a round of drinks. When everyone had been supplied, the Senora gave Livingston a nod, telling him the time had come.

"Well, I suppose you're wondering why I've invited all of you here tonight," he began.

"I hoped it was to eat some supper," Mr. Devoss joked.

Everyone laughed politely, and Livingston assured him that was definitely his intention. "But before we get to that, I want to tell you the reason we're having supper. You see, this lovely lady, the Senora Paulita Padilla y de la Fuente viuda de Chavez, has agreed to become simply Mrs. Daniel Livingston."

"You're getting married, Daniel?" Gideon's mother exclaimed as if she'd had no idea. She was such a good liar. Elizabeth was very proud. "What a wonderful surprise! And that means the Senora will remain with us forever. What a delightful benefit."

Livingston seemed surprised by this enthusiasm, but the others echoed it, offering their congratulations with seeming sincerity and joy.

"Thank you, all," the Senora said when everyone had voiced their feelings. "I'm afraid we must ask you a favor, however. You see, if Hernando learns I am engaged to be married, he might be disturbed enough to call off his wedding to Olinda, and that must not happen."

Everyone murmured their agreement with this statement.

"Why would he call off the wedding, though?" Anna asked with creditable innocence. "He benefits from it as much as you do."

"He might be afraid my new husband would mishandle my fortune, which is going to come to him and Olinda someday. Or who knows what he might think. At any rate, I don't want anything to distract from the beautiful wedding we have planned on Saturday."

"And with only two days to go, you shouldn't take any chances," Elizabeth said. "Although it's a shame you weren't engaged earlier. You could have held Olinda's wedding here. I'm sure it's been a while since you've had a wedding breakfast in this house, Mr. Livingston."

Livingston looked positively horrified at the prospect, as Elizabeth must have expected, but the Senora immediately came to his rescue. "We have a lovely breakfast planned at my hotel. But to confirm the secrecy of our own engagement, each of you was particularly chosen because we felt we could trust you not to speak of it."

"I would never dream of revealing your secrets, Senora," the Old Man said, and Gideon believed him. No one in this room was better at hiding things than Elizabeth's con man father.

"And we knew we could trust Hazel and Elizabeth and dear Miss Vanderslice," the Senora continued.

"And Bates and Devoss are lawyers, so they never talk about other people's business," Livingston added.

Mr. Devoss graciously nodded his agreement, and Gideon just took the last sip of his whiskey to fortify himself for the evening to come. This was, he realized, becoming a distressingly frequent habit.

"I have other good friends I would like to have shared this news with, but they are not as trustworthy," the Senora said, "so we will wait until after the wedding to tell them."

"Yeah, I can't wait to tell old Sebastian Nolan the news," Livingston said with great satisfaction. "He'll probably have apoplexy."

So Livingston couldn't even forget his competition with Nolan for one evening.

"Did you receive an engagement ring, Senora?" Elizabeth asked in what Gideon knew was passive retaliation.

To Gideon's surprise, the question seemed to startle the Senora or at least cause her a moment of dismay before she collected herself and held out her hand to reveal a very lovely ring. "Oh yes, Daniel surprised me with this tonight."

The ring was modern and quite obviously of the most recent fashion. Gideon supposed a lady always liked to have some expensive jewelry in case of emergencies.

Since the group was so small and so closely related, the seating arrangements were a bit informal. Elizabeth ended up sitting at the Senora's left and beside her father, whom she should not have been partnered with, but it was either him or her husband. As Elizabeth had predicted, Mother Bates was on his other side and to Mr. Livingston's right. Mr. Devoss was to the Senora's right, but Anna was beside him with Gideon on her other side and on Livingston's left. But the group was so small that they didn't observe the strict table rules and spoke to whomever they pleased.

About halfway through the fish course, the Old Man said, "Livingston, I hope I can count on your help. I've been asked to assist a consortium of businessmen to assemble a stable of race-horses."

"A consortium? Who are they?"

"They want to remain anonymous for the time being," the Old Man said. "Prices tend to go up if an owner thinks somebody rich is looking to buy, and they aren't interested in getting taken. They want some promising horses to get started with and they figure with a group, the losses will be spread around."

"The winnings, too," Livingston said a little grimly.

"These men aren't particularly interested in profiting immediately, although I'm sure they wouldn't mind. They are more interested in the thrill of the game, if you know what I mean."

"Yes, they want to be part of it without the risk," Livingston said a bit bitterly. "Do they want to buy some of my stock?"

"I'm sure they'd consider it, but I'd just appreciate you letting me know if you hear of anything promising."

"If I hear of anything promising, I'll buy it myself," Livingston said drily.

"Now, Daniel, you must be generous to Mr. Miles. He is our guest," the Senora said.

"I know, I know, but this is business, Paulita. Miles understands."

"I was surprised to receive an invitation to the wedding," Anna said in an obvious move to change the subject.

"Of course you are invited," the Senora said. "You are Olinda's special friend who always makes sure someone speaks to her at social events."

"I do try, but she is so very shy," Anna said.

"Except with Hernando," Gideon muttered.

"What was that, Gideon?" Anna said with a mischievous smile.

When Gideon just glared at her, she said, "Oh yes, that argument they had at your house. I do wish I spoke Spanish. I would have loved to know what they were saying."

"They were only saying what lovers everywhere say when they are upset with each other," the Senora said.

"Threats to murder each other, no doubt," Elizabeth said sweetly.

"Is that how you and Gideon argue?" Anna asked with genuine interest.

"Oh no, Gideon is too well-bred to say anything like that, but I'm sure he thinks it at least once a week."

"At least," Gideon agreed with a loving smile that made everyone except Daniel Livingston laugh. Plainly, he did not find death funny, and Elizabeth couldn't help but wonder if he was remembering his lost love.

IT'S BAD LUCK TO GET MARRIED IN THE RAIN," MOTHER BATES declared over breakfast on Saturday morning.

"Everything about Olinda and Hernando's marriage is bad luck," Gideon replied. "A little rain won't make any difference."

"Can't you at least give us an idea of what is going to happen, dear?" Mother Bates asked Elizabeth.

"I'm not even sure myself. Your reaction is always better if you don't know what to expect, so we shouldn't know anything at all."

"I wonder if Olinda will slap him at the altar," Gideon mused over his coffee. "That girl has a good arm. I wonder if she plays baseball."

"I'm sure Spanish girls do not play baseball," Elizabeth informed him sternly, making him grin.

"I never imagined Spanish women were so interesting," he replied. "Maybe I should have held out for one."

"You can decide if you ever really meet one," Elizabeth said sweetly.

"We'd better get moving," Mother Bates decided after glancing at the clock on the sideboard. "We don't want to be late and miss something."

As always, cabs were at a premium in the rain in the city, giving Elizabeth another excuse to lament their lack of a personal motorcar. Gideon, as usual, ignored her and managed finally to find them transport to the small Catholic church the Senora had secured in the Irish section of town. Gideon wondered how much the Senora had paid the priest to reserve the site, since the Irish weren't known for welcoming other ethnic Catholics into their houses of worship. But it was just a wedding, quickly over and done, so perhaps that had made the difference.

The church was far less opulent than St. Patrick's Cathedral, and Gideon knew a moment of regret for the couple whose married life would begin in such a dim and down-at-the-heels place. Then he remembered this was all a sham and almost laughed at himself for getting caught up in the fantasy of the con.

The pews were already filling with some of society's denizens who must have frowned at the invitation and scowled at the address of the church, but whose curiosity had overcome their reluctance and brought them here today. Since most of them had loaned the Senora money against the inheritance this marriage would bring her, they'd want to witness the ceremony.

The Bates family saved seats for Anna and the Old Man, who had not arrived yet.

In the meantime, Gideon entertained himself by watching Sebastian Nolan and Irene come into the church. Nolan scanned the pews as if looking for someone, probably Livingston, because the Senora would be in the back with Olinda until the ceremony was ready to start. The Nolans took seats a few rows in front of the Bates party, which suited Gideon just fine. Better view of the show.

Livingston came in a little later. He also scanned the rows before choosing his seat. He had the advantage of knowing where his rival sat. He made a little show of moving briskly down the aisle and sliding into the pew just in front of the Nolans. The two men exchanged a vicious glance, each no doubt thinking they had gotten the advantage over the other, if only he could say so, since they both believed themselves engaged to the Senora. What would happen at the wedding breakfast when they would undoubtedly meet at some point? Gideon could hardly wait.

As at all weddings, the sense of anticipation increased as the appointed hour drew near. The crowd eventually fell silent and the organ music began to swell. The Senora came down the aisle, escorted by what appeared to be an altar boy. How strange when she had not one but two fiancés who could have accompanied her, but Gideon wasn't going to mention it.

When the Senora was seated, Hernando and the priest came out of a side door to await the bride. Another man Gideon didn't recognize was with Hernando. He must be the best man. Who would stand up with Olinda? This was like a play and he found himself unabashedly curious to see who would fill all the parts.

But he should have known nothing would go as expected.

The organ music changed to what sounded like a march, probably the bride's cue to enter and begin processing down the aisle. Every head turned to catch the first glimpse of her, but instead of a beautiful young woman they saw no one at all.

Then they heard a bloodcurdling scream and a few hoarse shouts and a brief struggle and the horrible sound of breaking glass.

Gideon was on his feet in an instant. He had to push past Anna, who had taken a seat between him and the aisle, but the Old Man, seated at the end of the pew, was already hurrying out so Gideon had only to follow. Many of the other men were also racing to see what had caused the commotion, but Gideon knew they would be too late. Before they could reach the church door, whose stained glass panel now lay on the floor in shards, they could hear the roar of a motorcar racing away.

Someone threw open the broken church door, but nothing remained outside except a crumpled bouquet of white lilies lying on a rain-puddled sidewalk.

"What happened?" more than one voice demanded.

Gideon had an idea, but he didn't voice it. Instead, he was trying to figure out why the glass door panel was broken.

"What's this?" someone asked, picking up a fist-sized rock.

"Olinda? Where is she?" the Senora demanded, having just fought her way through the crowd of men now clogging the church foyer and the outside doorway. The rest of the female members of the congregation were quickly converging behind her.

"I don't know," someone said.

"She's not here."

"Her flowers," the Senora exclaimed, shoving some men aside so she could get outside. The bouquet still lay where it had landed, and she scooped it up, clutching it to her bosom protectively as she desperately scanned the street for a glimpse of the girl. "What happened to her? Did anyone see?"

"We were all inside," someone said.

"I heard a motorcar roaring away," another said.

"And there's this," the Old Man said, handing the Senora the large rock that had apparently smashed the window. Someone had wrapped a large envelope around it and tied it securely with some heavy string. The word "senora" had been crudely lettered on the envelope.

"What on earth?" she murmured, pulling ineffectually at the string.

Daniel Livingston produced a penknife and cut the string for her. The Senora plucked the envelope free and dropped the rock.

"What is it? What does it say?" Sebastian Nolan demanded.

Nolan had also worked his way to the Senora's side by now, and both suitors looked over her shoulder as she read the letter she had pulled from the envelope.

"It's a ransom note," Livingston said in wonder.

"Shush!" the Senora cried, crumpling the note against her so no one else could see. "We must not say. Olinda is in grave danger."

"What's happened? Where is she?" Hernando cried, having finally worked his way through the crowd from the front of the church.

"She's been kidnapped," Nolan informed him, having obviously read the note, too.

"Do not say so," the Senora said. "We must not say a thing. She could be killed."

"Then we need to contact the police," Livingston said.

"They say no police or she will die. Please, I must speak in private to Hernando. We will decide what to do."

"I will come with you, Paulita," Livingston said.

"No, I will!" Nolan insisted, giving Livingston the kind of look a prizefighter gave his opponent just before the fight began. He even closed his hands into fists, making Gideon a bit nervous.

"No, I must discuss this with Hernando alone. I will . . ." She took a shuddering breath, obviously on the verge of tears. "I will send for you when I need your help."

"You know you can depend on me, Paulita," Nolan said. "Day or night."

"I am ready for whatever you need," Livingston said more loudly.

"Yes, I know. I thank you most humbly, but now I must . . . Oh dear, all these people. Will you send these people away? There will be no wedding today. Come, Hernando, we must speak in private."

The Senora took Hernando's arm and led him back into the church. She'd dropped the bouquet at some point and now clutched only the note to her bosom. The crowd in the aisle parted for them. Many people asked them what was going on, but neither of them replied. Nolan and Livingston followed behind, jostling for position and informing everyone practically in unison that the wedding was canceled and they could leave.

So much for the wedding breakfast, which, of course, was really a lunch. Gideon wondered if the Senora had even ordered it. What an economical way to hold a wedding. He idly picked up the discarded bouquet and moved back inside with the rest of the crowd. The men found their female companions and began to file out. The buzz of voices filled the usually quiet room. People were asking each other what had happened and what they had seen, but no one knew anything his neighbor didn't know. Somehow the bride, all alone in the foyer and preparing to make her entrance, had been taken away in a motorcar after issuing one terrified scream. Her abductors had managed to heave a rock through the door panel, although that seemed a bit dramatic. But what did Gideon know about conducting a kidnapping? Perhaps rock-throwing was a regular part of them.

Some people were wondering aloud how kidnappers would know about the wedding and the Senora's great wealth, but others reminded them of how rumors flew in the city, which was really just a small-town hotbed of gossip if you only considered the people in society.

Gideon handed the bedraggled bouquet to Elizabeth when he reached the pew where she and his mother and Anna had chosen to wait, knowing they would learn nothing of importance by following the crowd.

"Olinda is gone, apparently," he reported. "Kidnapped with a ransom note and everything."

"And on her wedding day," Anna exclaimed with just the proper amount of outrage. "How tragic."

Gideon managed not to roll his eyes.

"What is the Senora going to do?" Elizabeth asked, ignoring Anna's little outburst.

"Consult with Hernando, it seems. The wedding breakfast is canceled, I gather."

"Honestly, Gideon, how can you think about the wedding breakfast at a time like this?" his mother chided.

He wanted to say, "easily," but decided that would be inviting another chiding from his mother so he tried to look contrite and said, "Do you suppose the Senora could use our assistance?"

"I'm sure she'll ask for it if she does," Elizabeth said with a little touch of warning. She wouldn't want him to ruin the plan.

"Now, fellows, I think we need to leave the family to their privacy," he heard the Old Man saying. Gideon looked over to see Elizabeth's father trying to reason with Livingston and Nolan, who both seemed determined to be the last man remaining in the church.

"I should be here for her," Nolan insisted.

Irene was tugging on his arm. "Father, Mr. Miles is right. The Senora said she would send for you when she needed you."

"And she doesn't need your help at all, Nolan," Livingston said. "I'm ready to give her whatever she needs."

"I'm sure she doesn't want anything from you," Nolan said.

Gideon noticed his hands were closing into fists, which was never a good sign. "Gentlemen," he said, adding his voice to the Old Man's, "I think we should all honor the Senora's wishes and leave her to it."

"But if Olinda was kidnapped, someone should go looking for her," Nolan argued.

"Where would you look?" the Old Man asked.

"Or send for the police," Livingston tried.

"The note specifically said no police," the Old Man reminded them. "Really, these are decisions for the Senora to make. If she wants our advice, I'm sure she'll ask for it."

"She actually said she would send for you if she needed your help," Gideon reminded them. "How much more assurance do you need?"

Plainly, neither of them wanted to be the first to leave, so they just stood glaring at each other until the Old Man said, "Let's be on our way, shall we? I'm sure the priest doesn't appreciate our standing around here arguing in the sanctuary."

A meaningful look at the glaring clergyman still standing rooted near the front of the church confirmed this opinion, so however reluctantly, Livingston and Nolan finally allowed themselves to be escorted out.

"And who is going to pay for the broken window, I'd like to know?" the priest asked as soon as they were gone. Was that his main concern when a bride had been kidnapped on the very steps of his church? Apparently so.

Gideon glanced around and realized he, his wife, mother and Anna were the only ones left in the sanctuary. "You'll have to take that up with Senora Chavez, I'm afraid," Gideon said.

"But she left."

"She left?" Gideon echoed stupidly. One glance at Elizabeth told him how naïve he really was. Of course she would have left.

"Indeed, she did, her and that fancy man and his buddy. Lit out like their tails was on fire. Did they think they'd find the girl out in the alley?"

"I have no idea what they thought."

"Well, then, but who's going to pay for the window?"

His mother started coughing suspiciously, so he knew she was finding this very amusing. At least Elizabeth and Anna knew how to keep a straight face. Gideon reached into his pocket. "Here is my card. I'm the Senora's attorney. If you send her the bill through my office, I'll see that she gets it."

The priest seemed satisfied with that, although Gideon was pretty sure the Senora wouldn't do anything with it when she got it. He didn't mention that to the priest, though. Instead, he escorted his womenfolk out of the church as quickly as he possibly could.

THE SENORA DECIDED TO SUMMON DANIEL LIVINGSTON first, and then ask Gideon to lend her his legal expertise. When the Bates family arrived back home with Anna and the

Old Man in tow to scavenge what they could in the way of a luncheon, they found a message from the Spanish woman requesting that Gideon attend her at her hotel suite.

"Maybe you should go, too," he suggested hopefully to Elizabeth. "I'm sure the Senora would appreciate a female presence in this difficult time."

"She didn't ask for me," Elizabeth reminded him with a teasing glint in her eye. "I'm perfectly willing to offer her comfort if she feels the need. I'll wait here in case I am summoned."

"But what does she need *me* for?" Gideon asked of no one in particular.

"One never knows what legalities might be involved," the Old Man said, helping himself to Gideon's whiskey.

Since nothing about this was in any way legal, Gideon had no reply.

He did take the time to eat before making his way to the Senora's hotel, since who knew how long this might take. She and Hernando were sitting with Livingston in the parlor of her suite when Gideon arrived. They all looked suitably glum, an expression Gideon felt was probably appropriate when a young woman in the flower of her youth had been cruelly kidnapped.

"How may I assist you, Senora?" Gideon asked. Did she know that he was not participating in the con, at least not to deceive anyone? Surely, Elizabeth had warned her.

"As you know," she said, fighting to maintain her composure although she was obviously under a tremendous strain, "Olinda was kidnapped. I received this letter with instructions on how to ransom her. You had better read it so you will understand."

Gideon took the now-wrinkled paper she offered him. Raindrops had caused the ink to run in spots, but the message was still clear. Olinda was being held until the Senora paid a ransom of half a million dollars. This amount, the kidnappers were certain, would be easy for the Senora to borrow against the fortune in the safe, which she would inherit as soon as Olinda was released and able to finally marry Hernando.

"Half a million dollars," Gideon murmured, nearly breathless with the audacity of it.

"They are insane, of course," the Senora said. "I do not understand American money, but I am sure half a million dollars is far less than ten million pesetas, but it is still far more money than most people have. Is this not correct, Mr. Bates?"

"That is correct," Gideon confirmed, his voice a little less firm than he would have liked. "Do you have any idea how you will borrow this amount of money?"

Now, any sensible man and certainly any reputable attorney would suggest summoning the police at this point, but Gideon wouldn't think of muddying the waters with talk of doing something helpful. Besides, they would just ignore his sage advice.

The Senora gave Daniel Livingston a fond smile. "Mr. Livingston has offered to lend me a substantial portion of it. Half, I believe he said."

"Yes, a quarter of a million," Livingston said quite proudly. Obviously, horse racing hadn't bankrupted him, at least not yet.

"That's a lot of money," Gideon felt compelled to say.

"It certainly is, but since the Senora and I have a . . ." He glanced at Hernando, who looked as if he was in too much distress to be paying close attention, but who could really tell? ". . . a special friendship, I feel I must offer her my assistance. She will, of course, repay me when Olinda and Hernando marry."

"Of course," the Senora said, giving him another look, this one full of gratitude. "The letter says the money must be in cash. Will that be difficult for you, Daniel?"

"I won't be able to get the money until the bank opens on Monday, but it shouldn't be a problem."

"I cannot tell you how grateful I am," the Senora said with what Gideon imagined was complete sincerity. Then she patted his hand, which seemed to send him into raptures. Gideon had to look away.

They discussed some details, and the Senora insisted that Gideon draw up a promissory note for the funds Livingston was going to provide. That, too, would have to wait until Monday, when Gideon's office was open, but he was able to note all the provisions. Hernando didn't even appear to notice that one of those provisions allowed the loan to be forgiven if Livingston and the Senora married. Gideon figured this was just a technicality, since Livingston would share in the Senora's fabulous wealth after their marriage. He must be mentally counting his fortune already.

When they were finished discussing everything, the Senora said, "My poor Olinda. Who could have done such a thing?"

"Anybody who read about you in the gossip columns," Livingston said. "People haven't been talking about anything else for weeks."

"Then it is my fault," the Senora said, dabbing her eyes. "I will never forgive myself."

But Gideon was pretty sure she would.

Livingston didn't want to leave, but the Senora reminded him in an urgent whisper that she still had to obtain the remainder of the ransom and his presence might discourage others from being willing to assist her. After much cajoling, he finally agreed to depart after making her promise to summon him if he was needed.

"Half a million dollars?" Gideon said in amazement when the three of them were alone.

"What is the point of asking for less?" the Senora asked. "You will only get less."

Which was an interesting philosophy, Gideon had to admit. Before he could say so, the Senora had gone to telephone Sebastian Nolan. Now they would find out just how much money he really had. Gideon hoped Elizabeth was wrong about him, since her share of Nolan's money would go to Irene and Cal Regan, but he wasn't getting his hopes up. Elizabeth was usually right about things like this.

Nolan arrived alone and surprisingly quickly. He was apparently staying at this very hotel until the situation with Olinda was resolved. Gideon had half expected Irene to accompany him. She did think the Senora was engaged to her father, after all. But he wouldn't want Irene around, Gideon realized. He would want to handle this himself.

"I am so sorry, Paulita," he said when Gideon had let him into the suite. Nolan sat down beside her on the sofa and took her hands in his. She was, he noticed, wearing a different engagement ring than the one Livingston had given her, so Gideon had to assume this one was from Nolan. How did she keep it straight?

"Do you know how much they demand to return my poor sweet Olinda?" the Senora asked, her eyes moist with unshed tears.

"I saw the note. A half a million. They'll probably take a lot less. I'd give them a few days to stew and then—"

The Senora said something in Spanish that might have been a curse but which certainly was angry. "You cannot think I would bargain for Olinda's life? She is my flesh and blood!"

"Oh no, I didn't mean . . ." He stammered to a halt, because, of course, he did mean that. "But where will you get a half million dollars?"

Hernando took his turn being angry at such an attitude. "If you will excuse me, I cannot listen to this anymore, Paulita. I must go lie down." With that he went into the suite's bedroom and closed the door, giving Paulita the ability to speak freely to Nolan.

"My dear Sebastian, I thought perhaps I could depend on you, my fiancé, to lend it to me. As soon as Olinda and Hernando are married, I can repay you."

Nolan blanched. Gideon didn't think he'd ever seen anyone turn truly white before, but Nolan did. Then he opened his mouth like a fish seeking bait, closed it and opened it again. Finally, he found his voice. "I don't . . . I don't have that kind of money."

The Senora looked horrified. "Have you deceived me?"

"I don't think so," he said without much conviction. "I mean, you never asked me about money, and I figured with your fortune . . ."

"You thought you would live on my money?" she asked, still horrified.

He tried to act affronted. "I expect my horses will start earning soon and it won't matter."

"But now it does matter because my dear sweet Olinda's life is in danger, and I must have the ransom to save her."

"I . . . I could let you have about . . . uh . . . ten thousand."

This was so absurd, the Senora didn't even attempt to reply.

"Maybe fifteen if I sold some horses," he allowed after another awkward minute.

"You would sell your horses?" the Senora asked, brightening at the thought.

He swallowed audibly. "A few platers, I guess."

"But you could sell all of them. How much would that bring?" she asked eagerly.

"I can't sell all of them. I'd be out of business."

"But I will have my inheritance. I can buy them back for you."

"It doesn't work that way," he protested. "Nobody will sell me back the good horses, and Trench—"

"Then I will buy you better horses. You must sell them to save Olinda."

"I couldn't . . . I mean, it would take too long to arrange and—"

"It will not take long at all. Mr. Miles, Elizabeth's father, he said he is buying horses for something. What was it, Mr. Bates?"

Gideon started a little at being consulted. He'd almost forgotten his role in this. It took him a moment to remember what she was talking about, though. "Oh yes, he said he was buying racehorses for a consortium." Which is what he'd said at the dinner at the Senora's other fiancé's dinner party. "They're . . . uh . . . looking for bargains, I think."

"That is what you must do," the Senora said. "You will save Olinda by selling your horses and afterward I will buy you a stable fit for a king."

# CHAPTER THIRTEEN

PLAINLY, NOLAN DID NOT THINK THIS WAS A VERY GOOD IDEA at all, but the Senora didn't give him much of a chance to object. "Mr. Bates, do you know how we may contact Mr. Miles?"

This was something he could easily answer. "He came home with us after . . . after we left the church. I'm sure he's still there." In fact, he was positive. The Old Man must have expected this development and would have remained where Gideon could easily reach him.

"Will you telephone him, please? Perhaps he can help us."

Gideon went to telephone his father-in-law. Elizabeth answered and she didn't seem at all surprised when he told her what he wanted. The Old Man came on the line and assured Gideon he would hasten over to the Senora's hotel to assist him.

The Senora had ordered some refreshments, which arrived while they waited. Gideon wasn't particularly hungry, having eaten at home, but he noticed Nolan didn't hesitate to sample the small sandwiches and tea cakes that the Senora had obviously considered sufficient.

The Old Man arrived in good time and accepted the Senora's offer of coffee, which she had to order special for him since the tea on the original order was now stone-cold.

While they waited for it to arrive, the Old Man explained to Nolan that he was representing a group of businessmen who wanted to purchase a stable of racehorses that they would own in common. They were prepared to pay what the horses were worth, but they didn't want to be gouged.

"We will need to get the most we can for the horses," the Senora said, "for Olinda's sake." Her large eyes were swimming with tears again, Gideon noticed. Who could refuse her?

"I understand," the Old Man said. "You must ransom Olinda. Which horses are you willing to sell, Nolan?"

Nolan swallowed audibly and he said, "None of them, really, but I've got to help Paulita. Can't let that poor girl spend any more time with those kidnappers, can we?"

"Certainly not," the Old Man said, looking every bit as concerned as the Senora would have wanted. "Perhaps you'll tell me about the horses you intend to sell and their records, so I can make you an offer."

"Sebastian will be selling all of his horses," the Senora said, taking Nolan's hand in both of hers. "He is willing to make this sacrifice for me, and I am very grateful."

The Old Man looked suitably surprised, but he accepted her assurance without question. Nolan may have looked like he had swallowed a brick, but he made no protest. The Old Man asked Nolan some questions about his stable and the records of the horses and made notes in a small notebook he pulled from his inside jacket pocket. Nolan had an idea of what each horse was worth, and the Old Man either agreed or argued, depending on factors Gideon could not decipher. When they were finished, the

Old Man said, "Looks like you've got about seventy-five thousand worth of horseflesh here."

"More if I had time to run them a few more times," Nolan said almost bitterly.

"This is not enough, is it?" the Senora said. She still held Nolan's hand, although he didn't seem to even notice.

"It's not the quarter million you're short," the Old Man confirmed. "Not even close."

The Senora dropped Nolan's hand and covered her face as she broke into sobs.

"Paulita, don't cry," Nolan begged, suddenly focused on her instead of his lost horses.

"How can I not?" she said brokenly. "Olinda is at the mercy of horrible men and those who are supposed to love me cannot help."

"I'll help. I'm selling my whole stable. What more can I do?"

He hadn't actually asked the Old Man, but he seemed to think he'd been consulted. "You must have some cash tucked away, Nolan. Remember, the Senora is a wealthy woman. She can repay you twice over."

"I already told her, I have about ten thousand."

"But you must have—"

"Your farm," the Senora said, dropping her hands from her tear-streaked face and turning to him. "You could sell your farm."

Plainly, Nolan didn't like this idea at all, but he was also loath to say so. "I . . . Where would we live?"

"We can buy a mansion in the city. We can buy another farm, and you can fill it with your new horses," the Senora said, plainly desperate. "I am a wealthy woman, Sebastian. You cannot cling to some little farm when my sister is in mortal danger."

"It's not a little farm," he argued. "It's prime pastureland.

Where will I keep my horses if I . . ." He seemed to suddenly realize this would not be a problem. "Oh."

"It is only for a few days, my love," the Senora said. "Only until we have Olinda back and she can marry Hernando. Then the money will not matter."

"But Trench . . ." he tried. "Irene raised him. What will she say?"

"She will say we saved Olinda," the Senora said with confidence she had no right to feel. "How much do you think the farm is worth? Would it be enough to reach the ransom?"

"I . . . I doubt it, but it would go a long way," Nolan said.

"Will your friends want to buy Sebastian's farm as well?" the Senora asked. "They will need a place to keep the horses when the racing season ends."

The Old Man seemed uncertain, which was unusual for him, but he said, "I can certainly ask them, and you're right, they will need a place to keep the horses and train them. I assume your farm is in good condition."

"The very best," Nolan insisted.

"They'll want me to look it over, I'm sure," the Old Man said. "But I promise to get you top dollar for it, Paulita."

"What is top dollar?" she asked with a puzzled frown.

"The most money possible. My loyalties should be to the men I represent, but in this case, Olinda's safety is what matters most. These men can afford to contribute to the cause, even if they don't know what the cause is."

"But what shall I do for the rest?" the Senora said, realizing she still had not reached her goal. "How much more do I need?"

"I don't know," the Old Man said. "We'll have to see how much we can charge for the farm and if I can talk them into buying it as well."

"But you can," the Senora said. "You must."

"I know how important this is, and I will do whatever I can to help you save Olinda."

"But what if I sell everything and you pay the ransom, and they still don't let her go?" Nolan asked.

The Senora and the Old Man looked at him in horror and even Gideon couldn't believe he'd said such a thing to the woman he supposedly loved.

"We'll certainly make sure they don't get the money until we know Olinda is safe," the Old Man said after a long, awkward moment of silence.

"Do you have a lot of experience dealing with kidnappers, Miles?" Nolan asked sarcastically.

Gideon thought he just might, but he didn't say so.

"Of course not," the Old Man said. "But it just stands to reason. They can't expect to get paid if they can't produce Olinda."

"The ransom note says the money must be in cash," the Senora reminded them. "Will that be difficult?"

"It will take some time, I'm sure," Gideon said. "And selling the horses and the farm will require some paperwork, but my staff is at your disposal to handle everything as quickly as possible."

"How much time?" the Senora asked, her voice quivering. "My poor Olinda . . ."

"We can't get any of the money until the banks open on Monday," Gideon said. "The paperwork for the sale of the horses and farm can be done fairly quickly, since you have a buyer in place."

"And my clients have the money in hand," the Old Man said. "They wanted to be prepared to act quickly if necessary to get what they wanted."

"And you'll speak with them today?" the Senora asked.

The Old Man smiled. "I will certainly try. I don't need to

speak with all of them, so that will help. I will have an answer for you by Monday. What will you do for the rest of the money, though?"

The Senora shook her head. "I will return to the friends who have helped me before. They all know Olinda is kidnapped. They will take advantage of me, but it cannot be helped."

If she'd been expecting Nolan to rise to the occasion and suddenly announce that he had been holding back, she was disappointed. Nolan looked a bit sick instead, and Gideon guessed that he was giving the Senora everything he possessed of value. If Gideon hadn't known of Elizabeth's plans to return her share of the con to Irene, he would have been forced to protest this impoverishment.

Nolan would probably bounce back from this. Men like him knew how to make money, and he'd rebuild his fortune using whatever means were available to him. And Gideon reminded himself of the way Nolan had treated Cal Regan, who had been crippled in service to Nolan and then abandoned. He'd been just as cruel to his own daughter, too, although, knowing Irene, she would probably take her father in, disregarding what was sure to be Elizabeth's counsel against it.

Hernando suddenly emerged from the bedroom, glancing around expectantly. "Are you finished? Have you found a way to ransom Olinda?"

"Almost," the Senora replied. "We will still need some help from our friends, but Sebastian has agreed to sell his stable of horses to help us."

Hernando seemed shocked at this. "His entire stable?"

"And also his farm," the Old Man confirmed. "You are very fortunate that he is willing to be so generous."

Hernando stared at Nolan in wonder for a long moment, and

Nolan refused to meet his eye. Plainly, this was killing him, but he was much too proud to back down now.

"I'm doing it for Paulita," he said.

"And I will always be grateful," she told him.

W HAT HAPPENS NEXT?" GIDEON ASKED THE OLD MAN when they were in a cab on their way back to Gideon's house.

"Just what you told the Senora. You'll meet me and Nolan at your office on Monday to complete the sale of the horses."

"Who is he selling them to?"

The Old Man cleared his throat. "American Horse Breeders."

Gideon couldn't help being impressed. "And who is that?"

The Old Man shrugged. "Me."

Gideon was no longer impressed. "You'll own the farm and the horses?" This couldn't be good.

"Don't look at me like that, Gideon. I have no interest in the farm or the racehorses. I have promised Paulina I will return them to Irene for a reasonable fee."

Gideon managed an apologetic smile or what he hoped looked like one because he didn't feel apologetic, but he'd discuss this with Elizabeth before he drew up any paperwork. Besides, he had another concern. "Who is supplying the money to buy all this?"

This time the Old Man's smile held a trace of pity. "Why, Mr. Boodle, of course."

T HE OLD MAN DECLINED GIDEON'S INVITATION TO COME IN-side with him. He had already overstayed his welcome at the Bates house, he claimed, and he left Gideon on the sidewalk as the cab carried him away to wherever it was he lived. Gideon suddenly realized he had no idea, which was probably just as well.

"Didn't Buster come with you?" his mother asked when he reached the parlor.

Gideon tried to ignore the fact that his mother was now calling Mr. Miles by his childhood nickname, a name he had heard only the Old Man's sister use. They were getting far too cozy for Gideon's taste, although how he could prevent that, he had no idea. "He said he had some business to attend to."

"I'm sure he does," Elizabeth said. "Let me get you something cool to drink and you can tell us all about your visit with the Senora."

Thus fortified, Gideon shared what he knew and his concerns about the ownership of the horses.

"I'm sure Mr. Miles can be trusted to do the right thing," his mother said.

Which was exactly what Gideon did not trust him to do. "I know Elizabeth would make sure everything is going the way it should," he said, knowing Elizabeth was not really in charge of this con.

Elizabeth gave him the same pitying look the Old Man had given him. "Is there some way that you can make Irene one of the owners of this Horse Breeders thing?"

"I could make her the only owner with the right paperwork, but she'd have to sign."

"Could you really? Oh, darling, that would be so perfect!" Elizabeth said, squeezing his hand that she had been holding throughout his report.

"Except for getting her to sign."

"Don't worry about that. Mother Bates and I will see to it that she signs whatever is necessary. How much time do we have?"

"I expect it will take a few days for Livingston to get the cash together. Your father said he has the cash ready to buy the horses. The Senora needs to make up the difference between what the kidnappers want and what Livingston and Nolan are able to provide, too."

"Oh, darling, she doesn't need to do that. It's not like Olinda is really kidnapped, and I guarantee, the person collecting the ransom is not going to stop to count it."

Gideon blinked in surprise. "Oh yes. I forgot."

"I forget, too, dear," his mother said. "It's very confusing."

She had no idea.

E LIZABETH DECIDED SHE WOULD JUST HAVE TO BUY HERSELF a motorcar with her own money and surprise Gideon. He was much too fond of her to be really angry. He probably wanted a motorcar as much as she did but just considered it an extravagance. In the meantime, on Monday morning, she and Mother Bates had to take the train out to the hospital where Cal Regan was still a patient, since they no longer knew where the Nolans were living now that the racing had moved to Empire City in Yonkers. A telephone call to the hospital had reassured them that Irene still visited Regan daily, so they hoped to catch her mid-morning, after she would have observed morning workouts and before the actual races started at two thirty.

Cal Regan was alone when they arrived, and he was understandably surprised to see them. They hadn't been to visit him for nearly three weeks. Since they weren't family or even close friends before Mr. Nolan invited them to watch the Belmont Stakes, this wasn't particularly surprising. Their showing up today was probably more surprising.

Mother Bates presented him with a cake she had carried all the way from the city and asked about his progress. After getting over his surprise, he admitted he'd been using crutches to get around some of the time and hoped to be walking out of the hospital soon.

They kept him chatting far longer than Elizabeth would have thought possible—society ladies really knew how to spend a lot of time talking about nothing at all of consequence—until Irene finally arrived. She was even more shocked to see them than Regan had been.

"What a nice surprise," Irene said, although she looked as if she thought it was more of a surprise than it was nice. Still, she couldn't complain about visitors to the man she loved.

Except Elizabeth couldn't help noticing the decided tension between Irene and Regan. She had gone to the bed where he lay after greeting Elizabeth and Mother Bates, but she didn't kiss his cheek or even pat it, and she definitely didn't make eye contact with him. And were her eyes a little red?

For his part, Regan did look at Irene but with more sadness than affection. Had Irene finally confessed about the baby and Regan had taken the news badly? But no, that would be an entirely different kind of tension. This was two people unable to reach an agreement but still unable to separate. So, a lovers' quarrel. Elizabeth could deal with that.

They made polite conversation for a few minutes, or as polite as it could be with Cal and Irene still obviously uncomfortable with each other.

"Perhaps you'd like to take a walk with me," Elizabeth said to Irene. "I'd like to speak to you about your father."

"You can talk in front of me," Regan said with a scowl. "Especially if you haven't got anything nice to say about him."

Irene ignored him. "I'd love to take a walk."

They ended up at the bench where they had sat before, and Elizabeth waited until she was sure no one else was around.

"Now tell me what you and Mr. Regan are quarreling about."

Irene stiffened, but she tried to look surprised. "I don't know what you're talking about."

"Yes, you do. Did you tell him about the baby?"

"Heavens no! He doesn't deserve to know about the baby." She was furious now.

"I knew it. You're quarreling. If it's not about the baby, what is it?"

Irene looked as if she might deny it again, but then her eyes filled with tears. "He wants me to forget him."

"Forget him?"

"Yes, forget him and get on with my life. He'll never be able to ride again, and he can't support a wife, and he's ashamed and he can hardly bear to look me in the eye knowing how I'm wasting myself on him."

Elizabeth automatically handed Irene a handkerchief as she broke down crying. After a few moments, Elizabeth said, "Is that all?" surprising Irene into a tearful laugh.

"Isn't it enough?"

"I suppose it is, but he's being very silly. We can excuse him because he must feel very helpless right now, but he's still being silly."

"Yes, he is, but how can I tell him about the baby now, when he's already convinced he'll never be able to marry me?"

"I can see why you'd hesitate."

"And you can see why I'm furious with him. I come here every day and every day he tells me to stop coming. Sometimes I think I should just smash him over the head with his bedpan."

"I can see how that would appeal, but it wouldn't help at all."

Irene gave a final sniff and mopped the last of her tears. "No, it wouldn't."

"And now I'm here to give you more bad news."

Irene looked at her in alarm. "What could be worse than that?"

"Your father has agreed to help pay the ransom for Olinda," Elizabeth said.

Irene sighed. "I'm not surprised. I think he'd do anything for the Senora, but I don't know how much he can contribute. He doesn't confide in me, but I know he hasn't been making much money these past few years and training racehorses is very expensive. He's even been trying to economize."

"He is talking about selling the horses to raise the money," Elizabeth said.

Irene jumped to her feet and glared down at Elizabeth. "You can't mean it!"

"I do mean it. That's why I'm here. Gideon was horrified when he was asked to assist with the contracts, so we discussed how we could protect your interests."

"My interests? I don't have any interests in the horses. Father owns them, and he's made sure I understand that I have no part of that."

"You would be amazed at what attorneys can do." Elizabeth was certainly amazed. Gideon had worked all day on Sunday to prove it. "Gideon has drawn up some papers that will make it impossible for your father to sell the horses or the farm—"

"The *farm*!" she cried, outraged.

Elizabeth glanced around to see if they were attracting any attention. "Perhaps you should sit down and listen to what I have to tell you. You'll feel a lot better if you do."

Irene sat down in a huff. "I know that woman looks like my mother, but that's no reason to give her everything we own!"

"In her defense, she has promised to replace the horses and buy your father a new farm when she comes into her inheritance."

"She can't replace the horses. How could we replace Trench?" Irene demanded.

"I'm not saying it's a good idea. I'm just telling you what they discussed. So, as I said, Gideon has drawn up some papers. All you need to do is sign them and your father won't be able to do what he is planning."

Irene frowned in confusion. "I don't understand any of this."

"You don't need to understand it. You just need to sign the papers, so you'll be protected."

"Are you sure if I sign, then Father can't sell everything?"

"That's right."

Elizabeth reached into the satchel she had carried from the city and pulled out the papers. "You sign and I'll witness your signature."

Elizabeth held out the sheaf of papers, but Irene leaned away from them. "Father always says you should never sign something without reading it."

"Then read it."

"I won't understand it even if I do!" she cried in dismay.

"Then take my word. We're doing this to protect you."

"But the Senora is your friend. Why would you choose me over her?" Irene protested.

"Because you're my friend, too, and you need my help more than she does."

"If my father really is selling everything he owns, then that last part is probably true."

Elizabeth smiled. "So, sign the papers. I even brought along a pen." She was pleased to see the fountain pen hadn't leaked, and she had to dab off only a little bit of ink on the tip before it was ready for use. Irene made a show of reading a few lines of the top sheet before giving up. Gideon had made the wording nearly incomprehensible to the layperson, but he had promised Elizabeth it was exactly what would serve. Irene signed in the places Elizabeth indicated, and then Elizabeth signed as witness. When the ink was dry, she tucked the papers back in her bag.

"Now let's see if we can talk some sense into Mr. Regan, and failing that, I promise you that as soon as Olinda's kidnapping is cleared up, things will greatly improve for you and Mr. Regan. Oh, and one more thing. You will need to come into the city on Wednesday and spend the night at my house."

"Spend the night? Why?"

"I'm afraid I can't tell you, but it involves the transfer of the ownership of the horses, and you need to be in the city early on Thursday morning. Trust me, Irene. I'm doing this for you."

S MITH, GIDEON'S CLERK, WAS HAPPY TO ESCORT GIDEON'S wife and mother into his office that afternoon. They didn't exactly have an appointment, but Gideon had warned Smith he expected a visit from them. Smith was a stickler for appointments.

"Did she sign?" he asked without even bothering to greet them.

"Of course she signed," his mother said with a disapproving frown. "When has Elizabeth ever failed?"

Gideon jumped up and skirted his desk and took Elizabeth in his arms. "Never," he said, and kissed her soundly, making his mother laugh in surprise.

"I'm so glad Smith didn't see that," Elizabeth said a bit breathlessly. "I'd never be able to look him in the face again."

"He'd never be able to look you in the face again," Gideon corrected her.

"I still don't understand how you can make sure the ownership of the farm and the horses passes to Irene," his mother said. "I know lawyers can be very clever but—"

"Mother, when have you known *me* to fail?" Gideon chided.

His mother was obviously less impressed with his successes. "Once or twice."

"Well, not this time. Sit down and I'll explain."

He started, using the terminology he'd use with one of his colleagues, but both women raised their hands to stop him.

"In plain English, please," Elizabeth cried, laughing.

He sighed and started again. "Your father has some company called American Horse Breeders. He claims it's a partnership, except he doesn't have any partners. He expects me to draw up the contract for the sale of the horses and the farm to this company."

"Or more correctly, to him," Elizabeth said.

"Exactly. So I created a company called *America* Horse Breeders and made Irene the sole owner of it. The contracts for the sale are made out in the new name. One of the documents Irene signed was a power of attorney allowing your father to sign the sale documents on her behalf. When he signs tomorrow, Irene will own the horses and the farm."

"And hopefully, the Old Man won't notice the change in the name of the firm," Elizabeth said. "Oh, Gideon, I can't believe you're going to con my father."

He blinked in surprise. "I didn't think of it that way."

"And isn't it lying?" his mother asked, obviously fascinated by her son's ingenuity. Gideon's aversion to lying was well-known.

"Not at all," he said, although he wasn't nearly as certain as he was trying to sound. "I'm simply correcting a mistake, since the Senora's intention is that ultimately, Irene own the horses and farm. This eliminates any possible issues that might interfere."

"And isn't that why people consult attorneys in the first place?" Elizabeth asked his mother, who had to agree.

"But couldn't Mr. Miles use the power of attorney to do other things in Irene's name?" his mother asked.

"No. It's limited to this one transaction."

"Gideon," Elizabeth said, frowning suddenly. "Have you

considered what my father's reaction will be when he realizes you have tricked him?"

"I have," Gideon said. "I am prepared to deal with it."

"He might be furious," Elizabeth warned.

"Then I hope he wouldn't take it out on you."

Elizabeth smiled again. "I'd like to see him try. This will be very interesting. Has Mr. Livingston given you his share of the money yet?"

"Not yet, but I expect him tomorrow morning. He sent me word he needed a day for his bank to get the funds together. Not many banks can give someone that much cash at one time without running short themselves."

"But I thought banks just kept everyone's money in their safe in case they needed it," his mother said.

"It's much more complicated than that, I'm afraid. At any rate, Livingston must have some influence to get that much on such short notice. Makes me think he could have funded the entire ransom."

"But why should he?" Elizabeth said. "The Senora has already agreed to marry him, but if something goes wrong, he might not get repaid."

"Financing a ransom demand cannot be considered a sound business decision," his mother said wisely, making Gideon and Elizabeth laugh.

"It certainly cannot," Elizabeth agreed. "When are you expecting the Old Man and Mr. Nolan?"

"Tomorrow morning. I told them I'd need a day to draw up the sale documents."

Elizabeth smiled mysteriously. "And then we'll be able to rescue poor Olinda from the clutches of her evil kidnappers."

Gideon smiled back. "That's what we're all looking forward to."

IDEON FOUND HIMSELF ODDLY NERVOUS AS HE PRESENTED the documents for Mr. Nolan and Mr. Miles to sign on Tuesday morning. He hoped it didn't show, and he was pleased to see his hands were steady as he placed the papers in front of each man.

The Old Man gave no hint of what he was feeling. In fact, he was probably not feeling anything at all. This wasn't his con, either, and he wasn't even getting a cut of the score, just a flat payment for his role in it. Elizabeth had explained that the Senora would pay him out of her share. The Senora's share would be much, much larger since she had "borrowed" money from several rich socialites long before Olinda even thought about being kidnapped. She wouldn't share that money with anyone beyond paying the expenses she had incurred and paying the folks who had helped her a flat fee. The ransom money was a different story. She would split that with Elizabeth, who would get 45 percent. Elizabeth had been vague on how they would split the cost of the horses and the farm, but she had ensured that Irene would own it all outright in any case, so dividing it up would be impossible. He wondered if the Senora knew what she'd done and how angry she'd be when she found out.

"I've just signed away my heart and soul," Nolan said as he passed the last of the signed documents back to Gideon.

"I know this must be difficult, Mr. Nolan. You've devoted a large part of your life to building your racing stable," Gideon said.

"And yet, it hasn't brought you financial success, has it?" the Old Man said. He somehow managed to make the question sound merely curious and not insulting.

"Not as much as I expected, but nothing can match the feeling you get standing in the winner's circle, Miles."

"I'll make sure to do it when one of our horses wins, then," he said with a smile.

"And you've got the money?" Nolan asked a little belatedly.

"Oh yes." The Old Man picked up the small bag he'd carried in and opened it, displaying fifteen bundles of hundred-dollar bills wrapped with bank bands that indicated each contained ten thousand dollars. This would supposedly pay for the horses and the farm, although Gideon knew closer examination would show each packet contained only a hundred-dollar bill on the top and bottom of the stack. Everything in between was just blank paper. This type of deception was called boodle, which is why the Old Man had joked the purchaser would be Mr. Boodle. "I'm sure Mr. Bates will count it when we're gone, but I assure you, it's all there. I would never shortchange a lady, especially when someone's life is at stake." Oddly, this was all probably true, although it didn't apply in this case.

"Of course not," Nolan said, a bit chagrinned at having been thought petty enough to have questioned the payment on this deal. "When . . ." He swallowed and tried again. "When would your clients want to take possession of the farm?"

"They understand that this has been rather sudden for you and the horses probably aren't even at the farm at the moment."

"That's right. Most of them are at Empire City. The ones I'm racing anyway."

"Someone will be by to take a look at them and make arrangements for the fees to be paid in a day or so, I'm sure. In the meantime, you don't have to rush to move out of the farm. No one in the consortium is planning to live there, so take a month to find a new place. I'm sure the Senora will have some ideas on that."

"Yes, I'm sure she will," Nolan said somewhat sadly.

Gideon knew a pang of regret. Nolan looked like a broken man. Nolan had treated Irene and Cal Regan poorly, but did anyone deserve what they'd done to him?

"Well, I'll leave this with your clerk, shall I?" the Old Man said, rising and indicating the bag of money he held. "I understand Livingston left his contribution here as well and the Senora will pick up the money on her way to ransom Olinda."

Nolan perked up at that. Angry color flooded his pale face. "Livingston? He's giving the Senora money, too?"

"She had to borrow it from someone," the Old Man said. "He was able to provide a good portion of it."

"That son of a—" Nolan was half out of his chair when Gideon interrupted him.

"Yes, Mr. Livingston was quite generous, and you weren't able to help her, Mr. Nolan." At that, Nolan sank back down in his chair, defeated by his lack of funds. "The Senora will pick up the money here. I believe she is only awaiting instructions from the kidnappers. She was to place an advertisement in the newspaper when she had the funds, something about needing to meet with Mr. Jones about an urgent matter. She can do that now."

"I'm sure she's terrified for her poor sister," Mr. Miles said. "Even if they get her back unharmed, she will never be the same."

Gideon didn't think that was a comforting thing to say to the Senora's fiancé, even if he didn't care a fig for Olinda, but Nolan said, "Let us pray she's unharmed."

Gideon caught the twinkle in the Old Man's eye. "Oh yes, let us. Thank you for handling this, Gideon. My clients are very grateful."

"Don't worry, they'll get my bill," Gideon replied, earning another twinkle.

"What do I owe you, Bates?" Mr. Nolan asked, rising a bit unsteadily to his feet. Gideon fought the urge to take his arm. He wouldn't like that.

"Mr. Miles's clients will be responsible for the entire transaction," he said quite generously and showed both men out.

Now all they had to do was wait.

# CHAPTER FOURTEEN

HE WAITING WAS ALWAYS THE WORST, ELIZABETH OB-
served. The beginning of a con was exciting, identifying the
mark and figuring out how to rope him in, telling the tale and
making sure he's convinced. Then came the difficult part, sending
the mark to get his money and then waiting for the final play. At
least this time the money was already in the safe at Gideon's law
firm. All they were waiting for now were the instructions on how
to pay the ransom and recover Olinda.

The Senora's ad appeared in the *New York Times* on Wednesday morning, and she received another message from the kidnappers by the afternoon mail. She and Hernando were alone at the
hotel when it arrived. The Senora, having two fiancés, couldn't
very well keep either or both at her side without betraying her
perfidy, so she had instructed them to leave her in peace. Since
Nolan was actually staying in the same hotel, keeping him away
was more difficult, and she was forced to inform him that she had
received her instructions, although she summoned Gideon before
doing so.

"What does it say?" Nolan demanded the moment he entered the suite.

The Senora sat on the sofa in the suite's parlor, dressed all in black, her eyes wet from tears. She looked suitably tragic. "Tomorrow at dawn, we are to deliver the money to a certain place in Central Park." She glanced at Gideon for help.

"A clump of bushes near the bandstand. The note says Olinda will be tied up and waiting in the bandstand itself, so all we have to do is drop off the bag with the money in it and go straight to her."

"Mr. Bates assures me we should be able to see Olinda from the place we are to leave the money, so we will know she has been freed."

"At dawn, you say," Nolan mused. "Then we should go early and wait for them to bring her. We could catch them then and they'd never be able to do a thing like this again."

"And risk Olinda's life?" the Senora cried in horror. "It would be the work of a moment for them to cut her throat if they thought we had betrayed them."

"I would like to catch these men, too," Gideon said quite honestly, "but we must honor the Senora's wishes. The plan seems simple enough. We can even drive right up to the bandstand since no one will be in the park at that hour."

"You have a motorcar?" Nolan asked in surprise.

"Mr. Miles has offered to drive me," the Senora said.

"Miles?" Nolan echoed in disgust. Plainly, he didn't like the idea of another man assisting his fiancée. "I should go with you."

The Senora took his hand and gave him a look so loving, Gideon almost believed it himself. "You are so gallant to offer, my love, but we cannot bring too many men. The kidnappers might think we are planning to overtake them."

"And we should, but I will respect your wishes, Paulita, and not go along. I can still go to the park, though. I can come in by another entrance and walk to a place where I can see what is happening and come to your aid if necessary."

The Senora really did look alarmed at this prospect, but Gideon and Nolan discussed the layout of the park, and Gideon suggested a spot that he later assured the Senora was far enough away that Nolan wouldn't be able to interfere or quickly reach the bandstand.

"And the kidnappers will not see you waiting there?" the Senora asked, plainly still not convinced.

"I promise to stay hidden. I wouldn't risk Olinda's life for anything," he said, raising a hand as if taking an oath.

Gideon didn't think he really cared that much for poor Olinda, but he was wise to pretend he did for the Senora's benefit.

They had barely gotten rid of Nolan when Livingston arrived without being invited. He said he figured the Senora would have gotten a response by then and she was able to convince him it had just arrived.

They had much the same discussion with him as with Nolan, and as expected, Livingston also insisted on accompanying the Senora to rescue Olinda. Gideon was able to suggest yet another spot where Livingston could observe without being close enough to interfere or be seen by Nolan.

"You should go with me, Bates. If things go wrong, we'll need all the help we can get," Livingston said.

Gideon turned his questioning gaze to the Senora. "Yes, Mr. Bates, you should go. You can make sure Mr. Livingston does not do anything *heroic*." The emphasis she put on the word "heroic" clearly meant *foolish*, and Gideon got her message.

"I would be happy to go." He wouldn't miss this for anything.

GIDEON HAD A DIFFICULT TIME FINDING A CAB TO TAKE HIM to the East Sixty-Fifth Street entrance to Central Park on Thursday morning since it was still actually the middle of the night. He didn't relish the idea of walking, which would have taken him at least an hour, but he ended up having to traverse several blocks before finding a cab parked, the driver snoring in his seat. He seemed annoyed at being awakened, but Gideon promised to double the fare, so he wouldn't be late, at least.

The sky was still dark when he reached the entrance to the park, and as promised, he found Livingston waiting there for him. He had half expected the man to go on alone, so he'd be free to do something *heroic* if the opportunity presented itself, and he was gratified to see Livingston had obeyed the Senora's instructions, at least so far.

"What have you got there?" Gideon asked when they'd exchanged greetings, gesturing to the oddly shaped case that hung by a shoulder strap at Livingston's side.

"Binoculars. We'll need them if we hope to see what is happening, since we'll be at least a half mile away."

Gideon wasn't sure the Senora really wanted Livingston and Nolan to see what was happening, but there was nothing he could do about it now. "Let's go, shall we? We have just enough time to reach our spot before dawn."

The newspapers had reported dawn would occur at 4:43 that morning, and the rising sun wouldn't be doing much to illuminate the park at that point. The long promenade that cut through the middle of the mall and ran past the colorful Mould Bandstand at the north end was known as Elm Alley because it was lined with huge elm trees. The leaves of those trees would shade the area from moon- or starlight as well as the encroaching sunlight. Even with binoculars, it would be difficult to see anything, which was probably what the Senora was hoping.

They reached the spot they had agreed upon for Livingston to wait, but he kept moving. "Where are you going?" Gideon demanded, hurrying to catch up.

"To the promenade. You can't see anything from here. We'll have a clear view of everything if we're at the promenade."

Gideon reminded him of the Senora's wishes. "And what if the kidnappers see us?"

Livingston gave a scornful grunt. "They won't. It's dark. Haven't you noticed?"

Gideon had no argument for that. They reached the promenade at four forty-five, according to Gideon's wristwatch, just in time for the official dawn. Gideon thought he saw a faint glow to the east, but he was probably imagining it, or it was an electric light burning in some building nearby. At any rate, the promenade was still in darkness and the bandstand merely one slightly darker shadow among many.

"Who's there?" a voice called from their left, and Gideon winced. Just what they needed. "If you're the kidnappers, I'm armed!"

"Nolan, is that you?" Livingston called in disgust.

"Of course it's me. Who else would be here?"

"Me, for one."

"Who's that with you?" Nolan demanded, emerging from the darkness.

"Bates."

"I should have guessed. Is Livingston paying you to be here?" Nolan asked with just a trace of bitterness.

What a good idea, but Gideon didn't say so. "I came because the Senora asked me to."

"She asked me, too," Nolan claimed.

"She didn't ask either of you," Gideon said to forestall an argument between the two suitors. "You both insisted on being here and—"

"Something is happening," Livingston said, pawing at the case he carried to retrieve his binoculars.

"What have you got there?" Nolan asked, but he got no reply because Livingston had lifted the binoculars to his eyes and the answer was obvious.

"It's a motorcar coming down the promenade." Usually, this area would be closed to motorcars and clogged with pedestrians come to enjoy the natural beauty or to hear a concert, but now the whole park was deserted except for the occasional bum sleeping it off on a bench.

Gideon and Nolan could see the headlights now. The motorcar was moving slowly, and then it stopped. The lights were rather blinding, so it was difficult to see what was happening, but the passenger door opened.

"Did someone get out?" Nolan asked anxiously.

"Yes, but I can't tell who. Now they're back inside."

"They must have dropped off the ransom," Gideon guessed.

The door closed and the motor began to move again. It stopped beside the bandstand. The steps leading up to it faced the promenade and in the glow from the headlights, they could see something was on the steps.

"What is that? Is that Olinda?" Nolan asked.

"Something white, like a large bundle," Livingston reported. "But it's not moving."

"The instructions said she would be bound so she couldn't run away," Gideon reminded them, fighting an urge to snatch the binoculars from Livingston.

But then even Gideon and Nolan could see what was happening. Both doors of the motorcar opened and three people emerged.

The Old Man would have been driving and one was clearly the Senora. The third was probably Hernando, who would naturally go to rescue his fiancée. The three figures hurried to the bandstand steps where the white bundle lay.

An eerie sound pierced the silence, a woman's scream of anguish.

"What is it? What's wrong?" Nolan demanded.

"I don't know. I can't see," Livingston said. He lowered the binoculars as if he couldn't bear to look anymore. Gideon snatched them away. It took him a moment to focus on the right spot.

"It must be Olinda," he said. "One of the men picked her up and is carrying her to the car."

"We can see that, but look at her," Nolan said with horror.

Indeed, her body was completely limp. No one was trying to revive her, either.

"She looks . . . dead," Livingston said.

"Maybe they drugged her," Nolan said a little hopefully.

"Why are we standing here?" Livingston said suddenly, and began to run toward the motorcar.

But it was already moving, making the awkward back-and-forth movements to turn around.

Nolan took off after Livingston, leaving Gideon to follow, hampered by the heavy binoculars, which he had to carry in his hands since Livingston still had the case.

They didn't run far because the motor soon disappeared down the Transverse Road to East Seventy-Second Street. Livingston stopped when he realized the chase was hopeless. "Where are they going?"

"A hospital, probably," Gideon said. "They'd want a doctor for Olinda, I'm sure."

"Where's the nearest hospital?" Nolan asked.

They argued about that for a few minutes. By then dawn had

really come and the night was fading into a washed-out morning. Every day this week had been in the mid-eighties, and today would probably be the same. The city had really never cooled off from yesterday, and all three of them were sweating from the brief run.

"They could've gone anywhere," Livingston said finally.

"Why don't you just go home and I'm sure the Senora will contact you," Gideon tried.

"Since my home right now is the same hotel where she is living, I think that's an excellent idea," Nolan said. "No matter where else she goes, she'll go back there eventually."

"And if that's where you're going, then that's where I'm going," Livingston decided and headed off.

Gideon caught up long enough to return his binoculars and then allowed the two men to stalk off, together but obviously hating it, leaving Gideon to wonder that neither of them had yet revealed that he was engaged to the Senora. They were such rivals that it was only natural for at least one of them to brag to the other about his victory. The Senora must have a strong hold over them to have won their silence. Before he could even finish the thought, he was distracted by the sound of running feet.

Livingston and Nolan were returning in an alarming hurry.

"The ransom!" Nolan called as they passed him, heading toward the bandstand.

Of course! They hadn't seen anyone come to collect it yet. They'd been distracted, that was true, but if there was a chance . . .

Gideon followed at a more leisurely pace, admiring the way the rising sun illuminated the golden dome of the bandstand as the various bright colors of its design became visible. What an interesting place to leave a kidnap victim, he mused.

Nolan reached the clump of bushes first and emerged with a Gladstone bag. It was open and he held it for them to see. "Empty."

"What? That can't be," Livingston insisted. "Nobody's been here."

"We weren't really paying attention," Gideon reminded him. "We were watching them find Olinda."

"But how could someone have come in and taken it without being seen?" Nolan argued.

"I have no idea, but remember how dark it was and the motor's headlights were blinding, and we were so far away." He turned and looked south on the promenade. "I can't even see where we were standing from here."

Livingston was thrashing around in the bushes, and he came up with one stray hundred-dollar bill. "It was here, all right, and now it's gone."

"They didn't even take the bag so they wouldn't be spotted carrying it," Nolan marveled.

"Probably dressed like a bum and dumped the money into a gunny sack," Livingston said bitterly, as if such cleverness were a personal affront.

"They outwitted all of us," Nolan said.

Gideon didn't point out that was the whole point of kidnapping someone. "So it seems."

"I guess we better get to the hotel," Livingston said after a moment of awkward silence. "There's no telling when the Senora will return, and I want to be there to greet her."

"You?" Nolan scoffed. "I'll be the one she turns to now, especially if Olinda is dead."

They were still bickering as they walked off, leaving Gideon once again to contemplate the beauty of the park. Since he was now almost to the Seventy-Second Street Transverse Road, and that was the one the suitors had used, he took his time, not wanting to catch them up.

He found a cab on Fifth Avenue after only a few blocks. He imagined things were getting very interesting at his house by now.

ELIZABETH HAD BEEN TRYING TO FIGURE OUT HOW TO JUS-tify waking poor Irene at literally the crack of dawn after she had been so reluctant to stay at the house overnight in the first place, but as usual Mother Bates had the answer.

"The Senora is returning here after ransoming Olinda," she explained, which also had the advantage of being the truth. Mercifully, Irene had not thought to ask why on earth the Senora would come here, probably because she wasn't quite awake yet.

Now Mother Bates sat with Elizabeth and Irene in the parlor, jumping at every sound, which was silly because when they finally did hear the motorcar approaching, there was no mistaking it. They all ran to the front door. Elizabeth threw it open just as the Senora emerged from the motor. Hernando held the door for her and then reached out to help Olinda. Both women expressed their thanks and headed up the front steps while Hernando got back in the motor and the Old Man drove them both away without another word.

"Olinda is rescued," the Senora said, smiling a little mysteriously.

Olinda was smiling a little mysteriously, too, but Irene didn't seem to notice.

"I'm so glad you're safe," Irene said when the two women were inside. "What a horrible ordeal."

Olinda did look as if she'd been through a horrible ordeal. Her white wedding dress was soiled and torn in a few places. Her hair was a tangled mess, and her face was dirty. She did, however, look happy to be rescued, at least.

"Come upstairs so you can get cleaned up," Mother Bates said to Olinda, who went with her without a word.

With a look of wonder, Irene watched her go. "She seems so calm. I'd be hysterical."

"Perhaps not," the Senora said with a smile. "Shall we go into the parlor? I have some things to tell you."

"Tell me?" Irene said in surprise.

"And you will come, too," she said to Elizabeth. "You need to hear this as well."

Elizabeth happily followed the two of them and got them seated together on the sofa. She took a chair opposite the sofa so she could watch them both for what promised to be a remarkable conversation.

But now that the time had come, the Senora seemed reluctant to start. She was clenching her hands together and she actually started to wring them. "Where to start? There is so much to tell."

"Start with the most important thing," Elizabeth suggested.

"The most important and the most difficult to say," the Senora said, but she visibly braced herself and continued, "Irene, the real reason I came to New York is because I wanted to see you. I wanted to see how you had turned out."

"Me?" Irene asked, bewildered. "How did you even know I existed?"

"Because"—she drew a deep breath—"because I do not just look like your mother. I am your mother."

Elizabeth gasped, but it was more because her suspicions were confirmed than because she was surprised.

Irene blinked a few times and then shook her head. "No, that . . . that's impossible. My mother is dead."

But the Senora shook her head, too. "Your father did try to kill me, but I managed to survive. I'm not dead, Irene, and I really am your mother."

"You died in childbirth," Irene tried weakly. "Your grave is at the farm."

The Senora smiled sadly. "Sebastian was very thorough, wasn't he? I wonder what is in that grave. I not only survived childbirth, but I raised you for almost a year. You were trying to walk by then. I would put out my fingers like this." She demonstrated. "And you would grab them with your little fists, and you would walk and walk until you fell down and then you would get up and walk again. So determined even then."

Irene stared at her in wonder. "I remember a woman's face, smiling at me."

"I always smiled at you. I loved you beyond reason, and I still do."

"Then why . . . ? Why did you disappear?"

The Senora sighed. "You know the story of how I jilted Daniel and married Sebastian."

"Yes. I've heard it all my life, although my father never liked to hear it."

"I'm sure he didn't. You see, it didn't take me long to realize I'd made a terrible mistake marrying Sebastian. He was . . . violent."

"Violent? You mean he hit you?" Irene asked, horrified.

"Yes, he did."

"Why didn't you leave him then?"

"I used to ask myself that, but I knew the answer, even then. The first time he hit me, I think he was as surprised as I was. He was so apologetic, begging me to forgive him and promising it would never happen again. Then he was so loving and kind and so devoted. For months. No woman ever had a better husband. By the time he hit me the second time, I was expecting you. I might have left even then, but he had moved me out to that awful farm. He had quarreled with my parents and told them they weren't welcome in our home. We had no close neighbors and he refused to let me make friends, even with the people at church. He'd make me stay home and tell people I was ill. I had no money and no one to help me, and then I had a baby to think of. I didn't know where to go or what to do."

Irene's anguish was plain to see. "But you did get away."

"Yes, when your father killed me."

Elizabeth thought her heart would stop. Irene let out a cry and tears flooded her eyes. "He couldn't."

"Oh, but he could. He tried to strangle me, and I must have passed out and he thought I was dead. I gather that he panicked and threw me in the back of a wagon and drove me to the river. It isn't far from our farm."

"No," Irene agreed faintly. "It isn't far."

"I woke up when I was in the wagon, but I didn't know where I was or what was happening. I couldn't make a sound, probably from the strangling, and I guess he didn't notice I was still alive or maybe he just didn't care. Anyway, he picked me up and threw me in the river. He must have thought my body would sink or float away and never be found."

Elizabeth had so many questions, but it wasn't her place to ask them. Fortunately, Irene did. "But didn't someone see?" Irene argued. "What about the men who work with the horses?"

"It was the middle of the night. He loved keeping me awake all night, telling me all the ways I fell short as a wife and mother and slapping me and punching me until I screamed in pain. Then I would have to stay awake all day taking care of you when I was exhausted and injured."

Irene just stared at her mother for a long moment, trying to take it all in. "But you didn't die."

"The cold water revived me enough that when I snagged on some tree roots, I was able to pull myself up onto the bank. I don't know how long I lay there, but long enough to realize I couldn't go home because if I did, he would just kill me again and this time he'd make sure I was dead."

Irene silently shook her head, not wanting to believe, but the tears running down her face betrayed her acceptance of the story. Elizabeth wanted to reach out to her friend, but she held back, knowing the Senora needed to finish her story.

"After sunup, a tinker found me. He was driving by in his wagon and saw what he thought was a dead body. He told me later he thought to steal any jewelry I might have, but I didn't have anything except my engagement ring. I decided to offer it to him, to bribe him to take me with him, but it was gone, lost in the river, I believed."

"But it wasn't lost in the river," Irene said, newly horrified.

"No, Sebastian must have taken it off what he thought was my dead finger."

Elizabeth gasped. "He gave you that ring again, thinking you were another woman."

"I almost fainted when I saw it. Luckily, he thought I was just surprised."

"And you didn't have the ring to bribe the tinker," Irene said, reminding her of the story.

"I had nothing but myself, so that was what I offered him, and he took me in."

Now Irene was angry. "You ran off with a strange man and left me, left your child behind!"

"Irene, you have to understand. Your father tried to kill me. I knew if I returned, he'd kill me for sure, and I'd be no use to you at all. But I knew he would never hurt you. He adored you. The reason he beat me, or at least the reason he always gave me, was that he knew I really loved Daniel Livingston. He never forgave me for choosing him first, even though I left him for Sebastian.

But you were innocent. Even when I was carrying you, he was always careful not to hit me in the stomach. You were his child, and he loved you in his way."

His way wasn't always good, Elizabeth couldn't help thinking, and she knew Irene must be thinking the same thing. She didn't say it, though.

"But you left me," Irene said instead.

"I intended to come back, I truly did, but my life has not been easy. The tinker was a snake oil salesman, and he taught me how to cheat people. After a time, I realized I was smarter than he was and better at cheating people, so I left him for a con man who taught me that trade. I learned to cheat people for a living, and I traveled all over the world, spending years at a time in different places so far from here that I couldn't even think of coming back. I know you can never forgive me, but please know that I never stopped thinking about you or loving you, and when I had a chance to come to New York, I decided the time had come."

"You decided the time had come to steal my father's money and ruin us," Irene said. "And now we have nothing and I'm going to have a baby and the father is a cripple who can't even support us."

"I did want to ruin your father, that's true," the Senora said. "But I never wanted to hurt *you*. Remember what your father has done. He fired Mr. Regan when he got hurt. He beat me time and again. He tried to murder me and thought he'd succeeded. He deserves what I've done to him."

"But I don't!" Irene cried.

The sound of the front door opening distracted them all. Elizabeth jumped up and opened the parlor door to find Gideon had just arrived.

"Where are your two cohorts?" she asked.

"They went to the Senora's hotel to wait for her to return. That should keep them busy for a while."

"Your timing is perfect, darling. Irene has just asked the Senora why she has left her penniless."

Gideon grinned, making Elizabeth wish she could kiss him, but there would be time for that later, when they were alone. He had done such a good job and he needed to be rewarded.

"But first," she said, "you should know that the Senora is really Mary Nolan."

He looked stunned. "How could that be?"

"It's a long story I will tell you later, but for now, I thought you should know."

"It does explain a lot about her behavior, doesn't it? And why she was so generous with Irene."

Elizabeth had to agree.

He followed her into the parlor and greeted Irene and the Senora, who were too busy staring uneasily at each other to even notice.

"Should I explain what we did with the farm and the horses, Paulina?" he asked.

"Please do. I'm not sure Irene would believe me."

Gideon took the chair beside Elizabeth's and said, "Your mother arranged to have you purchase the farm and all the horses your father owned." This was a little stretching of the truth, since Gideon had arranged it and simply told the Senora what he had done, but it wouldn't hurt to give Paulina the credit.

"But that's impossible. I don't even have any money of my own," Irene said.

"Don't worry about that. It's already happened and the Senora provided the, uh, payment," Gideon said, glancing at Elizabeth to remind her he couldn't lie, and he also couldn't quite tell the truth here, since no real money was provided.

"Those papers you signed for me?" Elizabeth said. "They cre-

ated a company called America Horse Breeders to buy everything. You are the owner of that company."

"That's . . . impossible," she said weakly.

"Not at all," Gideon assured her. "And we have the paperwork
to prove it."

"But when Father finds out, he'll be furious. He'll insist on
buying everything back."

"You can refuse to sell to him, but it doesn't matter because he
doesn't have the money anymore," the Senora said. "We used it
to pay the ransom and now it's gone."

"But you're going to pay him back," Irene remembered. "When
you get your inheritance."

"Except that I am not Paulita Padilla y de la Fuente viuda de
Chavez and there is no Chavez estate and I have no inheritance.
I am a con artist, remember? None of that was true."

Irene blinked a few times as she absorbed all this. "I . . . I
guess I do know that now. So, you aren't going to repay him."

"No, and he can't insist that you sell everything back to him,
even if he had the money to buy it. We also can't expect you to
run your stable of racehorses with no money, so you will also receive the rest of the ransom money as well."

"But you said the ransom money was gone," Irene said, obviously confused.

"And she's really only getting part of it," Elizabeth reminded
the Senora, also confused.

"No, she will receive all of it. I am giving her my share as
well."

Which made perfect sense now that Elizabeth knew her real
identity. The Senora had probably intended to do this all along.
She would come away with the money she had "borrowed" from
the New York socialites foolish enough to imagine they could

take advantage of her, so her time was not completely wasted, and her daughter would be provided for. No wonder she had been so quick to join forces with Elizabeth after the Old Man had told her about Elizabeth's charitable instincts.

"But I can't take money from you," Irene said.

"Why not? I'm your mother. If your father offered to give you a sum of money as a dowry, you'd take it, wouldn't you?"

"Yes," she admitted reluctantly.

"Then you can take it from me. You and your Mr. Regan and my grandchild will have your farm and your horses and a good chance of making a success of your lives."

"I don't . . . I can't . . . I don't know what to say," Irene said. She was crying again. "You cheated all those people and"—she looked at Elizabeth and Gideon—"and you helped her do it!"

Elizabeth hadn't expected to be condemned, but the Senora was unfazed. "Do not blame them. I lied to them and tricked them into helping me, and nothing they have done is illegal."

"I can vouch for that," Gideon said.

Irene still looked unconvinced as she swiped at the tears running down her face.

"Gideon," Elizabeth said, rising from her seat, "I think we should leave these two alone for a while." If anyone could convince Irene, it was Paulina. They just needed to give her a chance.

Gideon wasted no time in taking her hint. They retired to the library, where they found Mother Bates knitting.

"You have no idea how tempted I was to listen at the door," she confessed, "but I knew if I did, someone was bound to catch me. Now tell me everything."

"First tell me how Olinda is," Elizabeth said, sitting in one of the chairs arranged comfortably around the cold fireplace.

"*Freddie* is just fine, although she said she got cold sitting on those metal stairs for nearly an hour and next time she's kidnapped, she will wear long underwear, even if it is July. She changed into her own clothes and went home. She and Anna have plans today, I believe."

Elizabeth glanced at the clock. "The Senora has a train to catch, but we decided to give her and Irene a chance to talk alone. It will probably be their only chance, since the Senora won't be returning to New York ever again."

"What an interesting life. She comes to New York, makes a lot of friends, causes a huge scandal, and then disappears, taking hundreds of thousands of dollars with her."

"Don't get any ideas, Mother," Gideon said with mock sternness.

"I just said it was interesting, not appealing," she chastened him. "I do hope Mary told Irene she is really her mother."

Elizabeth and Gideon gaped at her.

"You knew?" Elizabeth asked.

"How could you?" Gideon demanded. "We just found out ourselves."

"I didn't at first, but when she was so kind to Irene, well, I could see it in her eyes, and there was no other explanation for her being so generous to her."

"Mother Bates, I must remember never to underestimate you," Elizabeth said.

"I have to admit, this was a particularly entertaining adventure," Mother Bates said. "I didn't even know Jake knew how to speak Spanish."

"You mean when he and Olinda had their big argument? He doesn't. Freddie apparently has a gift with languages, and she taught him some phrases. I'm sure he pronounced everything wrong, but no one knew since no one speaks Spanish, not even the Senora."

"Jake certainly looked nice in his fancy clothes, though," Mother Bates said. "Be sure to tell him I said so."

"Never in a million years," Elizabeth replied with a laugh. "He's already conceited enough."

"I keep forgetting to ask you," Gideon said. "Why did he need that scar on his face?"

"Because people will either just look at the scar or avoid looking at his face at all. That makes it more difficult for people to remember what he looks like, so it's a good disguise."

"How very clever, dear," Mother Bates said.

Gideon just shook his head. "How long do you think Nolan and Livingston will wait at the hotel?"

"I don't know. How long would you wait for the woman you love?" Elizabeth asked with a teasing smile.

"I would wait for you forever, but I'm not sure those two have the same feelings for the Senora."

"You can't think they were after her money," Elizabeth said with mock outrage.

"I'm sure that added to her appeal."

"You are so cynical, darling."

"But right, nonetheless. What is the rest of the plan?"

"After Paulina convinces Irene to keep the farm and the horses and the money, which shouldn't be too difficult, she will go directly to the train station. She already sent her luggage ahead."

"You mean she'll just disappear?" Mother Bates said in surprise.

"She must. She'll leave a letter behind for each of her suitors explaining that they found Olinda dead in the park. With Olinda dead, no marriage can take place, which means she will not receive her inheritance. She must return to Spain to negotiate a new arrangement with Hernando's father."

"Is she taking that magnificent safe with her?" Mother Bates asked.

"Absolutely not. It is a silent promise to return when she can to repay her debts."

"Which will give her plenty of time to make sure no one can find her ever again," Gideon said.

"You *are* very cynical, dear," Mother Bates echoed Elizabeth. "But what about the money in the safe?"

"And you are very naïve, dear," Gideon chided right back. "There is no money in that safe."

"Oh my goodness, of course there isn't. What was I thinking? But what will become of the safe?"

"Someone will probably figure out that they can sue the Senora to open it, even if she's no longer around, and they'll discover it's empty."

"And that will cause a whole new scandal," Mother Bates said, obviously relishing the possibility.

"Don't be so sure. The people who loaned Paulina money won't want it known that they were tricked, so it might get hushed up," Gideon said.

"In any case, it doesn't matter," Elizabeth assured her. "All that matters is that Irene and Cal Regan will have everything they need to live happily ever after."

"If you can get Cal Regan to agree," Gideon said.

## CHAPTER FIFTEEN

WHEN IRENE AND PAULINA EMERGED FROM THE PARLOR, it was obvious they had both been crying but that they had reached some sort of peace with each other.

"I'm glad you told her, Mary," Mother Bates said, taking the Senora's hands in hers.

"Elizabeth revealed my secret, I guess."

"She already figured it out," Elizabeth said. "She saw the way you looked at Irene."

"I wish you could stay," Mother Bates said. "At least for a little while. I'd like to hear what you've been doing all these years."

"And I would like to tell you, but that will be another time, I am afraid," the Senora said with obvious regret.

She went upstairs to change for her trip. Elizabeth and Mother Bates convinced Irene to join them for breakfast, which seemed late even though it wasn't even seven thirty yet.

"How is Olinda?" Irene asked as she was digging into her eggs.

She looked up in surprise when only silence greeted her question.

"What is it?" she asked, obviously confused.

"You will soon learn that Olinda was murdered by her kidnappers," Elizabeth said.

"But she wasn't murdered. I saw her myself a little while ago."

"I said you will learn that, but, of course, there really was no Olinda at all," Elizabeth said.

Irene frowned. "No Olinda? What do you mean?"

"I mean she was someone Paulina hired, and now she will disappear, just like Paulina and Hernando will disappear."

"She hired Hernando, too?" Irene asked in surprise.

"Don't try to figure it out," Mother Bates advised her. "It will drive you crazy."

Irene touched her forehead. "I believe you are right about that."

"She is," Elizabeth confirmed. "Just think happy thoughts, like what you and Mr. Regan will do with the farm and the horses now that you own them."

Irene frowned at this. "I don't know. He's so strange about money. He thinks he's not entitled to it unless he earned it."

"I'm sure you can convince him, dear," Mother Bates.

Irene didn't look quite so confident.

They had just finished eating when a shabbily dressed old woman entered the dining room.

Everyone looked up in surprise although only Irene remained confused.

"No one will ever recognize you," Elizabeth said to the woman.

"I hope not," Paulina said.

"Mother?" Irene asked in surprise. "Why on earth are you dressed like that? And what have you done to your face?"

"A little makeup. If Sebastian and Daniel figure out that I'm leaving, they might come to the station before my train leaves. I can't let them find me."

Everyone understood, so no one questioned her. They said their good-byes, which involved more tears from Irene and Paulina, but Paulina promised that they would meet secretly somewhere in a year, so Paulina could see her grandchild.

"Oh, and one more thing," Paulina said, slipping a ring off her finger. "This should be yours." She dropped the engagement ring Sebastian had given her into Irene's hand.

Then she went out the back door like the poor woman she appeared to be, carrying a worn Gladstone bag that probably contained hundreds of thousands of dollars.

Irene stared at the ring for a long moment. "I need to see Cal."

"How much of this will you tell him?" Elizabeth asked.

"None of it. He's completely unaware of what's been happening while he is in the hospital. I didn't even tell him my father got engaged. I'll tell him my mother came to see me and told me how Father tried to murder her. She convinced him to sign over the farm and the horses to me or she would go to the police. Then she gave me a large sum of money for a dowry because she somehow managed to earn a fortune in her new life and wanted me to be taken care of."

"That's a very good story," Mother Bates marveled.

"Mother thought of it," Irene said, disabusing everyone of the notion that she might have been a bit of a con artist herself.

"Of course she did, dear," Mother Bates said. "I'm sure you're anxious to see Mr. Regan. Come along, I'll help you gather up your things."

Repacking Irene's overnight bag was the work of a few minutes and then she was out the door after thanking them for everything they had done for her.

"She didn't seem as grateful as I would have expected," Mother Bates said.

"She's had a shock," Elizabeth excused her. "Several shocks, in fact. And sometimes people aren't as grateful for help as you might think."

Gideon went to his office, since no matter how many ransom deliveries he might have been involved with that morning, it was still a workday. The Old Man arrived in time for lunch. "How did it go with Irene?" he asked when they had exchanged pleasantries.

"She was very emotional, but she seemed to accept Paulina's story," Elizabeth said.

"Poor girl was very shocked, though," Mother Bates added.

"How did things go from your end?" Elizabeth asked.

"I waited several hours, then went to the hotel as Paulina had instructed. Sure enough, Nolan and Livingston were both still sitting in the lobby waiting for her to return. I pretended I didn't see them and went straight to the desk to ask for her, which they hadn't bothered to do because they knew she wouldn't be back from rescuing Olinda yet."

"You mean they sat there for hours and never even asked?" Elizabeth said.

"Why should they? In any event, the desk clerk told me she had checked out, and I acted very surprised. By then Livingston and Nolan had seen me and were demanding to know what had happened. I took them aside and told them Olinda was dead when we found her. I said the Senora was so upset that I put her and Hernando in a cab to return to the hotel while I made arrangements for Olinda's burial. I fully expected to find the Senora here, but the clerk just told me she had checked out."

"They must have been astounded," Mother Bates said.

"They were stunned, but the desk clerk recognized Mr. Nolan because he was staying there and informed him that he had messages for him and Mr. Livingston. The messages explained the

Senora had to return to Spain to make new arrangements with her brother-in-law and would be in touch with them."

"Did they rush to the train station to stop her?" Elizabeth asked.

"They rushed to the port to stop her. They assumed she'd be sailing to Spain, I think," the Old Man explained.

"How very sensible of them," Mother Bates said.

"The most sensible thing they've done, I think," the Old Man agreed. "Do you know if they found the bag we left in the bushes?"

"You left the ransom money in the bushes?" Mother Bates exclaimed in surprise.

"Of course not, Hazel," he chided her gently.

"They left the bag, but it was empty," Elizabeth explained. "And yes, Gideon said they remembered it at the last minute and went to look for it. They found the bag and a hundred-dollar bill."

"Which I left stuck to a branch as a convincer."

"It apparently worked," Elizabeth said.

They had an interesting conversation over lunch, answering all of Mother Bates's questions. She had been one step ahead of them in realizing the Senora's identity and had almost figured everything else out, too, so her questions were few.

Elizabeth and Gideon were snuggled up in the parlor that evening, having seen Mother Bates off to bed early after her long and exciting day, when someone started pounding on the front door.

Gideon instructed Elizabeth to stay in the parlor and went to answer it himself, half expecting one or both of the Senora's suitors to have come demanding some kind of satisfaction, but to his surprise, he found Irene Nolan standing on his doorstep.

"Cal won't marry me if I'm rich," she informed them.

"WILL IT WORK?" ELIZABETH ASKED HER FATHER. SHE'D gone down to his office in Dan the Dude's Saloon the next morning to tell him how unreasonable Cal Regan was being. He said he couldn't marry a woman for her money when he was penniless. It went against everything he believed in. That meant they had to figure out a way to get him rich by his own efforts.

"I don't know," the Old Man said. "I never heard of conning somebody to get them to *accept* money. We're always trying to take it away from them."

"He has to believe he earned it somehow, too," Elizabeth said. "Can't you think of a racing con that would work?"

"I can think of a dozen racing cons, but they never work on people who understand horse racing. No jockey would ever believe in a fixed race, for instance. They know it's impossible to really fix a race."

"What *would* he believe?"

"How do I know? He sounds like a really stubborn man. He won't even marry the woman who is having his baby."

"How did you know about the baby?" Elizabeth asked, outraged.

"You can tell by looking at her."

"No, you can't!" she argued.

"I don't mean her stomach is sticking out, but she's got this . . . I don't know what you call it, but a woman just gets this glow when she's expecting."

Elizabeth frowned. "How do you know so much about it?"

Was he blushing? "Let's get back to the problem at hand, shall we? Cal Regan is a stubborn son of a—"

"Who doesn't know about the baby," Elizabeth said.

The Old Man was genuinely shocked. "He doesn't?"

"Irene refuses to tell him. She wants him to marry her because he wants her, not because he has to, and apparently, he doesn't know about this glow business."

The Old Man shook his head at such foolishness, but he said, "I don't know what he might believe, but the *most* believable of all the fixed-race cons is probably the ringer."

Elizabeth considered this for a moment. "Yes, I can see that, but how do you guarantee that the ringer will win, since obviously we don't have any control over which horses run and there isn't really any ringer."

"Let me think," he said, rubbing his temples as if that would help. "If you can make somebody believe they lost, there must be a way to make somebody think they won."

"Yes, because we'd have to trick him into believing it since we can't guarantee it."

"Let's see," he mused, closing his eyes as if picturing it. "We tell him one of the owners has look-alike horses. One is a plater and the other is the fastest horse alive."

"Or fast, at least."

He ignored her. "They run the plater in some races, and he proves he can't win a race even if all the other horses pull up lame."

"That's good."

He still ignored her. "Then, when the odds on the plater get really long, he switches to the fast horse and wins the race."

Elizabeth was nodding. "That's what you tell the mark, except there really is no ringer and the plater doesn't win, so he loses his money."

"Which the grifter never even bet in the first place, so it's safely in his pocket and he disappears."

"If we could somehow make the plater win, though, we don't

need to even place a bet, just like in the regular ringer con. We can use some of Irene's money to pay off the bet and make Cal think he's suddenly a rich man."

The Old Man was shaking his head. "But you can't make the plater win, Lizzie. If you could really fix a horse race, all con men would be rich."

But Elizabeth was still trying to figure it out. "What if . . . ?"

"What if what?"

"We don't really need for the plater to win. We just need for Cal Regan to think it did."

The Old Man frowned. "How will you do that?"

"We'll just tell him. He's in the hospital. All he knows is what he reads in the newspaper, and he hardly ever gets any visitors anymore, according to Irene, so who will tell him otherwise?"

"We might have to print up a phony newspaper. Does he see the *Daily Racing Form*?"

"I'll ask Irene. She'll have to make sure he doesn't see that one, at least."

"You need someone to tell him the tale, though. Someone he'll believe."

"Oh dear, that could be a problem. Who would he trust?"

The Old Man shook his head. "It can't be somebody he trusts because a trustworthy person wouldn't know about this kind of thing. Who does he hate?"

"Oh my, I'm sure he hates the jockey who hooked him in the race the morning before the Belmont Stakes."

"Wasn't that the same day Trench was sponged and Regan broke his leg?"

"Yes. So, he'd hate whoever sponged Trench, too."

The Old Man considered. "Do they know who that was?"

"They think it was an exercise boy named Toby. He left to work for Daniel Livingston shortly afterward."

"Now that's an interesting thing to do."

"And not something you'd likely do if you were innocent," Elizabeth said.

"Who has the most to lose if they were exposed, the jockey or this Toby?"

"Regan and Nolan did consider reporting the jockey, but it would have been Cal's word against the jockey. His name was Hawkins, I think. And you know how those things go. Even if they decided Hawkins was guilty, he'd just get suspended from racing for a week or two, and they might decide not to punish him at all. That was why they decided not to even report it."

"But this Toby fellow, if somebody saw him sponging Trench, he'd be barred from racing for life," the Old Man mused.

"The problem is nobody saw him."

The Old Man looked surprised. "But didn't somebody just come forward? Somebody who was afraid to before, but now he's told some people and if word gets back to Nolan . . ."

"Oh, I see. We tell Toby that someone saw him and threaten to report him unless he helps us trick Cal."

"Which he should be glad to do since he's responsible for Cal being crippled and maybe not being able to ride again."

"Which is why Cal will believe him when he tells him Livingston has a ringer and is going to make a killing."

"How will he know which horse to tell him it is, though?"

"He doesn't tell him. He can't take a chance that Cal will tell someone else who would then tell someone else and so on, because if word gets out, everyone will bet on the ringer and the odds will drop. But Cal doesn't need to know the name of the horse. Toby will place Cal's bet for him when the time comes. It's the least he can do to make it up to him. Then he'll deliver his winnings."

"This is a brilliant plan," Elizabeth said quite sincerely.

"It's a crazy plan. Who wastes their time making somebody else rich?" he scoffed, but she could see he was pleased.

"Now all we have to do is convince Toby he's got to tell Cal about the ringer."

"And then make sure he actually does it. People like Toby aren't exactly dependable."

Elizabeth looked at her father with a critical eye. He was dressed in one of his bespoke suits, his silver hair brushed into an attractive style. He looked important and imposing, as he usually did. "Suppose someone claiming to be from some official-sounding charitable organization pulled Toby out of the stable and told him he'd been reported for sponging Trench and then explained how he could redeem himself by helping with this charade, which is the only way you could get Regan to accept help."

"Did you say 'you'?" he echoed with a frown. "By 'you,' do you mean 'me'?"

"I don't know anyone else who could pull this off," she said quite sincerely.

"And for free, I imagine."

"You've already been handsomely compensated for your part in the Senora's con. You should do this one just for fun."

"My work is not fun, young lady," he informed her.

"Balderdash."

He tried to look stern, but she could see right through him. "All right, but this is the last time."

"Of course it is. You don't think I'm going to make a habit of running cons, do you?"

For some reason, this made him laugh uproariously.

GIDEON AND ELIZABETH FOUND CAL REGAN ALONE IN HIS hospital room on Monday morning. Gideon was going to have to work late to make up for spending the morning visiting a crippled jockey, but Elizabeth had assured him it was for a good cause. Her only instructions were to be himself and to go along with whatever happened. This meant he didn't have to lie, but he also shouldn't express skepticism of whatever scheme someone was going to propose to Regan.

Cal greeted them with less enthusiasm than Gideon felt was warranted, considering he'd taken half a day off work and traveled an hour on the train to get here, but he swallowed his annoyance and tried to be pleasant.

"Is Irene coming to visit today?" Elizabeth asked.

"I, uh, I don't know," Cal said somewhat self-consciously. "She hasn't been here in a couple days."

"A couple days?" Elizabeth echoed doubtfully.

"Well, since Thursday."

"My goodness, I thought she visited you every day." She glanced at Gideon for his opinion, so he nodded just to be agreeable.

"She did but . . . We had an argument."

"Oh dear, I'm sorry to hear it," Elizabeth said. "It must have been serious if she hasn't been here since Thursday."

Regan offered no clue as to how serious it might have been.

Gideon asked him how he was getting on, and he told them he was using the crutches to get around and was afraid he'd always need them. Gideon offered a few words of encouragement, and then a young man appeared in the doorway. He was short and dressed like one of the exercise boys from the track, in canvas pants and a ragged shirt. He held his battered hat in both hands and was working the brim nervously.

Elizabeth recognized him from that day at the track when Regan had the fall, so he must be the infamous Toby.

"You've got some nerve showing up here," Regan said by way of greeting.

"I know but . . . I need to tell you something."

"If you've come to say you're sorry for sponging Trench and breaking my leg, you're a little late."

"I never . . ."

"You never what?" Regan demanded. "And don't lie and say you never sponged Trench."

"I never meant for you to get hurt," Toby said. "You gotta believe that."

"And what if I do? It doesn't change anything."

"No, but I come to tell you something that might." He glanced at Gideon and Elizabeth. "But I see you got company."

"We'll be glad to leave if that's what you want, Mr. Regan," Elizabeth said.

"I don't know what he's got to tell me, but I think I'd like a witness to whatever it is," Regan said with a thunderous frown.

Before the young man could speak, Irene Nolan appeared behind him.

"Toby, what in heaven's name are you doing here?" she demanded angrily.

Poor Toby looked crestfallen. He knew how to stand up to an angry jockey but apparently an angry female was too much.

"Irene, let's go for a walk. The men have something to discuss," Elizabeth said.

"I hope it involves reporting Toby to the racing commission," Irene said. She pointed at Cal Regan, who looked a bit nonplussed by her arrival. "You had better do what needs to be done."

"Come along," Elizabeth said. "I want to know all about your visit with your mother."

That was for Regan's benefit, Gideon guessed. Irene would have told Cal the phony story about her mother returning and giving her money and forcing her father to sign everything over to her. Naturally, Elizabeth would want to hear all about it.

"Do you still want me to stay?" Gideon asked Regan when the women were gone.

"Yeah, so if I murder him, you can say it was self-defense."

Toby paled at that, but he lifted his chin as if to show he wasn't afraid. "I know you might not be able to ride again, and I have some news that might help you."

"Help me ride again?" Regan scoffed.

"No, but . . . Well, it might get you a lot of money."

"How would you know something that could get me a lot of money?" Regan asked, still skeptical.

"Because Mr. Livingston is going to run a ringer."

"What's a ringer?" Gideon asked, although he knew. He figured he needed to appear completely ignorant so no one would suspect he was in on this.

"It's a fairy tale," Regan said in disgust. "If it was real, it would be two horses that looked exactly alike or close enough that nobody would notice. One never wins a race and the other can win any race."

"What would it matter if they looked alike then? Wouldn't you just run the fast horse and sell the slow one?"

Regan smiled at that. "Not if you were greedy. You could run the slow one in enough races for the odds on him to get really long. Then you run the fast one in his place and bet a lot of money on him. You'd make a killing."

Toby was nodding enthusiastically. "That's it. That's what Mr. Livingston is going to do."

But Regan was shaking his head. "Even if it's true, why are you telling me?"

"Because . . ." Toby swallowed. "Because I feel guilty for what happened to you, and I want to make it right somehow."

"You can never make it right," Regan said bitterly.

"No, but I can make you rich. You can bet on the ringer and make a fortune."

Regan gestured to his leg cast. "I can't bet on anything. Haven't you noticed I'm stuck here?"

"I'd place the bet for you," Toby said eagerly.

Regan laughed at that. "Oh yeah, so you could take my money and then tell me the horse pulled up or something and I lost everything."

"You can send somebody with me then. Somebody you trust. Miss Nolan, maybe."

"Not Miss Nolan," Regan snapped. He was either still mad at her or thought she was still mad at him.

"Then whoever you say," Toby said. "Please, let me do this for you, Cal. I can't hardly sleep for thinking about how bad hurt you were and it's all my fault." He did look distraught, but more likely he was thinking about getting reported to the racing commission.

"Why don't you just tell me the name of the horse and which race, and I'll see the bet gets placed myself," Regan suggested.

"But I can't tell you," Toby almost wailed.

"Why not?" Regan challenged.

"Because you might tell somebody and word like that spreads awful fast. Everybody'd bet on the horse and the odds would drop and the whole thing would go bust. You can see that, can't you?"

"Yeah, I can see it, but I wouldn't tell anybody."

"I can't be sure, and if the odds dropped, Mr. Livingston might figure out that I knew and told somebody."

Regan considered this for a long moment. "All right, I can see why you won't tell, but that still doesn't make me believe you. Besides, only a fool bets on the horses."

"But this is a sure thing. Mr. Livingston is planning to bet ten thousand dollars. I heard him say."

"No bookie could handle a bet like that with steep odds," Regan said.

"He's going to spread his bets around the country, so nobody knows how much he's betting."

"And what about you, Toby? Are you betting on this sure thing?"

"I sure am," he declared, raising his hand as if taking an oath. "Trouble is, I don't have much to bet. I'm trying to scrape up a hundred dollars, but I'm going to bet every cent I can find."

"And when does this race happen?" Regan asked.

"Mr. Livingston hasn't decided yet. He's waiting until the odds on . . . on the slow horse get really long."

"And you've seen the ringer?" Regan asked.

"Oh yeah. They're almost exactly alike. It just takes a little blacking on the left foreleg to finish the job."

"And you've seen him run?"

"He's like lightning. I'm telling you, Cal, you'd be a fool to pass this up. I'm trying to do a good thing here. Mr. Livingston would kill me if he knew I was telling you. If he knew I was telling anybody, come to that."

Regan looked unimpressed, but maybe he was just trying to aggravate Toby. "And how do you propose getting the money from me to bet?" he asked, surprising Gideon.

Toby brightened at this. "Any way you want, Cal. I can come here and get it or—"

"You can't leave the track any time you like," Regan pointed out. Since the racing was at Empire City now, it would be a long trip.

"Then I can meet somebody there. They can even place the bet if you want. It'll have to be at the last minute so they can't tell anybody else which horse it is."

"But we'll know it's one of Livingston's," Regan said to Gideon.

"He's running a lot of horses lately. What do you say, Cal? Do you want in?"

"I . . . I need to think about it."

Toby frowned in disgust. "Don't think too long."

"How will you get me word when the time comes?"

"I can telephone you here, at the hospital, I guess."

"How much notice will you have?"

"A couple days. We'll have to switch the horses, and I'll know when that happens that it's getting close."

"All right. You telephone me, and I'll tell you what I've decided."

"You'd be a fool to pass this up," he said again. "If you can't ride any more, you'll need—"

"Get out of here," Regan said, angry again. "You're lucky I can't walk, or I'd throw you out that window."

Toby took the hint and scampered away.

Regan swore and then sighed wearily.

"That was quite a story," Gideon said. "Do you think it might be true?"

"I wouldn't put anything past Livingston. I'd be more inclined to believe it if he was trying to beat one of Nolan's horses, though."

"Maybe that's what he's waiting for," Gideon said.

"Except that all the Nolan horses belong to Irene now." His tone indicated he was testing Gideon to see if he knew this.

"Do they? How did that happen?"

"Her father signed everything over to her."

"That was generous of him," Gideon said. "I guess he decided to retire from the racing business."

"He . . . yeah, I guess he did," Regan said, apparently not wanting to explain. Gideon couldn't blame him.

"That makes Irene an heiress of sorts, I guess," Gideon said. "She seems to like you well enough. You should snatch her up."

Regan frowned. "I don't need her money, and besides, what would she want with a crippled ex-jockey?"

"Women are funny," Gideon said with all the wisdom of a happily married man. "You can never figure what they might do. You should just ask her and see what she says."

"She won't say anything. She's not speaking to me," Regan said with a sigh.

"She spoke to you when she was here a few minutes ago. In my experience, a woman doesn't get angry unless she cares a great deal."

Regan frowned. "I won't be a charity case."

"Who said anything about charity? You know a lot about racehorses. You'd be a big help to her running the operation, even if you couldn't ever race again."

"But I don't have much money saved, and what I do have will go to the hospital. I can't go to her with nothing."

Gideon grinned. "You could always bet on the sure thing."

Regan didn't reply. He just stared out the window as if he was trying to decide.

IRENE WILL CONVINCE HIM," ELIZABETH TOLD GIDEON AFTER he had reported the conversation to her on the train back to the city.

"And what if she can't?"

"Then we'll think of something else."

"I have a feeling that Regan would start to get suspicious if he turns down one get-rich-quick scheme and then another one happens along."

"People aren't as smart as you give them credit for being," Elizabeth informed him gently. "Sometimes they believe they deserve good fortune and aren't surprised at all when it comes their way."

"That must be an interesting way to live."

'Yes, imagine always being hopeful." She sighed wistfully. "I think it would be delightful."

IN THE END, IRENE DID CONVINCE CAL REGAN TO PLACE A BET. He wouldn't bet every cent he owned, but he did consent to risk a thousand dollars of his savings. Irene was instructed to retrieve it from under the floorboards in his room at the Nolan farm, which she dutifully did, or rather she dutifully told Cal that she did, since it was a long trip to the farm and she had the remainder of a quarter of a million dollars after expenses in a safe in Gideon's office. So, she just kept it there for the time being. He wouldn't need the money until race day, and she certainly wasn't going to let him keep it at the hospital.

Everything seemed to be going well, until Irene telephoned Elizabeth the next day, which was the day they had decided that Toby would notify Regan the race was on Thursday, because that was the very last day of racing at Empire City. He couldn't do this if they had to travel all the way to Saratoga Springs, which was the next spot on the racing calendar. Gideon would just have to take another day off work if he was needed, and he very obviously wished to be needed. Elizabeth feared he might be forced to lie to Mr. Devoss about where he was going.

"Cal insists on going to the track himself to place the bet," Irene told Elizabeth, her frustration evident even through the phone lines.

"But how will he get there? And he can't manage to make his way around the stands at the track on crutches. He'd get knocked down if he didn't fall."

"He said the hospital will let him take a wheelchair to use."

"A wheelchair?" Elizabeth knew how large and unwieldy those chairs were, with their high caned backs and large wheels on either side. "How on earth would he get a wheelchair there?"

"He wants me to hire a car to take him, since he obviously can't go on the train. Just getting him to the station and back would be impossible. Oh, Elizabeth, this will ruin everything. He can't place the bet himself."

Since no one would be placing a bet at all because there was no ringer running and they actually had no ringer to even run, Cal could not possibly be allowed to go to the track, where he'd find out all of this.

"What are we going to do?" Irene wailed.

"Don't worry, we'll figure something out. And don't hire a car. I'll get someone to drive us," she promised rashly. She had another trip to Dan the Dude's Saloon in her near future. She just hoped the Old Man was available.

# CHAPTER SIXTEEN

A RE YOU SURE THIS IS GOING TO WORK?" IRENE WHISPERED
to Elizabeth as they followed the men down the hospital
corridor Thursday morning. Gideon was pushing Cal in his
wheelchair with the Old Man by his side.

The Old Man had reminded her that he had already performed his last free favor for her by browbeating Toby into going
along with their scheme. Now he was driving Cal Regan and
company all the way to Empire City Race Track for another
wasted day of his time when he could have been taking someone's
money. She had told him he was doing it for his sins. He had no
argument for that.

"Of course it will work," Elizabeth said. It was a good plan
and it relied on only chance and luck and a bit of stardust.

"But how are you going to—"

"It's best if you don't know, dear," Elizabeth assured her.

Getting Cal out of the hospital was the first obstacle. They
had to use a rear entrance that had only a few steps because the
front was too difficult, having been designed to impress with a

long set of stairs to the front door. The Old Man and Gideon had to carefully lift the chair with Cal in it down the steps, which they did manage without upsetting anything.

Cal looked pale and he was already sweating, probably because he was in pain, but he kept touching his breast pocket, not from discomfort but to check the packet of money that Irene had brought him that morning, which was ostensibly his savings from the farmhouse. Gideon had, in fact, retrieved it from his office, along with the money Cal would win from the imaginary bet if things went well. That money was safely stashed in the trunk of the Old Man's motorcar.

The trip from the hospital to Empire City in Yonkers was a little over twenty miles, so they should need about an hour. They were leaving in plenty of time so they could push Cal's chair through the crowded park and find Toby, get the name of the horse and be able to place the bet. Not that any of that would happen.

The men transferred Cal to the front passenger seat and then set about figuring out how to tie the chair to the back of the motorcar. Through the years, the "trunk" of the average motorcar had become not just a trunk affixed to the rear of the vehicle, but a part of the vehicle itself, although it still looked and functioned like the original trunk on this particular model. The Old Man had brought rope to tie the chair to the top of the trunk, and he and Gideon needed an inordinate amount of time to get it secured. Elizabeth and Irene kept Cal occupied during that process, so he didn't notice the Old Man using a wrench on the wheelchair. If he had, the explanation would have been he was making sure the wheels were bolted on tightly.

The Old Man had put the top up on the motor to protect them from the sun, but the breeze coming in the sides was welcome on this warm day. The forecast was for another afternoon in the mid-eighties. A good day for racing but not so good for riding in a hot vehicle.

Gideon took a seat behind the driver and Elizabeth sat in the middle next to him, leaving Irene to sit behind Cal.

"How are you doing?" she leaned forward to ask him, shouting to be heard above the engine and the blast of air roaring through the motorcar.

"I'm fine," he replied through gritted teeth, telling them he wasn't fine at all. "It's going to be all right, Reenie. We're going to be able to get married when this is over, and everything will be wonderful, so stop worrying about me."

Irene leaned back with a disgruntled frown. "The doctor didn't really tell him he could make this trip," Irene told Elizabeth softly so Cal couldn't hear her. "Cal asked if we could take him out for a drive and to get dinner, and that's what he said would be all right."

"Oh dear. I hope this isn't too much for him."

"If it is, he only has himself to blame. I knew he was stubborn, but this is ridiculous."

"He has his pride, Irene," Elizabeth said, patting her hand. "We're trying to let him keep some of it, so pretend you don't notice how much pain he's in."

Irene closed her eyes as if marshaling her strength. "I'll try."

The drive took a little more than an hour since the roads were poor and when they got close to the racetrack, traffic grew heavier. More and more people were driving to the track now that they had enlarged the parking areas.

"I know a shortcut," the Old Man said when they had to stop for a third time. He pulled off onto a side road that was indeed free of other vehicles, but the sudden acceleration jarred something loose or maybe it was caused by Gideon pulling the rope end that had been tucked into the corner of the window opening beside him. At any rate, the wheelchair came loose and went crashing onto the roadbed, breaking into several pieces.

Irene actually screamed, and everyone cried out in some manner as the Old Man brought the motor to a sudden stop.

"What on earth?" several of them demanded, and the Old Man and Gideon jumped out.

Irene and Elizabeth followed to see what had become of the wheelchair, which now lay, wheelless, in the middle of the road. One of the wheels had continued to roll and lay off in a field while the other lay somewhat smashed beneath the chair itself, the pushrim crushed from having absorbed the impact of the fall.

Elizabeth saw the Old Man pick up what appeared to be a nut or a bolt that would have held a wheel in place and drop it into his pocket. In case there was a danger of actually being able to put the chair back together in time, this essential part would never be found.

"What happened?" Cal was shouting from the front seat, where he couldn't really see the damage. "Is the chair all right?"

"Oh, Cal, it's smashed to pieces," Irene cried.

"It can't be! I have to have it. I didn't even bring my crutches!"

"Maybe we can put it back together," Gideon said. His words sounded sincere, but it was a good thing Cal couldn't see his expression, which was mischievous in the extreme.

"We can try," the Old Man said gamely, and he sent Gideon to fetch the wheel from the field.

It didn't take long to determine that one wheel was broken beyond their ability to repair, and the missing bolt also posed an insurmountable problem.

"What are we going to do now?" Cal moaned when Gideon explained the problem and showed him the damaged wheel to prove it. "If I don't place that bet . . ." He shook his head in despair.

"We can still do what we came to do," Gideon pointed out. "I can place your bet for you. Toby knows me. I'll tell him what happened and that I'm taking your place."

"What if he won't tell you the name of the horse?" Cal argued.

"He'll tell me. If he wants to have a clear conscience, he'll tell me."

"What choice do we have?" Irene said, taking his hand in hers. "We can't carry you into the racetrack. Please, let Mr. Bates help, Cal."

Cal looked up at her, his pride and his love shining in his eyes. Luckily for him, the love won. "I guess you're right, if you wouldn't mind, Mr. Bates."

"I'll be happy to help. If Toby questions me, I'll bring him out to you, but I don't think that will be necessary," Gideon said, knowing it wouldn't be.

"I'll go along, too," the Old Man said. "Gideon will need a bodyguard to protect him from pickpockets when he comes out with all your winnings, Cal."

Everyone forced a chuckle at that, even Cal.

By the time they gathered the pieces of the chair and tied them securely to the back of the motorcar, it was almost time for the first race. This time the Old Man accelerated much more slowly, and they made it to the racetrack without further incident.

"I hate leaving you out here in the hot sun," Gideon told Elizabeth as he slung the satchel of money he'd brought over his head so no one could snatch it from him.

"We'll survive. There are vendors all around selling hot dogs and lemonade. I'll see that Cal and Irene don't expire."

"See that you don't expire, my darling. I might bet some money on this ringer myself and buy you something nice," he added with a wink.

"Oh yes, a diamond necklace," she said in case Cal was listening.

"What have you got there?" Cal asked Gideon as he and the Old Man set out for the entrance.

"A bag to carry your winnings in," Gideon said with a grin, patting the satchel. "You didn't think I'd stuff them in my pockets, did you?"

Cal managed an answering grin even though his face was gray with pain. "I didn't really think about it."

"Well, think about it. It will be a pretty big bundle."

"It better be a big bundle," Cal said to Irene when the other men were gone. "It's our future."

Irene bent down and kissed his forehead. "Try to get some rest. Elizabeth and I will get us something to eat."

Cal was actually asleep when they returned with hot dogs wrapped in newspaper and Dixie cups full of cold lemonade. Irene woke him to take a drink but then let him sleep again.

They walked over to the meager shade of a sapling planted to produce real shade in about a decade or two and enjoyed their impromptu picnic.

"I haven't had a chance to tell you, but I heard it at the track. Mr. Livingston is telling everyone that Olinda was killed by the kidnappers and the Senora left for Spain to negotiate for her inheritance."

"Yes," Elizabeth said. "Mrs. Westerly was asking Mother Bates what she knew about it."

"Did they lend my mother money, too?" Irene asked.

"I believe so."

Irene sighed. "I don't know what to think about her. She stole that money she gave me, didn't she?"

"Mr. Livingston provided it," Elizabeth said. "And he owes Cal for sponging Trench and crippling him."

"But the money she took from all those other people . . ."

"Doesn't concern you. She told you she is a con artist. That's what they do, and none of it is your fault."

"Father will never forgive me. He was furious when I told him I own the horses and the farm now."

"You've done nothing you need to be forgiven for, Irene. You accepted a gift from your mother, money and property that is rightfully yours. Your father is the one who needs forgiveness, and unless he asks for it, you shouldn't give it. He tried to murder your mother, remember."

"He never hurt me, though."

"Didn't he? He stole your mother from you, and he was going to take Cal away from you, too." Not to mention all the casual cruelties she had endured from him.

"I . . . I didn't think of it that way."

"You should, Irene. Good fortune has come to you. Most people would be happy."

"But I've lost my father and now I've lost my mother all over again."

"If your father is worthy of your love, he'll come around and make up with you, and your mother has promised at least another visit. That's more than you ever hoped for before."

"I suppose you're right."

"And you and Cal can be married now, assuming this ringer really wins the race," Elizabeth added with a grin.

Irene grinned back. "I can't believe Cal agreed to place this bet. He's always so careful."

"Maybe he's feeling desperate to be with the woman he loves. He might not know about the baby but he does love you, Irene."

"I keep reminding myself that's why he refused to marry me. He didn't want me stuck with a cripple for life."

"As I said, he has his pride. I just hope his winnings will be enough to satisfy it."

"I, uh, I didn't tell him how much money Mother gave me," Irene confessed. "He didn't ask, so I didn't volunteer."

"Oh, how clever of you, Irene. You can manage the books and he'll never know."

Irene smiled. "That's what I thought, too. Maybe I have more of my mother in me than I thought."

"Sometimes being a little sneaky is a good thing," Elizabeth said from experience.

Time seemed to drag, although they could judge the passing of the races by the cheers from the crowd. Three had passed, Elizabeth thought, when she saw Gideon and her father trudging across the parking area toward them.

"Regan, wake up!" Gideon called when they approached the motor and found him still snoozing.

He woke with a start. "What happened? Did you win? Did I win? What happened?" he demanded, wiping the moisture from his brow.

"You won, all right," the Old Man said. "Do you want to tell the story?" he asked Gideon.

But Gideon couldn't tell the story without lying, something he never used to do at all and now did only in emergencies. He shook his head. "You'll tell it better."

Which was very true, since the Old Man had probably made it up.

By now Elizabeth and Irene had abandoned their patch of shade and joined them at the motor.

"We ran into Livingston in the stables when we were looking

for Toby," the Old Man began. "He looked awfully cheerful, which he never does, so we thought we must have the right day." He slapped Gideon on the back, making him grin. "We had to make conversation with him. He asked if I'd heard from the Senora, and I had to say I haven't. He's wondering about getting his money back, I imagine."

"I'm sure he is," Elizabeth said.

"What money and who is the Senora?" Cal asked. He was still a bit groggy from sleep and the heat and his pain.

"No one you'd know, dear," Irene said. "So did you find Toby?"

"It took us a while to shake Livingston off, but Toby had seen us, and Gideon told him you were out in the parking lot. He couldn't get away, but he told us the name of the horse so we went to the betting area."

"It was quite busy, as usual," Gideon offered, giving what true information he could.

"No one really noticed us, I'm sure," the Old Man said. "We decided to split up. Gideon took half of your money, and I took the other half. Then we bet with two different bookies each. That was so we wouldn't break their bank when we won and get stiffed," he added with a chuckle.

"I didn't win that much, did I?" Cal scoffed, half hopefully.

"Pretty nearly," the Old Man said. "I wouldn't have taken a chance with one bookie on a two-thousand-dollar bet when the odds were that high."

"*Two* thousand?" Cal shook his head to clear it. "Reenie was only supposed to bring one thousand."

"I took a chance," Irene said. "I figured I'd pay you back out of the money my mother gave me if you lost."

He gave her a look that was half-exasperated and half-admiring, but he turned back to the Old Man. "What were the odds?"

"Well, you know how chaotic things are now with the bookies. They make their own odds and they change by the minute, but it averaged out to around twenty-five to one."

"*What?*" Cal yelped, shaking his head again. "That can't be right."

"We haven't counted it, but we think you got nearly fifty thousand dollars," Gideon said quite truthfully, opening the satchel so Cal could see the bills jammed into it. No boodle here, not even wrapped bills, because the bookies would just count out the winnings and hand them to you. All of it came from the ransom money Mary Nolan had given her daughter.

Gideon slipped the strap of the bag over his head and placed it into Cal's lap. Cal stuck his hand in and pulled out a wad of bills. "Fifty thousand dollars, Reenie! How much did your mother give you?"

Irene smiled beatifically. "Not fifty thousand dollars," she said as honestly as Gideon would have.

Cal's grin was pure triumph. He stuffed the bills back in the bag and reached for her hand. "Now we can get married."

Everyone laughed at that, Irene the hardest, but there were tears in her eyes when she said, "Only if you ask me nicely."

"Don't worry. I'll do a grand job of it as soon as we're alone."

"Then we better get you back to the hospital as fast as we can," Gideon said.

No one argued with that.

Cal was much too proud to complain, but everyone knew he was in agony by the time they got him back to his room. The doctors and nurses were furious at him for tricking them into allowing him out and especially for breaking the wheelchair, but he generously agreed to buy a new one to replace it, since he was now a rich man.

The doctor told Irene he'd be keeping Cal too doped up for

the next few days to give him a chance to think of any more excursions, so she didn't worry about him asking to see a newspaper or the *Daily Racing Form* to check out which horse had won his fortune. That would forever remain a mystery, and Gideon and the Old Man would delight in teasing him by never revealing the name.

As soon as Cal was recovered from his exertion, Irene told him about the baby, and they agreed to marry as quickly as possible. They asked Elizabeth and Gideon to stand up with them when the hospital chaplain performed the ceremony in the tiny hospital chapel. Mother Bates stood in for Irene's mother, and the Old Man gave Irene away since her father was still too angry to see them.

The nurses prepared a small reception for them, with cookies and punch in Cal's room.

At one point, the Old Man cornered Elizabeth and Gideon while a group of doctors and nurses congratulated Irene and Cal. "I'm thinking I won't charge Irene and Cal very much for the horses and the farm. Maybe twenty-five thousand."

Elizabeth exchanged a look with Gideon, who seemed to turn a little pale. "Why would you charge them anything at all?"

"For my trouble. I think I earned it, and I have no use for a stable of racehorses."

"I think Gideon needs to explain something to you," Elizabeth said.

Gideon looked even paler. "I . . . The Senora wanted Irene and Cal to have the horses and farm."

"I know she did. That's why I'm willing to sell them so cheaply. I told her I would."

"But I changed the paperwork. I created a new company that Irene owns, and you actually bought them on her behalf."

"But I signed the papers," he reminded Gideon.

"She had given you power of attorney to do that for her. She already owns everything."

"*Everything?*"

"Everything," Gideon confirmed.

"You . . . you did that?" the Old Man asked.

"Uh, yes."

"So, I get nothing from that deal?" the Old Man asked, stupefied.

"You get what the Senora paid you. I know she was generous," Elizabeth reminded him.

He looked at her as if he'd never seen her before, and then he looked at Gideon as if he had seen a ghost. "You conned me."

Now Gideon looked a little green, but he lifted his chin and said, "If you insist, yes, I suppose we did."

For a second, Elizabeth held her breath, waiting for the explosion that was sure to come. The Old Man stared at both of them for a long moment and then his shoulders began to shake. Was he having apoplexy? But no, in another second he was laughing. He threw his head back and guffawed until nurses from other rooms came running to see what was wrong.

It was a few minutes before he was able to control himself again, and when he did, he slapped Gideon on the back and said, "Welcome to the family, son."

# AUTHOR'S NOTE

I KNEW VERY LITTLE ABOUT HORSE RACING WHEN I STARTED this book, but I found the research fascinating. I hope you enjoyed reading about it as much as I enjoyed learning about it. Thanks to the archives of the *Daily Racing Form*, I was able to recount actual races and even get the weather report right. I fudged only a bit on the races where Nolan's and Livingston's horses ran, since those horses never existed.

Sir Barton is now recognized as the first American Triple Crown winner, even though there wasn't an official American Triple Crown for years after his accomplishment. At that time, few horses were entered in all three of the races that now comprise the Triple Crown because of the distances involved and the short time between the races back then, so Sir Barton remains the only winner for a long stretch of racing history.

Sir Barton was an outstanding horse, but the reason you probably never heard of him was because Man o' War came along a year later and won all but one of his races. After much wrangling and negotiations, the owners decided to settle once and for all the question of which horse was better by holding a match race. Man o' War won that race by seven lengths, relegating Sir Barton to the ash heap of history and cementing Man o' War's fame forevermore.

The United States did virtually shut down racetrack betting for a period of time in the early 1900s, and betting was chaotic in 1919 when this story takes place. This finally led to the adoption of pari-mutuel betting, which is now the system used at racetracks.

In the days before public address systems, the crowds did yell, "They're off!" at the start of each race. The starting barrier was just as described in the time before the modern starting gate was invented. The barrier did occasionally injure a horse or rider, and no one was sad to see it replaced.

History does not record the exploits of many female con artists, but one successful example was Thérèse Humbert, a Frenchwoman who pretended to be the heir of an imaginary American millionaire and cheated dozens of people over a period of twenty years, using the same con that the Senora uses here. Only when someone thought to sue her and open the empty safe was her ruse discovered. She did not make as successful an escape as the Senora and ended up in prison.

Please let me know how you enjoyed this book. You can sign up on my website to receive notices when my new books are released so you don't have to miss a single one! You can contact me at victoriathompson.com or follow me on Facebook at Victoria. Thompson.Author or on Twitter @gaslightvt.